THE LIFE OF
HEROD
THE GREAT

THE LIFE OF
HEROD
THE GREAT

A NOVEL

ZORA NEALE HURSTON

EDITED AND WITH COMMENTARY BY DEBORAH G. PLANT

AMISTAD

An Imprint of HarperCollinsPublishers

THE LIFE OF HEROD THE GREAT. Copyright © 2025 by The Zora Neale Hurston Trust. All rights reserved. Printed in the United States of America. No part of this book may be used or reproduced in any manner whatsoever without written permission except in the case of brief quotations embodied in critical articles and reviews. For information, address HarperCollins Publishers, 195 Broadway, New York, NY 10007.

HarperCollins books may be purchased for educational, business, or sales promotional use. For information, please email the Special Markets Department at SPsales@harpercollins.com.

FIRST EDITION

Designed by Yvonne Chan

Library of Congress Cataloging-in-Publication Data has been applied for.

ISBN 978-0-06-316100-9

24 25 26 27 28 LBC 5 4 3 2 1

There is no agony like bearing an untold story inside you.

—Zora Neale Hurston

CONTENTS

Editor's Note   *ix*

Preface   *xi*

Introduction   *xvii*

Chapter 1: Antipater and His Sons   1

Chapter 2: Herod, The Over-Bold   23

Chapter 3: The Accused   51

Chapter 4: New Moon over Judea   75

Chapter 5: Herod at Home   79

Chapter 6: Voice from the Past   94

Chapter 7: General Herod   101

Chapter 8: Test of the Metal   124

Chapter 9: The Road to Rome   155

Chapter 10: Home Again   241

Chapter 11: Herod at Jerusalem   256

Chapter 12: King of Judea   264

Chapter 13: Mariamne Accused   275

Chapter 14: Trial of Mariamne   281

Chapter 15: Games, Gold, Generosity   296

Chapter 16: Love Again for Herod Magnus   300

Chapter 17: Herod Builds   307

Chapter 18: Return of the Two Princes   310

Chapter 19: Reunion in Ionia   317

Epilogue: Back upon the Grille   319

Commentary: A Story Finally Told   *321*
A Note from the Cover Artist   *339*

EDITOR'S NOTE

The Life of Herod the Great is the presentation of Hurston's unfinished and salvaged novel. Synthesized versions of Hurston's preface and introduction are included. Presentation of the narrative text and the preface and introduction reflects the work-in-progress state of Hurston's novel and edits have been made to align with conventions of spelling and grammar. The history of Hurston's manuscript includes it being rescued from a fire. Many pages were burned or singed. Where the missing words and phrases of salvaged pages could be determined by context, they have been edited into the narrative. Where major sections or whole pages are missing or indeterminable, asterisks (* * *) within the body of the narrative indicate missing text.

PREFACE

Why a life of Herod the Great?

For many valid reasons, the first being that the West, whose every nation professes Christianity, should be better acquainted with the real, the historical Herod, instead of the deliberately folklore Herod. Outside of Herod's connection with Christianity, rarely has an individual appeared who gleamed and glittered from so many facets. He has impressed himself upon the pages of history as an athlete, a soldier of the first class, an equally able administrator, a statesman, a devotee of higher learning, as a great and tragic lover, and as a friend as famous as Damon and Pythian.

Few if any other figures in history have been so fortunately endowed. Herod could not avoid prominence, since his father, Antipater, was of ducal status in Idumea, and of singular intelligence. Herod's father and grandfather before him were international bankers, and so esteemed for wisdom that they were everywhere sought as counselors to rulers, and so often the hosts or guests of monarchs, that both were spoken of as "the friends of kings." And the family wealth was counted second between the Euphrates and the Nile. By the wisdom and foresight of Antipater, Herod and his three brothers were superb athletes, with Herod excelling the others. By the time that he was fifteen, he was reputed to be the first horseman of southwest Asia, and first in the use of the weapons of warfare and the science of combat. Nor could he escape the snares of love with his personal charm and physical endowments. He was over six feet tall with a perfectly proportioned body, and with features so harmonious that he was said to be the handsomest man of his time on either side of the Mediterranean. And like both his father and his grandfather, he was an alumnus of the University of Damascus, which was devoted to Greek philosophy and other Greek concepts of learning.

Then there is the pretense that he was hated by the nation, when in fact, his popularity was enormous. One historian, Flavius Josephus, admits this grudgingly by the statement, "Because of his splendid appearance, and because he took such good care of them, and tolerated no nonsense." And, in spite of the fact that the names of Herod the Great and certain of his posterity have been more closely connected with Christianity in the first century of its existence, only the well-informed divine can distinguish him from his sons or grandsons. This confusion has been achieved by calling them all Herod when they had distinctive names of their own. The result is that the average reader cannot tell the acts of one from another. Nor has one out of a million in the Western world followed the descendants of this remarkable man to see some absorbed into the patrician families of Rome or various royal houses in Asia and Europe, and indeed a great-grandson to occupy the throne of Armenia.

Nor is the accusation justified that Herod, as king, corrupted the nation and led it into sin by his fondness for the arts and customs of the Greeks in employing Greek sculpture in the decorations of buildings, encouraging the Greek worship of athletics and the body beautiful, and the various forms of literature. In other words, the identical inclinations that we ourselves exhibit.

There was indeed a conflict in Judea, not between Herod and the people, but that eternal struggle which is inevitable in every nation between change and tradition; between priest and palace—the palace representing the wide world. Its course, or evolution, forever following the identical pattern:

Phase One: The palace ignorant and helpless before the priesthood.

Phase Two: Palace becomes literate and the fear of magic is overcome.

Phase Three: Priesthood erudite and bitterly prejudiced against the power of the palace.

Matters were in the third phase in Judea when Herod was born. The conflict cut through every class of society in Judea—the priesthood itself was divided; Pharisee and Scribe against Pharisee and Scribe and so on to the laborer in the field. It is inexcusable to pretend that it was Herod against the whole nation. His faction was in the majority.

For all religious cults are sectarian and jealous of other gods by necessity. Cults proselytize, overwhelm, but never consciously merge. The law of survival is forever in operation. The priesthood in Judea had become cold and cynical, but that did not mean that it no longer wished to survive. Vainly it fought to maintain isolation to prevent competition—geography at war with history.

A life of Herod the Great seems imperative at this time. In two thousand years, the wheel of history has come a full round. What *was* in Herod's day *is* again. The struggle for the mastery of Asia, which was ancient in Herod's time, and in which he played an important part, has been revived. We see history repeating itself. Once again is taken up the struggle between East and West; that ageless conflict which began with the siege of Troy by the Greek city states. The contest was seemingly ended for all time with the victory of Alexander the Great over Darius at Granicus and Issus when Macedonia became master not only of Persia, but all of western Asia besides, including North Africa by the conquest of Egypt. However, we see the conflict erupting again in the first century BC with Rome, that new power which had arisen in Europe, now the champion of the West, and Parthia—the old Persian empire under a new name and a new management—again scowling across the Mediterranean, then called the Great Sea, as defending warrior for the East.

By following Herod's career, we are brought into the company of the history-makers of that first century BC and are able to trace the pattern which established the way of life of the Western world of our times as to law and the relationship of man to man. We find Herod in active participation with the Caesars, Marc Antony, Cleopatra, Cassius, Orodes of Parthia, Aretas of Arabia, the last members of the Asamonean dynasty which was founded by the patriotic Maccabeans, and makers of history of the century. And that century was so similar to this, the twentieth AD, as to be startling.

For again the ideology of the whole world is in flux. Old institutions and old concepts are in the death throes, and the new being precipitated out; ideologies East and West fight for the minds of men. Identical circumstances provoke similar reactions, human nature being what it is. Herod drew his sword for the West. And now, at present, the United States, most powerful nation of the West, faces Russia of the East across the expanse of the world, with frowning mien, which is met with equal challenge. It is possible that conclusions beneficial to all can be drawn from the past.

Polybius, the ancient Greek philosopher, was convinced that he had the answer when he lectured to his disciples:

Be a realist and a rationalist. Seek the heart of matters. Know history, for there is "no more a ready corrective of conduct than knowledge of the past." "It is history, and history alone, which, without involving us in actual danger, will mature our judgment and prepare us to take right views, whatever may be the crisis or the posture of affairs." History may be a lantern of understanding held up to the present and the future.

And Herod the Great, like all other figures of history, can only be understood against the background and customs of his times. It is vain to reason on very ancient facts from very modern concepts.

Zora Neale Hurston
Fort Pierce, Florida
March 21, 1958
April 7, 1958

INTRODUCTION

A biographical novel of Herod the Great would be extravagantly justified by the presentation of his life of intense personal drama alone. As a story for story's sake, it is unsurpassed in history. Herod's life reaches the very summit of triumph and the utmost depth of tragedy. He was fated to have the pain and pleasure of a profound love affair and a most celebrated friendship. In fact, the man who became known to history as Herod the Great appears to have been singled out and especially endowed to attract the lightning of fate.

But the picture of his life cannot be clearly seen unless he is used as a window through which is observed the century which gave birth to a new world. The vigorous and resourceful young Rome had conquered classic Greece by force of arms, but was in turn overwhelmed by the learning and principles of government which were to set the pattern of government for the entire world of the West—and under which we live to this day. Relentlessly, Pax Romana headed east of the Great Sea.

But east of the Great Sea was Parthia, the Sassanian government of what had been the great and cultured old Persian empire. The name was unknown to history before 554 BC. These new Persians were a nomadic people from the Asian steppes east and north of the Caspian Sea in what is now the USSR. Some historians contend that they were the ancestors of our present-day Turks. In the first century BC they were rude, barbaric, courageous, and good organizers. By all accounts, these Parthians were very tricky, but superb horsemen and bowmen.

These tent-dwellers had migrated into eastern Persia in great numbers even before the time of Cyrus the Great, 536 BC. They were such a large proportion by 256 that, led by a man of noble birth among them, they successfully revolted from the Greek rule. They were anti-Hellenic, and having a hatred of all strangers, drove out Europeans from Persia and announced a program to recover Asia for the Asiatics. Thirty-two years later, Parthia was a strong, well-ordered, and consolidated kingdom. As the leader of the revolution, Arsaces was the first king, and all of his successors took the same name, as all of the rulers of Rome after Augustus Caesar were called Caesar.

Also, it is impossible to understand the life of Herod the Great unless there is some concept of the state of affairs in Judea. The movement for the re-establishment of a Hebrew nation in Palestine—which began in the reign of Cyrus the Great, was halted in the reign of Cambyeses, and actually took place in 520 BC in the reign of Darius Hystaspes—was not a return, as is invariably said and thought of in the Christian world. It was a restoration of a nation, and not the return of individuals, unless we conceive of the natural laws being suspended because the people concerned were Jews.

Seventy years—more than three generations—is too long for a "return" for it must be recognized that any individual old enough to remember anything when Nebuchadnezzar carried the nation off into slavery would be too old for the rigors of travel for such a long distance, or to remember anything much on his return. Their leaders of the Restoration, Zorobabel, Ezra, and Nehemiah, recognized what we appear to ignore—that the 42,462 Jews who chose to go to Palestine to attempt the new nation were, to all intents and purposes, Persians. While they had practiced their religion in Persia, they had all been influenced by Persian culture. The religion was definitely influenced by the Persian concepts of God, and the like. The Hebrew language had been lost by the people, and was known only to certain of the priesthood. The language of the people was now Aramaic, so widely spoken then all over the Middle East.

Even before the new nation was firmly established, the leaders found that something had to be done to fix the laws of Moses and the way of life upon the people. Hence the assembly of the Great Synagogue at Jamnia in northern Palestine, which went about the task of editing Hebrew literature and establishing a canon of what we know as the Old Testament. The decision was made as to what was to be regarded as sacred and of divine authority, inspired scriptures, and what was to be excluded from this category. This was of great importance, for these men recognized the influence of the long exposure to Persian concepts—that the prophetic age had ended with the Captivity; that Malachi, the youngest of the prophets, was the last; that Jewish literature had degenerated during the Captivity and must continue to do so because of this same Persian influence; that it now leaned upon the past more and more after the canon was established; and that having no productive power of its own, it must fall back entirely on the past. The most and best that it could do was to conserve the forms and, if possible, the *spirit* of what was ancient.

Hence, long before the arrival of the first century BC the practice of Judaism had become mechanical and rigid, the priesthood cynical and cold, and this consequent mechanical adherence to ancient form was the direct parent of the morality of the Pharisees which Christ so persistently denounced.

Moreover, in the Judea of the first century BC there was a schism of long standing which to all intents and purposes was a revolt against the empty scholasticism of Judaism eternally chewing on the cud of "the law." This conflict, which rent the nation from top to bottom, came about by the penetration of all western Asia by Greek philosophical concepts and learning. The story of this dissemination of Greek thought in Asia was very ancient and long by the time of Herod. Some Greek influences had been brought in with the Great Migration, or Greek Dispersion, which took place at a period so remote that no historical date can be set for it. Certainly it was long before the siege of Troy.

But the greatest stimulation came from the eruption of Alexander the Great into Asia in 326 BC. Along with Alexander's vast armies was a contingent of Greek scholars under the supervision of the nephew of Aristotle, who had been the instructor of Alexander. It is well known that the great Macedonian held the view—no doubt inspired by Aristotle—that wars would cease and the lamb and lion lie down together when all peoples had religion and customs in common. To this end, Alexander's scholars were kept busy planting Greek schools, libraries, and theaters wherever he marched. And for at least three centuries before Herod was born, there was the Decapolis, or Ten Greek Cities, of Asia east of the Jordan, none too far from Jerusalem, where life and custom went on as it did in Athens.

Three Jewish philosophical sects—Pharisees, Sadducees, and Essenes—were all in flourishing existence for at least two centuries before Herod was born. They came into being through the impact of Greek thought on Judea. Flavius Josephus was himself a Pharisee. The Pharisees were "kin" to the Stoics; the Sadducees were of the persuasion of the Greek pragmatists. These Sadducees, unlike the Pharisees and Essenes, denied that there was such a thing as arbitrary fate, but insisted that things came about through cause and effect. Therefore, men by their own attitudes and actions controlled their own fate.

Though Persian religious concepts influenced Jewish thought considerably during those seventy years, the Sadducees utterly rejected the Persian concept of life after death. It is not certain whether they accepted the political view of a powerful priesthood as was the case of the Persian Magi.

As for the Essenes, the youngest and least numerous of the three sects, their abstemious way of life was influenced by the Greek Dacae, and their thought by Epicurus: "The aim of philosophy is to free men from fear, and more than anything else, from the fear of gods. The gods are not to be feared; death cannot be felt; the good *can* be won; all that we dread can be conquered."

Sublimated through Jewish monotheism, the contract-minded and avenging Jehovah emerges as the loving, understanding, tender Father of the Essenes and later, Christianity. The second strong influence upon the Essenes came from India. Numerous of them lived and worked together for mutual aid in monasteries the same as those of the Catholics of our time. And from India came the Doctrine of Logos. In the early years of the reign of Seleucus I, around 300 BC, Megasthenes, ambassador of Seleucus I to the court of Chandragupta, Maurya, India, wrote back to the Macedonian ruler of Celesyria:

There is among the Brahmans, a sect of philosophers who hold that God is The Word, by which is meant, not articulate speech, but the discourse of reason—the second personality of God—that which is charged or entrusted with creation.

Logos had become very important in Jewish thought within a century—especially that of the Essenes. We find Christ identified as The Word in the introduction to the Gospel of St. John.

The rupture between those who relied upon the past and the Greek-minded had become so wide and so definite that when the Maccabees of Modin led the revolt from the Greek rulers, the Seleucids, so many Jews preferred the Greek way of life that Bacchides, one of the Greek generals, could gather together those Jews who had apostatized from the accustomed way of living of their forefathers and chose to live like their neighbors, and so had a powerful military force of Jews to oppose the Maccabees. For nothing so cements the minds of men together as the alliance of manners.

Judas Maccabeus, in retaliation, went over Palestine exterminating the *Apikoros* (apostates) with fire and sword, "but no sooner than he was dead, it all sprang up again." The cry of the opponents of change was, "Do not surrender to the Greeks and Satan." The retort of the Greek-minded was, "The Chasidim would dissuade us from civilization. Is a man then sinful because he is wiser than his forefathers?"

Long before Herod's century, the homes of wealthy Jews were of the Corinthian order of architecture; the interiors were decorated with murals painted on glass, and many other objects of art. Portraits were painted, and the like. Greek was spoken as a mother tongue by the upper classes, and even by freedmen, servants, and slaves, a Chasidim complains to history, though Aramaic was spoken all over Celesyria also. Hebrew had been lost to the people during the Captivity.

In the light of bountifully attested historical fact, it is ridiculous to point Herod up as "a Romanized Jew" forcing his inclinations upon an unwilling nation. He is merely a prototype of his class of the time. Judea was not, as Christianity keeps on representing it, no different from the tribesmen who received the Law at Sinai. The Sunday Schools of Christianity have neglected to point out the evolution of Jewish culture and thought from the time of Moses to the fall of Jerusalem to Titus in 70 AD. Therefore, it appears that the Jews had and have no life except in the Bible. Like a pressed flower between the leaves of a book, Judea was a very highly evolved nation of people.

The intended eternal isolation of the people by Ezra, Nehemiah, and Zorobabel had failed.

This was true because they, and Christianity of our time, had ignored a most important expression of nature—Jewish genius. Why should this be expected to be missing from the Jews when it is present in all other ethnical groups? And the Jews have produced a disproportionate amount of genius to their numbers. Individuals were bound to be born with intellectual curiosity, the inquiring mind, and the creative instinct. And since it is universally accepted that communication, the exchange of ideas, is the very soul of civilization and progress, how could they have been expected to reject everything but the past? And even their earliest history shows the Jews to have been an individualistic and free-minded people, as even Moses found out to his annoyance. They followed no man blindly.

This was the posture of affairs when Herod was born. He was not, nor could he have been, anything except a part of his time and of the customs of those times. There were certain political customs, which though they still exist in our day, are not so common as then. They figured in his career.

The first was political assassinations. This custom held true on both sides of the Mediterranean. In the first century BC, they hustled rulers and powerful political figures off the scene by sharp blades and dishes of poison in both Europe and Asia. Nor did close ties of blood stand in the way. In fact, the closer the tie, and the nearer to the throne a man was, the more he was apt to kill those of his bloodline. So sons did away with fathers, mothers, brothers, and even sisters commonly, to avoid the boredom of waiting for the incumbent to die a natural death.

The second pervasive custom of the age of Herod was the taking—even the extortion—of bribes by Roman officials in the provinces. It is only too obvious that officials who were awarded an appointment, especially in the Roman provinces of Asia, regarded the appointment as a license to make themselves independently wealthy. They made it impossible for provincials to ever get a dignified hearing before them unless and until they brought along a "present." It was the etiquette of the times. This practice was carried to extreme and sordid lengths. When Julius Caesar was consul for the first time, he exerted himself to get laws on the books to relieve the provinces of this evil, but it continued in the provinces of Asia anyway. Even that tough and suspicious veteran of the Roman camps in Gaul and Asia, the Emperor Tiberius, was horrified by the practice. He said, "A good shepherd shears the sheep, not skins it." Yet, he found himself powerless to stop it. So that a politically wise litigant, say in Judea, knew that his cause was lost, however just might be his claim, unless he was generous with the bribe. Nor was Rome the only power which went in for this. The Parthians and Egyptians also had their hands out. This addiction to "presents" was so influential that a serious work might well be written on the effects of bribery on the history of western Asia.

It is only right and fair to point out the reason for the unfavorable and equally untruthful legends put forth as fact concerning Herod the Great. He was certainly of Greek culture, and generally oriented towards the West. Nothing could be done about it during his long reign, for the majority of the nation was with and for him, but legends could be circulated after his death by the Ebionite influence during the first one hundred years and more of Christianity. It has continued, this influence on Christianity, to our own times. This flowed from Peter and his followers, who sought to tie Christianity to Judaism by interpreting the prophets of the Old Testament canon as foretelling Christ, and making out that Christ was only another of the old line of the prophets.

The known fragments of what we know as the Four Gospels were read in some of the churches, but were not held to be sacred nor of divine inspiration nor authority. This high place was reserved for the books of the Old Testament. The writings of Paul, as well as his preachings, were utterly rejected. What was bound by the viewpoint of the Old Testament was bound in Heaven, and what was loosed was loosed eternally. Herod was anathema to those who leaned upon the past because he did not descend from the priestly line, was not even a Jew by blood, and was of the "Greeks," however the masses of the nation might look upon him as a good and satisfactory king, which they certainly did.

Flavius Josephus, now the chief source of biographical material on Herod the Great, is a poisoned source. Where the priestly caste and the Asamonean dynasty are concerned, Josephus is violently partisan. He states that he will tell the truth, which he does in a way, but then in the next paragraph sets out to supply motives for the splendid acts of Herod that are in direct conflict with the fact previously stated. This occurs in so many instances that it becomes a pattern. Herod's motives Josephus could not know, for he was born forty-one years after the death of Herod, and therefore had no means of knowing anything outside of the recorded facts. Fortunately, he boasts of belonging to all of the elements in the nation who were against what Herod stood for. He even harps upon these things. He was an orthodox kind of a Pharisee, of the first of the twenty-four courses of the priesthood, a descendant of Jonathan of the Maccabees, from which was derived the short-lived dynasty of the Asamoneans, and an anti-Greek.

There is a startling parallel between the life of Herod the Great and Napoleon Bonaparte in this respect. The people of Judea had rejected the Asamoneans before Herod was grown, and they had been passed on by the Romans not only as enemies of Rome, but as having no abilities necessary to the history of the era. Herod poured into the vacuum created by the degeneracy of the Asamoneans. The French had discarded the Bourbons as not only useless as leaders, but also inimical to the preservation of the nation before Napoleon, like Herod, had come of age.

And the Bourbons, like the Asamoneans, were utterly persuaded that they were destined by God to rule whether they served any useful purpose to the people or not, and when ousted, looked upon it as a sacrilege, and intrigued endlessly to regain a power which they had become unfit to wield. Though the whole dynasty of the Bourbons never produced a single individual of the abilities of Napoleon, the discard set itself up as "Legitimists" and refused all compromise with him. It was the same way with the Asamoneans despite the sufferings of the nation by their misrule. They also had the identical, "Let them eat cake," inclinations. Divine right of kings notions. First by birth.

Being of this enchantment, Josephus indulges on every possible occasion—and some occasions childishly forced—in boasting of the "noble" birth of the Asamoneans and the "mean" or "low" birth of Herod because he was neither a Jew nor of the priestly line; when in fact the family of Herod was semi-royal, had ducal status in Idumea, and had had it for such a length of time that none of the historians who mention this family ever mention any lower standings. On the other hand, the Maccabees of Modin, though of the priestly line, were of extremely modest means, and no mention is made of them until the revolt from the Macedonians around 165 BC, and the first to set himself up as a king—Aristobulus, son of John Hyrcanus—did so only two generations before the birth of Herod.

Most of the works of the eminent historian Nicolaus of Damascus, including his biography, *The Commentaries of Herod the Great*, have been lost, so that the paraphrase of this life of Herod by Josephus in both his *Antiquities of the Jews* and *Wars of the Jews* is now the chief source of material on Herod the Great. But in all fairness, it should never be overlooked that the attributed motives and interpretations of

Herod's acts are by Josephus, in "legitimistic" spite. Fortunately, other reliable and objective historians have shed light on the life of Herod.

Since it is worse than useless to attempt to interpret very ancient facts through very modern concepts, it is necessary to draw attention to the conditions and customs of the world of the times of Herod the Great. He, like all other historical figures, is out of context unless seen against the background of his era.

Then and then only can we see this singular character who was said to be the handsomest man of his time, the hero of a famed but tragic love affair, the unsurpassed all-around athlete, first soldier of southwest Asia of his time, first administrator, bosom friend of Marc Antony, Augustus Caesar, sought after by Cleopatra. On the other hand, he was the great and magnificent builder of the temple in Jerusalem which Christ attended; of Caesarea, the overwhelming city of white marble on the coast of the blue Mediterranean, which the Romans employed for their administrative city later; the palaces in which Pontius Pilate and Antipas interviewed Christ at Jerusalem, and in which Festus and King Agrippa received Paul when he was accused; and numerous other points which touch Christianity. Herod the Great was to accumulate the epithets of Herod of the Sun-Like Splendor, Herod the Over-Bold, from his reckless daring in war, and Herod, the Beloved of God.

Zora Neale Hurston
Fort Pierce, Florida

CHAPTER ONE

ANTIPATER AND HIS SONS

The Common Court of the temple of Zorobabel at Jerusalem was crowded to capacity but in complete silence. But silence has many personalities. This profound absence of sound was filled with the hysteria of hope, for the people gathered here had been hastily summoned by Antipater, the most powerful citizen of Judea, who now stood in the erect posture of a soldier on the speaker's platform, with his left hand stretched out and resting on the lectern.

Standing thus before the congregation, his physical power spoke. In his middle years with a slight brush of gray at his temples, he showed no other sign that he was past his youth. Six feet of brawn and steady, determined eyes. A strong, handsome face and dignity of poise. And now without any preliminaries, Antipater began to speak. Behind him, the Seventy sat in a large semi-circle with Hyrcanus, the high priest, in the center making the required Seventy-one. As if driven by a wind, the semi-circle leaned forward the better to hear. Before him, the vast throng bowed forward likewise. The clusters of large candles illuminated the platform and threw everything on it in high relief.

"As you know, the Great Caesar was in Syria to settle the affairs of our nation, and you are aware of the disposition he made. And further, that I have but recently escorted him as far as Antioch from which port he sailed for Rome. My most recent activities, on my return from Antioch, have consisted in going over the country and quelling the disorders which I found, and which, if left to continue, would have plunged our country again into the horrors of civil strife."

Antipater . . . swept the room with grim eyes. "The current chaotic state of affairs, I, as your governor, appointed by Caesar with full support of the senate, will in no wise tolerate. It was upon my recommendation to Caesar that Hyrcanus has been restored as your high priest, of which office he was wickedly deprived by Aristobulus, his brother. And if you will abandon the wicked and destructive practices of this Aristobulus, who is now dead, and behave towards Hyrcanus as is right and proper, I guarantee that you shall live happily and live your lives without disturbance in the enjoyment of your possessions; but if any of you are addicted to the frigid hopes of what you might gain by innovations and aim to get wealthy by such means, you will find in me a most severe master instead of a gentle governor, and Hyrcanus a tyrant instead of a king, and the Romans, including Caesar, your bitter enemies, for be assured, the Romans will never bear to be set aside those whom they have appointed to govern you."

Instantly, a murmur like a fire in the woods swept the room, and almost as quickly it was changed to loud applause. This continued for two or three minutes unabated. Behind Antipater, Hyrcanus was doing his utmost to participate, but his efforts were confusing. First he smiled broadly with his head nodding and bobbing excessively to indicate that he not only approved, but had actually commanded Antipater to say what he did. Then he decided that this was the wrong gesture, as indeed it was for many took to tittering at him, then he overdid a stern frown at the populace, which caused many to titter more in derision. Finally the clamor for the return of peace, prosperity, and security as expressed by the tumultuous applause died away and Antipater continued.

"And to further make certain of the restoration of security and prosperity which we all so desire, I call to my assistance Phasaelus, my first-born son, and appoint him governor of Jerusalem and the places about. He will make it his obligation to restore the perfect order of former times so that each citizen, of whatever class, may enjoy security for himself, his family and his possessions, and second, to rebuild the walls of the city thrown down by Pompey. . . ."

Then even louder and more prolonged applause interrupted Antipater. Seeing himself unable to continue immediately, he turned his clean-shaven face to the right and nodded, and Phasaelus rose and stood and was acknowledged by the populace with thunderous applause and the calling of his name in praise and favor.

With Phasaelus still standing at Antipater's right hand, the procurator spoke again.

"And to the end that all parts and provinces of our nation be quieted and protected alike, I appoint my second son, Herod, to be governor of Galilee, our most northern province, to put down the tumults there which have come about through the civil strife in the nation and thus gave a handle to those who prefer to live by unlawful means to the injury of honest and pious men."

At his father's nod, Herod arose and stood at Antipater's left. He rose with a swagger and his broad, self-assured smile took the gathering into his arms. The place went wild. With a few bitter exceptions, men cheered, shouted, called out his name, and kept cheering. Why? Not one of them could have said exactly why he was so stimulated at the sight of this young man. Certainly Herod was a good two inches taller than his father or brother, but they were tall enough to satisfy. He was extraordinary in his handsomeness, but should they be excited about that? It was perhaps a freak of personality native to the theater where some, a very few, can command applause for doing practically nothing, while very competent actors can scarcely gain notice. Herod had that something.

"Antipater and his sons!" some voice shouted from the rear of the room.

"Galilee rise again!"

"Antipater and his sons!"

"Praise to Antipater, we are allies of Rome and not slaves as we were to the Macedonians. Antipater!"

"Herod the Over-Bold!"

"Herod the generous to the workers of Judea!"

Finally, Antipater raised his hands and quieted the tumult, his sons resumed their seats, and a most sober silence came upon the people, for the name of Galilee brought to their consciousness the terrible name of a man, Hezekiah, the bandit leader of Galilee. Hezekiah, wholesale murder, ruthless slaughter of unarmed men, women, and children. Robbery. Arson in the night. Horrible butchery and rape.

Now they looked with pity on the shining young man at Antipater's left. They looked from his gay, self-assured countenance to that of his father and back again. How could the kindly Antipater doom this so youthful and handsome young man to such a horrible death? And especially when he was reputed to be a most affectionate father, and equally loved by this second son of his? Many deliberately looked long and steadily to fix Herod's shining face upon their minds and memories so that they could later relate just how he appeared at this hour, for all were certain that they would never see him again. Hezekiah.

"And finally, my beloved countrymen, I congratulate you upon your courage and fortitude during the long period of our many misfortunes which began with the arrogant Aristobulus attempting to seize the birthright of our high priest, Hyrcanus, and led to the assault upon us by first Pompey, then others. I also am grateful to you for your willing assistance in restoring Judea to its former glory. With the kindest emotions, I now dismiss you."

And no sooner did he say this than Antipater, followed by his sons, headed for the door. People gasped. Everybody, even the Sanhedrin, had expected more. They left the temple slowly and reluctantly. They saw that everything necessary for the settlement of the government had been disposed of in less than a half hour. But where were the displays of rhetoric that the highly trained Antipater and his sons were so capable of? Where were the opportunities for others to exhibit? Not one question had been asked. This meeting, stripped of all drama by their new procurator, was the most dramatic and provocative thing that had happened in generations.

Real darkness had scarcely invaded the city, so what with so much to talk about, nobody even considered going home and to bed. The few very elderly men of importance who usually did so had no more notion than the others on this occasion. So according to social rank and financial rating, every man headed for his favorite club, tavern, or humble inn. Some of these spots were in the Upper City and patronized by the prominent and wealthy around the Upper Market Place. Some in the better streets of Accra, or the Lower City. Some less pretentious lay in the Valley of the Cheese-mongers, and still others in poorer neighborhoods. Some existed even in the suburbs.

The members of the Sanhedrin, for the greater part, resorted to a spot in the Upper City not too far from the temple. Pollio and his famous disciple, Sameas, were earlier than most at this club, and went to their favorite table in a corner where they could command a view of the entire room. They ordered an amphora of fresh-pressed wine

from the grapes of Gaul and soon a dozen others had crowded about
their table, as usual.

"Well, O learned Pollio, what of the happening of this night?"

"You saw and heard as much as I, O Eleazer."

"But the interpretation?" Eleazer persisted, stroking excitedly his
fulsome beard. His eyes glittered with expectation and hope. Pollio,
the prominent Pharisee and scholar, cut a quick glance in the direction
of Sameas and smiled minutely.

"You forget that I am a Pharisee like yourself, Eleazer, not an Essene.
I do not pretend to foretell the future. Whatever may be your hopes,
Antipater is a most resourceful and capable man of affairs. I would not
be surprised if he succeeded in his aims."

"Ah, but that is just the heart of the matter, Pollio!" another of the
elders all but shouted. "What are the aims of Antipater and his sons?
What are they? I—*we all*—should ask. Does that Idumean think to
make himself king? Now, I . . ."

But Eleazer was cut off by another of the Chasidim who equaled if
not surpassed Eleazer in vehemency.

"But did you look well at Hyrcanus there tonight? Why did the
highly intelligent Antipater use his influence with Caesar to have him
made high priest and king again? I will tell you why. He recognizes
as well as you and I Hyrcanus's vanity. Not being of the priestly line,
and an Idumean beside, the shrewd Antipater means to use him as a
tool to have absolute power over the nation. Antipater and his sons,
indeed! Those Greek-minded whelps of Edom." This man raked his
old, claw-like fingers through his beard as if he tore something to
pieces thereby. "Why, we will never allow it. And that brash Herod,
well, who is it that does not agree that making him governor of those
Gentiles up in Galilee was the best way of ridding the nation of him?
For Hezekiah will quickly do away with him."

"I am one who does not agree that his death at the hands of the bandit is inevitable," Sameas spoke slowly and coolly. "I am a realist and a rationalist, and since it is known that Antipater is unusually fond of his children, and Herod in particular, he would not be sending the youth to certain death. Being a scholar instead of a soldier, I have not much of an idea what possibilities are in Herod's favor. Oh, most will see the possibility and probability of Herod's destruction by Hezekiah with his army of cutthroats and robbers, but there must be some chance of his survival, or I am sure that Antipater would never send Herod against the monster."

"But it is madness, O Sameas. Consider that men of great experience in warfare have shunned an attack upon this Hezekiah. He is formidable. Even Sextus Caesar, president of Syria, despite Hezekiah's bold eruptions into adjoining Syria on occasion, has not dared to give the bandit leader the meeting. Oh, Herod will surely be destroyed, and in a most barbarous manner."

Several venerables around the table by nods, murmurs, and gestures of finality gave assent to this. Sameas glanced at Pollio to see if he also read between the lines. Seeing that his teacher did, he smiled faintly and spoke again.

"Perhaps it is because I take no pleasure in the death of our young governor of Galilee that I do not see the same conclusion as you do so easily. Often the wish is father of the thought."

After quick exchanges of glances among themselves, one of the elders murmured, "You speak strangely tonight, O Sameas. Have you, like the rash youth of Judea, been bewitched by this shining young Edomite? Antipater is a very rich, and now powerful man. Perhaps you too have been corrupted."

"Corrupted? Like yourselves, I see the power and abilities in Herod and the probability that he may go far in government. But unlike you, I see no threat to myself. Therefore, I have no wish for him to be removed from my path."

There was the clamor of numerous young voices at the entrance, and around fifty young men of the first families of Jerusalem burst into the room. They bore none other than Herod in their midst. There was shouting and much movement as the strapping figure of the son of Antipater was carried to the far side of the room to a long table already filled with many dishes and amphoras of wine.

"The shame of it!" One handsome youth whose father had a reputation for piety shouted, "We would feast our leader on his first night as governor of Galilee, but where do we find him? In the library of his home poring over the battles of Alexander the Great and Caesar's Commentaries. But we are going to feast him whether he wills or not. Here, help us place him at the head of the table, Alexander, and you, Dositheus! Let us be merry, for soon we march for Galilee to comb the beard of the barbarous Hezekiah."

But here Herod freed himself from the arms of his friends and stood erect and laughing in that magnetic way that he had.

"I will be feasted by you, my friends. A good soldier knows when he has met a superior force, and does not fling away his forces to no profit. Many great military leaders take the view that a skillful retreat is as glorious as the winning of a battle. He can fight another day at a time and place of his own choosing." He flung out his arms in surrender and marched to the head of the table amid loud cheers and seated himself. "However, I can merely taste the wines only, for my father says that dedicated leaders never have time for wine."

The rest of the group quickly seated themselves while they indulged in jokes and friendly raillery. The eyes of the others in the room were irresistibly fixed on Herod and his group. His head covered with a thick mop of light brown hair which curled fiercely, his upper garment of fine white linen of Cos, and his arm ornaments of heavy gold with jewels, and the clasp on his left shoulder of a most curious design accented by a large ruby.

"What a comely youth," Pollio sighed.

"And why not?" Eleazer snapped. "That family has bred like the Arabian horses they so treasure. I have it from a reliable source that the women chosen for mothers must not only be of a good family, but must also be tall, beautiful, and able to read and write Greek."

"Do their horses also read Greek?" Sameas, the youngest about the table, asked, facetiously, to soften the vehemence of Eleazer. And when his sally was rewarded with a burst of laughter, he added, "I am in need of an additional secretary, and if Antipater's horses are that highly bred, I might procure one for a scribe."

"But seriously," Pollio took it up, "it might be well if that custom became more common. It has been maintained by many learned men outside of our nation that marriage within the family fosters imbecility, and imperfections of the body. During many centuries the Greeks bred for human perfection. Now, to be sure, this careful breeding in the Antipater family has done them no hurt. They all have fine, tall bodies and perfect limbs, and none would be so rash as to contend that they are not of active minds."

"You mean to imply that that is the reason why Antipater can now lead Hyrcanus about like a dancing bear at the games?" This rhetorical query came from a Pharisee with pink cheeks showing above his thick beard and with a twinkle in his eyes. "If so, we ought indeed to think seriously of the matter. Perhaps, for the good of our nation, the Maccabean family should have ended with John Hyrcanus, for since his time, the family has produced nothing but trouble for our nation. It is due to their stupid and wicked acts that we are now subject to the Romans."

Now they were off, this nearly score of the principal men of Jerusalem. They brought up the past with bitter and scornful accusations while no more than forty feet away at the other end of the room was Herod and his friends—some of them the sons or grandsons of those who sat there lamenting—and all of the principal families of Jerusalem. These men trod sorrowing steps back over the road which had led to Antipater becoming procurator of Judea.

"The longest journey begins with the first step," Eleazer began. "At times I reason that something had to be wrong in the household of the pious John Hyrcanus for his sons to behave in ways so injurious to our nation."

"Possibly," Pollio commented, "but not necessarily so." He halted for a moment while regarding the gay company of young men at the other end of the room. "John Hyrcanus did forsake the sect of the Pharisees and joined the Sadducees, but some most excellent citizens belong to that sect."

Then from one mouth to the other, the recapitulation went on. On the death of John Hyrcanus, his oldest son Aristobulus promptly changed the form of government from the traditional theocracy under the rule of the priesthood to a monarchy by declaring himself a king. He began this by imprisoning his mother and three of his brothers to avoid any competition for the crown. Antigonus, the brother next him in age, he allowed to be free, but before the end of his short reign of a year, he had Antigonus assassinated. His mother, he starved to death in prison. Then he himself died.

The third son of Hyrcanus succeeded Aristobulus, and immediately killed the son who was fourth in age because he suspected him of royal ambitions. The youngest wisely kept his mouth shut and so survived. This third son was named Alexander Jannaeus, who further alienated the nation by crucifying eight hundred prominent citizens. For the first time in the history of the nation, a high priest had a partition erected between himself and the people while he served at the altar, as the public brought citrons and bombarded the high-priest king. After numerous other cruelties, Jannaeus finally died.

He left two sons. Hyrcanus II, the present incumbent, who was degenerate and feeble-minded, but inordinately vain and cunning. Hyrcanus always pretended that he cared nothing for public office. His younger brother, Aristobulus II, was openly ambitious for prestige and power. While their mother, Alexandra, was ruling, this Aristobulus attempted to seize power, justifying his rashness by continually pointing out the unfitness of Hyrcanus to govern. No sooner was Alexandra dead than he drove Hyrcanus off the throne and made himself king. Publicly, Hyrcanus pretended not to care, but poured out his grief and disappointment to his bosom friend, Antipater, who promised to, and did, assist him.

Antipater persuaded Aretas, king of Arabia and his kinsman, to aid Hyrcanus. He even paid him a large sum of money to do so. He took the willing and eager Hyrcanus to Arabia by night, and Aretas later brought him back into Judea with an army, and beat Aristobulus in battle.

Then entered the Romans. Pompey, planning to war with the Parthians, sent Gabinius and Scaurus into Syria ahead of himself. Scaurus took a bribe of four hundred talents, and Gabinius three hundred, to aid Aristobulus and ordered Aretas to get out of Judea immediately with his army, or go to war with Rome. The Romans and their love of bribes! Neither Scaurus nor Gabinius cared a green grape whether Aristobulus was the rightful heir or not. What they wanted was money, and seeing that Aristobulus had possession of the national treasury, they promptly decided in his favor.

But later, Pompey arrived in Syria. Antipater went as ambassador to Pompey for Hyrcanus, while one Nicodemus performed the same service for Aristobulus.

Now, with Pompey, Antipater was in his element, moving with assurance, while Nicodemus was like a fish in hot oil. Antipater, educated in the Greek manner, well-traveled and familiar with the courts of kings, and with a sense of the fitness of things, had no trouble in charming and convincing Pompey. Besides, as was acknowledged by Nicodemus as well, Hyrcanus was the elder brother and had been confirmed in the priesthood by his parents and the law of the land.

Nicodemus helped the cause of Hyrcanus further, though unintentionally, by exposing before Pompey the bribes accepted by Gabinius and Scaurus, and behaving as if he expected Pompey to seize upon his generals instantly and send them home to Rome in chains. Not only did the two generals show their rage, but they were supported by Pompey. Hurriedly he dismissed the claims of Nicodemus, but sent him off with the statement that he would talk with him later, and went home with Antipater as a house guest.

Aristobulus naturally doubted his chances of success now with Pompey and began to look around for other means to gain the crown. He was devious and resorted to bald untruths to put Pompey off until he could find help from some other source. Pompey's rage rose like a pillar of fire to Heaven.

"Does this insignificant provincial so deceive himself that he thinks he is of superior intelligence to the first citizen of Rome? He has no legitimate claim to what he is contending for, to the detriment of the nation, nor has he the strength to seize it by force. He begs for my consideration, then attempts to defraud me by stupid lies and stratagems. By Jupiter, I will pluck him and stew this Aristobulus like a pigeon!"

So to the distress of the nation, Pompey went to war against Aristobulus, pulled down the walls of Jerusalem to get at him, beat him, and carried Aristobulus, his wife, and his two sons and two daughters off to Rome in chains.

Antipater, who had set out to protect Hyrcanus in possession of his birthright, did not have to exert himself to remove the troublesome Aristobulus from his path. Pompey performed this task for him.

Alexander, the older son of Aristobulus, was married to Alexandra, the daughter and only child of Hyrcanus, but in this savage struggle for power, they became first estranged, then the bitterest of enemies. They had two children, Mariamne and Aristobulus III, whom he was never to see again.

So on this night, the first of Herod's as governor of Galilee, Aristobulus was dead by poison, and Scipio had cut off the head of Alexander at Antioch. Alexandra, his cousin-wife, when the news reached her at the palace of her father in Jerusalem, made no pretense of grief. The news had reached the palace in early afternoon. She hurried to the nursery where her small son played and clasped him to her breast in a lingering embrace.

"God be praised!" Alexandra exulted. "The arch criminal who would have robbed you of your throne is dead, my adored little son. Now, nobody nor anything stands in the way of your ascending the throne when Hyrcanus, my father, is dead. I must begin to take greater care to prepare you for your kingdom, for Hyrcanus is neither firm of mind nor body, and may not live very long now. But I, your devoted mother, will attend to the affairs of government until you reach an age that I consider fit for you to rule. I will appoint the noble Antipater to assist me."

The small boy was struggling to free himself from Alexandra's embrace.

"Oh, release me, Mother. Don't you see how you interfere with our game? These two sons of the household steward and I are birds and seeing which one of us can fly the farthest and the fastest. I was away over the Mount of Olives when you obstructed my wings. Go away, Mother! The others will get ahead of me."

"Hush and listen, son. I shall feast you at sundown in honor of the hour when we shall receive the government. Come and embrace me, my beloved. I shall feast you this evening on roasted young mutton and figs stewed in honey."

The little boy, enthralled with his play, thrust his mother away and went on moving about with arms extended in flight, but Alexandra left the nursery smiling. Let the boy play. She would keep him playing for at least thirty years or more while she exercised the power of government. And why not? She was only twenty-seven, while Alexandra, her mother-in-law, had been sixty-four when Alexander Jannaeus died and she took over the government and deprived her sons of it for nine years. She had held on until she died, at the age of seventy-three. Alexandra could see no reason why she could not follow her mother-in-law's example, with the assistance of Antipater and his sons.

With a light heart, Alexandra paused briefly at the apartment of Mariamne, her daughter, and ordered her to dress carefully for the occasion, and would have hastened on to her own rooms for the same purpose, but the girl, a very beautiful child approaching puberty, detained her.

"Will I be feasted also at another time, Mother? Is Aristobulus to be all in all forever with you, and I nothing?"

"Don't be foolish, Mariamne! What would be the occasion for such a thing? You are a girl, and the people would never tolerate a woman as their governor except as a regent during the childhood of the real king. Besides, there is no need to be melancholic. When your brother has obtained the government, I will then be able to find you a proper husband. Now, our fortunes are depressed and a suitable match would be impossible. You are not heir to the family fortunes. The best that can be arranged for you will come when the time arrives."

"Has Aristobulus been declared king then by the Romans?"

"Not at the moment, but no doubt it will soon occur. Both your wicked grandfather and father are removed from our path, and our excellent and faithful friend, Antipater, has raised an army and marched on to Egypt with Mithradates of Pergamus, the general of Julius Caesar. He has performed other splendid services for Caesar and will no doubt win his high approval. Naturally, he will ask in return for the elevation of Hyrcanus to his former position. The tidings may reach us within the month."

Alexandra was so overwhelmed by her dream of power that she could not resist removing another obstacle from her path that evening at the feast.

"Father," Alexandra began in a very solicitous voice, "the reports from Egypt, as you know, are very good. Antipater is gaining mightily upon Caesar. All the powerful Romans speak in praise of the excellent Antipater. Naturally, Caesar will be grateful, and since Antipater has performed so many and difficult things for your sake, he will beseech Caesar to restore you as high priest and king of Judea. Our fortunes improve."

Hyrcanus, gleeful and with eyes rolling in his head, exulted, "Ah, my faithful friend, Antipater! Yes, yes, he does not like to see me unhappy. He will persuade Caesar to place me at the head of government again, even though he knows my wishes to keep away from public affairs. How fond Antipater is of figs stewed in honey! He should be with us this night. He likes stewed figs. And he is ever good and kind to me. He alone of all my relatives and friends does not say that I am a degenerate imbecile and slothful and unfit to reign. Never has he mocked me with scorn nor laughed at me."

Alexandra saw the eyes of her father grow moist and was touched with pity for a moment, then became practical again.

"Yes, I know, Father. Your father and mother and brother Aristobulus all spoke that way of you, and numerous of the leading men of the city. Therefore, it would be better to have the kingdom confirmed to my son."

The eyes of Hyrcanus flung wide open in fright and injury.

"You, also, Alexandra? Everybody except Antipater wants to take my kingdom from me." Hyrcanus shed angry tears. "You are the one who is mad, Alexandra. Your son cannot lawfully receive the high priesthood until he is twenty-one. You are insane to think otherwise. Nobody else can even consider anyone but me so long as I am alive."

"Be quiet, Father. The serving men will hear you. You are getting old and besides you continually say that you have no taste for public affairs. Why not . . ."

"That is a lie! I love the honor and the glory of it. I love the raiment of office." He beat on the table with his fist and wept in rage. "They made me say that—my mother and the Pharisees. Only Antipater knew my heart. They made me say it or they would have passed me over entirely. They said I was too foolish and must submit to the rule of the Pharisees or . . ."

"You see, Father? Therefore, why not consider living a quiet private life where no one will be provoked to laugh at you? Pass the government on to my son, and secure a comfortable estate—say down at Merissa in Idumea beside that of Antipater and entertain yourself with the possession of a flock of beautiful doves?"

"What? What do I want with a flock of doves? No! I want to be . . ."

"Or rare white peacocks, Father?" Alexandra pressed.

Hyrcanus fixed a baleful glance upon his daughter's face and suddenly got to his feet. Alexandra ceased to speak with her mouth wide open . . . in surprise.

"Birds!" Hyrcanus said coldly. "What do I want with birds? I was born to be a king. I am first by birth and you like my brother and many other wicked men want me to hide myself and pass my life occupied with the feathers of birds. I want to be king. I want to be king! I want to . . ."

And he fled from the room shaking with sobs.

Now, the group of principal men about the table in the tavern had heard about this scene, for servants talk to servants and sometimes, when they have received presents for information, to men of importance who consider it prudent to discover what goes on in certain houses. They discussed the character of Alexandra and described her as a bold, ambitious woman who dominated the weak mind of her father. But what could she do? Judea was now under the Romans, and nobody knew that recent day in Syria what disposition Caesar would make of public affairs.

"And now the story told by the servants more than two years ago is confirmed," said Eleazer sadly. "We were all deceived by the man. He is unfit for public affairs, but vain and cunning. He is easily moved by vanity. There he sat tonight while Antipater spoke, nodding and smiling like the imbecile that he is, trying to persuade the people that he had commanded Antipater to do and say what he did when it is well known that he has no more power than a shadow on a wall. Except for the priesthood, everything is in the hands of Antipater. His pretentions are utterly ridiculous."

"Again, the generosity of Antipater is confirmed," Pollio nodded. "Recognizing his childish vanity, Antipater persuaded Caesar to allow Hyrcanus to wear the robes of the high priesthood, like a plaything. His fidelity is a thing of wonder. That Idumean is God's image of a friend."

"Antipater's fidelity I too saw as one of his components as I looked at him almost in a trance," Sameas broke in. "I saw his acts and attributes making an eternally moving series of pictures like the graven frieze about the Parthenon at Athens: His ancestry and the work of his ancestors, being the leading group of carvings. His childhood in Idumea, as he was in training to become an athlete and soldier and statesman; his education in mathematics, philosophy, rhetoric, and familiarity in the arts; his appearances at the various courts of Asia; his buying up the taxes of nations and thus gaining familiarity with everything in those countries, and making intimate friends of the rulers; his lifelong and faithful friendship with Hyrcanus, the war he waged against Aristobulus to protect Hyrcanus from being shoved aside; his gathering of all those great stores of corn, oil, and wine as soon as he discerned the possibility of the civil strife in Rome and so was in position not only to make enormous profits, but gain the friendship and gratitude of the great men of the earth, and so place them in his debt.

"A stirring group of carved pictures consists of his gathering and equipping three thousand men and joining Mithradates on his march to join Caesar in Egypt and all the benefits Antipater bestowed on the general like not only provisioning the army, but persuading Arabia, Gaza, Ascalon, Syria, Tyre, and Sidon to aid Caesar, while also removing all obstacles from the path of Mithradates. I particularly like the picture of the valor of Antipater at the Jews Camp in Egypt where he was the first to breach the walls of the city, and the first to enter, and his noble support of Mithradates when the Egyptians would have beaten him otherwise; his fighting close to Caesar himself, in Egypt, and winning the admiration of the great Roman by his daring successes. Then the picture when Antipater met Caesar in Syria in that gorgeous setting where his bearing and his rich apparel made him look more like an emperor than Caesar himself. His great dignity and handsome body became him."

"I thought his most persuasive moment was when that cringing Aristobulus accused Antipater of deceit with Caesar and Antipater flung loose his costly linen robe and exhibited the scars he had accumulated in the battles in Egypt, and exclaimed, 'My wounds and scars attest to my fidelity to Caesar!'" interrupted the Pharisee with the twinkling eyes.

"I was approaching that magnificent drama, Gorion," Sameas said with irritation. "I was the one who had this vision, and I should be allowed to reveal it in my own fashion. I went to Damascus to oppose any advancement of Antipater and his sons, but was overwhelmed.

Who among us had troubled himself to deserve so much from Caesar? Who else could have done so well for our nation? At enormous financial cost to himself, and even at the risk of his very life, he had purchased the goodwill of Rome for our nation, to the end that we emerged as the confederates of Rome instead of being made subjects. Considering all these things, and in spite of the urgings of many of my friends, I kept my lips firmly closed."

"Yet Antipater received enormous benefits for himself and his sons," Eleazer objected. "I heard Caesar announce that Antipater and his descendants were henceforth Roman citizens, free from taxes everywhere, and that he was free to choose whatever province in Asia that he chose to govern. With his fine Greek politeness, Antipater left the choice up to Caesar, who promptly made him procurator of Judea."

"Oh, Caesar knows how to be grateful," Gorion nodded. "But do not forget the practical and materialistic nature of the Romans. Caesar did not do these things because of the handsome body and face of Antipater, and because he is a magnificent host, but because he knew of no other man in this part of Asia who could hold it and administer it wisely for the Romans. In fact, Antipater received less than he deserved."

"Still," contended Eleazer, "his administering the civil authority is a violation of our laws. That Idumean is not of the priestly line. Our laws state that we are to submit to be governed by our priests."

"But what can Hyrcanus do?" Pollio asked. "You know his defects. Do not deceive yourself; Caesar saw them too. Nothing could have persuaded him to leave affairs in the hands of Hyrcanus. I was there also. Caesar merely indulged Antipater by allowing him to be high priest. He expects nothing of Hyrcanus or any of his family. With Parthia the enemy of Rome and a powerful enemy at that, Caesar would risk nothing like that. Never! Rome has rejected the Asamoneans."

Sameas took a sip of wine and leaned forward. "Therefore what we witnessed earlier this night is the result of the acts and components of Antipater. He has made himself our most responsible citizen. Since he has associated Phasaelus and Herod in his affairs for the past ten years by way of training and preparation for public office, he appointed them tonight as his assistants. Who among us is prepared to take their places?"

A heavy silence hung over the group while Sameas looked from face to face for an answer.

"And particularly," Sameas continued, "who among us wishes to go up to Galilee and contest with Hezekiah? It is a ferocious gamble, but you find Antipater willing to wager his young and favorite son. If he loses, it will be very tragic, but if he wins, it will add to his splendor. That is the man with whom we are confronted."

Nobody said anything. In the prolonged silence, a voice was heard from the other end of the room where were seated four divinity students at the table nearest Herod and his friends.

"Let us gather hundreds of men before the house of our new procurator and make a great tumult and clamor. This Antipater is no better than the heathens who worship idols and sacrifice their children to Moloch! He throws his young son to the monster Hezekiah as they once threw their infants into the fire. This night, we have been visiting all the taverns of the workers, and also those of Judea's esteemed families, and everywhere, people weep at the sacrifice of Herod. Everywhere, they place wagers, not on the survival of the unfortunate young man, whom they describe as very handsome and generous, but on how long he will escape the terrible tortures and death at the hands of Hezekiah."

There fell a dramatic silence over the whole room that was eventually broken by the hoarse voice of a heavy-built man at a table near Sameas who challenged, "Ten shekels that Hezekiah destroys Herod within a month!"

"Twenty shekels of gold that Hezekiah overtakes the son of Antipater within two weeks," another voice took up the challenge.

"I raise that to a mina!" another voice shouted.

"Five mina!"

"A talent of silver that Herod survives," said a voice at the table of Herod.

"What madness!" gasped one of the divinity students.

"Taken!" shouted the hoarse-voiced merchant. "I shall thereby increase my stock of purple and scarlet."

"Five talents of gold that Herod conquers Hezekiah no later than the third encounter!"

"Taken! Taken!" cried several voices at once. "But who is this madman?"

Herod slowly rose from his couch beside the banquet table and stood calmly that all might see him. A startled gasp broke from many throats.

"Herod himself," murmured several.

"Yes, Herod, son of the noble Antipater," Herod said in a proud, sure voice. "Ten talents of gold that I shall be too hard for Hezekiah! Ten talents. Who accepts my wager?"

Nobody did. They gazed upon the handsome, resplendent young man and broke into loud cheers. They kept it up. He was lifted by numerous men and stood upon the table, the cheering continuing. Herod, smiling defiantly, drew the fine sword of Damascus steel with the jeweled hilt that his father had given him on his graduation from the University of Damascus, and waved it triumphantly. The room went madder. The four divinity students rushed into the crowd around the table, carried away by the enthusiasm that Herod invariably aroused, and shouted that they were going to follow him as their leader.

"You see how that Herod corrupts our youth?" Eleazer demanded sourly.

But nobody was listening. For the moment, practically every man in the room was convinced that Herod was invincible. The vast army of Alexander the Great, with the great Macedonian at its head, could not have stood against Herod. That was the way he affected people. He was borne aloft by his worshippers and out of the tavern. The cheering kept up and gradually receded in the distance. The sober men about Sameas did not sit down again. When the voices, vastly augmented, sounded faintly from the Valley of the Cheese-mongers, Pollio looked at the others, lifted one brow half-smilingly.

"Perhaps it is time that we all went home to our beds." Then he smiled openly. "Did a heathen god pass us in parade, or did we merely imagine it?"

CHAPTER TWO

HEROD, THE OVER-BOLD

N o sooner did Herod leave the tavern than he changed character. He became the administrator and man of arms.

"Directly home and to your beds, those of you who will
march to Galilee with me. There is much to be done tomorrow if we
are to leave for Galilee the day following. Let me find no exhausted
men among you tomorrow. Victories, such as we plan, are won by men
of alert minds and fit bodies. Astride your mounts and homeward!"

Herod himself did not follow his own orders. He rode to the citadel to find out what was the situation there. Had the legion, the
veterans of the Egyptian campaign, who had fought under his father
with Caesar, all reported, and were they resting? He was gratified
to find that this was so. He went out upon the parade ground of the
fort and saluted the leaders and gave instructions that the horses be
grain-fed, rubbed down, and bedded well on straw. He would have
slept there among his men but for the fact that his bride, Doris, was
far gone in pregnancy, and he followed the instructions of both his
parents to be with her and comfort her as much as possible.

Then he rode to the baronial estate of Antipater in the Lower City, stabled his mount himself—as his father had taught all of his sons to do—and walked through the elaborate formal gardens towards the house.

A large, round old moon was still shining, making the fountain on the east side of the huge, sprawling mansion a glittering, jeweled thing as the spray rose and tumbled into the basin below. Always sensitive to beauty, Herod paused there to enjoy the spectacle for a minute before he entered the house. A night-blooming shrub poured sweetness upon the air. He stood there longer than he intended, utterly enchanted.

Then he started and instinctively, his right hand closed upon the hilt of his dagger at his waist, for a shadow detached itself from the darkness between him and the house. And came quickly, but directly towards the fountain. Herod saw that it was a woman, a young woman, and before she reached him, he recognized the figure as Cleote, the Greco-Egyptian girl whom he had acquired in Alexandria three months ago to attend upon his wife as soon as it was established that Doris was pregnant.

"Cleote," Herod spoke in a subdued voice, "what are you doing out here? I hired you as an efficient midwife to wait upon Doris, not to be a guard of the grounds."

The girl had now crept quite close to Herod. Her bare hands extended, perhaps to assure him that she had no weapon, and had no intention to harm him.

"I know, my kind and good master," the tremulous voice of Cleote replied. "You chose me for the honor of attending upon your wife in her condition upon the recommendation of the physician-head of the college in Alexandria, and gave me your commands. But, but, being restless, and Doris sleeping very soundly, I was at the window and saw you when you arrived, and came down to you here in the garden."

With that, Cleote flung her body against Herod's and rested her head upon his chest. But Herod thrust her from him.

"Ah, do not . . . do not . . . do not shove me away, master. Take me—do away with this virginity—this denial of love that troubles and tortures me so. Ah, take me!" Cleote clung desperately to his blouse.

"But I cannot. My father has forbidden his sons to take advantage of the young women of his house. You know that he will not have a slave on his estates. He abhors slavery, and frees slaves that he buys immediately. If ever a man loved, admired, and respected his father, it is myself. He forbids me to do such a thing. He arranges for his female servants to be married and be secure. He does not wish for that which makes a young woman precious to her husband to be taken away from her by his sons because you are of a lower social status. He says that it is cowardly and wicked. You are young, beautiful, and highly skilled, and I heard him tell my mother that he planned to marry you to his man of business who is now in Rome, but who will return in a few weeks. When Doris gives birth to my child, he said, you will be free to marry, and my mother has planned many costly gifts for you on your wedding day."

Cleote stood now with bowed head, as the moon began to give less light, and wept. "I know that you too are famished for love, Herod. I have loved you since your father's steward brought me here. Yes, loved you. You are the most perfectly beautiful of all men. Just this once, Herod. Doris is unable to comfort you now because of her pregnancy, but she will never give you the comfort you require, for the reason that she is cold by nature. We are taught the signs of it in our school. She is very beautiful, yes, but wanting in heat. You are strong, affectionate, and young. Allow me to furnish that which you must have to sustain you and make you a whole man."

"No, Cleote. Never has my father made use of a concubine, and he strictly enjoins such a relationship to his sons. Go now, Cleote, and go swiftly."

Presently, he stood in his apartment looking down on Doris by the light of a single large candle whose flame moved gently in the slight breeze of the air. There was that abundance of dark, silky hair clouding her face, her shoulders, and the pillow. There were the regular and harmonious features required of a bride of a son of his house. Yes, Doris was indeed beautiful but lacking in stimulation, because she herself was never stirred.

Parian marble, sculptured by Phidias, the tortured Herod thought derisively. *But she is my wife and I have allowed that Cleote to injure my opinion of her.* Doris slept on peacefully, and Herod began to undress himself. *That is a lie. I felt some lack in Doris from the very night of my wedding, but could not define it. But all will be well in the end because both my parents attest that if a man marries a good and proper woman and treats her with the proper tenderness and consideration, it is bound to be a happy and successful union. But this is no time for me to be going over the matter. Tomorrow will be a busy and fateful day in my life. The welfare of Galilee depends upon me.*

At an early hour of the morning, Herod presented himself at the citadel. He was on the parade ground when he heard the priest announcing the daily sacrifice from the tower of the nearby temple. He was putting his Arab horsemen through a maneuver that he had found in Caesar's Commentaries from his Gallic wars.

"What I require of you is to school your mounts to turn about in the shortest possible space and time. In that way, you will be at no disadvantage and prepared to defend yourselves from the enemy, no matter from what direction you are attacked. In addition, train your mounts to stay at your back when you dismount to fight with your swords at close range. Now, how many of your mounts have experience in battle?"

"O Herod!" the captain of the Arab horsemen exclaimed, "of all men to inquire such a thing of an Arab soldier? Not only of our blood yourself, but from a small boy trained in our ways of handling horses, and then make such a question. You have seen us in battle. You know that our horses rise on their hind legs and crush the skulls of the enemy with their front hooves; that they seize the enemy's limbs with their strong teeth and hurl them to death, and as to trampling them down, you know how terrible they are in battle in that way."

Herod grinned with satisfaction and asked again, "Yes, but will he stay at your back when you dismount to fight at close quarters?"

"Where else, Herod? When he has slept in the tent with you all of his life, eaten with you, and acted as nurse-protector to your children, he is ever at your back. He is ever a good brother to you. But now, we should practice that part about turning within his own tracks some, so that he will perform it whenever asked."

Herod watched this exercise for half an hour and then left to take counsel with his quartermaster. Having served under Antipater for many years, he too had gone ahead with what he knew had to be done. Not only did he have sufficient beasts of burden, but spares. There was also a bounty of wagons and carts. The beasts had already been examined to see if they were all sound, but had been put on grain-feed, brushed down, and stalled. Plenty of provisions for fighting men and beasts were being loaded into the vehicles. And a competent driver had been assigned to each vehicle.

"Ah, what fine, capable men I have with me," Herod exclaimed. "There seems to be nothing left to me but to announce the plan of march. On the stroke of midnight, the baggage train is to set out for Jericho. You, Joseph, who performed this same service for my father in the Egyptian campaign, will naturally be in charge. At the third hour, my footmen will follow, led by Aristo, who also served under my father. And when it is proclaimed from the pinnacle of the temple, 'The morning shineth already . . . ,' then I shall lead my horsemen through the gates of the citadel of the city, through the Gate of Damascus. We shall meet again in Jericho. My chief officers will there come to me and we shall work out the next move on our march to Galilee."

When the dawn appeared, Herod and his cavalry were all bathed and dressed in their dress uniforms. Herod had designed the costumes and they were good to look at. His men were very proud in them. Knowing for weeks ahead of the public of his appointment, Herod had ordered the uniforms at his own expense. As for his own, he had set the most excellent maker of armor of Damascus to work on it. His coat of mail was formed of tiny pieces of pure and polished silver, each in the shape of a tapering feather. The small units rendered the metal coat as flexible as wool. It glinted and glittered from a thousand facets. His short cloak was white silk of Cos, and lined with silk of royal blue. The clasp of it was an intricate design in gold and decorated by a sizable ruby. The arm-bracelet which he wore above his left elbow was gold in the shape of three strands of rope and ended in the form of the Lion of Judah holding a large ruby in snarling jaws. As he waited for the signal from the pinnacle of the temple, he, like all of his men, stood beside his mount.

At the cry of the priest upon the pinnacle, he mounted, flung back his cloak with a reckless gesture, and rode before his men through the gate of the citadel as it swung ajar.

"We ride now towards our destiny," he confided in a low, exultant voice to Nicator, his Arabian stallion, and pranced out into the street. His men rode out in the formation agreed upon during the night, four abreast. Nicator's rich accoutrements of polished silver on polished leather, and the semi-precious stones ornamenting all, responded to the youthful light of morning as he was guided up the hill to the highest point of the city, where stood the temple confronted by the sprawling palace of the Asamoneans.

If by planning to leave the city at such an early hour, he thought he would avoid a crowd, Herod was mistaken. A packed crowd stood opposite the gate of the citadel to see him emerge. The sidewalks were crammed on both sides up the hill to the temple and beyond. As Herod rode three horse lengths ahead of his men, they cheered him wildly.

"Herod the Handsome!"

"Hail, Herod the Magnificent!"

"Herod, the Defender!"

"Herod the Over-Bold!"

"Herod the Ever-Ready!"

"Herod Nicator, the Conqueror!"

Herod would not have been himself if he had not acknowledged this acclaim and played up to it. He waved his right hand in salute to the people, flashed his brilliant smile, drew his jeweled-hilted sword, and waved it above his head as he announced in a loud and convincing voice that the Lion of Judah sought his prey. The people went mad and cheered louder. That was their Herod!

But now that he approached the temple and royal palace, he went into the display that had been planned the night before. With the lifting of his right hand, every one of the thousand and more horses reared simultaneously, made three tight revolutions on their hind legs, pawed the air with the front feet, and descended. As Herod wheeled his spirited Palomino, the columns of four wheeled first right and then left on a pivot between the palace and the temple. Wild cheering broke out again. Then Herod stood stock still with Nicator's head facing the palace, drew his sword, and saluted the balcony of the palace smartly.

For there stood Antipater upon the balcony of the palace with Phasaelus on one side and Hyrcanus on the other. *What a handsome and impressive man my father is!* Herod thought as he held the salute for a long moment. Beside Antipater, Herod decided, Hyrcanus looked like a mule beside a Palomino stallion. The breeding just was not there. Antipater wore the parade uniform that he had worn in Egypt and had worn again when he had received Caesar in Syria. Force and intelligence and assurance shaped his face. *How fortunate I am to be the son of this man. I must, I will be victor in Galilee and act as the best administrator that any province in the world ever had. My noble father expects nothing less of me.*

According to plan, the men broke the salute in a gallop, each leaped from his mount and mounted again while the horses yet galloped, which brought a wild cheer from the spectators. Ah, that Herod was reckless but magnificent! Who was like him?

Eyes, which Herod did not see nor even think about, had watched him from before the moment when he arrived before the palace balcony. Two pairs of eyes in the palace, and neither knew that the other peered from behind the hangings of a front window.

Alexandra, the widowed daughter of Hyrcanus, had crept from her bed and hastily but secretly sought the cover of the hangings at a front window at the east side of the palace. Her daughter, Mariamne, also secretly gained a window in the west wing, her young body concealed by a heavy, red drape. The girl had hardly slept an hour during the night, waiting for the time when Herod and his horsemen should ride past.

Alexandra gasped as Herod rode up the hill. The shoulders, the proud erect carriage, his assurance in the saddle indicated to her general masterfulness. She began to feel possessive. And why not? He was of eminent birth, far richer than her family, able, and so beautiful of body and face. She was not an old woman, really. Less than ten years older than Herod, and her royal birth would compensate for the difference easily. And further, with Herod beside her, and the tremendous power of his father, she could be accepted as queen by the nation. In fact, they would be compelled to accept her if Antipater said so. He was the voice of Rome in Palestine. Who would dare to oppose the daughter-in-law of Antipater? And with that smile, handsome Herod would be so easy to love. Never at any point had she felt love for the arrogant, stupid Alexander. Now . . . and always she was clothed in a glory of her own making.

The adolescent Mariamne knelt behind the drapery of the window to the west and also dreamed. Ah, the handsome, strong, and masterful man who was riding up the hill towards the palace. Why was there no one like him to throw protective arms about her? Her grandfather was foolish and feeble. Her mother self-centered and cared for nobody except Aristobulus, her small brother. She was merely a troublesome girl who could never inherit the crown, and therefore of no value to anybody. She cared nothing about the government. Just somebody to love and protect her. Who would be more acceptable than the handsome Herod? Perhaps she could find a way to suggest the match to him.

From Jerusalem to Galilee was a three-day march if one went by the direct road which passed through Samaria. Herod took this route and the third day was at the southern end of Lake Gennesaret with his entire contingent safe after a very pleasant march. After Jericho, Herod had sent a courier with a letter each day, giving his father a report on conditions of places along the march.

Now, in Galilee, he made a temporary camp south and east of Nazareth and sent out messengers to summon the elders of the towns and villages to come to him there. They did, but each showed surprise and small pleasure at the youth of the governor. The old ruling "father" from Magdala spoke his concern.

"Antipater was in Galilee only a few weeks ago and saw our unhappy situation. He talked earnestly with us, and we explained many things to him. Evidently, living at Jerusalem, he is like all the Judeans, indifferent to our fate. Otherwise, he would not send to us an inexperienced youth of a boy."

But he too, like the others, finally succumbed to Herod's charm, his grasp of the situation, and his assurance that he would put down all disorders and restore security and prosperity.

"If you will only aid me with your wise counsel, Fathers. There is no hurry. I want you to remain here and talk with me as long as you have information and advice to give. I think that if you advise me well, you will find that my youth is no hindrance to me at all. My own father has gone to great pains to train me, and expects me to accomplish what you wish here. Look upon me as your own son, and instruct me in that spirit."

The eyes of the elders flew from one to the other in pleasant surprise.

"This is what we want to hear, son. We are no longer unhappy with the son of our great friend. Now, ask us what you want to know."

"First, it is necessary to deal with this cruel and destructive bandit, Hezekiah. I need to know everything about him possible. What is he like in a physical way? Where is his headquarters? How does he operate? About how many followers has he? Are they very loyal to him? How far west and south has he struck? Is he extending his field of activities? And anything else that you can think of."

A deep and apprehensive silence fell upon the enclosure of Herod's tent. Fearful glances were exchanged. Then a relatively young man, a Syrian from Capernaum, spoke up.

"It is usually very unwise to speak about this fearful human monster but since you appear ready to risk your own life to help us, we would be the most vile of cowards to shield ourselves quietly by refusing to risk speaking openly to you in our own interest."

"Galileans have never been cowards," another joined in. "But when a man finds himself powerless before a band of men without heart, soul, nor conscience, it is very difficult to be brave. More than that, Hezekiah has unseen ears in many places. You complain of his cruel depredations, and in a night or so, his horde sweeps down upon your town, and you and your family are robbed and butchered."

"That is just the trouble, son," the elder from Magdala all but shouted. "There are those in every community in Northern Galilee who earn money by informing on others to Hezekiah. There is no way of knowing who they are. But here, I assume a man may speak boldly."

"Do so by all means, Fathers, for rest assured that I shall destroy the monster."

The men talked. Hezekiah had easily five to seven thousand men behind him. He was nothing more than a petty thief before the disturbance arose between Hyrcanus and his brother, Aristobulus. With the lessening of enforcement, all those who would prefer to rob and murder rather than to gain a living by work ran to Hezekiah. Others were impressed by fear into his band. Others were secretly with him and earned money by informing the bandit leader as to who had hidden money or had spoken disparagingly of him. His band increased to thousands when Aristobulus was captured the second time by the Romans and was poisoned by Pompey's party, for he had operated as a pirate and bandit himself for a time. On his death, his followers had deserted the coastal cities and run to join Hezekiah, since they wished to continue to live by crime.

It was no secret that his headquarters were east of the lake where the Jordan River entered it. Why should he care who knew? He looked upon himself as too formidable to be attacked. But, oh, the horrible rapes, murders, burning of homes, the tongues of informers cut out, and the like. Virgins and young wives found beside the road and in fields after being taken in one of Hezekiah's raids. And after he himself had raped them, he had turned them over to his men. Some died from exhaustion, being raped so continuously that they had no opportunity for sleep nor food. Infants with their brains dashed out against stones, farms burned, cattle driven off. The oil, corn, and wine that was to sustain a family for a year snatched away and destroyed in orgies of feasting in the caves of the bandits.

"There are no words to tell of my horror and repugnance to such crimes," Herod said after more than an hour of listening. "Fathers, I give you my right hand that I shall destroy this beast. The last drop of blood in my veins is pledged to your security. I pray for the blessing of killing Hezekiah with my own hands."

One elder arose and rushing over to Herod, embraced him like a son. Tears of hope and gratitude flowed from many eyes.

"This youth is indeed our son. He speaks like a Galilean. Shall we show less industry in the matter than he?"

It was agreed that they could not. They zealously aided in making plans and recruiting volunteers to his standard.

"What I chiefly require is information. I know that my army appears unequal to Hezekiah's numbers, but what we lack in numbers is more than over-weighed by skill and courage. Fathers, what skill and courage is required to fall upon unarmed shepherds, husbandmen, women, and children?"

The men looked from one to another in pleased surprise, then back to Herod.

"Our son is wise indeed. There is no necessity to say more. We grasp the point. Never has he had to fight against trained soldiers. Still, we do not wish you to be overconfident. Hezekiah is brutal and cunning. He has twice your number of desperadoes and cutthroats behind him. But we are now inspired to defy him. If our son dies fighting the beast, let us die with him."

They recommended to Herod that he make it to the walled city of Sepphoris. It was the largest city of Galilee, protected by walls, but near to Hezekiah's field of depredations, which spilled over the border into Syria at times. Herod promptly moved into Sepphoris with his army.

Recruits began to trickle in at first, then as the days passed, became a steady stream, and Herod put his officers to training these young men as auxiliaries for permanent use in keeping order in Galilee.

One night, two young men, brothers, slipped into his camp. These two differed from the other recruits in that they were deserters from Hezekiah. Among other useful things, they warned Herod that Hezekiah, to show his defiance and scorn of the young Herod, planned an assault upon Capernaum on the third night following. He meant to make it particularly terrible to show the people of Galilee that Herod was no protection, and second, to scare "Antipater's pretty infant" back to Jerusalem.

Herod thanked the young men, but asked if they could rejoin Hezekiah without the risk of danger to themselves, and gain more information for him.

"It is dangerous, O Herod, for he has spies everywhere, in and outside of his camp, but we were threatened with the destruction of our home, the rape of our mothers and sisters unless we join him, and the terrible crimes that we have witnessed and been forced to take a part in, determines us to do what we can to put an end to the beast. We will return."

"You are to desert him again on the assault upon Capernaum and be secure from then on. But I want to be sure that we are at the right place to give the bully the meeting. If some other place is selected for the target, get the information to me in some way or other. That is what I require of you. Or in the case that he changes his mind about the raid, get me word."

Now Herod planned swiftly. He consulted with the ruling men of the province, and the racial elements who inhabited Galilee solemnly prayed—each in his manner—for the victory of Herod, and also, if he failed in overcoming Hezekiah, that his life might be spared.

For Galilee, as its name implied, was truly the "Ring of the Gentiles." The Jews were in the minority, but all lived happily there together. Neighborly and brotherly, tolerant of the religious views of the others. It was the melting-pot of Palestine. Further, the great crossroads of western Asia—east and west, north and south—crossed Galilee. The great caravans bearing goods even from far India, through Persia, Asia Minor, down through Syria, Palestine, Arabia, and on to Egypt, had been traveling with their military escorts along this road for a thousand years before Herod was born. Goods and merchants landed at Antioch and other port cities from across the Great Sea, moved eastward to the Decapolis east of the Jordan and on to Chaldea, Babylonia, and east of the Caspian through Galilee. The "nations" met no withdrawn, isolationist population in this most northern province of Palestine.

This was not Judea. Galileans met and talked freely with men from everywhere in the then-known world, exchanging goods and ideas. During the centuries, conquering armies had marched up and down, east and west through this province and left their signs and marks upon the people. Therefore, they were an independent-minded, self-willed people, which often distressed closed-in Jerusalem. So the rulers there asked rhetorically, "Can anything good come out of Galilee?" and poked fun at the peculiar, almost lisping accent of the Galilean.

"You are our son," an old Syrian elder said emotionally. "You are Galilean at heart, Herod. You are of and with us. You do not find our way of speaking ridiculous. You rashly expose yourself to great danger for our sake. We will carry out your instructions gladly."

Herod wrote his father of his plans, and added:

Tomorrow, I shall cross the Jordan and attack this loathsome bandit leader in his very caves. I feel no fear, for as you know, a rabble, however numerous, cannot stand against trained soldiers. It is very different from attacking and slaughtering unarmed husbandmen, women, and children. Having seen the work of this barbarian, I am determined to kill him and free these decent and lovable people from his crimes.

My most reverent and deep love to all of the members of my beloved family. Tell Pheroras that he trifles too much and therefore fails to devote his time and himself to the things you, and the rest of the family, would have him concerned about. How is Joseph getting along with his military training? I expect a great soldier in Joseph in time. Embrace my mother tenderly for me. Tell my little sister, Salome, that her love and admiration reach me over all the distance between. She is so intelligent and easy to learn, and so beautiful that my love of her is excessive. You are aware of my love and devotion to my elder brother, Phasaelus. Embrace him in my stead. Now, as to Doris, I am writing her a separate letter also, but remember, that in case I lose my life in the battle tomorrow, her child, if a boy, is to be named in your honor. If a girl, after my mother. In the unhappy case that I am slain, I know that you will take good care of both. Pray for my success.

Having dispatched this lengthy epistle, Herod bathed and went to bed. All arrangements had been made for his forces to march out of the encampment at dawn. The distance to be covered was approximately twenty-five miles. At noon, they were again at Capernaum waiting for the baggage train to catch up with them. His footmen rested from the fast march, cooked full meals and relaxed.

The people of Capernaum filled the streets and hailed the young governor. Many wept out of sheer relief and joy. Though they felt it a sharp disappointment that Hezekiah was still alive.

Herod wrote his daily letter to his father before he slept and sent it to Jerusalem by a swift courier.

Herod, Governor of Galilee, to Antipater, Procurator of Judea. Greetings. If this finds you well and peaceful of mind, I am glad. I am with the archers of my army at Capernaum. Herod then went on to give his father the details of the day's encounter, adding that he would not return to Sepphoris for a few days in order to protect the city in case Hezekiah returned to avenge himself upon Capernaum for his defeat of this day. *And if I fail in my duty and the trust you reposed in me, I shall strip myself of the love, honor, and glory, without which I cannot live, of being the son of the brave and noble Antipater, whose soul is the greatest in the habitable earth. Beseech my beloved brother, Phasaelus, Governor of Judea, to write me more often, advising me more fully of his progress there. So far, his epistles have been few and scant of information.*

Now came the hard part of Herod's letter. Both of his parents expected him to write to Doris often, and certainly to add an expression of comfort and affection when he did not write her directly. Dissimulation was difficult for his open nature, and now he frankly admitted to himself that there was no heat in his marriage. He was pleased but not transported at the prospect of becoming a father. He had no memories of moments in the begetting of this child in which the very stars stopped in their courses because of his ecstasy. So after the usual mental labor on this point, he wrote, *I hope that my wife is suffering no undue pain and discomfort, and will make me the father of a fine and healthy child.*

When four days had passed and Hezekiah had not returned to fight him, Herod was satisfied. His spy in the bandit's camp had brought him the information the following day that the bandit leader had uttered many threats and intended to carry them out. He ordered them to recapture and put to death any man trying to desert. More than a dozen had managed to slip away on that same night of the battle, or skirmish. Absolute success was no longer taken for granted now among his followers, and many more merely sought an opportunity to get away. Provisions were very low, and this was a sign that Hezekiah now felt timid, for he made no move to replenish. Besides, an arrow had grazed his upper left arm, and the wound was festering. However, an Egyptian physician who had fled to join Hezekiah a year previously after committing murder in Alexandria was attending him, and assured Hezekiah that he would be cured in a few days.

Back at Sepphoris, Herod went about preparing to attack. Each day Herod's horsemen practiced maneuvers on rocky ground in preparation. The archers, javelin men, and swordsmen practiced daily also for many hours. Then they changed weapons and started all over again so that all would be deadly with each.

Four weeks went on in this way, then Herod summoned all of the elders of the cities and villages of Galilee and conferred with them long and earnestly. Every phase of life in Galilee was discussed and planned for.

"Each of you, my Fathers, must see to it that houses destroyed by Hezekiah must be replaced. Once, it was my delight to pass through Galilee, because every foot of this rich black soil was cultivated. The land was green everywhere, and the people were happy, bold, and contented. Galilee must be returned to that condition. It has been my favorite province since my youth. I love it as if I had been born here. I trust you to undertake this labor while I go forth to destroy what has been the reason for your misfortunes for many years now."

A copy of Herod's written plans was handed to the head of each delegation, and each man embraced Herod and pledged himself to put things in order in his area. "Will we be less willing to promote our own welfare?" they said. One hundred of the best expert bowmen were positioned on the flat house-tops in twelve strategic spots, beginning with those in effective arrow-range of the gate. And no one, no matter what the emergency, was allowed to leave the city once the trap was set. Anyone who might have the intention of hastening to warn Hezekiah was thus balked.

The sun dropped and dropped and Herod began to feel the creep of disappointment. Sunset had come and no sign of Hezekiah. Fuming and fretting, the new governor of Galilee was considering withdrawing when an estimated thousand of the bandits, led by Hezekiah himself, came whooping and thundering up to the city gates. There was no hesitation, they rode in with their pot-bellied mounts on the gallop, for what cared they if they rode down the population?

But there were no people on the streets. The city fathers had commanded everyone to keep indoors. With no human obstructions, the horde came in fast, whooping fearfully their vile threats. Herod did not give the signal until more than half of the band was in.

Then the whining song of arrows lifted on the air, and men began to topple from horses. The invisible archers did their work as efficiently and as swiftly as the light permitted. Curses, screams of pain, maledictions, as the once self-assured robbers turned to flee. But this was not easy, as the ones in retreat collided with the ones, who, as yet unaware of the trap, whooped on in, only to try to turn but become tangled in riderless horses, and be further hindered by the piled bodies of the wounded and dead. Herod tried in vain for a shot at Hezekiah, but on account of the poor light, could no longer single him out. In the space of half an hour, the mad turmoil was over. Those who were able fled east and north to their secure hiding place on the eastern shore of Lake Gennesaret, leaving their dead and wounded and more than a hundred horses behind.

When the sound of the fleeing horses had died away, Herod was at once searching among the dead and wounded bandits for the body of the leader Hezekiah, who was not among them. "I am happy to see my men in such good heart," he kept saying as he hesitated at the fires. "Have you plenty of everything?"

"We have an abundance of everything, O Herod, the Over-Bold. It can never be said of you that you are not generous."

"Hungry soldiers do not fight with conviction. But what is the name of the amusing song that so many of you are singing?"

There was an embarrassed silence for a moment, as one man glanced from one to another with sheepish smiles. Then one man spoke up.

"Is it possible that Herod does not know of 'Joseph, the Camel Driver'? It is sung on all travels of caravans and in most armies. It goes from mouth to mouth and from one country to the other."

"I do not recall having heard it, men. Continue the singing of it. I am interested to know about this Joseph, who drives camels."

"Not camels, O Herod," another hastily interposed. "It was one camel . . ." Here laughter from many quarters broke out. "If the son of the noble Antipater will not be offended . . ."

"I am a soldier, am I not? Why deny me what is known in so many armies? Sing!"

"Well, you see, it is a kind of marching song, and the singers just sing the words they learn from others, and . . ."

"Sing it! My ears are not easy to be offended."

So an accomplished balladeer at the next fire began at the beginning and led the rest. Immediately thousands of voices fell in. The first stanza occupied itself with why the camel, with such an ugly shape, stinking breath and rear end, went about with such a haughty look on its homely face. It was said to know the most secret name of God. God had told it to nobody but the camel. From that point on, the ballad followed the pattern of the usual adventurous lover and Joseph had loves in many countries. The song was tuneful and it was bawdy, and Herod laughed and sang with the rest. But finally, even with the inevitable incremental additions and repetitions, the adventures and loves of the amorous Camel Driver came to an end.

"I know that we are in a very short march of the headquarters of the notorious Hezekiah," he said to his collected officers. "I plan to camp here for the night so that our men are well rested for the terrible struggle of the battle. However, see that everything is in perfect order in case we are attacked during the night. I wish that Hezekiah would attack us here, since it is much better fighting territory than among those obstructing rocks at the foot of the mountains, with the narrow beach at hand. But if he does not give me the meeting himself, I shall be upon him early in the morning."

But the wily bandit forced Herod to fight him on his own ground. His savage fighters, knowing the desperation of their plight, rushed out from their mountain nests and attacked with fury. Herod met the charge with even more fury and skill and prevented his men fighting with their backs to the lake. The training of his men began to tell, and slowly, and fighting desperately, the bandits were forced back and northward around the foot of the mountain, and they tried to reach the caves above. Herod's bowmen were invaluable to him in the first assault particularly, and in the last phase of the conflict. Now, when Hezekiah's men had retreated to the point below their caves, Herod's horsemen proved their worth. Twisting and turning within the length of their mounts, they were able to confront and prevent the bandits over the boulder-strewn terrain and inflict injuries at the same time. Up went blades, down they came in a flash.

Seeing how hopeless their case was, many of the bandits now fled away from the conflict and took the road leading through Bashan and on to Parthia. Herod wished then that he had had a thousand more men to overtake these men and cut them down, but he had none to spare. He comforted himself as best he could with the thought that at least they were driven out of Galilee and adjoining Syria, and would be no trouble in the area. But extermination was his goal.

And then at last he saw Hezekiah himself not far away, fighting a savage rearguard action to escape to the safety of the caves far above. Herod grasped his spear and yelled to the bandit leader.

"Stop, Hezekiah! If you are as brave as you boast that you are, halt your cowardly flight and fight the one you have called 'Antipater's beautiful baby.'"

The bandit wheeled and snarled at Herod, exposing his rotting front teeth. He cursed Herod roundly and coarsely, then suddenly gripping his heavy spear, hurled it. But it was a second too late.

Herod's own spear was on the way, it hit Hezekiah fairly in the chest and pinned him to the ground.

"Oh, allow me to finish him, Herod," one of Herod's young officers begged.

"He is finished," Herod said confidently making his way towards where Hezekiah lay. "I have been practicing that throw since I was ten years old. Never do I fail to inflict a fatal wound if I am in range. I have brought down deer in full flight with it a dozen times. That man is dead."

And he was, and what remained of his fighters were in full flight, hotly pursued by Herod's men—horse and foot. A very few escaped along the road, but the others perished to a man.

The figure of the bandit Hezekiah was loathsome. The under-bred body and face, unkempt beard, and rotting teeth, repelled Herod. He was so fascinated that he was scarcely aware when he was joined by two of his junior officers who had feasted Herod on the night of his appointment as governor of Galilee.

"What a marvelous hurl, O Herod!" one exclaimed, looking down at the point of the javelin.

"No," Herod returned, "I aimed at two inches further to the left. It was the width of the blade and the force of the thrust that saved me. After fifteen years of trial, it should have been perfect. But look at the loathsome creature! This horrible thing has forced himself upon countless innocent virgins who would not have endured him if their will had been consulted. Consider the horror of the action to the unfortunate girls. It might have been our own sisters, wives, or even our mothers."

The young men, outraged at the thought, would then have mutilated the body further, but Herod prevented them.

"No, my friends. Let the body remain recognizable. I intend to display it at the junction of the great highways at Cana, so that all the world will know that this horrible felon is really dead. His body shall be hung from a stake and put upon a wagon so that the people can see it as we return to Capernaum."

The officers hurried off to carry out the order, and Herod sought out Aristo, who was already attending to the securing of the bodies of those who had fallen, wounded or dead.

"Look at the sun, O Herod. It is mid-afternoon. You look surprised. The fury of the struggle made us forgetful of time. We fought well. Be proud of yourself, O Herod. Caesar himself never did better in Egypt."

"That is high praise, coming from you, O Aristo, who fought under my father, and close to the Great Caesar himself."

The two stood looking about them. Up the rugged slope of the mountain, at the talus-strewn foot, and down along the narrow beach to the waters of the lake, bodies, bodies, lying in every posture of death.

"We lost men, but few compared to the losses of the enemy," Aristo said thoughtfully. "That demonstrates again the value of training and experience. Our wounded are already loaded on wagons and on the way to Capernaum. Soon our dead will be loaded and on the road to Sepphoris for proper burial."

HEROD FOUND THAT the news of the destruction of Hezekiah and his followers had traveled fast. No sooner had his army passed the narrow gorge where the Jordan entered the northern end of the lake than they encountered cheering crowds. Battle-weary as they were as they proceeded round the broad end of the heart-shaped lake, Herod was forced to continually slow down and acknowledge the cheers of the crowds who had gathered along the line of march. Herod had planned to break his march at Capernaum for the night to give his men a chance to rest before proceeding on to Sepphoris, which he did, but there was little rest, for the admiring hysterical crowds poured into Capernaum from every direction, even from adjoining Syria. They were all about the house where Herod was quartered and writing a letter to Antipater, far into the night. They begged to glimpse him, to touch him, even to look upon his horse.

"My Galilean Fathers, next to God, Antipater, my earthly father, is my object of love and worship. My mother says that I would show the greatest excitement whenever he approached my cradle, and when I was only a few months old, would stretch my arms towards him, begging to be lifted up by him. No sooner was the battle over than I sent off a brief letter to him, informing him of the success of his son. My two couriers should be in Samaria by morning at least."

"A worthy son of a worthy father. Such fidelity heightens our own regard for you, Herod of Galilee. We think of you, our son, in that way. Now, we have a great favor to ask of you. Since the people of this area have suffered so long and so cruelly from the crimes of this Hezekiah, we are of the opinion that it would be a blessing if you would pass your army in review before them tomorrow."

"Granted. And now I go to bathe and seek some rest. This battle had its difficulties and challenges."

Accordingly, the next morning at nine, Herod, mounted on his stallion, Nicator, led his army past the city hall of justice where all of the local dignitaries sat on the balcony to feast their eyes on the splendor of the army. Herod wore the finely-made armor of silver again, and received an acclamation like wind over the sea. Groups of virgins dressed in white danced before him and put garlands upon him, and flung flowers under the feet of his horse. Bands of youths with garlands danced and sang songs hastily composed in his honor. People fought to even touch the bridle and the mane of Nicator, the stirrups, the tail of the stallion, wept for joy and in adulation, screamed and fainted in high emotion. No Roman general, voted a triumph by the senate, ever received such adoration. "Our Herod. Hail the conqueror. Herod the Glorious. Herod of Galilee. Herod has fleshed his sword in Galilee."

These and many other salutations struck his ears like thunder. The thousands who had brought garlands pressed upon him more and more and all but smothered him under the floral offerings. He had had the body of Hezekiah hung on a stake upon a wagon, and the multitude had to be restrained from tearing it down and offering it every manner of insult and mutilation. Men shuddered at the sight and screamed curses. Women screamed hysterically and fainted. Some shouted fiercely of when they had last seen the miscreant. When he was cutting out the tongue of a neighbor; raping a struggling, screaming virgin; dashing the head of an infant against a stone and raping its mother to death; and the like. So they acclaimed his destroyer more. Every contingent of Herod's troops was honored—even his baggage train as it passed in review and on out of the city gates.

Back in the walled city of Sepphoris, which he had reached at last after being acclaimed at every town, village, and hamlet along the route, and on approaching Sepphoris, the city elders had led out the entire population gaily dressed to receive the conqueror, Herod, bone-weary as he was, first wrote out a more detailed account of the battle, sent it off to Antipater, then slumped into a profound slumber. The sun was well above the horizon the next morning when he stirred and found admirers from all parts of Galilee gathered in Sepphoris to acclaim his victory.

"Will this acclaiming never end?" he grumbled to his aides, but dressed himself carefully and went out to receive his worshippers. The next day, he set out on a tour of both Upper and Lower Galilee to put affairs in order. Then he left for Sepphoris.

* * *

A courier carrying a letter from Sextus Caesar, second cousin of Julius Caesar, overtook Herod's party some miles from Sepphoris. Sextus Caesar was governor of Syria, and his letter spoke in highly flattering terms of Herod's destruction of Hezekiah and his followers. Then

Caesar said that hundreds of letters had come to him from that part of Syria which joined Galilee lauding Herod as their savior, and a young man of the highest courage and talents. Therefore, Sextus Caesar desired that Herod should appear before him at Damascus as soon as he could accomplish the journey. He ended his letter with warm words of praise.

Now Herod made one of those little gestures which further endeared him to the Galileans, and was to have tremendous influence on his future. Turning back to Sepphoris, Herod sent for the elders, showed them the letter from Sextus Caesar, lamented that if he went to Damascus, it would delay the plans for the restoration of Galilee for perhaps two weeks. Then asked humbly if they thought that he should obey Caesar and hurry to Damascus, or ignore him and go on about the plans which they had worked out together.

For a minute, the elders were so astonished by his humility and regard for their opinion that nobody could find a word. Then the first to recover ran to Herod and embraced him warmly.

"Ah, our eminent young son! You have been admirably trained by your noble father in the respect due to your elders. I know that all of us here agree with my words when I urge you to go on to Caesar at Damascus. It adds luster to us all here, who are your fathers. Go, son, and we will send letters to advise all of the Galileans of the reason for your delay. You have those qualities and generosity of soul which make you easy to love. Go with our blessings. It is possible that Sextus Caesar requires your counsel in the settling of the affairs of Syria."

Herod found the president of Syria a mild-mannered man in his mid-forties with a lively sense of humor, well informed generally, and kindly of spirit.

"I was told that you were very young, Herod, but I had no idea that you were as young as you appear."

"My youth is somehow always exaggerated, O Caesar, for I am in my twenty-fifth year. But never in my life has my youth, as my father scolds, been any hindrance to me."

They both laughed heartily at Herod's impudence, then Herod was led to give an account of all that had happened in Galilee, while a secretary took careful notes. He then reported on the state of affairs in Judea, Arabia, Samaria, and the Decapolis.

"What a wealth of information you have!" Caesar exclaimed. "How would a man so young come by it?"

Then Herod explained briefly that his father was an international banker, serving rulers by direct loans, or buying up their taxes. His father always making a thorough survey of the affairs of any nation or province who applied to him for money. He told how, since his fifteenth year, Antipater had always taken him and Phasaelus along and made them aware of every detail of such transactions. Indeed, he required them to do a great deal of the research work themselves, with assistants, of course, to take care of the details. Because of this, he was familiar with conditions in western Asia from Egypt, in Africa, to the provinces up to the Euphrates. Knowing, and being favorably known to the rulers in this area, it had been possible for his father to bring to Julius Caesar the assistance required in his Egyptian campaign.

"This is important information you furnish. I must write a letter to the Roman senate acknowledging your services."

Sextus looked at Herod long and critically, then said with a quiet smile, "You know, Herod, you have all the makings of a great king."

"I have?" Herod showed astonishment. "What persuades you of this?"

"First and most important, you *look* like a king. The people are not given to excessive thinking, and when their ruler looks like what they conceive that a king should look like, they are easily satisfied in other ways. You have shown yourself to be an excellent soldier, and now you reveal to me the preparation for a wise and informed administrator. You indicate that you have been schooled in rhetoric, and certainly you are capable of quick decisions, and the rashness to carry them out."

They both laughed again and, arm in arm, went off to the public baths, making light jokes as they went. They found excellent entertainment in each other. That evening, Sextus feasted Herod with all of the leading men of Damascus present. Among these was Saramalla, the wealthiest man between the Euphrates and the Nile, the only man wealthier than Antipater, and his close friend. In the course of the long banquet, he spoke in high praise of Antipater and his sons to Caesar. Herod, on his part, charmed the gathering to a man.

The following day, Sextus, having dictated his letter to Rome— and a most flattering commendation—took Herod on a hunting party of about a dozen men, where Herod won the admiration of the group with his accuracy and courage in the chase.

The following afternoon, Sextus took Herod to the games at the amphitheater, where he was acclaimed as the conqueror of Hezekiah and given a great ovation. Sextus Caesar was visibly pleased.

"Because of his wicked crimes and aware of his formidable reputation," said Sextus, "I was cautious in my preparation to assault him, to the end that the attempt could not fail. Then along you came and relieved me of the necessity."

Turning from the exhibition below, Sextus extended his right hand to Herod. "We must ever be the firmest of friends." The two clasped their right hands with deep sincerity.

Herod was to return to Galilee the next morning, and Sextus was so taken with his personality that he tried to delay Herod for yet another day, but finding that he could not, arranged an elaborate breakfast on the patio of the government house for themselves. He teased Herod in a good-natured way of being anxious about the affairs of his "kingdom," and when they exchanged the customary presents, he received from Herod the shoulder clasp which Herod had worn when he left Jerusalem, saying that Herod had splendid taste in his clothes. And in the spirit of jest, gave Herod a length of finest linen dyed royal purple.

"But should you take the notion to wear this, Herod, keep out of Rome. The Roman people are no more discerning than the people elsewhere, and I have no wish for them to acclaim you as king, and thus displace my eminent cousin, Julius, and thus bring on another civil war."

"Oh, I am not so ambitious, O Sextus," Herod replied with mock modesty, "I would not insist that I be given the title of king. I would be quite satisfied with being made dictator for life. Everybody in Judea is well aware of my retiring nature." They burst into loud laughter. "All I want is the best."

CHAPTER THREE

THE ACCUSED

Jerusalem was in an uproar brought on by Herod's successes in Galilee. First came Herod's report of his victory to his father, who went at once to the palace and showed it to his lifelong friend, Hyrcanus, then to various eminent men of the city. In a matter of hours, it was known all over the metropolis. Judea went wild with rejoicing, except for a minority which was morbid with disappointment, and made no secret of the fact that they had hoped things would turn out otherwise. Among them it had been said repeatedly, "Remove that brash and reckless Herod, and the intelligence of the trio, Antipater and his sons, will disappear." Certain that he would be killed by Hezekiah, they had comforted themselves, and so were most unwilling to believe that Herod had strengthened his own reputation and the family hold on the public mind by his unexpected and sensational victory.

"Don't be so credulous," they sneered. "Antipater is an extremely rich man. Herod has merely bought Hezekiah off. By a large gift of cash, Hezekiah has been persuaded to leave the country."

But confirmation of Herod's triumph came from many directions on flying hooves. One messenger arrived with the tidings, then another, and another and so on until it appeared that every city, town, and village in Galilee had reported to Jerusalem. Messengers with letters of praise of Herod for delivering them from the power of the bandits also came from places in Syria. Herod was made out to be almost a deity. Then a group of merchants arrived in Jerusalem telling of seeing the body of Hezekiah hanging at the crossroads at Cana. His death could no longer be doubted.

The first result of the sensational news came from Phasaelus. He had been going about restoring the walls of Jerusalem which had been torn down by Pompey, but in a rather nonchalant manner. Now, on the next morning, he was about very early and in the end had hired two thousand more laborers and put them to work. Two thousand more men gainfully employed raised his prestige considerably in Jerusalem. Phasaelus looked in every direction to see what could be done to benefit Jerusalem and its suburbs and the people responded favorably. He busily administered justice regardless of social standing and won more glory. But he was noticeably irritated to hear his name mentioned last in the trio. The old title, "Antipater and his sons," now read, "Herod, Antipater, and Phasaelus."

First Cypros, his mother, and then Antipater took notice of the jealousy of Phasaelus, and Antipater gently rebuked Phasaelus for it.

"Are you now deviating from what you have always been taught, Phasaelus? That the success of one member of the family is the success of all? Destroy this sickness of your mind, for in that direction lies disaster for us all. I am delighted with your new exhibition of energy, but do not allow it to arise out of jealousy of your brother."

"I am not jealous, Father," Phasaelus defended himself a trifle sullenly. "But I am your oldest son, and I think that you should have sent *me* to Galilee, it being the more responsible and dangerous task.

I know military science just as much as does Herod. I too could have beaten Hezekiah."

"That is neither fair nor just, son. Being the elder, I gave you the choice, did I not? At that time, you eagerly chose the governorship of Jerusalem as being of a greater dignity. Remember, Phasaelus?"

"Well, yes, but then I could see that you preferred Herod for Galilee."

"Yes, I really did, beloved son. The conditions required his greater energy and daring. You are entirely satisfactory to me, but each of you have different talents. You fit well where you are, and, as you see, Herod was suited for what had to be done in Galilee. Go ahead and equal or surpass him where you are."

"Please forgive me, Father," Phasaelus said humbly. "I was getting jealous of Herod's glory and splendor, but now I see how foolish it was of me. Our labors really complement each other in upholding your hands. You will see that it shall not occur again."

Antipater embraced Phasaelus warmly, then made several suggestions for his progress in restoring Jerusalem.

"Beauty never injures anybody nor anything, Phasaelus. Add beauty to the city wherever possible. For example, the Pool of Siloam could be adorned and made more comfortable for those who go there. With stone seats about, some blossoming shrubbery, it could become a thing of beauty. Plant trees wherever possible also. From the Upper Market Place down through the Valley of the Cheese-mongers and on to Accra, the streets could be lined with shade trees. Have the laborers sow flower seeds in every vacant spot in the suburbs. Encourage the people who live inside the walls, rich and poor alike, to plant gardens of flowers. Bring the city to be a place of lively beauty."

Phasaelus went to work with more vigor, and soon the people of Jerusalem took to singing his praises, also. He was kind, he was just and altogether concerned about the welfare of the people. How fortunate were they to have Antipater and his sons in charge of their affairs!

Here were no self-indulgent tyrants wasting up the public funds upon themselves. Never in the memory of living men had public affairs been conducted in such a beneficial manner.

As to Hyrcanus, it was obvious that nobody gave him a thought. He was merely a name in the palace. Who was it that did not know that Antipater had gained him the high priesthood and title of king as a toy for his feeble mind to play with? This was most generous of Antipater, but it was taken for granted that Hyrcanus would play away and not attempt to meddle with government affairs. After all, Caesar had trusted Antipater with responsibilities, and it was very fortunate for Judea.

So they roared salutes to Antipater when he appeared on the streets. He might have been an absolute but beneficent monarch for the respect and love they paid him and his sons.

"We can well afford to acclaim them," the heads of principal families conceded, "for they do not abuse their power, but always stay within bounds. Antipater is a man of great and noble soul."

However, there were those who saw that those very attributes endangered their hopes. Day by day Antipater and his sons were becoming more and more entrenched in the hearts of the nation, and thus confirmed in power.

They knew already that Hyrcanus was extremely jealous of the glory of Herod in Galilee and that this was aggravated by the success of Phasaelus in Judea, and the extreme popularity of Antipater everywhere. And knowing of the overwhelming vanity of Hyrcanus, they realized he could easily be persuaded that he had power and attempt to exercise it to the destruction of the family of Antipater, and the flower of that family, Herod. They cunningly neglected to remind Hyrcanus that the empty title had been granted him, on the insistence of Antipater, by Caesar, but went on to dilate his vanity and increase his sense of injury by pretending that he really *was* king and in charge of affairs in

Palestine instead of Antipater. They cleverly ignored the fact that Judea was now a Roman principality, and no longer had the power to choose a governor.

"Hyrcanus, you see that Antipater and his sons behave as if you were no more than a king in name. They ignore you and exercise all power themselves."

"Oh, oh, yes, I allow this because Antipater is my good friend. I tell him what I wish to be done and he does it for me."

"Why deceive yourself, Hyrcanus? And why attempt to deceive others? Everybody knows that you do not direct the actions of Antipater. You merely blind yourself."

"And from one end of Palestine to the other," one Simon joined the attack on the wavering Hyrcanus, "the actions of Antipater and his sons are acclaimed as glorious. Not you, but they are said to be the saviors of the nation. Who mentions your name—and you of the priestly line?"

Hyrcanus hunched over and began to cry in a childish manner.

"You are speaking the truth." More sobs. "They will allow me to do nothing. They prevent me."

"Shhh! Do not say that publicly, Hyrcanus, for that Antipater has been too cunning for you there. When he returned from conducting Caesar out of Syria, he did nothing, explaining that he waited for you to quiet the tumults over the country and restore the walls. Now people saw that you did nothing, and will say that you lie if you say that you were prevented."

"But they did! Antipater and his sons did! I would have led the army myself into Galilee and destroyed that Hezekiah, but nobody would allow me." He wept in self-pity and beat his fists upon the table as he wept.

"Stop weeping and listen, Hyrcanus. You must destroy them and be king. The heart of the family is that rash Herod. When he has been taken off, Antipater and Phasaelus will soon fall because both of them are easily deceived. Antipater will believe evil of few, especially of his closest friend—yourself. That Herod is suspicious and very hard to deceive. You must rid yourself of him."

"But how? He is possessed of a very quick temper, and as you see, he is very able in battle. If I hit him, he will kill me."

"You are an old man, older by many years than Antipater, Herod's father. It would be madness for you to attempt to slay him with your own hands. However, there is a device by which you can procure his death by others, and appear not to be willing to do it."

"How?" Hyrcanus cried with great eagerness. "But tell me, and I will do it."

"But it is useless, Hyrcanus. Your mind has always been persuaded by your closest friend, Antipater. You will not remain firm."

"But, but, that was before he showed himself to be my enemy, and stole my government away from me. Now, I hate him thoroughly, and all of his family."

"If that is the case, then listen with your ears. All that is required is to summon him, I mean that reckless Herod, to his trial for the unlawful slaying of Hezekiah."

"But, but everywhere he is acclaimed as a hero for it."

"That is true, but if the Sanhedrin condemns Herod for killing Hezekiah without having brought Hezekiah to trial for his crimes before the Seventy, we will not only rid ourselves of Herod, but cause his great victory to be looked upon as a crime. All can be accomplished in one day, Hyrcanus. Herod is brought to justice and condemned by our law which says that no one, however guilty, can be executed without the sentence of the Seventy. Did Herod regard this? No! He took upon himself to kill this man before we even knew that he had won the battle and gotten hold of Hezekiah."

The eyes of Hyrcanus widened in the joy of victory. He cried for joy and his body rocked back and forth like a pendulum.

"Ah, I have them at last. That will quiet the foolish tongues who heap praise and adoration upon this Herod. Let the summons be written at once and sent on to Galilee to him."

"No, no, no, Hyrcanus. The nation would accuse us. We must allow him to be accused by others."

"That is foolish, for none will accuse him. Aside from the destruction of Hezekiah, they now praise him as a magnificent governor of Galilee. Letters of praise come to Jerusalem almost daily. And Sextus Ceasar regards him as a jewel without price."

"Nevertheless, Rome has said that we can continue to be governed by our own laws. We can get him accused before us. We shall send a man of discretion and persuasive powers to Galilee and get the widow of Hezekiah, and the widows and children of others of the bandits, to come to Jerusalem and linger around the temple daily weeping and accusing Herod of having killed their husbands unlawfully. His destruction cannot be accomplished in a day, but it can be done."

"But, but the multitudes of Judea would never bear it," Hyrcanus said sadly.

"It will all be done so swiftly that he will be dead before the multitudes are aware. And once he is dead, he is dead. His splendid appearance will not be here to persuade them."

"It makes them drunk like wine now," Hyrcanus observed sadly. "Who shall I send to get the women and children?"

"Leave that to us, Hyrcanus. Place in our hands a mina or so to take care of the expenses of transporting the women and maintaining them while they are in Jerusalem, and be silent about our plans. Rather, you must be loudest in praise of Herod and his family. That is all that is required of you until we tell you when to summon Herod to stand trial."

Less than a month later, the widow of Hezekiah and ten more of the widows of the slain robbers were found on the road between Jericho and Jerusalem, weeping and lamenting, as they walked with their children, the unjust killing of their husbands. They arrived at Jerusalem crying aloud and soliciting alms for themselves and their children made destitute by the high-handed Herod, who showed no regard for the law at all. They hung about the temple daily with their cries and accusations. Hyrcanus would not listen to them at first, but after two weeks of this, sighed and said that the Sanhedrin must hear their story.

The hearing was immediately arranged, and after their story was heard, Hyrcanus broke into weeping and said, "I love Herod, he is the same as my own son. It was so that I was a guest on the Idumean estate of his father, my dearest friend, when Herod was born. Ah, he was a beautiful, healthy infant. He was born at the exact moment that the new moon appeared in the heavens." Here, Hyrcanus was overcome by tears. "But, as much as it grieves me as the closest friend of his father, he will have to be summoned to his trial. Our laws must not be disregarded because of the deep affection between us."

Pollio, the eminent Pharisee and scholar, sat beside Sameas, his distinguished pupil, and whispered to him, "What goes on here? Try to imagine Herod in the midst of his desperate battle, crying out to the bandit leader to submit himself to arrest so that he could be brought before us for trial."

Sameas smiled briefly. "You know the answer. Some here are intent upon the death of Herod. I am very interested to see what comes of this matter. Do you think that Antipater is blinded to the intent of it all?"

"He should not be, O Sameas, yet the innocence of the man's soul prevents him from seeing evil in men. Especially in that degenerate Hyrcanus. I have often wondered at the fidelity of Antipater."

"More testimony to his cleanness of heart. Look at Phasaelus. I often wonder if he is as pure of suspicion as his father, or just lacking in perception. Herod, however, is a different matter. Perhaps that is why they are determined to take him off. He is, in reality, the guardian of his family. Well, we shall see what happens."

Both Antipater and Phasaelus were deeply troubled, however. They saw through the ruse completely. Antipater quickly retired to his home in Jerusalem and wrote a letter warning Herod not to come to his trial until he had arranged his affairs in Galilee to his satisfaction, and not to come with such a big army as to frighten Hyrcanus, but sufficient to protect himself. He got his warning letter off by a swift messenger, then slumped in grief.

"What do you make of it, Father?" Phasaelus asked glumly. "I am surprised and cast down at Hyrcanus—for whom you have performed miracles—for even listening to these miserable widows, and sharers-in-crime, who have been set on by those who envy us, let alone summoning Herod to stand trial."

Antipater said nothing for a while, then in a contemplative voice he murmured, "My son, you do not examine the actions of a friend under a harsh light. The relation of friendship is the most sacred in the world. There is nothing in Heaven, in the waters beneath, nor upon the earth so holy as the bonds of friendship, as I have ever instructed you. Nor is there anything so loathsome as a foul friend. Therefore, I am bound to withhold judgment upon Hyrcanus until he proves himself my enemy. His mind is very weak. He had been persuaded into this by more intelligent minds. I am certain that he will acquit Herod as soon as the case is heard."

"Father, my beloved and noble father, I am even more concerned, for you seem to be trying very hard to convince yourself that Hyrcanus is really your friend. Personally, I feel deep suspicion of your friend in this matter. It appears to me a flimsy excuse for Hyrcanus to attempt to set aside the decrees of Rome and doing away with you and your family, return to the theocratic rule." He paused, finally drew a deep sigh, shrugged his shoulders, and went on. "Well, Herod is not easily imposed upon."

"It is a very unhappy state of affairs. The midwife has informed your mother that Doris's time will come within the week," Antipater brooded. "And now, they summon Herod to stand trial for murder."

"But I take comfort in the knowledge that Herod will not allow these treacherous men to behead him like a sheep brought to slaughter. Herod will fight them, and despite the fact of that degenerate but cunning Hyrcanus pretending to be your friend, if Herod is forced to that extremity, I will join him."

"And I also, Phasaelus. And that is just what I fear. It will be claimed by our enemies that we set off a civil war. I have no wish for Caesar to decide that his faith in me and my abilities has been misplaced." Antipater rested his brow in his hand for a minute, shook his head and lifted his large, strong body to a standing position. "I feel a headache. I suppose that I require more sleep, now that I am getting older."

Phasaelus looked after his father anxiously as he slowly left the room. After a thoughtful few minutes, he spoke aloud. "It is a very good thing that Herod, worshipping Father as he does, did not see his face at this time. The civil war that Father dreads could not have been put off."

In that hour, Phasaelus acknowledged to himself what he had refused to see before. Herod was his superior. Both in thought and action, his younger brother was always his superior. He was governor of Jerusalem and with an army at his back. Why did he assign the defense of their father to Herod instead of to himself? Because even Antipater had come to wait upon the decisions of Herod. Therefore, Herod was in fact the head of the family. What use then to feel jealous of him anymore? The intelligent thing was to fall in behind and follow Herod. In that lay the future of the family. What difference did it make that the conclusion was repugnant to him when it was so, and necessarily so? He got to his feet slowly, left the home of Antipater, and made his way the short distance to his own house.

It being early in the evening, he found his wife in the nursery, amusing their year-old son until he should fall asleep. He greeted both with kisses, and entered the game of entertaining his son. As nearly as he could, he followed the example of his father, who went against the social pattern by being close and intimate with his family. When the child went to sleep, mother and father tiptoed out of the nursery and went to their own room with the arm of Phasaelus about the waist of his wife. Behind closed doors, he told her about the unjust charge brought against his brother.

"Nothing but vile envy!" the wife of Phasaelus exploded. "Those mossy-chinned fanatics cannot get into their foolish heads that nobody wants them to govern them. They have not had a new thought since the Flood. So they think that it is very clever of them to put Herod to death through a fraudulent scheme, construe his glorious victory into a crime, and thus destroy his body and eradicate his shining memory from the people. The young of the nation adore Herod, and even most of the aged look towards a better day. The age of the fierce old meddling prophets is many centuries past. For the good of the nation, these men who seek to destroy Herod ought to be exterminated."

"And they will be, Well-Beloved, if they continue to provoke Herod, despite my father's efforts to restrain him. You know Herod. He dares *anything*, and carries the day. Hyrcanus and his advisors are more than foolish to disturb him." Phasaelus chuckled. "He despises those vengeful old moss-backs for their false accusations against our father before Caesar. They should not tempt him too far."

In Galilee, Herod was in conference with many of the elders from all parts of Galilee when the warning letter from Antipater arrived. He read it with astonishment, then outrage, and leaped to his feet with clenched fists.

"Something disturbs our son," one elder observed. "He should tell us what it is that so provokes him."

Herod read the letter aloud to the assembly and the response was instant and united.

"Such evil audacity, but typical of Judea. Lead us against them, Son. Lead us! Do they think Galilee will submit while they plot the death of our valiant son?"

"Be not misled, my Fathers. I will fight them. You see that my father advises us to put the government of Galilee in the best shape possible. I must rely upon your advice and counsel in choosing the most able men to assist me in carrying out the plans we have worked out for the welfare of our province."

"Most assuredly, for it is to our own advantage to bring that about. Of course, you will acquaint Sextus Caesar of this piece of villainy and revolt from Rome. Prepare to travel to Damascus as soon as the summons reaches here. Conceive of those wretches accepting the perjury of the widows of those criminal wretches—who lived upon our blood themselves—against a noble character like you! It exposes their own wicked intentions. But we shall defeat them."

On the following day when the summons arrived, half a hundred of the most influential men of Upper Galilee were on hand at Herod's headquarters. All burst forth in rage when they heard read the charge of murder. It was all that Herod could do to restrain these men from gathering an army of Galileans and marching on Jerusalem.

"Do nothing until I return from Sextus Caesar," Herod begged. "I give you my solemn word that I shall take many Galileans with me when I go to Jerusalem to answer the charges. I shall have them closest to my person as my most trusted guards."

The ruling men accepted this, and allowed Herod to depart for

Damascus, when they saw that he had arranged for Aristo, and others of his seasoned officers, to begin training the recruits who poured into his headquarters. Many had rushed to Sepphoris from Syria.

The governor of Syria received Herod happily, and told him the witty sayings which he had accumulated since their last meeting, then when he inquired the cause of the unexpected visit, Herod answered by handing him the letter of Antipater and the summons from the Sanhedrin. Sextus flew into indignant rage.

"The lying insolence of this attempt upon your family, which is, in effect, a revolt from Rome. It must be dealt with, with severity. Pay no attention to this fraudulent summons. In case they have the effrontery to send to Galilee to seize your person, deal with them as you dealt with Hezekiah."

"I am more than willing to visit punishment upon these ambitious criminals, but my father being procurator, not of the priestly line, and not even a Jew by blood, they would represent to your noble cousin that my father had the intent of destroying the nation. You recall how these same men came to Syria when Caesar entrusted him with the government and accused him and his sons of tyranny and oppression?"

"I do indeed, O Herod. And I remember how your noble and generous father pled with Julius Caesar to restore the high priesthood to this wretched Hyrcanus. Caesar had no need whatsoever of a high priest, and one who is degenerate and feeble-minded, but out of his deep regard for Antipater, he granted it. Now see how both Antipater and Caesar are repaid! The evil, cunning monster thinks to take the life of his benefactor and his benefactor's sons by stealth. And my intelligence informs me that those criminal widows did not repair to Jerusalem of their own accord. I wager you a talent, gold, that they are there on monies supplied by this same ulcerous Hyrcanus. In Greece, they punish ingratitude by severe imprisonment, and they are right in this. But I shall write this Hyrcanus and the conspiring Sanhedrin a letter that will make them know that Rome is not so stupid as to be deceived by their wicked but brainless devices."

While Sextus Caesar dictated his heated letter to Hyrcanus, Herod strolled in the spacious gardens of the palace of the president. Being of the nature he was, he took notice of the plants and trees and shrubbery, fountains and statuary. Many items were of extreme interest to him. He decided to copy many details in his own garden. Returning to the interior and finding Sextus still occupied with the letter, he left word that he was going to visit the bazaars of Damascus, which were varied and rich in merchandise.

He went, and as always, was enchanted with the offerings and the shops of the various workers in precious metals and the lapidaries. How skilled were these men! Remembering Doris, he ordered for her anklets of fine gold adorned with sapphires and three tinkling little bells. Then a necklace and bracelet to match. He bought six lengths of the richest silk, each of a different color, for her also, and a flask of rare perfume that had been brought from China. Herod admitted to himself that these expensive offerings were intended to quiet his sense of guilt in not loving his wife, who was perhaps at this moment in the pains of birth, bearing him a child. For himself, he ordered sandals of gold leather with three straps that brought the top up to his lower calf. Then he ordered a sword of the finest steel of Damascus, with a richly jeweled hilt, for his son, in case Doris brought forth one. Then a fine chain of gold with a pearl pendant, in case she bore him a daughter.

The stroll through Damascus benefitted his spirits. The ranging hills to the north of the city, the ancient highways, where it appeared that caravans from far places were forever approaching, bringing rich and rare objects, or departing to distant lands which he yearned to see. He visited briefly the university where he had been educated and saluted warmly his former instructors. Soon he was surrounded by cheering crowds of students who honored him because of his fame as the conqueror of Hezekiah, and governor of Galilee, and besides, the friend of Sextus Caesar.

A tall figure burst from a classroom upon the cloistered walk, took off with a flying leap across the campus and flung himself upon Herod.

"Nicolaus!" Herod cried and heartily embraced the tall, spare-built Nicolaus. "Nicolaus, my classmate and friend of my bosom!"

"Herod, owner of the fidelity of my right hand! What brings you to Damascus? Your glorious actions are filling the world with your fame."

"The story is too long to be told in a moment, Nicolaus. Is it possible for you to get leave of your instructor and accompany me back to the palace of the governor?"

"Certainly, if you will come with me and allow me to present you to him. He is one of your most enthusiastic admirers, and laments that he was not here when you were."

The presentation was made and Nicolaus allowed to accompany Herod to the government palace. Along the way, Herod told his intimate friend all, and Nicolaus explained why he remained at the university.

"I have fallen in love with history, and intend to become a very able and truthful historian. So now, I am absorbing the materials and methods of recording history."

Sextus received Herod's friend graciously, and invited him to eat with them. As they took their places, Sextus quipped, "This is a very fortunate combination. On the one hand, Herod seems to be unable to prevent making history, and you prepare to set it down. Excellent!"

"Only the Sanhedrin in Jerusalem seems bent on preventing my making any more."

They laughed at this, then Sextus read his letter to Hyrcanus.

"It has come to my ears that you, in association with the Sanhedrin at Jerusalem, have summoned Herod, Governor of Galilee, and charged him with murder for exterminating the notorious bandit leader, Hezekiah. I, Sextus Caesar, president of Syria, by command of the Great Caesar and the Roman senate, demand to know by what right you attempt such an audacious and insolent action.

"Under the decree of Caesar and the Roman senate, all powers of the government of Palestine are vested in Antipater, made procurator by Caesar. Nothing was left to you except the exercise of your temple rites, and that only at the pleading of Antipater, your faithful friend, whose eminent son you now contrive to murder by a senseless device. Even you, as weak of mind as you are, must see that there could be no peace and security anywhere if such outlaws as this Hezekiah could not be turned from their murders and other depredations by summoning them before a Sanhedrin. If you and your Sanhedrin are persuaded that this could be done, why did you not summon him while he was still alive and bring him to justice, and thus pacify your country and make it secure? Because you knew that it could not be done. And now, when Herod, at great peril of his life, has secured that blessing, not only to his own country, but to Syria as well, out of jealousy, you seek to rob him, not only of his life, but of his glorious reputation.

"I accuse you of not only attempting to murder Herod under a clumsy pretext, but also his father, the noble and eminent Antipater, and all of his family, which amounts to a sedition against the power of Rome, whose representative, Antipater, is in Palestine.

"I therefore order you to dismiss this foolish and wicked charge against Herod instantly when Herod arrives at Jerusalem to stand his trial. If this is not done, I, as the representative of the power of Rome in Syria, shall visit a terrible punishment upon you and the Sanhedrin, for daring to take into your hands rights and powers which you no longer possess, your government now being subject to Rome. To that end, Rome has chosen to place the government in the hands of Antipater, and any attempt on your part, or the Sanhedrin, will be regarded as a revolt from Rome, and you will be looked upon as the enemy of Rome."

Sextus looked up from the scroll at the end and queried Herod with his eyes.

"How accurately and magnificently you have stated the case," Herod exclaimed. "The Asamoneans, having made themselves obnoxious to the people of Palestine by their crimes and extravagance, and fighting among themselves, bribed the Romans through Pompey to intervene, and then being beaten by Pompey because of this same type of trickery, and scorned by Rome, now attempt to sneak the power denied to them. My own father is at fault for beseeching Caesar to reinstate this treacherous Hyrcanus in the priesthood. But fidelity in friendship is a religion of my father, and he has inculcated it into his children. However, when a man has given me his right hand and then behaves towards me like an enemy, I then deal with him as an enemy. My father seems to be unable to see this low-cunning Hyrcanus as he really is. But a time will come when I shall pay him for his treachery to my generous and innocent father."

"And my eminent cousin, Julius Caesar, will certainly support your actions; for if there is a man whom Caesar loves, it is Antipater. And being aware of Antipater's actions on behalf of this treacherous leech, nothing will prevent him from supporting your actions."

"That is all I require, O my kind friend. Someday I shall certainly call this bumbling degenerate to accounts."

"Excellent! Now as to this present case, go to Jerusalem when you see fit. I see no necessity for haste, since there is some very good hunting and other sports in this area, and we must enjoy it together. Perhaps Nicolaus, your old friend, will come along. And next week, a troupe of very famous dancers from the Decapolis—well, they are really out of Athens, but presenting their shows in the cities of the Decapolis at present—and we must not miss that . . ."

"And some excellent wrestlers from Macedonia," Nicolaus broke in with enthusiasm.

Sextus smiled, welcoming a new enthusiast, then continued.

"That is, if affairs in Galilee can wait on you for that long."

"Certainly! The elders of the towns are very earnest about good order and serving under me. They look upon me as their son and take pride in seeing my plans carried out."

"And that is a triumph of administration, Herod," Sextus said. "I tell you that you have the qualities of a king. When you can get the people to enjoy supporting your measures, you have the genius of government. But back to your visit to Jerusalem. Appear before the Sanhedrin in as pompous a manner as possible . . ."

"Ah! Perhaps the opportunity has arrived for me to put on the purple vestments that you bestowed upon me."

This provoked loud laughter for a minute, and then Sextus said, "The very thing! Appear in purple, your hair barbered faultlessly and with your costly ornaments on. The very sight of you will throw that collection of quaking old geese into a whirl." Caesar snickered, and continued, "I really would like to be there when you arrive. The sight would outdo the amphitheater."

Herod enjoyed a happy fortnight with Sextus and Nicolaus, but kept in constant contact with both Sepphoris and Jerusalem. So he knew that Doris had borne him a son, and he had been named for his father. He also knew that everything was in perfect order in Galilee. The deal had gone through for smoked fish from the lake. A large group of men had formed a fishing and shipping combination, and were selling to Rome. Another group had combined to make harnesses and saddles as he had suggested. They waited on his return to secure them some contracts. Abrahim's fine riding-mule had an attack of colic from too much grain, but was recovering. Tasso's ewe had given birth to twins.

Phasaelus reported that Jerusalem was tense over the coming trial of Herod. Among their enemies, the odds were ten to one that Herod would be beheaded before sunset on the day of his appearance. They went about with smug smiles on their faces, and the joke was current among them that the Sanhedrin was more terrible than Hezekiah. The widows of the bandits were seen everywhere now, well-dressed, and boasting that Herod would soon pay with his head for his crimes. Of the Sanhedrin, only Pollio and Sameas had nothing to say. As for Hyrcanus, he was talking like an absolute monarch and boasting (behind Antipater's back, of course) of what he was having the procurator to do, or what he was forbidding. It was laughable.

"Herod is coming!" Crowds raced along the sidewalks, trying to keep pace with Herod's stallion as it picked proudly across the Valley of the Cheese-mongers and upwards towards the Upper Market Place. "Herod is coming. Hail valiant Herod!"

Inside the hall of justice, the members of the Sanhedrin stood about in groups, speaking in low tones, but with satisfied faces. At the cries from the street, they quietly took their places in the wide semi-circle. Hyrcanus moved in a pace between a swagger and a dodder as men often do, indicating the gap between the goal and the accomplishment. Reaching the seat in the center of the semi-circle, he stood for a moment, trying to awe the spectators before he sat down. He gave several wiggles of his hips the better to settle into position.

"Hyrcanus seems to be acting out what he conceives as being very kingly today," one spectator observed to his neighbor, "when all he achieves is an old fussy hen returning to her nest."

Those who overheard this man sniggered quietly. But their eyes were glued to the wide door for the first sight of Herod.

"Herod is near. I can make out the tread of many horses. Listen! Yes, horses. Many horses. But where are Antipater and Phasaelus? Have they been secretly murdered?"

The query was immediately answered. The young and handsome governor of Jerusalem entered with a bodyguard of no more than a dozen men, and took a seat three rows from the front. As soon as he was seated, in came the procurator of Judea with twenty-five men only as his guards; he stood for the mighty ovation, smiled and lifted his right hand in salute to the people, and seated himself in the front row with his guards disposed in a way to protect him. An embarrassed silence fell on the platform as Antipater seated himself. Several of the Seventy mentally rehearsed the speeches of indictment they would make, and the supreme moment when they would give the condemning vote. Self-styled Ciceros bloomed all around the semicircle. Hyrcanus rehearsed his sentencing speech with soundlessly moving lips.

"Herod is mounting the hill!" And Jerusalem followed and cried out. Shopkeepers had abandoned their shops recklessly; the shoemakers had run away, some with their lasts still clasped in their hands; women hung from windows; the rabble cried and ran on. Herod and his horsemen had to proceed with care lest they trample the tumult down. Toothless old crones fought fiercely for a foothold in the rush and crush. The weak, male and female, were elbowed aside. Some went down and were trampled by the hurrying feet.

Herod, followed by his armed guard of two hundred and fifty men, began to mount the stairs. Their steps were unhurried, but firm and determined. The Sanhedrin took on a solemn and dignified look. None turned a head as the firm footsteps reached the landing and approached the wide door.

Herod entered the chamber and advanced in a determined manner to the spot before the platform facing Hyrcanus. A wordless sound of admiration swept the room. For there the handsome Herod stood clothed in rich royal purple; rich jewelry glittered from his shoulder clasp, the heavy golden chain about his neck, his armlets, and the hilt of his sword. His feet were enclosed in gold-leather sandals. His head, held high and defiantly, was perfectly barbered.

It was now the turn of Hyrcanus and the Sanhedrin to gasp, and that was the last sound heard from them until after Herod had left the room. Where was the supplicating accused murderer in torn, cheap black raiment crawling in and prostrating himself on the floor before them, begging for their mercy? This spectacle of the richly clad, defiant Herod was too astonishing. But there he stood—glaring arrogantly into the face of Hyrcanus. The bearded face of the high priest went chalky. Herod glared on. The mouth of Hyrcanus began to slacken and gape, and Herod still stood with feet wide apart, right hand on the hilt of his sword, and glared into the face of Hyrcanus. The two hundred and fifty soldiers were ranged closely behind Herod, cutting off any assault that might arise from the spectators. The lids of the eyes of Hyrcanus began to flutter, and the eyeballs rolled up until the pupils disappeared. His body shook with tremors, but Herod still stood before him, daring him silently to open his mouth.

Now, Herod began at the extreme left of the Seventy and dared each face singly and individually to speak. Eyes were averted, heads dropped as if to examine something in their laps, or eyes closed. With two exceptions. The eyes of Pollio and Sameas met his steadily, but they did not speak. Sameas, the youngest of the Sanhedrin, even appeared to be suppressing a smile. When Herod's challenging gaze reached the center of the line again, Hyrcanus was not in his place. He had fainted from terror, and slid to the floor. There he lay twitching his arms and legs in a fitful way. And not one of his assessors dared to rise and go to his assistance.

Herod swept his daring gaze on to the extreme right, but it was the same. Not a man there dared utter a word, let alone arise to deliver a pompous accusing speech. Rather, they seemed to try to make themselves less visible. Herod challenged each man with his eyes and stood in this place of silence.

Then the spell was broken. Some man in the rear of the room could not suppress a snigger. Then several more let go. Now Herod stalked back to the place before the seat of Hyrcanus and spoke in an imperious voice.

"My generous nature permits you to escape my wrath this time, but if ever again you interrupt my duties as governor of Galilee to ride to Jerusalem to answer your foolish and old-womanish charges, you shall feel the weight of my sword."

Herod made a sharp right-about in a military manner and stalked from the chamber; his guards, with naked swords first challenging Hyrcanus, the Sanhedrin, and the spectators with cold and determined eyes, followed after, two abreast, in precise military step and rhythm. Down the stairs they emerged upon the street to the wild cheering of thousands.

As yet, no account of what had happened in the Chamber of Justice had reached the massed crowds outside, but Herod's smiling, triumphant appearance told them enough. The tremendous volume of the acclaim could be heard in the Lower City. Aristo rushed past the smiling, saluting Herod and signaled to the body of Galileans to whom he had entrusted the horses. The first hurried over leading Nicator, Herod's stallion. He accepted the bridle from the youth's hands and said, "We Galileans are not to be conquered, eh?"

At this flattering acknowledgment of kinship, the Galileans— several hundreds of them who had come to Jerusalem voluntarily to give what assistance they could to their young governor—went into wild cheering. Unknown to Herod, the elders had armed these young men with short, curved knives which they carried concealed under their jackets, ordered them to place themselves around the door of the chamber, and, in case Herod was convicted by the Sanhedrin, to draw their weapons and deliver him from the arresting officers. Now that Herod had delivered himself, it was unnecessary to fight, but fierce loyalty still moved these men. They all but split their throats with cheering as Herod and his soldiers mounted and rode first north then east until they came to a place that permitted them to wheel their horses without danger to the multitudes in the streets, then retraced their course past the chamber.

There was still tumultuous sound, but now it was different, and Herod was concerned when he saw that his band of Galileans were the center of the disturbance. He reined in to ask of Phasaelus what was the occasion for the disturbance.

"Oh, as the defeated Sanhedrin descended to the street," and here Phasaelus, as governor of Jerusalem, suppressed a grin, "one of your Galileans, out of fidelity to you, began to shout, 'Away with the Fringes!' referring, of course, to the fact that only the Pharisees are allowed to wear a fringe upon their robes. Others joined in the cry, and I am afraid that many of my Judeans took part. Then one of your young men went to the extreme of pulling down his pants, turning his back to the dignified members of the Sanhedrin as they emerged, and, squatting down, he patted his naked behind at the Fringes in obscene invitation. Some of the more sedate men of Jerusalem took affront at this insult to the Sanhedrin, and set upon the young man, who was instantly supported by the whole body of Galileans, who had *sicaris* concealed about them, drew them and drove their attackers back. Fortunately, I came down to the street with my bodyguard at that moment and my presence stopped what might have been a serious disturbance."

"Good for my Galileans! Naturally you must take the offender into custody. For the sake of your own prestige, lay a heavy fine upon him, say a mina, and I will send Aristo to pay his fine."

"Agreed, beloved brother. And you were magnificent before the Sanhedrin. Never will that picture fade from my memory. But we can talk further at home. Now, with a stern face I will have your Galilean seized. See you within the hour at Father's house."

Now, Herod beckoned Aristo to him, whispered into his ear, passed a mina from his pouch to him, signaled to his guard to follow, put Nicator into a rearing prance to please the people, and cantered away to the sound of cheers.

Herod had stood his trial for the murder of Hezekiah, and this was the verdict.

CHAPTER FOUR

NEW MOON OVER JUDEA

Not a muscle even twitched in the face and figure of Antipater as Herod made his dramatic exit from the chamber. With an expressionless mask and unmoving eyes, he nevertheless took in every slightest change of expression on the faces of the members of the Sanhedrin before him. Without turning his head, he noted what went on among the intended witnesses, the widows of the bandits. What was intended to be a whisper reached his keen ears.

"Quiet! You senseless daughters of a mule and a Bactrian camel! He did not see us. Do you want Herod to return and slay us? Hush!"

But terror forced another to complain, "The goat-headed sons of swine have betrayed us. Now Herod will find us in Galilee and slay us."

"Did I not command you to be silent?" The wife of Hezekiah shot back in a threatening whisper. "Shall I awaken the sleeping blade under my robe? Fools! I shall force them to supply the money to take up a new life in Parthia. We shall lose nothing by coming here to serve them."

No more than I suspected, Antipater said to himself behind his impassive face. Then he concentrated on the drama being acted out by the dignitaries. Secret amusement stirred within, but his face told nothing.

When the last footstep of Herod's guard faded from the ear, and the cheering rocked the streets, the Seventy and One seemed to awaken from a sleep. Paces came alive, men stirred, three moved to the assistance of Hyrcanus and got him again in his seat. Sameas got calmly to his feet and spoke.

"I wonder if any of you, my assessors, really comprehended what has happened here today."

"Do you think that we are all deaf and blind, Sameas?" Simon demanded testily. "How could we avoid comprehending what was done here?"

"You saw with your eyes, you heard with your ears, but are you certain that you really realize what happened?"

"Well, what happened, Sameas?" Eleazer asked with heavy sarcasm.

"Have any of us here ever witnessed such a case as we have seen today, that a man who is called to take his trial before us, ever stood in such a manner before us? Every other man who has come to trial before us presents himself in a submissive manner and like one in fear, and endeavors to move us to pity and compassion. He has his hair disheveled, and wears a black, mourning garment, and prostrates himself with his face to the floor before us until we give him leave to arise."

Sameas paused and swept the faces of his colleagues with a searching glance.

"But how did the admirable Herod appear? Accused of murder, he stood before us clothed in purple, with his hair finely trimmed, and adorned with the most costly ornaments. His armed men were about him. Neither the president of this body, nor yet Hyrcanus our high priest, dared open the trial for terror."

"Why waste time telling us what we already know, O Sameas?" Eleazer snapped. "We were only about to begin the trial when Herod fled the place."

"Then I ask your humble pardon for my hasty conclusions, my colleagues. Let us summon this Herod to return and be tried. The day is getting old."

A quick rumble of dissent swept the body, and Sameas smiled in a knowing way.

"No, no!" Hyrcanus objected strongly. "We must postpone the matter to some other time."

"Very well, O Hyrcanus and my assessors, hear this: The future master of Lower Asia stood before us this day. He exhibited his superiority over us by the disdain with which he treated this body. He recognized that the power had shifted to other hands, a fact which you refuse to admit. I sought to dissuade you from this foolish action when it was conceived, for I saw clearly that no power to enforce your demands resided in your hands, did I not? And for this impotent, audacious scheme, Herod will someday punish you all with death. Hyrcanus has stated on one occasion that he was at the home of the father of Herod when Herod was born, and that his birth occurred at the exact appearance of the sickle of the new moon. It is possible that it foretold the future of the infant. I do not insist upon it, I merely state that it is possible. Of this I am persuaded, that one stood before us this day who shall be the master of this nation in no long time."

A growl of dissent broke upon the chamber, and all stood on their feet and without more ceremony, left the room. Here and there Sameas was accused of being bribed by Antipater's money to make the statement that he had made.

His tutor, Pollio, disputed this vehemently and showed his own hand by saying, "Sameas is a truly honest man. If you have power greater than Herod, why then did you allow yourselves to be made the laughingstock of the nation today?"

In this muddle, the dignitaries hurried from the room and down the stairs to the crowded streets. In confirmation of the predictions of Sameas, they descended into a volcano of acclaim for Herod. There was not one voice raised in their honor. But a Galilean bared his behind to them. All but a few then saw that a new moon had indeed risen over Judea.

Antipater, about to mount his horse, saw Pollio and Sameas so close to him that the sleeve of Sameas almost touched his own in the crush. Antipater smiled and spoke, then turned his horse over to his groom and, together, the three made their way through the human mass, and walked, conversing pleasantly, towards his luxurious home in the Lower City. Antipater had graciously invited the two to view his new grandson and sip a cup of wine cooled by snow brought from Mount Hermon. The two accepted with alacrity. Not one word was spoken of the event of the day, but being men of understanding, it was accepted on both sides that a new alliance had been formed.

CHAPTER FIVE

HEROD AT HOME

W hen Antipater arrived, he found the whole family assembled on the patio, or inner court, which was surrounded by trees, flowering shrubs, and playing fountains. A long table had been set out there, and was already loaded with fresh fruit, wines being cooled, and a great bowl of fresh figs stewed in honey.

The two eminent Pharisees then witnessed a scene which, to them, was almost unbelievable. Cypros, the wife of Antipater, his two daughters-in-law, and the small son of Phasaelus were there along with Antipater's sons, Joseph and Pheroras, and the young daughter, Salome. All rushed in a veritable storm of affections upon Antipater, crying out their pleasure at his return and hanging upon him. The presence of the females and the children was not to be expected in an Asian home. Further, Antipater, flushed with pride and pleasure, presented his guests to each member of his family, or rather, presented them to his distinguished guests. Pollio and Sameas stood amazed.

"A revelation, O Antipater," Sameas said half seriously. "We follow the lion to his den and discover the secret of the marvelous unity and

fidelity of Antipater and his sons. He binds all together by close association daily and provides his children constant opportunity to ab-
sorb his wisdom and his virtues. It is against custom, but good. There
is no room for jealousy of son of his father's eminence, nor brother of
brother. That is the evil which destroys too many eminent families. It
overthrew the Asamoneans."

"True, O Sameas," Antipater responded modestly. "I teach my sons
from infancy that jealousy is a vile crime in families. The success of
one is the success of all. They must support each other to the death;
not give way to envy and destruction of each other. Eternal fidelity."

"The highest virtue," the graying Pollio commented. "And it is
bearing its fruit."

Antipater smiled, and then became the thoughtful host.

"Now, I shall keep my promise by showing you my second grandson. Herod is in the nursery now worshipping him. After you have
seen this infant who is named after me, we shall wash our hands and
dine."

The three men entered the spacious house chatting gaily while
Cypros examined her younger children to see if they had washed their
hands and faces carefully. "And Salome, please do not join the conversation while your father and older brothers talk with our guests. To do
so will appear very rude and inappropriate. Keep quiet."

"But Mother, I read the fable of Aesop about the frogs gaining a
king perfectly today. My teacher said so. I will show them how well I
can read. They will be delighted like Father."

"You will do no such thing, I tell you. Children should be seen and
not heard. If you much as utter a word, I shall take away the foal that
your father gave you yesterday. Not one word!"

In the nursery, Herod sat beside the richly-adorned cradle and fed
his eyes upon his son. The infant was very healthy, but Herod was
disappointed. The child seemed, even so early, to resemble the father

of Doris. Herod had hoped and expected that it would be a faithful copy of himself. Would it be cold and phlegmatic like its mother? God forbid!

That brought him to the all-important question: Would he have the kind of happiness that he sought in his future with Doris? His mother assured him glibly that he would. Doris was so calm, placid, and kind, she had insisted. Exactly the kind of wife that he needed, to offset his reckless nature. But that was what he himself did not want. He neither wanted to be calm nor placid. The pairing seemed like a lion yoked with a sheep. Well, his parents were wise and correct, perhaps all would be well, but he seriously doubted their conclusion in this matter. He required ecstasy, not calm.

It was at this moment that he heard the approach of Antipater with his guests. Instantly, he put on an air of being enraptured with his son. But nothing prepared Herod for the surprise in finding Pollio and Sameas in the home. What were they doing here? Two of the men who had conspired to take his life. Rightfully, he should slay them on sight. But observing the warm relations between them and his father, he was guarded. He welcomed their inspection of his son, and their praise of its health and beauty, and as they left the nursery to wash their hands, Sameas dissolved Herod's suspicions by taking hold of his left arm in a friendly way and making a joke.

"It was resolved by the Sanhedrin, O Herod, that you do not appear before that body for a long, long time. Hyrcanus informed us that he was just coming around to the proceedings when you so abruptly left, and being the youngest of the judges, I offered to run after you and beg you to return, but my generosity was unanimously voted down."

All burst into laughter, and Herod joined them heartily. He looked at Antipater, whose eyes informed him that these two were his allies.

"And my eminent pupil was no help in dispelling the terror that you threw over the assembly, O Herod," Pollio grinned. "He arose and predicted that you would grow greater instead of less, and that a day would come when you would punish them all for their insolent attempt on your life this day."

"And Sameas was a good prophet," Herod grew grim for a minute, then relaxed. "Hyrcanus and his conspirators can catch me very easily, but they will require the assistance of Caesar's famous Tenth Legion to turn me loose."

This brought another burst of laughter as the men emerged from the bath and headed again for the patio.

"Yes," agreed Antipater, "I am afraid that the predictions of Sameas added greatly to their terror."

"But my famous pupil was justified, for we tried to discourage the project when it was first conceived by Eleazar and Simon. Hyrcanus would not listen to our arguments against it. The vainglorious little toad!"

"So Hyrcanus really approved of the trial?" Antipater asked sadly.

"Oh, yes, Antipater. He only sought an excuse to bring it about. He would have nothing to do with caution and wisdom," Pollio added.

"Pollio is caution, while I am wisdom personified," teased Sameas.

Now they entered upon the courtyard, but Herod stopped abruptly in his tracks and extended his right hand, first to Pollio, and then to Sameas. Not a word was spoken, but each understood.

Arrived at the table, Antipater graciously seated Pollio at the head, placed Sameas at Pollio's left, and seated himself on his right. Herod was placed next Sameas, and Phasaelus the neighbor of his father. Swift and well-trained servants passed about and served them with broiled fowl, boiled onions, roast mutton, herbs, beans, melons, chilled wine, and finally the figs preserved in honey.

And while they ate leisurely, they talked. The women and children were massed at the lower end of the table, from where Cypros directed the service in whispers. For the first time, Herod learned what had occurred after he left the Chamber of Justice, and the entire table burst into laughter at Sameas's lively description of the fright of Hyrcanus as Herod threatened him with his eyes.

"Shame, shame, shame upon you, O Sameas," Pollio pretended to scold. "A famous man of learning and a philosopher, provoking so much laughter with your description of our high priest."

Sameas, who was only two years older than Phasaelus, continuing to chuckle, retorted, "But I did not make Hyrcanus ridiculous, O Pollio. Either his parents did it, he did it himself, or shall we place the responsibility with God."

"Or shall we lay it at the door of Antipater for using his influence with Caesar to return the puffed-up clown to the high priesthood?" Pollio prodded slyly.

"Exactly," observed the wife of Phasaelus surprisingly. "And so the little puffed-up frog plots to destroy our brother, Herod. We find now that he has no sense of fidelity and gratitude as does my noble and eminent father-in-law. Only criminal vanity."

"The eternal schemer," Sameas added.

Antipater sipped lightly from his cup of chilled wine, and spoke slowly and deliberately.

"The obligations of true friendship demand all. Friendship is an expression of sacred worship. I gave my right hand to Hyrcanus many years ago."

"But never have I trusted him," Cypros said with feeling.

"The case of Hyrcanus is tragic," Antipater defended. "His mind has been overwhelmed by men of evil counsel. He has no idea what a monstrous thing he has attempted. Those ambitious men!"

"Whose minds cannot conceive of change," Pollio commented slowly. "Change. It was the philosopher Heraclitus who appeared to be ever concerned about the mystery of change and who said, 'Nothing is; everything becomes; no condition persists unaltered, even for the smallest moment. Everything is ceasing to be as it was, and is becoming what it will be.' And no intelligent mind can continue to deny the truth of his observations. The eternal laws cannot be thrown down. I saw them in operation this day, and realized that I could no longer pretend that Judea has natural laws peculiar to itself. Change."

"Continue, please," Antipater spoke humbly. "It is my most earnest desire that my children be surrounded with wisdom and learning, and those who have acquired it. You have done my house a great honor to come here; consider me deeply indebted to you for your generosity with your treasures."

Pollio took a full sip of wine, regarded Antipater solemnly, then swept the table with his gaze.

"It is you, Antipater, who instructs us. You have taught that if a man of abilities would make men of his sons equal to himself, then he must keep them close beside him and allow them to learn from him, rather than keep them at a distance as is our habit. Again I say, today I have discovered the secret of your successful family. It points out the slavery of custom, for how has anyone at this table been injured by all eating together as we have? It is a very pleasant and affectionate association. I shall imitate it myself."

"Perhaps another viewpoint of my father's will not find acceptance with you," Herod offered, and studied the faces of Pollio and Sameas closely as he went on. "My beloved mother reads and writes Greek with the same ease that she speaks it. She is familiar with the Greek dramatists, poets, and philosophers also to an extent. My sister is being educated also. Both my wife and my brother's wife read and write Greek."

"And why not?" the beautiful wife of Phasaelus demanded defensively. "Antipater is absolutely right in his views. Are we to be shut away from the beauty and pleasure of the classics only because we happen to be female?"

"The custom of shutting women away from the treasure of reading is indeed mistaken, O Pollio, and you, Sameas. It affords me untold comfort and pleasure when my husband is away from home—as he must be so often. We do not aim to attain the status of the *hetairai* of Greece by it, but to make ourselves more companionable to our husbands and sons. And knowing many things by being able to read, we can tell if our children are being properly instructed."

Cypros stated this with the utmost poise and assurance, and beamed from one of her daughters-in-law to the other. Herod looked encouragingly at Doris, but she merely flushed and kept silent.

"Shut away," Sameas said slowly with his eyes half closed in thought. "That is exactly the concept that had me obsessed during that unfortunate occurrence today. Shut away. I gained a new view of the world. Suddenly I became alarmed about the fate of Jewish genius. How many brilliant minds must have been born and remained unknown by being shut away from the world and fresh ideas and concepts by being isolated. An Alexander the Great, a Socrates, a Plato, a Phidias, Euripides, Caesar, and many other noble types of mind, living and dying without giving to the nation and the world of the great treasures within. Now, from centuries of being shut away, these associates of ours think . . ."

"No!" Herod burst forth with vehemence. "That is exactly the difficulty, O Sameas. They do not think. Worshipping custom, their minds run in the ruts cut by the chariot wheels of the past, so in reality, they do not think at all. The very life of the nation is to be sacrificed to the handicaps of First-by-birth, even when First-by-birth has shown itself utterly incapable of doing or being anything except a danger to the life of the nation, and a burdensome expense with no profitable return to the country. They stand ready to murder in a cold and cynical manner those who can and do benefit the people. It is equal to casting the young of Judea into the fiery mouth of Moloch."

"That same thought occurred to both myself and my eminent pupil when we were first made aware of the scheme. Being a lover of my country, I rejected the scheme then, and continue to do so." Pollio looked at Sameas for confirmation, and the younger man nodded vigorously. "I said to Sameas that the project was merely a copy of the custom of those barbarous Parthians of killing the general who wins too many battles for his country, and thus becomes popular with the people. You recall the Surenas, as they call their supreme commanders, who won the sensational victory over the Roman, Crassus, was soon executed by the reigning Arsaces, under the charge, 'His services to his sovereign (Orodes) had exceeded the measure which it is safe for a subject to render to the throne.' Because of this corroding jealousy of the royal master, never will the Parthians achieve their ambition of conquering Rome. What is to be gained by killing off all of the most able in a nation? That is exactly what Hyrcanus and his advisors aimed at."

"I was aware of their intentions," Antipater said sadly, "and I was distressed as to what posture to assume. Never did I doubt that they could be put down easily by any one of the three of us alone, but I recoiled from seeming to begin an oppressive civil war. Well, happily the threat is now behind us."

"I do not think so," Pollio mused. "Despite their rejection by the people and then Rome, you will find that if the slightest opportunity arises, these plotters will seize upon it. These Asamoneans are obsessed. Guard yourself from deceitful wiles."

The soft eyes of Antipater went quickly from the face of Herod to that of Cypros, and found what he expected—a gloating and confirming look.

"You have played into the hands of my wife and my son, Herod. They distrust Hyrcanus strongly."

"How else can we see him except as he presents himself by his own acts and attitudes, noble Antipater?" Herod queried. "Hyrcanus has no concept of the meaning of friendship. His word means nothing."

"A slimy, cunning, crawling thing!" Cypros denounced. "How many times have I implored my beloved husband to leave him to his own impotence. But, no, he judges that Asamonean by his own high qualities, when there is nothing of my husband's nobility of character about the weakling. In fact I become enraged when I think that the creature considers that he is bestowing a blessing upon Antipater to allow him to sacrifice his time, money, and abilities on his behalf."

Smiling broadly, Sameas lifted his eyebrows and winked at Antipater.

"Women are very descriptive creatures, O Antipater. They have a way peculiar to themselves. The esteemed Cypros sounds just like my wife describing the person and qualities of my relatives. Do you suppose, O Pollio, that there is a school which teaches them how to describe those whom they do not care for?"

"Very possible," Pollio chuckled. "If so, then my wife must have been a distinguished pupil. You should hear her on the wife of Boethus. She would provoke the envy of Cicero."

Antipater smiled and spread his hands in a way to say, "I told you so," and looked teasingly at his wife. Then he observed dryly, "You observe that my wife has fallen off from the worship of the Asamoneans. You could rightly call her an apostate."

"Laugh if you will, but I can in no way overlook a man who has taken advantage of the generosity of my husband on numerous occasions, and now, after he exerts himself to persuade Caesar to make him high priest, seeks to undermine his benefactor's power bestowed on him by Caesar, and at last, to take the life of my son. Royal indeed! The family of Antipater was rich and ennobled in Idumea for generations before Matthais, father of those Maccabees, quit herding sheep around Modin. And am I not the niece of Aretas of Arabia? Why should my husband and sons demean themselves by serving Hyrcanus? The slobbering degenerate!"

Herod got up from the table swiftly and hurried to embrace Cypros. "Rest contented, Mother. I will not overlook his crimes. Pretending eternal friendship with father, then scheming to kill his son. If ever he plots to summon me again, I will not be hindered by Father and Phasaelus. I will kill him. In fact, my sword cries for his flesh at this moment for calling me to stand this trial. He deserves death, and but for my father, I would destroy him before I return to Galilee."

"That would be the injury of your father, and also yourself and your brother, with Caesar." Pollio cautioned. "Such an action would serve your enemies well. You will do for them what they were unable to do for themselves."

"As I pointed out to him," Antipater concurred, "but Herod is utterly devoted to his father. He readily forgives and forgets an offense against himself, but he is almost impossible to restrain when he considers I have been injured. He declares that Hyrcanus is a foul friend who repays my fidelity to him with treachery. In fact, I fear that Herod is persuaded that he is the father and protector of the entire family instead of myself. We sometimes jest with him on that by calling him 'The Patriarch.' He defends us all valiantly. However, he must take into account that we are now in public life, and cannot behave as if we were still private citizens. Caesar has entrusted me with the welfare of the nation, and we must not allow him to be persuaded that he has misplaced his confidence."

"But, Father, even Caesar does not lie quiet while enemies, both to himself and to the nation, carry on their villainies. It is far from prudent to do so. Sooner or later, I shall punish Hyrcanus and his conspirators for their evil ways and intentions. You are far too innocent, Father. You dislike to believe that any man is intentionally evil, and especially one who has given you his right hand, as Hyrcanus has done. But you see how lightly he regards his sacred oath. His actions belie his words. So why continue to excuse him?"

"Herod's analysis of the situation is correct," Sameas said earnestly. "But that is not the point in contention. What is under consideration is whether it is the right time to take action, is it not, O Pollio and Antipater?"

"That is the point, O Sameas. You have stated it well. Herod will have our support when he takes action, but he must be certain that it is the proper time. We shall, of course, not show our alliance with you, O Herod, since what we might urge upon others would be stubbornly rejected if it were suspected that we have become less traditional, and more concerned about the welfare of our country. However, we shall keep Antipater informed of anything of importance which he could not learn through the usual means."

The two eminent Pharisees were escorted to the gate by Antipater and his sons in a most courteous manner, where right hands were given without words.

And no sooner had these influential men departed than Antipater threw his arm about Herod's shoulders as they walked back into the house.

"A truly brilliant stoke, O my Herod! The Sanhedrin plotted your death by a fraudulent trial. You came and acquitted yourself magnificently, and by your courageous action, won the two most influential men of Jerusalem to your side."

While Antipater rested both of his hands upon Herod's shoulders and looked with wonder, almost awe, into his face, Herod beamed into the eyes of his father in a most worshipful way.

"To have won your approval, beloved Father, is the crowning victory of all. You see, I have not forgotten the saying of Demosthenes which you so often dinned into our ears: *What is the chief part of a statesman? Action! And the next? Action! What next again? Action! It fascinates and binds hand and foot those weak in judgment or weak in courage, which constitutes the majority.* Do I give you back your own instructions accurately?"

"There is no need for words when you have used action so splendidly. An act of courage is never lost, even though the venture fails, for the valor of the man is recorded upon the majestic scroll of Heaven. It will never die."

Now the party had re-entered the house and Herod said with urgency, "And now, I must go quickly to Damascus to report the outcome of my trial to Sextus Caesar. He urged me to do so with all haste. Therefore I shall instruct Doris to be prepared to leave with me tomorrow at the latest." Herod almost ran to his own apartments.

But Doris protested stubbornly. "My pride in my brave and eminent husband is without bounds, O beloved Herod. You surely do not expect the wife of such a famous and eminent person as you are to appear within your government in so casual a manner. Your wife and young son should be seen first by those you govern, and where you have earned a name that sheds glory over the habitable earth, in a most pompous manner."

For a stunned minute, Herod stood speechless staring at the placid face of Doris.

"Are you mad, Doris?" Herod burst out finally. "To make a great show of wealth is the least thing to be desired at this time. My father made me governor with the express instruction to pacify the province, put down the disorderly, and restore Galilee to its former prosperity. My people there have suffered much through no fault of their own. Now, both the elders and the people love and trust me. I must not give any there the suspicion that I am come to burden them with taxes and otherwise distress them. No, no pompous show at this time."

"It is plainly to be seen that you love those Galileans with their barbarous way of speech . . ."

"I do, and why not? They are kindly, honest, hardworking husband-men, fishermen, and artisans without the bigotry of Judea. I love to be among them to the extent that my duties as governor do not lay heavily upon me at all. My earnest wish is to see Galilee the green, pleasant land it used to be, with every foot of the rich black soil again under cultivation, the fishermen going about their business around the lake, well-fed and in security; the artisans engaged about their tasks in their shops content and prosperous, and all showing their pleasure at sight of me. I do not wish to find fear or hatred of me in a single face."

"What you say is reasonable, O my beloved husband, but I see no reason why the wife of a governor, a man who is possessed of such enormous wealth as you, famous everywhere for his astonishing suc-cess against the bandit leader, should not appear to be what she really is. You have not even built a house to receive me in Galilee."

"But I shall build one there one day when the province has recov-ered, and I have come upon the very spot that suits my plans best. That takes time, Doris. It must be like a finely cut gem in an exquisite setting. I love Galilee. It is the home of my heart. There I feel as if I had returned after a long journey in strange lands."

"But why? Your family is not of the Galileans."

"We are not too certain about that, Doris. There is an old legend that the line is really Pheonician of many centuries ago. That we were successful in commerce across the Great Sea, that our ancestral estates were between Sidon and Tyre. But, facing ruin when trade fell off after the Ten Tribes were carried off into captivity beyond the Euphrates, our ancestors moved southward into the land of the Idumeans, where trade with Egypt and the Greek islands kept us prosperous, and finally we came to be looked upon as of their blood after some generations.

Just as now we are regarded as Jews. There are no written records, so we look upon it as possible legend. But anyway, that northern province seems home to my soul."

With bowed head, Doris sat silent for several minutes, while he studied her intently. Finally, Doris lifted her head, adjusted the jeweled band which bound her hair, and murmured sullenly:

"I am your wife. I will go with you tomorrow if you command me to do so."

"That I will not do, Doris. The custom in my family is that our women be allowed to exercise their own will as well as speak their own minds freely. If you do not wish to spend every possible hour with me, whatever the circumstances, you remain here with my parents until I prepare the kind of residence that you hunger for, and take you there in a showy manner."

Herod dashed outside and began to give orders for a hasty departure with only his men of arms. Antipater questioned him about it, and he told his father briefly of Doris's decisions. Antipater hurried to Cypros with the unpleasant news, and Cypros ran to Doris.

"What are you about, my daughter?" Cypros asked anxiously. "What madness are you up to?"

Doris stated her case in a few sentences. It was the death of her dream not to proceed to Galilee as the wife of the renowned governor of that province. With rich, *new* garments and jewels, with a new and richly decorated carriage, and so on and so forth, and many personal attendants.

"But my son is not a king, Doris. This concerns me deeply, for as you remember, it was I who selected you to be the wife of Herod. Your calm nature appealed to me to be excellent to offset the hot head of Herod. You should be with him all the time possible. Suppose he should take up with another woman? What could you do? What could I, his father, or anybody do about it? That I do not wish to happen among my sons. I hunger for them to follow the example of their beloved father. Never, to my knowledge, has he indulged in concubines and outside women. You do not seem to know your own duty, child. Leave no hole in the fence for them to go through. Unknown to them, keep them bound. Marriage gives a woman numerous secret advantages. For example, you are brought to your husband a virgin, but there is no necessity to continue eternally inexperienced and uninteresting. Go to, and become a *pornai* (whore) in bed, a *hetairai* (entertaining girl) in your reception hall, and every other thing which he desires. Leave no room for any other female to occupy. I want no improperly-born grandchildren. Get up now, and make haste to go with your husband."

A full hour had passed since Herod had quitted his apartment. Traveling as a purely military contingent, in that time, his men were mounted and they were about ready to head north when Doris sullenly decided to obey her mother-in-law. A messenger to the citadel quickly returned saying that Herod was on the point of departure, and could not now change his plans.

The placid Doris, whose opinion and influence no one took into account, had made a monumental decision. Herod, Doris herself, Antipater, Cypros, the whole family, and the nation were to be affected by it, but nobody could conceive of it at this moment. Doris had pled to her mother-in-law that she was trying to protect her son from the dangers of travel at this early age. But even her son would suffer infinitely ruder shocks because of his mother's decision.

CHAPTER SIX

VOICE FROM THE PAST

Herod's officers could not conceal their surprise and pleasure when the order came that they were to go by the coastal road instead of by the shorter route through Jericho and Samaria. The sun was setting as they rode out four abreast through the Gate of the Essenes, with the Tower of Hippos a darkening upthrust against the evening sky to the north and east.

They traveled at a brisk walk for miles—until they met the carts loaded with produce moving towards the city for the markets in the morning. Then they galloped for miles into the night. Everybody showed the high spirits induced by the outcome of Herod's trial. Ribald jests and snatches of the kind of songs that soldiers are apt to sing when free of city life were flung back and forth among the ranks.

Now and then Herod laughed briefly, but inside he was very thoughtful and grim. The tumult stirred by the circumstances of the trial raged within him. The next move was his. What was to be done?

The red-flamed sun was freeing itself from the mountains to the east and north as his contingent approached Jamnia. The nearness of the sea lifted his spirits slightly.

"We will rest here until dawn of tomorrow," Herod announced. "Rest and entertain yourselves in any way that pleases you that does not injure you as a soldier nor offend the people of the city." Then he bestowed five drachma Alexandrina to each private and five shekels temple value to junior officers and dismissed them. He himself repaired to the house of a friend to rest and think.

Before sundown, refreshed by a bath and long sleep, he sent off a letter to his father.

Please do not scold Doris for not sharing the hardships of the type of travel that is a necessity to me at present. I wanted my son to be with me as you have had us with you. But at present, he is much too young to gain anything from the association. In any case, he will be with you and my honored mother, who will no doubt be more beneficial to him than I could. As for Doris, you must recognize that she has not the temperament to assist me as my mother is capable of doing for you. I confess to you that I cannot feel that same necessity for her presence as you do for my mother. However, I shall be that kind and considerate husband that you have ever taught me to be. To say all in all, I confess to you that she arouses nothing in me. Please forgive me.

I travel back to Galilee by the coastal road, because that area holds so much of the important events of the history of the nation, especially Lower Galilee. I want to see it all again with my now mature eyes and perhaps resolve some matters which now disturb me. I feel a strong urge to visit the site of Saul's last battle. You said once that this Saul was the tragic hero of a great story, but was misrepresented by the records set down by his betrayers. I wish to tread over the ground where he fought so valiantly, but so uselessly—Saul and his sons. Perhaps there is a parallel between them and you and your sons. Therefore, I shall not hurry back to Sepphoris, but go leisurely and visit that area which has seen the war chariots of many nations in deadly conflict. I shall report to you my conclusions perhaps reached there. Then I shall perhaps grasp the soul of what Isaiah speaks of as "Galilee of the Gentiles," the Delilah of the Philistines, who may be our ancestors, who fought against the valiant Saul on the triangular plain of Esdraelon with Carmel on the west, the Nazareth of bare, white chalky hills on the north, and Gilboa to the east. Then I shall ride over the Valley of Jezreel towards the Jordan, which is the gate to Palestine from beyond Jordan. I undertake this to the end that I know thoroughly the province which you have sent me to govern.

Having at last spoken openly to his father about his marriage, Herod was immensely relieved. Officers and men commented on his gaiety as he proceeded northward along the coast. Herod laughed and sang with his troops, went into the inns, and was liberal with the dancing girls.

At a decayed old structure behind a stone enclosure which bore the flattering name of Strato's Tower, Herod stopped long enough for the men to refresh themselves and turned eastward from the coast. As he mounted, he turned to two of his officers and said, "Everything is here for the most beautiful city of the earth. The beautiful blue waters of the Great Sea, a wide, sloping hillside with exactly the right gradient for a city by the time it reaches the summit, and . . ."

"Everything but a natural recess for ships to enter your port," one of his companions laughed.

"But a way could be found. I am not an engineer, but they now perform wonders. All that is necessary is sufficient money on the one hand, and sufficient skill and ingenuity on the other. Someday, it will be done."

"If the planner can recruit a cohort of angels," said Captain Alexander, the handsome and dashing son of one of the principal families of Jerusalem. "And under the command of the impetuous Herod, son of Antipater, and governor of Galilee."

"That is possible," Herod quipped in return. "Like Eaneus, once I touch the nourishing soil of Galilee, nothing is impossible to me."

Swinging westward now, Herod brought Nicator to a gallop which developed into a mild race. Herod was stimulated by the smooth motion of Nicator beneath him. After a time, he slowed to allow Alexander to come abreast.

"Why such speed when we have plenty of time?" Alexander asked peevishly.

"Long inaction does not suit my temperament. In addition, on this occasion, I am upon a journey of the soul."

"Of the soul, O Herod? You are indeed a man of many humors."

"Perhaps you are right. Soon we will leave Judea behind us, cross a narrow point of Samaria, and enter Lower Galilee. Do you realize that each piece of soil represents a different spiritual element, companion of my childhood days? Of the three, Galilee is the richer. In Lower Galilee, nations, very great and powerful nations, many of whom no longer exist, have fought for dominion on the plains of Lower Galilee. Armageddon, Esdraelon, Jezreel, have known the thunder of thousands of chariot wheels, the loud clash of arms, the tragedy of utter defeat, and the cries of triumph. Kings whose names are dim now in history, calling on gods no longer held worthy of worship for victory, and discovering that the gods of the weak are deaf. The mood is upon me to set my feet upon this historic soil and to listen to the voices of the past."

"Only to find, O dream-filled Herod, that where the chariots of Assyria, of Babylon, of Greece and Macedonia wheeled and turned, is now green with the eternal pulse and varied gourd vines of your Galilee. Not a trace remains of the great battles fought there. Pulse and gourd vines—that is what Galilee means to me."

"But I do not agree that nothing of the ancient tumults is left. Call it superstition if you will, but it seems to me that great actions impregnate the very soil and air where they occurred. And because I am persuaded that this is so, I earnestly wish to traverse the Plain of Esdraelon to Gilboa, where that most patriotic and valiant Saul fought his last battle. To me, Saul, first king of Israel, is the greatest of his race and nation."

"Greater than our David?"

"Infinitely so, O Alexander. The story of Saul is one of the greatest and most tragic in the history of the world. Acclaimed and beloved by the people of the nation for the sound reason that never did he refuse the enemy the meeting. Ever in defense of the people, and for that reason, deplored by the power-loving priesthood, who even as now never intended that absolute power should pass from their hands. Now, let us come to that final battle against the challenging Philistines. David, the subservient, had been secretly anointed and given every assistance to undermine the rule of Saul; his fighting men decreased and subverted as far as possible by the priesthood, and the Philistine pushing into the borders of the country.

"Saul, well aware of the conditions, nevertheless, resorted to arms to drive the enemy back, went with troubled heart to the priesthood to inquire of his chances of success. He was told that 'God' will not answer him. One must inquire if the name of God was not used here as a forgery. Saul turned away even more depressed in spirit where those who felt the same devotion to country as did Saul should have done everything possible to elevate his soul in such a rare hour. The valiant king then resorted to the Witch of Endor, and was further cast down. But did he then flee away to safety outside of Israel, leaving his people to the mercy of the Philistines? Heavy of soul because of the odds against his success in the conflict, he nevertheless gave the invaders battle, fought as few warriors have ever fought, saw his brave sons hacked down beside him, and only when all was irretrievably lost, sought death rather than live to see the defeat and enslavement of his country."

"But David . . ."

"And where was David at that terrible hour in the history of his country? In the camp of the enemy, eager to fight against it, and only prevented from active hostility by some influential officers of the Philistines because they did not trust a man who had shown his willingness to fight against his own country. I know only too well what has been written down by the Scribes, who are, after all, prejudiced witnesses, but the facts of history are useless without analytical interpretation. David arrived at his death, honored by the priests and glorified by the Scribes, and was buried in an elaborate memorial tomb, in which he had arranged to have buried with him an enormous sum of gold and silver which might have been used for the benefit of his nation—from which it had been robbed—but who now knows the last resting place of the patriotic and valiant Saul?"

"Frankly, O Herod, never had I thought about the matter in that way. You leave me without argument. It required great love of country and a great and valiant soul to take the steps that King Saul did. The only parallel is the Lacedemonians at Thermoplea."

"If not even greater. Therefore, I yearn to tread the soil of Esdraelon, to stand at Mount Gilboa and invite his great soul to speak to me—not by any necromancy, but to breathe up from the soil."

"But why, O strange Herod?"

"A grave decision is before me. It is possible that I shall come to the solution on such historic soil. Therefore, I am now eager to be again in Lower Galilee."

Herod found the historic triangular plain as his friend Alexander had predicted—after a thousand years, even tradition did not attempt to say where had stood the villages of Shunem nor Endor. Oblivion, ever present with her mouth wide open, devours all with the same indifference. Despite the great human dramas enacted here, now everywhere were the well-tended homesteads, each with olive trees, small vineyards, vegetable gardens, sheepfolds, and pastures covered with pulse. And certainly prominent were the great variety of gourds climbing over fences and trees flowering, fruiting, and dangling in numerous shapes. There were the typical flowers in the front yard of the white-washed mud and stone houses with their flat roofs. There was the rich black basalt soil covered with the luxurious green of Galilee. The mountains to the north and west still tilted towards the east, and the chalk-white, bone-looking low mountains which formed the Ridge of Nazareth.

Herod had no difficulty in quartering his men in the villages, but he spent the remaining hours of the day riding slowly about the plain and, with what he knew of military strategy, reconstructing the movements of the great battles of long ago. By the westward drive of the Philistines, where the clash must have come; where Saul must have waited to accept the challenge of the invaders; where he had been forced to give ground—halted the retreat here and reformed his scant forces as his terribly outnumbered men grouped about his towering figure with their backs to the wall of the mountain until the terrible end. Involuntarily, he gave forth a bellow of rage, and put Nicator to the charge. Then, quickly recovering himself, rode slowly to the nearest village and ordered his tent pitched on the spot which he calculated to be in the vicinity of where the valiant Saul in his agony of soul must have contrived his own death.

CHAPTER SEVEN

GENERAL HEROD

On his return to Sepphoris, Herod was overwhelmed by the adulation of the people. The pomp with which he was greeted after his victory over the Sanhedrin at his trial could scarcely have been greater had he defeated the Great Caesar fighting before his renowned Tenth Legion. Again he was garlanded, sung about, and again virgins dressed in white danced before him and flung blossoms under the feet of Nicator.

Further, the province had assumed a war-like posture. Men skilled in the making of weapons were at it night and day to provide arms for the citizenry able to bear them. After working hours, men were being drilled under the officers appointed by the elders. Everybody yearned for a place behind Herod when he marched on Jerusalem to punish "those Fringes" for their insolence in calling their "son Herod" to trial. The air was heavy with the cries of war. "Death to the Asamoneans! Stone the Fringes! March on Jerusalem! Dominion to Herod! Galileans are never cowards! Death to the Sanhedrin!"

Still mounted upon his Palomino stallion, Herod bared his head and sat looking over the vast throng which had gathered to greet him. He bowed his head briefly, and when he lifted it, tears were in his eyes. Then he spoke to the people briefly.

"My beloved fathers and brothers, your demonstration of love for me and concern for my safety moves me to seldom-shed tears. It also binds me by unbreakable bonds to you. May I destroy myself with my own hands before I become unworthy of your great love and faith in me. May I be cast into the utmost depths of Hell before I arrive at such infamy. If I did, it would amount to base betrayal of man and impiety towards God who has granted me the blessing and honor to come among you as your governor and to share your noble and courageous spirit."

Here Herod was interrupted by such wild cheering that he was not able to continue for several minutes.

"Be assured that we shall not overlook the wicked and the vile of soul when the time is ripe for their punishment. We Galileans would not deserve our well-established reputation for manhood and courage when we are in the right if we did. But we must be certain that we are prepared in every sense when we make the attempt. I must go immediately to Damascus to confer with the president of Syria first, and acquaint him of our intentions and moves. I trust you to continue with your preparations, but withhold action until I return to lead you. I commend you on the prosperous and orderly state of affairs in Galilee, and the manner in which you all have obeyed the counsel of your elders. My estimate of you as fighters is such that with you at my back, I would march against the most celebrated fighting men of the known world were it necessary."

Herod dismissed the people after distributing many presents and commendations. Then he summoned the governors of the various places over the province for their reports, and sent each away with a gift.

Most likely, it was conscious, for Herod never was accused of lacking in intelligence, but conscious or not, Herod had this day and in this manner struck a blow of state. He had laid the foundation for the political machine that was to stand him in such good stead later on. Galilee was solidly in his pocket. It was to remain so for the rest of his life.

At his headquarters, he found four letters from Jerusalem. He read the one from his father first. Antipater wrote him of the overwhelming goodwill of the nation towards him. It amounted to something like idolatry. Then he informed Herod of the terror of Hyrcanus and the Sanhedrin. Hyrcanus was in such a state of fear, not only that Herod would throw him out of office, but also punish him with death, that he had collapsed twice in public in the short time that had elapsed since the trial. This fear was aggravated by the fact that he and his confederates knew that Herod not only had the military power to overwhelm him, but the goodwill that the nation bore Herod would more than sanction such an action should Herod decide to do so. The members of the Sanhedrin were also in terror—with the exceptions of Pollio and Sameas—and some contemplated fleeing from Judea. He hoped that all was well with his beloved son, and that the affairs in Galilee were satisfactory.

Cypros, Herod's mother, complained of Doris. It was hard, she wrote, to understand how Doris, who only a few days before could not see her way to accompany her husband to Galilee unless she traveled in the manner of a queen, had now taken to hours at a time in association with the household servants. She was sitting in the quarters of the female servants every afternoon, conversing with the maids as if they were her social equals. That was bad enough in itself, but was not the extent of her injuries to the family. The house steward had revealed to her that Pheroras was having criminal conversations with at least three of her young maids, and Doris was not only aware of this, but was encouraging Pheroras. Herod knew only too well that this was something in which Antipater never indulged, and strictly forbade to his sons, holding that it was taking a vile advantage of the girls.

Now, she could not sleep for fear that Antipater would learn of this conduct of Pheroras. The nineteen-year-old boy was to be pitied in a way. He had been born lacking in the mental qualities of her other three sons, and also without the same energy of body, though he was handsome enough to look at. Further, as the boy reached his manhood, Antipater was too occupied with public affairs to force him to pursue his studies and his military training as he had with the others, especially Phasaelus and Herod. She had no complaints to make of Joseph, since he willingly went to the gymnasium, read books on military science, and associated with military men. But it appeared that all Pheroras wanted to do was to lurk around the young female servants and indulge his passions of the body. What was to be done? Herod knew that it was a rule in the family of several generations to choose the parents with great care, both for intellectual as well as physical perfection. She could not bear to think of indiscriminate grandchildren, nor of a grandchild brought up in the servants' quarters. Could Herod send for Pheroras and thus force him into military discipline under his guidance? At any rate, she was displeased with Doris, and suggested that Herod either send for her to be with him in Galilee and thus restore her home to order, or send her home to live with her parents in Idumea until he had such a palace for her that Doris would be pleased with. Salome was making wonderful progress with her studies. Strangely, her mind seemed equal to that of a boy. She sent her brother worshipful love as always.

Joseph's epistle was brief. He burned to join Herod in Galilee. He had decided to become a professional soldier, and it would be pleasing to him to gain experience in Herod's army. Would beloved and admirable Herod allow him to come? He would be happy to accept any assignment, however minor at first, to train under his beloved and distinguished brother. Pheroras was behaving very badly, but he would tell Herod the details when they met again.

Herod dashed off a brief note to Joseph to join him immediately, but not to bring Pheroras, as he could not bear for a brother of his to set a poor example before his men.

The last letter was from Sameas, who gave him the same information about the state of affairs in Judea that Antipater had sent, but with bits that his father could not have known. Of particular interest to Herod was the item that Hyrcanus and several other members of the Sanhedrin were considering fleeing to Parthia in case Antipater could not persuade Herod to spare them, if and when he returned to Jerusalem. Knowing the extent of Herod's love of his father, and faith in his wisdom, they were waiting on that before taking final steps. Was it possible that both Antipater and Phasaelus were too ready to believe that everything told to them as truth to be truth and without guile? Did Hyrcanus contemplate being brought back into Judea by the Parthians and given supreme power under them in case fate favored them over the Romans? But who could tell what an inordinately vain imbecile might conceive with the assistance of certain associates who were convinced that they had divine sanction to rule the nation whether they had the ability to do so or not? Perhaps it was well that Herod was not so credulous.

After four days of rest from the saddle, during which he was in daily conference with the local governors of the province, Herod set out for Damascus by chariot. He was accompanied by only his special bodyguard of two hundred and fifty picked men. As usual, Herod put on quite a show of elegance and made a stir as he entered the ancient city and swirled up to the residence of the president.

Sextus Caesar made no attempt to conceal his pleasure at seeing Herod again, nor his satisfaction and amusement at the turn of the trial at Jerusalem. Then the lean, ascetic face sobered.

"Have you any comments, any suggestions to add, O Herod? With Parthia only awaiting a chance at the Roman throat, and many able men of Rome still alive who are enemies of Caesar, we must be eternally alert here in Lower Asia. Who knows what turn affairs might take?"

For answer, Herod opened the portfolio, extracted the letters of his father and Sameas, and passed them to Sextus Caesar. Herod watched with concealed eagerness as the president bowed his balding head and read. At the end, Sextus flung up his head like a stallion who scents danger.

"How many really able fighting men have you, and how many auxiliaries could you raise in a short time?"

Herod smiled. "Oh, I had forgotten this," he continued as he withdrew a lengthy scroll from the portfolio and extended it to Caesar. "My pleasure in seeing you made me forgetful."

Caesar broke the seal and unrolled the script at once. A long look, then he flashed Herod a warm smile.

"How carefully written, and how detailed! Has your esteemed father seen it yet?"

"I had two copies made and sent one off to him before I left Sepphoris. He has it by now."

"Excellent! But I would expect that of you, I am very eager to read it. It will require long and close study. Amuse yourself in any way that you choose. We sup here at nine."

Herod entered his chariot and was driven to the suburban home of the father of Nicolaus and Ptolemy. There he had enthusiastic welcome.

"Ah, but you thoughtless miscreant!" Nicolaus charged as he embraced Herod affectionately. "You leave me here pursuing the vagaries of history while you go conquering around. You must realize that the time has come for me to join you as your historian, yet not one word to that effect have I received from you."

"But what would you have to record, O brilliant Nicolaus? Nothing but the routine of governing a small province of a small nation? There are no more Hezekiahs for me to fall upon."

"That is correct, O Herod. None who can approach the rapacity of Hezekiah except Roman officials, and you will not be allowed to lay hands upon them."

They laughed heartily, then laughed more when Herod described the abortive trial with words and gestures.

Then abruptly, Herod was grim. "But their shabby trick is going to cost them their lives. I am going to Jerusalem after I finish with Sextus Caesar with sufficient forces to overwhelm and drag them out and cut off their goatish heads."

"Then I am going along," Nicolaus said with determination. "While I drone away here learning about history, you are actually making it. I am going!"

"And I too," Ptolemy chimed in.

"Shut up, you young whelp!" Nicolaus shouted. "You are all of five years my junior. You have plenty of time to wait. Why ruin my chances by pushing yourself forward? Go away while men talk. Go and see about the wolf hound who has just whelped out in the kennels. In any case, go!"

Ptolemy was not disconcerted. Instead of leaving the room, he made himself more comfortable upon the long chair, took a sip of the mild, sour wine, and lifted his well-arched brows in mock indignation.

"To what a degree of insolence my aged brother has arrived. Is it possible that the disability of senility comes upon him at the age of five and twenty? Look, O Herod, he attempts to dismiss your confidential scribe from your presence when in fact, I should have my stylus and tablet in hand, taking down your immortal words as they fall from your lips. One who is proficient in both Greek and the barbarous Latin tongue, and who through the pursuit of learning, at nineteen, already knows something of Roman law."

"Something," Nicolaus commented dryly, "but very little, having only matriculated in the study of law this very year. Herod does not require a lawyer at all. He is making law himself. He needs a historian, a chronicler to set down what he does. And as he will hardly find room for one of us, I as his former classmate and intimate friend should . . ."

"Enough!" Herod exclaimed with mock severity. "Both of you shall go with me to Jerusalem, but my conscience will not allow me to detain Ptolemy from his studies for more than a month. Learning is a religion with my father, and he would reprimand me for luring Ptolemy away from school."

The two handsome young Greeks cheered and leaped to their feet. The family chariot was ordered, and the three went to the foremost gymnasium which was patronized by the men of the first families of Damascus, where Herod showed off his skill as wrestler, at which sport he was superior, then they bathed and were rubbed down by the attendants. It was now seven-thirty by the water clock. And Herod decided that it was time that he return to Sextus.

"How fortunate you have returned a little early," Sextus exclaimed. "Your report indicates that you have exceptional abilities as an administrator as well as a soldier. I am so impressed that I have already dictated a letter to Rome on it and notified my distinguished cousin and the Roman senate that I have advanced you to commander of the armed forces of Celesyria, and it was my wish that you would see my letter of recommendation before it was sent."

Sextus looked up to find Herod's limpid brown eyes alight with happiness, but he expected Herod to say just what he did. Politeness required it.

"But O noble Caesar, you do me too much honor. It is possible that you grossly overestimate my capabilities."

"Ah, no, O gifted Herod. You must accept lest you be my ruin at Rome. If it became known there that I had under me the finest soldier and administrator of Lower Asia and did not bind him, not only to Rome, but to the party of Caesar, by unbreakable bonds, I would be dismissed in disgrace. And justly so. Rome has become the greatest power in the inhabitable earth because of its flexibility, its adaptation, its ability to recognize talent anywhere, and to make use of it. In this important respect, we excel ancient Greece, who despised non-Greeks and made no use of skills in the provinces. We are so superior to Parthia in that field that there is no comparison. As you know, they have the custom of beheading their generals who win many victories for them under the device that the general has rendered a greater service to the throne than was required. Think of that!"

"Perhaps our Sanhedrin borrowed their viewpoint." Herod chuckled. "Judaism was certainly influenced in religious matters by the Persian magi. Why not in other things? Certainly there exists a kind of Parthian party among us. Cyrus the Great and Darius Hystaspes made an everlasting impression upon the nation by their generosity in not only allowing Ezra, Nehemiah, and Zorobabel to restore the nation at Jerusalem, but in returning the temple's vessels and other favors. Only, some tend to overlook the fact that these barbarous Parthians are not the great, ancient Persians. These tent-dwelling shepherds do not build anything worth seeing, nor tolerate culture. They have no scholars, architects, nor philosophers. No man looks down upon such heathens more than I."

"For which you are to be admired, O Herod. And yet, these barbarous tent-dwellers have challenged Rome in Asia. They cannot conquer. It is the flexible West against the unchanging East. The struggle which began at Troy is active again in our times. There lies Arabia and Egypt to our south. Who holds Celesyria holds the key to the south. *It must be held for Rome.* That is our responsibility. That is why you have been made imperator of the armed forces of Celesyria. You must be bound to Rome."

"But I am already bound, O Sextus Caesar. I am in chains by similar ideas and outlook, as well as a sense of history. My father has been drilling it into his sons for many years that Rome is and will be the center of the world for another thousand years. I am well aware that Rome has not been the mistress of the world for the millennium past, however. I mean another thousand years of progress in human advancement. The center of history is Rome. I am exceedingly proud of my Roman citizenship."

"And Rome is equally fortunate and proud that you are a Roman. Now that you have read my letter, is there any omission to be added before I send out a special courier to Antioch tonight to take ship for Rome?"

"Yes, O Caesar. The treaty of alliance drawn up by your eminent kinsman and my father is much too limited and vague for these troubled and threatening times. I suggest that it be rewritten to meet the conditions with which we are now confronted. My nation requires to be bound more than I."

"But excellent, O Herod. See? You prove your worth to Rome at once. I was not aware of the terms. The addition to my letter shall be made this moment. The courier has already been instructed to ride hard and be on the ship that leaves from Antioch for Italy in three days."

The courier sent upon his journey, Herod and Sextus went in to supper. No sooner were they dining than Herod did what was expected of him. He was too aware of Roman custom to neglect or delay.

"In the face of your great generosity to me, you must not pain me by refusing a slight gift which I wish to make you."

"But there is no necessity for you to give me presents, my admired friend. In fact, I have given you less than your due. Your abilities demand recognition. Oh, some trifling keepsake will be acceptable."

"That is my misfortune, O beloved Sextus. What I wish to give you is an Arabian foal. He is the son of my Nicator, a Palomino of the purest and finest strain. But the young animal is at my father's estates in Idumea. With all my responsibilities, I had no time to have the proper harnesses and trappings made for it by a leather worker who is sufficiently skilled. I myself can have the colt delivered to you here at Damascus, but you will please indulge me by accepting a trifle to have it done yourself. Please do not refuse me in this matter."

Before the men slept that night, Herod had "forced" Sextus Caesar to accept a talent in gold to cover the expenses of the furnishings for the colt. Official Roman etiquette in the provinces had been observed. The fact that Rome was strengthened in Lower Asia and that Herod was more than equal to the task had nothing to do with the subject. It was the form to be followed. Like breaking a bottle of champagne on the prow of a vessel at the launching. Certainly, provincials, especially of Asia, got nowhere unless they knew their manners. Sextus was pleased to see that Herod knew his way around. The young governor of Galilee could look forward to further advancements, and Sextus could look forward to that villa on the Island of Capri for which he had yearned for six years.

Herod spent the following two days acquainting himself with the state of the Roman forces in all Syria. Five legions were garrisoned at Apamia north of Damascus near the Euphrates. They were kept there to prevent any surprise moves by the Parthians. Herod did not disturb these forces, but took two other legions in Syria with him to Jerusalem in addition to his Galileans.

Before he marched out of Sepphoris, Herod had written his father of his intention to come to Jerusalem and to punish those who had plotted against his life there, but he was surprised to find Antipater and Phasaelus surrounded by their bodyguards waiting for him at the eastern approach to the city. General Herod made a show of his filial affections as usual, but from the very first moment, was aware of a certain restraint in both his father and his brother. There was no lack of affection, and their praise of his advancement was fulsome, but still, something was lacking.

The matter of the new agreement of mutual assistance with Rome was disposed of, then Antipater began to speak of the state of Hyrcanus.

"That is but natural and just," Herod snapped. "Rightly he suffers from a sense of guilt. But the miscreant feels no remorse for his vile attempt upon my life, but only that it did not succeed."

"Listen, my son, do not destroy the poor man. He is not really competent mentally, as you know. He was the tool of evil men. Spare him."

"That type of man should be left in public life where he can bring about every kind of mischief without even knowing what he is doing, Father?"

Phasaelus now entered the controversy. "Hyrcanus had been the friend of our father from before the time that Father was a grown man. His case is pathetic. From your great power, be lenient and merciful to the weak."

"How you do talk, beloved brother," Herod retorted coldly. "This is far from a personal matter, as your intelligence must advise you. It concerns the welfare of our nation, to say nothing of the Roman empire, of which we are not only citizens, but officers entrusted with its common good and preservation. We will be traitors to our oath of office if we condone such treasonable conduct. No, I cannot spare him nor his confederates in this plot."

"But consider the matter from another view, Herod," Antipater pled. "We have enemies, as has been demonstrated. By your seizing and executing these men, you give handle to our enemies to accuse us before Caesar of having betrayed his trust and taken the government completely into our own hands without consulting with Rome. We can be made to appear greedy adventurers . . ."

"That is not true, O esteemed Antipater. Sextus Caesar is aware of everything contemplated, and has given his sanction. Indeed, the president of Celesyria has urged this course upon me. You fear Rome unduly. In these times of peril to the empire, Rome cannot afford to overlook traitors and revolutionists. This is no time for disturbers of the peace."

The controversy went on and on for the better part of an hour. Finally, Herod slumped in his shoulders, sighed, and turned to his father.

"You know that I love, respect, and honor you to an extravagant degree. I cannot contend with you. I am disarmed by my love. But it is against my intelligence and the safety both of Judea and Rome to overlook these traitors to everything that is high and noble. We shall all suffer from your softness of heart. On the battlefield where fell the noble Saul and his sons, it came to me the folly of preserving one's enemies to the end that they destroy you. You make of me a traitor to my oath of office, Father, and you, my brother. I do not like the feeling that it brings."

Both Antipater and Phasaelus quickly embraced Herod and spoke with deep affection and relief.

"You do well to spare the old man," Phasaelus cooed. "He has been taught his lesson."

"You will not lose face with Caesar, beloved Herod," Antipater added. "You can make a show of force, threaten, and then withdraw, son. That is all that I ask of you. You have the goodwill, no, the worship of the nation. You certainly have the power. None will think that you were afraid. That would be impossible under the circumstances. Show grace and mercy and further bind the people to you."

"Only later to betray them to internal warfare, but I bow to your wishes rather than to my duty and judgment."

Herod entered Jerusalem in a most pompous manner. First rode Antipater, procurator of Judea, followed by his guard in parade dress, Phasaelus, his handsome oval face with the long, drooping lashes, and almost feminine mouth, chin up, followed by his own guard, then nothing. Herod waited until there was a space of perhaps a hundred feet that separated him from the last of his brother's guard for dramatic effect. Then Nicator, with his jeweled harness and trappings, came lifting his feet, proudly bearing Herod, riding before his vast contingent, through the historic Gate of Damascus. As he had promised them, his fanatically loyal Galileans were at his back. Then followed the other two legions composed for the greater part of Greeks and Germans.

The beholders were struck with awe. It impressed like a great display of natural forces. The thousand on thousands of blades flashed like continuous lightning, and the tread of men and horses was grumbling thunder. Such a show of power to destroy induced in the spectators a feeling of worship as ever with humanity in the face of overwhelming power. Hence the tendency of men to attribute to their gods the power of irresistible destruction, the tendency to deify destructive forces of nature, and even animals like the lion, tiger, poisonous serpents, and the like. Herod, in command of such a force of destruction, could never again be conceived of as the gay, handsome youth they had always known. So they cheered wildly as the great parade moved through the thoroughfares of the city, Upper City, across the Valley of the Cheesemongers, through the Lower City, and practically circling Jerusalem, returned at last past temple and royal palace and on to march into the citadel, where the troops were to be quartered.

With few exceptions, the nation today identified itself individually with Herod and his army, as nations always yearn to do with leaders. Today the people saw themselves as they wished to think of themselves—glamorous and invincible. Hooray for Herod as themselves!

However, a dozen of the most prominent of the Sanhedrin were gathered in the home of one along the line of Herod's march, and gazed at the spectacle without showing themselves too plainly. They could visualize nothing but death and destruction to themselves in the spectacle.

"Have we been blind?" one murmured in awe. "Is this Herod something more than a man?"

"Certainly not! Do you wish to blaspheme?"

"No, but how does he bring about so much? His father sends him an unexperienced youth to Galilee as governor, where we are all certain that he will be destroyed by Hezekiah, and yet in a few weeks he has destroyed the bandit leader and become the hero of Lower Asia. To overcome this, we summon him to take his trial for the murder of Hezekiah, he appears before us like a king, frightens us into impotence and silence, then goes before the president of Syria and now returns to Jerusalem as a general of the armies of Celesyria, and with the means to destroy us all in a moment. From his very dangers he draws splendor. Herod appears to be beloved of God. But why?"

There was a troubled, stinging silence, then at last an answer came.

"Is it necessary to consider the possibility of Herod's divinity? He is sufficiently troublesome to us as a man. Has or will Antipater persuade him to withhold his hand? If not, will we be summoned to stand our trial before him, or will he merely seize us after this demonstration of his armed might and strangle us?"

"As late as yesterday we might have set out for Parthia where we would have found security, and had the assurance of being brought back into Judea when circumstances favored the restoration to power of our party. But that Hyrcanus . . ." The sentence ended in a snarl of terror, a passionate beating of the breast.

"But there is reason to hope in the plan of Hyrcanus," another swallowed painfully and after a long minute continued, "it is well known that Herod loves and worships his father to a most extraordinary extent, and has never failed to obey Antipater . . . but of course, now that he has grown so great . . ."

It was obvious that these men, the most influential of the Sanhedrin, had gone over this ground many times in the last few days but found little comfort in the circumstance. Outside, the rumble of the tread of horses and war machines and the glitter of blades went inexorably past. Inside this room was futility and desperation.

And yet a glimmer of hope shone through their despair. "But unless we are destroyed now, a time will arrive when we can dispose of him and his house. You will see."

However, the sounds and sights of Herod's might drowned out their desperate hope. The group melted down into a gasping, weeping, breast-beating mass. The sounds of the passing soldiers appeared endless.

Hyrcanus appeared in formal dress upon the balcony of the palace, but not having heard from Antipater, he was boneless. He would not even have dared to appear but for the driving of his daughter. "Get up, Father! You are of the royal line. Conduct yourself like a king. Make it appear that Herod makes this display at your command. Put on your robes of state and stand there as if reviewing your troops. Get up!"

So Hyrcanus, gelid in his limbs, took his place upon the balcony. He tried to look like Caesar entering the Gate of Pomp at Rome, but soon collapsed into a chair. He was struck down when Herod was abreast of the palace, but failed to salute or take notice of his presence at all.

"Ahhhh! Herod means to throw me down from the throne and slay me."

Mother and daughter in the palace also keenly observed the passage of Herod before his armed legions. Alexandra could easily be seen by the multitudes, for she stood, finely dressed, thinking of herself as a powerful queen—like Cleopatra of Egypt for example—proudly reviewing her armed might passing before her. She thought of herself in the heroic role of the Hebrew woman of history saving her nation. She was Esther dealing with Haman; she was Jael removing Sisera, but with this difference: Alexandra had no desire to destroy this example of masculine perfection astride the blond Arabian stallion. Her whole body cried out against such a thing. In addition, and most important, Herod would be her instrument of government. Her plan would be wrecked without his abilities and his power over the people.

She had a great admiration for Cleopatra. Observe what she had accomplished through Caesar by female charm. And before she slept, she would have placed herself in the position to begin. For doubtless, Antipater would appear with Herod at the palace, and Hyrcanus, under her coaching, would propose the union of the families by marriage, and at the right moment, she would skillfully place her own name in nomination by graciously letting Herod and Antipater understand that she would consent to join her royal person with Herod's. There was not the slightest doubt in her mind that both would be overwhelmed by her condescension. What use would Mariamne be to the Asamonean interests? Beautiful and young she was, yes, but only slightly less stupid than Hyrcanus. Supported by Herod's abilities, she would go down in history as a much greater ruler than her mother-in-law, Alexandra. Her plan was perfect. ·

Mariamne, unknown to her mother, also watched the passing of Herod. He aroused in the softly-beautiful young maiden no dreams of empire. His handsome face and strong body stirred her. She was in love with the man. In addition, Herod filled a great need in her life. In the shadow of his arms, she envisioned a protective tenderness. As his wife, somebody would want and value her. Her soul could creep out from its hiding place, and she could at last stand equal with her spoiled younger brother Aristobulus. How she detested her arrogant and selfish brother at times! Ah, to hover under the wings of such strength and manly beauty!

When the long procession arrived at last at the gates of the citadel, Antipater approached Herod and drew him aside.

"I must hasten to the palace and assure that poor, demented Hyrcanus that you will do him no violence. Relieve his anxiety. Do you wish to come with me and tell him in person?"

"Not at all, beloved Father. I have done him no favor. It is you whom I served. I will practice no deceit with him. I positively will not go."

Seeing that Herod would not be persuaded, Antipater went on alone. He was moved to deep compassion when he witnessed the state of terror that Hyrcanus was in. As ever, he was stirred to protect and overlook the frailties of his old friend.

Hyrcanus was maudlin. He wept with gratitude that Antipater was there to protect him. Any dignity that he possessed had been frightened away, and he talked too much, too fast, leaving no room for his own advantage, and Alexandra was not in the reception hall to guide him.

Ever after, Alexandra felt that fate had deserted her by causing her to be in her own apartment closeted with her lady's maid. Immediately after that procession had passed, she hurried to re-dress herself with particular care to appear at her very best when Antipater and his two sons arrived. She had ordered a very rich banquet, and planned to invite the three, as if an afterthought, to dine at the palace. But when she emerged from her dressing room, all had been dealt with. Hyrcanus, so relieved when Antipater told him that Herod had given his word not to molest him at this time, had fallen on the bosom of Antipater and begun to speak hysterically.

"It is well that Herod will not harm me, beloved Antipater, and my closest friend of many years. I love the boy. I have always loved him as if he were my own son. And for weeks, I have thought of nothing else but to have him for my son-in-law."

"Son-in-law?" Antipater gasped. "You wish to give him Alexandra for a wife?"

At this moment, Alexandra was before her bronze mirror noting with satisfaction the jeweled band for her hair. Nodding with pleasure, she nodded to her maid and asked: "Have the procurator of Judea, the governor of Jerusalem, and the general of the armies of Celesyria arrived?"

"I will go and inquire," the expert Egyptian lady's maid replied.

In a few minutes she returned. "The esteemed procurator of Judea has been in the hall of reception with Hyrcanus for half an hour, O exalted Alexandra, and daughter of a king, but his sons are not with him."

"Very good. They have been delayed by government affairs. I shall now be ready to receive them when they arrive. Anoint my wrists with that costly perfumed oil which arrived from Alexandria last week."

With the underside of her wrists anointed skillfully, Alexandra swept from her chambers and moved as she envisioned Cleopatra doing as she approached her reception hall where Caesar waited. Then the elements collapsed about her head. For as she entered, she overheard the chattering Hyrcanus urge, "I will give my Mariamne to your Herod, and with whatever dowry he wishes. And why not? It will only be in his safekeeping, will it not? He must protect us all anyway, and it will be as if I handed Mariamne over to my own son."

Now, Hyrcanus indulged in fatuous laughter. "Our daughter will wed our son. Marvelous, eh? Ha, ha, ha! I'm just like a fox. He, he, he!"

The crushed Alexandra would have withdrawn and sought the refuge of her bedchamber, but she had come too far and had been glimpsed by both of the men. Still laughing, Hyrcanus called her to join them and she had to listen to it all told again at great length by her father. Then hope arose in her, and she turned her eyes on Antipater.

"And what says Herod, O eminent Antipater?"

Antipater spoke very slowly.

"My son knows nothing about the matter. Hyrcanus has only now spoken of it to me. I will, of course, tell Herod immediately and find out his wishes."

"Oh, it will be most agreeable to my son, Herod." Hyrcanus chuckled with complete assurance. "Naturally anyone would be proud to marry into the royal house. Yes, yes, yes. I wish him to come to the palace so that I can reveal my plans for him myself. Oh, yes, yes, yes."

"I am aware of the great honor conferred upon my son, and through him, upon my house." Antipater murmured. "I shall return to the citadel, where Herod is quite busy with the arrangement of his troops and . . ."

"Urge him to come and sup with us," Alexandra cut in. "He well knows that he does not have to observe ceremony here. Have we not always been as of kin, our families?"

Herod's reaction shocked even Antipater. "What madness! Why should I feel it an elevation to marry into a discarded royal house? Hyrcanus indeed exalts an empty title when he thinks to cover up his grave malefactions by offering me his stupid granddaughter. I am not flattered by the proposal, nor will I go to the palace to sup."

Herod halted, seeing the shock in Antipater's countenance, then hurriedly embraced his father and continued in a soft persuasive way.

"Beloved and honored Father, do not be enchanted by a shadow. I see that you are bewitched by the word 'king.' But what is the real meaning of the name? It is the most potent man of the nation. It no longer means anything so far as the Asamoneans are concerned, as you know. It would have been well for both the nation and the family if the dynasty had ended with John Hyrcanus, who was the last able man of the line. You are blind or you would see that you yourself are the strong man of Judea. It is you who gives a false look of power to Hyrcanus because he is your friend, supposedly. At any rate, you are sorry for the weakling. The Asamoneans are a mass of trampled grapevines with you and your sons used as an arbor to give them form without substance. I would be merely furnishing the false appearance to the nation of a virility in the worn-out dynasty and provoking the nation to place a confidence that would but betray. Further, I strongly suspect that that is their intention in trapping us into a marriage. Tell them that I refuse the offer."

"But, my dear Herod, the hand of a royal princess is not rejected like that. What, how can I say . . . ?"

"Remind them that I am already married and the father of a son. The fact that I regret my marriage to Doris has nothing to do with the case. Before I leave Jerusalem, I shall send her back to Idumea with a fine escort and many presents, but certainly I shall send her, but send her without a divorce at present."

Seeing his father's distress, Herod began to pace up and down his apartment in the citadel. Finally he spoke.

"Under the tremendous pressure of my career, it is possible that I ought not be a married man, Father. Perhaps I do not have the time to give sufficient time to a woman, or I am too generous with them. Recently I had a most interesting encounter with an Essene. Had I been born of a less prominent family, I can see, after a lengthy discussion by the brethren, that I might easily have joined them."

"I too am inclined towards their philosophy, but like you, deterred by circumstances. However, that need not exclude our help and sympathies. Many eminent men are secretly affiliated."

"I am deeply impressed, Father. And they get along very well without women. In such a mood, you can see that I do not require more involvement, but less. When you return to the palace, you can ease yourself by saying that I am too occupied at present to give proper consideration to such a grave matter. Let Hyrcanus betroth his Mariamne to somebody else."

After a long and serious consultation with Cypros, who objected strongly to the match and sneered, "So the vine now generously offers to support the tree. Are we to be thought of by that family as nothing more than tools for their use? One day, they set out to murder my son, but failing in their evil design, they now propose to make use of him to protect them from the wrath of the multitudes, and not only that, expect us to be uplifted by the suggestion. Nor can I bear that stupid, cruel, and arrogant woman, Alexandra. I say no!" But go to the palace Antipater must and find diplomatic words to deliver Herod's answer.

Hyrcanus was astounded at the refusal and showed his outrage, but before he could get together the words to make it clear, the shrewd Alexandra cut him off.

"You are mistaken, Father. Herod does not refuse. As he so wisely said, he is merely too disturbed and occupied at the present to discuss it as it should be discussed. There is the matter of the dowry, which requires serious thought, and . . ."

"Why, why does the matter of dowry cause so much difficulty? My old friend here, and also his son, ought to know that he can have whatever he desires. Therefore, what else is there to delay the announcement?"

The diplomatic Antipater withdrew from the palace as quickly as possible and returned to Herod.

"Now that foolishness is disposed of, I can turn to the matter of sending Doris back to her ancestral home under the shadow of Mount Seir. Perhaps I shall bring her and my son back to the city later. I do not know exactly what I think at present. And my official duties are so heavy at present that I have small time for reflection. But in any case, the Asamonean scheme is defeated."

However, Herod had not been back in Galilee a week before Antipater sent him a hurried missive telling him that it had been formally announced from the palace that Herod, governor of Galilee, commander of the armed forces of Celesyria, was betrothed to Mariamne, the granddaughter of Hyrcanus.

"Never have I heard of a case of a man denying a report that was made by a ruler that he was betrothed to the ruler's daughter. It would shame her before the whole nation, beloved son. What is to be done I do not know. Even your mother can think of no remedy except time. No doubt if you delay in consummating the marriage long enough the Asamoneans will make some other arrangement. That will free you without your shaming the young girl before the world."

Herod pressed his teeth together in anger and frustration. "That is the work of that cunning Alexandra," he stormed. "Well, she shall see that this marriage will never be finished. But what a bold stroke from her!"

CHAPTER EIGHT

TEST OF THE METAL

However, Herod found that this unorthodox betrothal did not weigh heavily upon him. In fact, it tended to divide and to frustrate his opposition in Judea, for the childish Hyrcanus was eternally boasting of his powerful son-in-law, and requiring small favors of Herod to show the warmth between the families. Herod unfailingly indulged him and smiled at his childlike requests. Otherwise, the matter just dragged on.

There were some though, who could not give up the hope of overthrowing him. Malichus, the head of one of Jerusalem's wealthiest and influential families, was the leader of this never-say-die faction. It had dwindled to almost nothing, for the nation now saw Herod as a permanent fixture in public life. From resenting him they had come to resignation, and finally pride. That was what had become of the party which Malichus once led. Malichus himself was relentless.

"What, or who is this Herod? Does he possess some powerful demon? Now, he is betrothed to the princess, daughter of the high priest. What next? I fear that some turn of fortune will place the diadem upon his head. Everything—all events—somehow turn to the elevation of this young man."

Then like a threatening flash of lightning came the report that Sextus Caesar, president of Syria and the intimate friend of Herod and his family, had been assassinated at Damascus. This younger cousin of Julius Caesar was slain by Cecilius Bassus. Bassus was of the party of Pompey. His act was to plot the demise of Sextus Caesar to avenge the overthrow and death of Pompey.

Lower Asia exploded like a gasoline drum. Bassus seized command of the legions garrisoned at Apamia, northwest of Damascus not far from the Euphrates. No sooner did the news reach Sepphoris than Herod began preparation to attack Bassus. Phasaelus, with all the forces he could gather, prepared to go. Antipater remained at Jerusalem to see after affairs, but urged his sons on and sent every reinforcement that he could gather, and still leave Judea protected. "Avenge the death of our friend!"

But the responsibility for punishing the party of Pompey did not rest upon Herod alone. All of the Roman commanders in Asia also converged upon Apamia. Caesar, alarmed at the strength of the opposition and the duration of the struggle, sent out one Murcus with additional troops to succeed his murdered cousin.

Additional hope came to those who wanted change. An infinitely greater detonation shook the world. Herod went deadly pale and his legs grew weak when the tidings reached Apamia that Julius, the Great Caesar, had been murdered in the senate house at Rome by Brutus and Cassius and their conspirators. The world heaved under his feet like a ship in a violent storm. The very climate of the world was in disorder.

"What is to become of us?" the less resolute Phasaelus moaned. "Shall we flee to . . . to . . . Egypt, perhaps, O my brother?"

"Where in the habitable world could we go that the names of the sons of Antipater are not known, Phasaelus? And any part of the Roman empire is safe, or as perilous, as another."

"Yes, I can see that, now that you point it out. But, but what is to be done?"

"Conduct ourselves like men. Fill out the clothing of grown men. Carefree youth is forever behind us from this day onward, O beloved Phasaelus. Events themselves will naturally decide our course, but in this tremendous cataclysm, only the strong man—both of body and soul—can survive. Only the resilient and resolute can advance. Our family has arrived at a certain eminence over the past three generations. We must not, cannot recede from what our forefathers have done for us. We must make our own contribution to the coming generation. In a few words, we must fight."

"But suppose that the party of Caesar is overcome?"

"Then fight with our wits. We are still Roman citizens and Judea is allied to Rome by a treaty of mutual assistance, is it not? Whoever governs at Rome, we are still Romans, the mightiest nation which has ever trod the earth. Therefore, nothing is changed for us."

Phasaelus brightened visibly. He flung his arm about Herod's shoulders. "You continually astonish me with your resourcefulness and courage. However, you do make me feel futile at times. Even a little jealous, but not for long. I always remember what our noble father has taught us—never to be jealous of the success of another member of the family, since the success of one is the success of all. That is true. It continually proves itself on all sides."

"Naturally. Our father is never wrong except his belief that all men are essentially good. That is a most dangerous notion to men in public life. It worries me continually, Phasaelus. And you serve him badly by encouraging his innocent trustfulness. Ambition and envy make hate-filled beasts of men. When a man achieves great eminence, he also acquires deadly enemies. I constantly pray for Father to accept this ugly truth."

There grew up a heavy silence between the brothers now. Finally Phasaelus mumbled skeptically, "Are you very certain that you are not overly suspicious and mistrustful?"

"No, Phasaelus, no. My attitudes are the result of hard fact."

"But how can you know always, beloved Herod? You could be . . ."

"Rulers found more than a thousand years before that it is foolish to attempt to govern without knowing everything possible concerning what goes on in and out of the nation that might have an effect upon the country. So spy systems were developed. They sound ugly to speak of, but they are very necessary to stability of government, beloved Phasaelus. There can be no considerable attempt at revolution without the multitudes, the common people. The people must be induced by one means or another to be the muscle, the sacrificial body of the struggle, or it cannot happen. So they must know that it is contemplated before the governor does. Therefore, I am a member in good standing of the Stone-Cutters' Guild."

"Herod! How astonishing! But how could you bring it about?"

"Very easily, Phasaelus. During my first year as governor of Galilee, I saw the necessity, and talking with a stone-cutter in Sepphoris, I told him that I admired the occupation, and were I not who I was, would love to be one of them. He himself suggested that the guild would be flattered to record me as an honorary member if I would appear in the working clothes. I did so, and was welcomed very warmly. I fattened the treasury by paying ten times the amount assessed, occasionally slip off in disguise and pass an evening at their hall. It is very amusing and informative. So they sent a letter of introduction to their guild at Jerusalem, and I am a member there also. So I gather the secrets of the ambitious and bitter men who would like to see our family bloody in the dirt. Without naming my source, I pass what I have learned on to Father and you. That is why I warn Father that Malichus wishes his death as well as mine and yours. He must beware of that man."

And shortly, Herod had need of all the resignation and resourcefulness that he could muster, for the slaughter of Caesar at Rome produced unimaginable turmoil. The mightiest men of Italy exploded into a vast struggle for personal power, and each went where he considered that he could get hold of money and men to make himself master of Rome. Brutus, Cassius, and their immediate associates who had expected to profit most and immediately from the death of Caesar were disappointed, for Marc Antony, distant kin of the slain Caesar, exhibited a certain genius in his resourcefulness by seizing the initiative and turning bleak disaster into a triumph.

As the body of Caesar was being borne from the senate house to his own home, Antony had halted the procession in the marketplace and there delivered such a eulogy over the body of the dead dictator that the common people of Rome turned on the conspirators with such murderous fury that both Brutus and Cassius were compelled to flee Rome. Antony made himself master of Italy. Belatedly, Brutus and Cassius learned the truth that, forced to choose, the poor, like the rich, love money more than political liberty. The Roman people remembered vividly Caesar's numerous triumphs, the enormous wealth and treasures which his triumphs had brought to Rome, and the free shows and the distribution of free wheat. What had Cassius and Brutus brought them, Marc Antony asked the people. Nothing! Then the scoundrels had murdered the man who did bring them food, entertainment, and glory. Kill them!

Cassius fled to Syria to raise an army and funds to fight Antony and Octavius Caesar, the grandnephew of Caesar and his heir for the mastery of the Roman empire.

With a heavy heart, Herod saw Cassius come to Apamia, take

over the legions there, and raise the siege which the party of Caesar, to which he belonged, had been maintaining. So he retired with his forces to Sepphoris, and Phasaelus to Jerusalem.

The days now passed Herod in procession, variously garbed wild figures seen through gray-black mists. His underground sources informed him that a delegation of five, headed by Malichus, had hastened to Syria to inform Cassius that Antipater and his sons were of the party of Caesar, and so violently partisan that they could never be brought to reconciliation with Cassius and his party. The only chance for peace in Judea was to put the family to death. This was particularly necessary with the cruel and arrogant Herod, the special favorite of the Caesars. Cassius had listened briefly, but made the short reply that his present mission was to raise money and troops with which to return to Rome, but in the case that Herod and his family made any attempts against him, they would find that he had a heavy and impatient hand. The audience had not lasted ten full minutes, thus offending Malichus.

The elders of Galilee gathered about their "son" to comfort him, and at the same time to find out what was the situation, and what were they to expect.

"My beloved Fathers, I can only quote the Greek philosopher Heraclitus, who was ever concerned with the mystery of change: *Nothing is; everything becomes. No condition persists unaltered even for the smallest moment. Everything is ceasing to be what it was, and becoming what it will be.* All that we can do is hold ourselves in good heart to meet whatever condition develops. Whatever it turns out to be, we Galileans will face it with our customary valor."

After a lengthy, frustrated silence, the headman of Nazareth murmured, "If only we could get some idea of what is likely. For example, do you think that this Cassius and his party are likely to become masters of Rome?"

"Frankly, I do not, Fathers. Antony is a very shrewd politician, and has already gotten the Roman people against Cassius and Brutus. And in addition, he is a very able soldier. The struggle may be prolonged, but in the end, Antony and the young Caesar seem bound to win. Of course, while this heartless man is in power in Asia, it would be highly indiscreet to voice such an opinion in his hearing. He is a hungry wolf, raving for money, and through money, political power. Already, he is going into all the cities, demanding such sums as will work terrible hardships upon the people. There is no doubt that he will soon come into Judea and make demands upon us. We can only hope that it is possible to raise what he demands of us. In the meanwhile, let us all contain ourselves with patience, and give no handle for him to exercise the cruelty of which I believe this Cassius to be capable."

All agreed that this was the prudent course since they had no hope of being too hard for the great mass of Roman legions. Then they went away in dejection.

No longer than a week passed before Herod was hastily summoned to Jerusalem to confer with his father.

"Look at this," Antipater said with a long, pale face as he handed Herod the letter he had received from Cassius.

In the communication, Cassius told Antipater that he had already been advised of the unalterable attachment of Antipater and his sons to the dead Caesar. However, he, Cassius, had no time at the present to punish them justly. He demanded 700 talents out of Judea shortly, and in case Antipater—out of loyalty to the party of Caesar—did not raise it promptly, he and his sons would forfeit their heads.

Herod raised his eyes from the document and gazed at his father and brother, both paralyzed by fear. His heart constricted painfully, and his protective instinct expanded.

"The case is very hard, Father. Seven hundred talents is far too much to extort out of a country as small as Judea. Yet the fault lies with

Cassius, not you. We cannot hope to defeat him in battle. Therefore, the money must be raised. As you perceive, the hostile tone of this letter is due to our relentless enemy, Malichus. He traveled to Syria to play the sycophant laying up a stock of merit with Cassius in hope of replacing you as procurator."

"Yes, I know," Antipater mumbled miserably. "Oh, to be forced to place such a miserable burden upon our nation! We, who desire so much to further prosperity."

"And more is demanded of us than others when you consider the population," Phasaelus moaned. "Perhaps Cassius, in addition to his greed, is highly prejudiced against the Jewish people."

"Very likely," Antipater groaned.

"Very well," the practical Herod said. "The sum must be raised or that rapacious Cassius will not only kill us, but do more awful things to our people. Naturally, you will assess the raising of the money by areas. How much am I responsible for in Galilee?"

Antipater thought a while, then took up a stylus and clay tablet and began to figure.

"Galilee is poor compared to Judea. Bring me 100 talents. That is an enormous sum, I recognize, but I cannot see how it can be avoided."

"It shall be raised somehow, Father. And since Malichus is one of the wealthiest and supposedly most influential men of Judea—or as he represents himself to Cassius—assign a heavy sum for him to produce. And especially since he wants Cassius to believe that he is of old an enemy of Caesar and a partisan of Caesar's enemies, it will naturally be expected by Cassius that he will exert himself mightily to bring in his assessment."

Antipater relaxed; his large soft eyes flew wide open, and he smiled broadly. Phasaelus threw back his head and laughed.

"Perfect, Herod! Let his pretensions confront the realities. Oh, even disaster has its rewards. Father, set Malichus down for 200 talents. He no longer has any following, and Cassius will discover exactly how influential he is. Herod, you are a jewel without price."

"Done," Antipater grinned. "Now, let us see what territory to assign Malichus to gather money from. Hmmm. The Upper City where he claims that he is so powerful. Naturally, Phasaelus and I will collect it after he fails. I could have assigned him Samaria, but then he would have the excuse that the Samaritans do not like orthodox Jews. Let him roast right here in Jerusalem."

The nation was then divided into ten areas excluding Galilee. Eight other men besides Antipater and Joseph received assignments. Antipater sent for them and advised them within the hour.

Herod hurried home to Sepphoris and called all the headmen of Galilee to him.

"Fathers, now that I have read Cassius's letter to my father before you, it is not necessary for me to enlarge upon it. You recognized the terrible threat to our small nation. Since there is no hope of our disputing the issue with arms—the Roman armies under Cassius being too overpowering for us to even hope for success against them—we must somehow raise that 100 talents, and immediately. Having only recently recovered from the derangements of the civil war between the Asamoneans and the ravages of Hezekiah, it would be tragic indeed if this ravening wolf Cassius destroyed us again. And we are fortunate in being assessed only 100 talents out of the 700 demanded from Judea. I therefore beg that we exert ourselves to raise and deliver it to Cassius before the discrepancy in our favor has been noted elsewhere. I am only too aware of the cruel oppression in being required to raise such an enormous sum at all, but what can we do? Tell me, Fathers, if you can discover any other course."

In the record time of ten days Herod was able to deliver to Cassius the 100 talents raised in Galilee. Cassius leaned far back in his seat and fixed Herod with his cold, tormented gray eyes and stared at him for a very long minute.

"And you are of the family which I was told was inimical to me. It is no wonder that Caesar thought highly of your family. It is true that he was overly ambitious, but no man in his senses would say that he did not know how to choose the men to assist him. Your alacrity shall be remembered in your favor, O Herod. Now, let us see how soon those who traduced you to me will come with their share."

So pleased was Cassius with Herod, that he took upon himself to go down to Jerusalem to meet Antipater and Phasaelus. Their share and all the rest was on hand except the portion to be raised by Malichus. The Roman summoned Malichus before him and, in the presence of Antipater, Phasaelus, and his staff, denounced Malichus in the harshest terms. Cassius even descended to coarse abuse.

"And you are the villain who came to me at Apamia with scurrilous lies concerning these honorable men, you son of a mongrel dog! I am going to kill you this day to cleanse the earth of such evil-smelling dung!" The enraged Roman turned to his guard and shouted, "Seize this ball of dung and drag him out and cut off his head this minute. Away with him!"

But the over-gentle Antipater intervened and, by promising to go among the people himself and secure the money, finally persuaded the maddened Roman from taking Malichus off immediately.

"But this camel's spit should not be allowed to live any longer," Cassius objected. "What enraged me most is the effrontery with which this dung of a camel thinks that he can deceive and trifle with me, Cassius, the co-master in no long time of the Roman empire. Who and what does he think he is? The anus of a pig!"

However, Antipater finally prevailed, but still Cassius drove Malichus from his presence like a dog. Only the assurance of the money cooled him sufficiently to depart northward without slaying Malichus. He pointed out that he had already made slaves of the inhabitants of Emmaus, Gophna, and two smaller cities for not bringing in the tribute he exacted, so who was this vile Malichus to trifle with him?

But as Herod had predicted, the kindly intervention of Antipater increased the hatred of Malichus towards the family instead of lessening it. Malichus had been humbled before the nation, and Antipater and his family exalted. He was not the kind of man to forgive this.

"What? Is it true that Cassius and Marcus, persuaded that Herod is the ablest man in Lower Asia to assist them, have made him procurator of all Syria and have given this Herod a vast army of horse and foot and a navy under his command, and promised him that when Antony and the young Caesar have been crushed, to make him king of Judea? Hear O Israel! Has God forsaken His own?"

And he was answered that God had not forsaken the nation, but that Herod was indeed so elevated. The Romans were a very practical people, and elevated those who could be of service to them. It was possible that Heaven was in no way concerned nor involved.

"Then I shall bring them to their destruction. It cannot be borne," Malichus screamed. His disturbance had reached that degree where he had lost discretion. He began to plot against Antipater.

Learning of the supposedly secret machinations of Malichus and his confederates from his confidential sources, Herod hastened to Jerusalem and warned his father.

"An asp is never persuaded by kindness, Father. You were in error in trying to benefit this man. Nothing will soften him but his death. And further, your bosom serpent, Hyrcanus, is secretly supporting Malichus."

"Oh! I cannot conceive of such a lack of loyalty and ingratitude on the part of Hyrcanus, Herod. I cannot believe such a charge."

"You had better, beloved Father. This vain, driveling Asamonean knows no such emotion as loyalty nor gratitude. He is full of evil cunning. The fear of being displaced moves him. I tell you that he is very active in the camp of your enemies. Let me dispose of him once and for all."

"You are really persuaded that this is true, my son?"

"Make a test and see for yourself, beloved Father. The vanity of that dolt is all-surpassing. My informants are certain. But make a test yourself, and see if he does not slither about like a serpent in the grass. Prove matters for yourself." Herod turned his head away to hide his tears. "In the meanwhile, I will linger about Jerusalem to guard you. I have no intention of allowing you to be slaughtered like a sheep by men who should be grateful to you, but who plot against you in the darkness. I love you more than anything else on earth."

Antipater hurriedly embraced Herod. Neither at this moment were anymore the stern public figures which the world knew. Here in the spacious library of Antipater's palatial home in Jerusalem, they reverted to an especially fond father and son. They were back in mood to the old days on the ancestral estate in Idumea, in that close association. The athletic Antipater was forever with his two older boys, teaching them the science of war, boxing, wrestling, running, hiking, swimming, archery, the expert use of the javelin and sword. Or in summer, they were together in rose-red Petra of Arabia on the estate of the father of Cypros, who was very near of kin to King Aretas, where Herod was being skilled in horsemanship among the Arabians. Of course, Phasaelus was there also, but Herod was always the more intense, the more eager to learn, and the most loved by all. For this brief time, Herod and his father were reliving that old intimacy. Now Herod, loosening the embrace, put words to their emotions.

"Do you remember that fancy of mine that at sundown every day, Mount Seir, far off to the south and east of us, returned to earth after spending the day in Heaven with God—having spent the night watching whatever went on, on the earth during the night? I conceived that the mountain kept watch over the world all night, and when the sun rose, went off to Heaven to tell God what men had done during the night."

Phasaelus, seated comfortably, laughed with affectionate reminiscence now.

"And when our uncle Joseph insisted that mountains did not travel so easily, you picked up a small stone and placing it in your sling, hurled it at him with such force that you crippled his ox?"

"Served him right," Herod laughed. "A man should have enough poetry in him to imagine a flying mountain at least. Nor would he concede that our father was stronger than God. Such a spoilsport."

"Little apostate," Antipater said fondly. "But somehow, you always loved me to excess, my Herod. Before you were even three months old, you could distinguish my voice and become agitated in your cradle in the hope that I would take you up for a while."

"Aha! So you should not now risk your life so recklessly among deceitful villains and allow them to deprive me of your presence. I guard my own life to preserve you from the extreme pain of losing me. I think how you, my mother, my beloved brothers and sister would be desolated by my loss. So protect and preserve yourself for our sake, Antipater. Have a care."

All the play and fancy was gone from his voice and manner now. He appealed to Phasaelus with his eyes, and Phasaelus responded.

"I agree with Herod, Father. There have been enough peculiar incidents to convince me that what my beloved brother says is true. Malichus is certainly plotting your death by stealth, and Hyrcanus could not be innocent of his behavior. Lose no time in testing out the sincerity of both."

"Very well, beloved sons. I will confront Malichus, and accuse him of deceit and designs against my life."

"But you must allow us to be present, Father," Herod insisted. "If he is not very convincing, I shall slay him on the spot."

This plan was tried, but Malichus not only took oaths of admiration, friendship, and eternal gratitude, but wept copiously at even being accused. Antipater was easily convinced, but Herod said on leaving that he was far from satisfied. It was tried again and again, but with the same results.

"Are you satisfied now, Herod?" Antipater asked.

"The protestations do not cause me to have every faith in Malichus; I simply do not trust him. My trusted, and justly so, informants tell me that he and Hyrcanus are working night and day to bring your armed men to the point where they will desert to Hyrcanus at the crucial moment. My advice to you is to gather an army from those beyond Jordan rather than depend upon those around Jerusalem. Are we not tied to the Arabs by blood? There is your answer."

Cypros, the former Arabian princess, agreed with Herod, so Antipater did go over the Jordan and began to put together a large and loyal force.

Seeing this, great panic seized upon Malichus and his associates.

"Shall we sit still until Antipater has gathered a force so great as to return and destroy us?" Malichus screamed. "Certainly he no longer believes my protestations of loyalty and friendship to him. That is the work of that skeptical Herod, who may become king over us very soon. Both Cassius and Marcus have given him their right hand on it. Antipater must be removed shortly."

"But how? He no longer is careless of his safety. He knows what we had no intention of his knowing until it would be too late. Now he prepares to destroy us. We have been betrayed."

"By whom? It would be well for us to know who is the traitor among us. But every man among us swears to have kept our secret. That Herod must be possessed of a demon. Somehow, he discovers everything."

In haste of desperation, a new plan was formed. Antipater still trusted Hyrcanus. Hyrcanus's part was to induce Antipater to attend a great feast at the palace where many of the most prominent men of Judea were to be present. That was all that was required of him. The rest was up to Malichus.

The drama was brief and brutal. Antipater, happy to make a gesture of peace and unity, brushed aside the warnings of Herod and, attired splendidly, attended the banquet in the palace. He was overwhelmed by the expressions of happy welcome by both Hyrcanus and Malichus, but before the feast was half over, he was served a cup of wine by the chief butler of Hyrcanus, and collapsed and died almost instantly. The butler, well rewarded by Malichus for the deed, departed the palace at once and fled to Parthia. Hyrcanus fell from his seat in a screaming fit, and Malichus rose and, with a triumphant smile, retired to his dwelling in the Upper City.

Jerusalem flamed with outrage at the deed, and Malichus was forced to realize that his plot was not as secret as he had supposed, for mobs clamored for his blood as the citizens of Rome had cried for the death of Brutus and Cassius. Herod was wild with rage and the desire to lay hands upon the malefactor, but was persuaded by his brother to hold off until after the funeral.

Antipater was given a most magnificent funeral, with eulogies by many of the most eminent men of the country. Both Herod and Phasaelus were outraged to find Malichus making the loudest clamor of grief. To deceive both Antipater's sons and the public, Malichus insisted on erecting a costly monument to the man of great piety and patriotism. But none were deceived by it.

"Let us lose no time in bringing the murderer of our father to justice, Phasaelus," Herod spoke from between clenched teeth.

"I am not deceived by his wicked deceits either, beloved brother, but we must proceed with caution. You saw how he seized upon the armed men who had been under our father, and attempted to gain possession of the government, yet he weeps that he loved our father and mourns his death. My blade cries for his blood, but we must take care not to throw the nation into a sedition."

It was hard, but the counsel of Phasaelus finally prevailed with the hot-blooded Herod. Malichus lied hard. He lied from deadly terror of the vindictive, father-worshipping, powerful commander of the armies of Celesyria. Yet, his lifelong dream of power would not die. While he made the most abject oaths of innocence to the sons of Antipater and extravagant public expressions of grief and outrage at the poisoning of the late procurator of Judea, still he plotted. He plotted to achieve his ends to take over the government of Judea. The hatred of Malichus knew no bounds as the hot-tempered Herod stood in his path like a rough-backed mountain.

There was another handicap beside Herod and the disfavor of the public. Cassius had seized Malichus's son and held him as a hostage at Tyre. Any overt act, and Malichus knew that the flint-hearted Cassius would immediately kill his son. How to attempt to make himself ruler of Judea without sacrificing the life of his son was his problem.

Cassius was now in the north making frenzied preparations to meet and defeat the combined forces of Antony and Octavius Caesar who were moving eastward through Europe to attack him in Asia. Brutus was in Macedonia and urging him by almost daily messages to hasten and join him lest he be compelled to meet Antony and Octavius alone. In the meanwhile, the enraged Herod lay along the path and awaited an opportunity to fall upon Malichus like a wounded leopard.

But the times were troubled everywhere. Samaria erupted, and Herod hurried there to quiet the place, which he quickly and easily accomplished by bringing about a reconciliation between the warring parties so as to be free to strike at Malichus. Phasaelus still urged the policy of getting hold of the murderer of Antipater by some scheme that would not allow them to be charged with beginning a civil war.

To this end, Herod came with an army to Jerusalem at the festival of the Passover, while still pretending to believe the loud protestations of innocence of Malichus. Lest Malichus flee to regions where he could not lay hands upon him, Herod pretended that he was the friend of Malichus, hoping to seize him before the holidays were over.

However, Malichus was not misled by Herod's strategy. In a panic of terror, Malichus ran to Hyrcanus and persuaded him to exclude Herod from the city. How to accomplish this occupied many anxious hours on the part of both men. At last, Hyrcanus with a straight face told Herod through messengers that a vast mob of Gentiles—meaning the non-Jewish mercenary soldiers of Herod's army—should not be in the city while the Jewish nation was purifying itself.

"You observe now," Herod raged to Phasaelus, "the proof that Hyrcanus was the secret enemy of our father. What a flimsy and contrived excuse to protect the murderer of our parent! However, Hyrcanus does not now deal with a soft-hearted and easily deceived man like Antipater. I brush aside his deceit like chaff. This very night I shall enter the city and lay hands upon Malichus if he can be found without razing the city."

Phasaelus still stood firm against any violence, but urged Herod to wait for a better opportunity. This stand provoked Herod to the first angry outburst against his brother since their adulthood.

"Do not waste your time and my own filling my ears with cowardly trash! This type of avoiding action on your part and that of my father brought him to his violent death. Say no more! With or without your assistance, I am going to avenge the murder of my father."

"Then I do withdraw," Phasaelus retorted. "If you insist upon not only destroying yourself, but myself also with the people by your so-called magnificent temper and refusing to be persuaded by reason, then I will have nothing to do with the matter. Nor do I relish being spoken of as a cowardly weakling."

Phasaelus turned shortly and went to his own home, calling back over his shoulder that one of them had to remain calm and retain the family prestige with the nation.

Herod let Phasaelus go without protest, and went about searching for Malichus. After hours of search over Jerusalem, he had to admit defeat.

"I cannot find this Malichus," Herod said to one of his officers, "because he is concealed in the royal palace. But if they think that I will abandon my resolve to kill the murderer of my beloved but foolishly-trusting father, they are mistaken. Not only will I slay Malichus, but someday I will settle the long score that I have with that driveling but cunning Hyrcanus. You will see."

Boiling with rage and frustration, Herod sent off a lengthy letter to Cassius. In it, he told the Roman of the circumstances of Antipater's tragic death and of his determination to punish Malichus with death. "I have received information that he escaped from Jerusalem and is now in the neighborhood of Tyre, where his son is held as a hostage by your orders. I pray your leave to allow me to seek him there and kill him."

"I am aware of the vile morals of this Malichus," Cassius wrote Herod immediately. "You would be less correct in your filial duty and as a Roman officer if you failed to avenge your noble father's death. Do not fail to destroy this detested Malichus. I will send to the Roman officers in the vicinity of Tyre to assist you in your noble purpose in any way possible. But kill him, you should."

The bitter Cassius promptly wrote a letter to his officers stationed along the seacoast instructing them "to give Herod every assistance in a worthy design of his." At the time, Cassius was besieging Laodicea and, anxious to join Brutus and face Antony in battle, he pressed the attack upon Laodicea savagely, and took the place.

"Aha! Fortune favors me," Herod exclaimed when he heard of the fall of Laodicea. "Everyone who seeks the favor of Cassius will hasten to Laodicea to bring money and garlands to Cassius. The evil ambitions of Malichus will drive him there surely. And there he will fall into my hands."

But Malichus reckoned otherwise. He knew that Herod would go to Laodicea, and he had no intention of coming face to face with Herod anywhere. As to Cassius, if the plan he was nurturing matured, there was no necessity to flatter him at present. Maybe never. While Herod and the others were giving presents to Cassius, his design required him to go no further north than Tyre to steal away his son, then double back to Jerusalem and make himself master of Judea while Herod was in the north and Cassius was hurrying away into Asia Minor to meet Antony. The scheme was perfect in his eyes. He could see no fault in it. Everything seemed to favor his hopes.

Malichus reckoned without Herod's spy system. While he moved north and west with the delegation from Judea which included Hyrcanus, Herod was kept informed of every step that Malichus made. Therefore, he halted the journey of the delegation at Tyre, when he might easily have continued on towards Laodicea, on the excuse that he yearned to feast the officers and his delegation there. Hyrcanus and the others were installed in the most luxurious inn at Tyre for the night. And while the lavish feast that Herod had ordered was being prepared, and the delegation rested and gave themselves over to pleasure, Herod left them and, in company with a dozen officers in on the secret, went quietly along the moonlit beach.

Nine furlongs, a little more than an English mile, south of Tyre, Herod saw Malichus, hooded and heavily cloaked to disguise his identity, coming swiftly but furtively up the beach.

THE LIFE OF HEROD THE GREAT

"It is he!" Herod whispered to his war party. "Let us dispose ourselves back and front of him so that he cannot escape us in the imperfect light."

In a very brief spell this was done without attracting the attention of the hurrying Malichus and his four companions. Then Herod stepped boldly in the path of the furtive man.

"Hail, O great and sinister Malichus! This is Herod, son and ambassador from the murdered Antipater. What message have you for him?"

The only reply was an astonished, choking gasp, and as Herod charged with his drawn dagger, a loud and despairing scream. Herod struck while his companions took care of the four guards of the man who had poisoned his father, then all joined in the execution of the fallen Malichus. In a matter of seconds, Malichus was dead of many wounds.

The war party then returned to the city, and Herod to his room at the inn, where he said nothing of the incident, but bathed carefully, changed his bloody clothes, and went cheerfully to rejoin the delegation in the dining hall of the inn.

He was just in time, as the meal was now ready, and the servitors began to place the meats and wine upon the table the moment that Herod appeared. In seating his guests, Herod placed Hyrcanus on his right where he could study his reactions.

Perhaps a half hour had passed before the innkeeper entered in great agitation and announced that Malichus of Judea had been slaughtered on the beach. Herod held his gaze upon the face of Hyrcanus, who in the act of lifting a piece of roast beef into his mouth, rose stiffly, then fell speechless to the floor. So profound was the shock and astonishment of Hyrcanus, that it was more than half an hour before he could be revived. Then he turned frightened eyes upon the watchful Herod and, with halting speech, finally made out to inquire of him what was the matter, and who had killed Malichus, and why. Herod dissembled and told him that it had been done by the orders of Cassius, without explaining at that time that it was he who had executed the slayer of his father. Herod took this way to test the fidelity of Hyrcanus.

"Oh, oh, how justly has this wicked Malichus been served," Hyrcanus exclaimed as he shakily resumed his seat at the table. "He was a deceitful, lying man who plotted against his own country. Judea is well rid of the scoundrel. Cassius acted wisely in ridding the world of such as he."

The effect of what Herod observed did not, however, absolve Hyrcanus. "This Hyrcanus is equally guilty of the blood of my father," Herod said in his heart. "But I will allow him to believe that he has deceived me until the hour arrives when I can dissipate his ignorance and measure out his punishment."

With all speed then, he sent off a letter to Phasaelus at Jerusalem, telling him of the death of the murderer of Antipater. And Cassius having received the delegation kindly and commended Herod at Laodicea, Herod returned to his headquarters now at Damascus, while Hyrcanus and the others returned to Jerusalem.

He was confirmed in his suspicions of Hyrcanus, for now he discovered that Hyrcanus had left the brother of Malichus, Felix, with an army when he left Jerusalem for Laodicea. Upon the return of Hyrcanus to Jerusalem, Felix attacked Phasaelus with determination. A certain element of the people had been roused to revolt also in support of Felix. Herod was down with an attack of dysentery, but nevertheless, he rushed to Fabius, now president of Syria, for permission to hasten to Jerusalem to support his brother. But he found that he was too enfeebled by dysentery to make the journey. However, in a few days, a letter from Phasaelus informed him that Phasaelus had defeated Felix with great slaughter, and he was comforted.

But the greatest comfort came from a paragraph in his brother's letter:

Events have shown me the wisdom of your course, beloved Herod. The death of our adored parent, and the fighting with Malichus and Felix, prove that you are wise. Never again will I accuse you of being too mistrustful and hard. I send you my warm embraces.

And soon, Herod learned that Phasaelus had gone to the palace and denounced Hyrcanus to his face as a faithless and ungrateful man. He threw it in his teeth that while he had received an untold number of great favors from Antipater, been restored to the high priesthood at enormous financial and political expense, and in blood by Antipater, and thus also by Herod and himself, he was nevertheless eternally plotting against both them and the security and prosperity of the nation. Never did he miss an opportunity to slyly support their enemies. Then he warned that he had better have a care lest Herod march against him. As ever, Hyrcanus dissembled and denied it all.

Mighty events marched on that were to affect the life and career of Herod. The armies of Brutus and Cassius came to grips with the forces of Antony and Octavius Caesar at Philippi in Macedonia and were annihilated. Both Cassius and Brutus were slain. The party of the Caesars was again the master of the world.

First, on recovering his health, Herod marched into Judea where Hyrcanus had entrusted Felix with the care of the strongest forts in Judea, beat Felix, took the forts away from him, but spared his life on the condition that he quit Judea forever.

But the disturbed times afforded him no rest. For Ptolemy, prince of Chalcis, in the hope of extended power for himself, was persuaded to bring Antigonus, youngest son of Aristobulus, brother of Hyrcanus, who had begun the civil strife which had destroyed the power of the Asamoneans and brought Antipater into preeminence, back into Judea and had furnished him with money with which to raise an army. Fabius, because he was connected by marriage to Antigonus, had given his consent. Marion, tyrant of Tyre by the consent of Cassius, also invaded Galilee in support of Antigonus.

Herod went to war with his customary vigor and soon drove Marion out of Galilee, marched on to Tyre itself and took it, and executed Marion. Since the majority of the Tyrians, out of hatred of Marion for his crimes of oppression, had done whatever was possible to assist Herod, he treated the Tyrian garrison in a most generous manner, even giving sums of money to many of them. He turned about then, with the assurance that the officers there would prevent any further trouble against Herod.

Herod smiled bitterly when he received the frantic message from Hyrcanus to save him and Jerusalem from Antigonus. This foppish nephew of Hyrcanus was marching southward towards Judea, and Hyrcanus knew that the hatred which Antigonus had for him would bar him from no cruelty, once he had Jerusalem and his uncle under his power. Hyrcanus reminded Herod that he was practically his son-in-law and, therefore, could not leave him to the mercy of Antigonus.

"But he only remembers obligations and fidelity when his ox is gored," Herod wrote Phasaelus. "Otherwise, he sides with our enemies. I am going to expel Antigonus, not to protect this deceitful and cunning monster, but for the salvation of the nation."

Herod the determined and seasoned soldier confronted the courtier Antigonus near Dora, at the very borders of Judea. The two armies faced each other across a small river that flowed to the sea there. It had its beginning in the mountains of Galilee.

In a pre-battle conference with his officers, many of them his Galileans, Herod said, "This stream which rises in Galilee is our ally. This foppish Antigonus, the simpleton, has allowed us to maneuver him with his back to the stream. We shall force him into it. A good soldier never accepts battle where the terrain and circumstances are unfavorable. He should have retreated across that stream before he gave us the meeting. He shall pay for his arrogant folly this day with his worthless life."

The battle was a rout. Herod's seasoned and fanatically loyal troops attacked with frenzy. They vanquished the enemy in a matter of minutes. The slaughter was immense. However, Antigonus did not lose his life that day. Abandoning the contest, he fled away in the garb of a woman and left his troops to the mercy of Herod's blades and arrows. After it was over, Herod allowed his men to enrich themselves on the enormous booty that was abandoned by the frantically fleeing army of Antigonus. Numerous of the survivors promptly deserted to Herod, who received them kindly.

Herod now marched to Jerusalem where, with Hyrcanus himself as the leader, he was acclaimed with garlands and presents as he had been in Galilee after his victory over Hezekiah. The ancient city rang with the clamor of his praise. Some indeed, of the party of Malichus, gnashed their teeth at his success, but they dared not make their discomfiture public, lest they be torn to pieces by the public.

On Herod's third night in Jerusalem, he was accorded an elaborate feast at the palace.

"No need to stand on ceremony," Hyrcanus said as the entire family appeared at the table. "My granddaughter is your wife already. In any case, from the intimacy of our families, you have seen our Mariamne often enough over the years."

But having never really seen her before, Herod meditated, struck by her soft beauty and maturity. That brought him up short. He had not seen her in several years now, and had been thinking of her as an immature, flavorless child. Why, this girl had been born before the death of Pompey. That would make her approximately ten years his junior. The tradition in Herod's family was against the marriage of the child brides considered so desirable by most men. Herod kept stealing glances at the girl while he conversed on public affairs with Hyrcanus. Her straight black hair glittered from oiling and brushing, her eyes were large, liquid, and almost black, lips full and well formed. Her apparel was costly, but short of the taste to which he was accustomed in the women among whom he moved. That was something, however, easily remedied. He could not expect the sophistication in her of a well-traveled lady who associated with the upper classes of the world. Too shut in and limited in scope, but that also could be overcome. And she was perhaps three inches short of the height which he admired, and desired to be inherited by his children.

The thing which marred the occasion for him was the brash and spoiled behavior of Aristobulus, Mariamne's younger brother. Petted and adored by his mother, he had not been disciplined. He was a noisy, demanding little monster who frequently did things to attract attention to himself and to interrupt the conversation of his elders. He yearned to turn him over his knee and blister his bottom for him. But, he noted, nothing that he did distressed Alexandra. Her harshest rebuke was, "Is that how you will behave when you become king? Oh my beautiful son, you must use more restraint than that before your subjects."

One incident stamped itself upon the mind of Herod, and was to have influence upon his later life. There was a large bowl of peaches on the table. Before time for dessert, the boy, then around ten or eleven, reached and took one, and demanded that Mariamne peel it for him. She refused quietly until, with blazing eyes, her mother commanded her to do what the prince told her to do. The girl, with an air of oppressed submission, peeled the peach and handed it to her brother. Perhaps twenty minutes later, Herod's eyes were pulled in Mariamne's direction, and found her gazing at him in a kind of mute appeal. It was a most unhappy, defenseless look.

His protective instinct flared. He wanted to rise and go to her and assure her that she had no need to fear anything anymore, and to box the ears of the spoiled brat soundly. He was almost persuaded to take up the matter of consummating the marriage at once, but caution prevailed. Past experiences with the family made him timorous of mixing his life with theirs. From what he knew, he could look forward to nothing more than deceit, cunning, and treachery. That he recoiled from in a wife. That undying ambition to rule and the unscrupulous means to achieve their ends made the Asamoneans abhorrent to him. He yearned for what his father had possessed in a wife, tender love and trust and intelligent and comforting companionship. Knowing what he knew, how could he expect it from Mariamne? It was possible that her nature was different, but if so, then her birth in this family was indeed tragic. So he kept quiet, though Alexandra furnished him two opportunities to conclude the matter.

But as they left the dining hall, somehow, Mariamne was close beside him. Her small, delicate hand brushed his wrist, as if by accident, he assumed. It sent a spark through Herod's body. Involuntarily, he shot an inquiring glance down at her. For a full week, he kept inquiring of himself if he had not for a moment experienced a passion which he had never known before. Was this what he had been seeking ever since his maturity and never found?

Events captured his attention and drove Mariamne from his mind. Octavius Caesar and Antony had settled their differences after the brief battle of Mutani, and the Second Triumvirate had been formed. Octavius, Antony, and Lepidus had all thrown in for liquidation the men who were enemies to one of the three. The young Caesar had thrown in Cicero, who had been not only his instructor, but a close friend and champion since the death of Julius Caesar. He had raised the army for Octavius which had defeated Antony, and forced the older man to accord Octavius his due. Now Antony demanded the head of Cicero, and Octavius, a more hardened and practical politician than was expected, turned in Cicero. The head of the distinguished Roman was fastened to the wall over the speaker's platform in the Roman senate house. The proscriptions over, Octavius returned to Italy, while Antony took over Asia.

Antony came to Bythinia and there received the potent men of Lower Asia. Herod and Phasaelus appeared there among others. Hyrcanus accompanied them. Also present was an opposing delegation from Judea.

Antony received Herod warmly, and spent some time recalling his association with Antipater in the Egyptian campaign, and also in Judea against Aristobulus and Alexander.

"What a fighting companion your father was, O Herod. Magnificent. Of the highest courage, ingenuity, and reliability. And what a superb host. As soon as the pressure of the affairs permit, I shall be your guest and discover if you are as consummate a host as your noble father."

This went on and on as the opposing delegates waited and fumed to make the accusations against Herod and Phasaelus. Finally, Antony signaled for the men to come forward and speak.

"O noble Antony, Herod, and his brother, Phasaelus behave like kings. Hyrcanus is really king, but these two leave him nothing more than the title. They take upon themselves to manage all public affairs. They have all the power."

"Which is as the Great Caesar designed it. You must know that he only granted Hyrcanus the title to please Antipater, who asked it of him. Being deeply obligated to Antipater, he granted it. He has not right nor claim to anything more. It was to Antipater that Caesar entrusted the care of Judea. If now, Hyrcanus is attempting to usurp what was not granted to him by Caesar, I shall certainly deal with him in a hard manner."

"But O Antony . . ."

Then Messala, a patrician Roman, and acquainted with the family of Antipater from many years, stepped forward and not only defended

Herod and Phasaelus, but reflected upon their accusers. Hereupon, Antony harshly told their accusers to shut up. He had no wish, and saw no necessity for them to say anything more, and wished them to get themselves out of his presence.

However, the efforts to unseat Herod and Phasaelus did not end there. When Antony arrived at Daphne, near Antioch, a delegation of 1,000 prominent men of Judea came there to again accuse the sons of Antipater. Antony listened wearily as the orators of the delegation assailed the sons of Antipater with accusations of usurpation of power from Hyrcanus, and Messala defended them. Finally he turned to Hyrcanus.

"The declared purpose of the men of this delegation is to defend you from the encroachment of Phasaelus and Herod and to thus bring about good government in Judea. Now, whom would you say governs best?"

"Herod and Phasaelus and their associates," Hyrcanus answered readily.

"I am delighted to hear you say that, O Hyrcanus, because I am certain that you speak the truth. Therefore these others have come here on a deceitful, malicious mission, and I shall punish their leaders with death."

The hard-campaigning Antony would have had them killed forthwith, the fifteen most active of the delegation, had not Herod begged for their lives. But Antony could not be deterred from placing them in prison for later consideration. The rest of the delegation went out on the beach and set up a tremendous clamor of protest. Seeing the rage of Antony mounting at this, Herod ran out on the beach to them and begged them to desist and go away quietly before Antony took steps to destroy them all. Herod was ignored and their clamor increased. Then Antony, extremely irritated, sent a body of his soldiers out among them with daggers. Around a hundred of the protestors were

killed outright and many more than that seriously injured. The rest
ran away in terror in every direction. Those who reached Jerusalem
safely lived in terror for a while.

"That is the way to deal with seditious swine!" Antony snarled
when the beach had been cleared of the Jews. Then he laughed heartily. "But how they ran when the soldiers got among them with their
daggers! It was equal to a contest in the arena. How amusing!"

Herod was far from amused. But discretion forced a smile upon his
face. He tried to analyze his emotions. These men had come there to
destroy him; had Antony decreed his death they would have celebrated
it as a triumph. Yet he felt indignation at the cruel and cynical manner
with which Antony had treated them. Perhaps he was too much ruled
by that protective paternalism of which his family teased him. The father of Palestine, Phasaelus called him jokingly.

When quiet had been restored to the assemblage, Marc Antony
struck a solemn mien upon his tribunal and spoke like an oracle.

"And now to conclude the business of Judea. I hereby create Herod
and his absent brother, Phasaelus, sons of the noble Antipater, tetrarchs
of Judea, making these two *alone* responsible for the security of Judea,
and for the administration of all public affairs in that country. I shall
immediately send letters to all places necessary, testifying to this action."

Cheering broke out, and under the noise of it Antony leaned towards
Herod, who was standing close to the tribune, and said in an undertone,
"I expect you to sup with me at my headquarters this night. I hope that
this is agreeable to you."

Herod was surprised to find that he was the only guest at the meal.
The talk became frank and easy on several political matters, and as the
hours passed on, became personal. The kind of talk that men indulge
in when unobserved and trusting. Women, pleasure, and preferences
and dislikes. Reminiscences. Frequent laughter. At length, Antony,
after recounting a brief but fervid affair of the heart after the battle

of Philippi, rose and went to a traveling-chest, and returned with an armlet. It was of beaten gold in a very odd design worked out with precious stones.

"This I acquired as booty after the battle. There is an interesting story behind it, which I will not go into at present. I wish you to take it as a gift from me."

"But it is too expensive, O noble Antony. You are much too generous."

"The gift indicates the value I place upon your friendship, O beautiful Herod."

Inwardly Herod flinched. He hoped that the warrior Marc Antony had not acquired that Greek custom of love affairs between men. But he gave no sign of his query. After all, he did not have to submit to such. He was many years the junior of Antony, and physically twice as fit.

But he knew his etiquette and had come prepared. With flowery phrases, he insisted that the exalted Roman accept five talents in gold as a small acknowledgment of his own regard for the friendship of the valiant and patrician Roman. Would Antony kindly allow him to send his servant to the inn for a certain chest?

Antony in turn protested that Herod was too generous, but dispatched four men of his guard to fetch the chest. Then as Herod stood and tried on the armlet, he looked on with admiration.

If Herod could have read the thoughts of Antony at that moment, he would have known that his suspicions were correct. The Roman was admiring Herod's physique, as he stood adjusting the ornament on his upper arm. Antony was silently appraising Herod's masculine perfection, his large, luminous eyes and superb lashes, his muscular limbs well developed by military use. But he did not sense that Herod's mind would be capable of persuasion. And so Antony dismissed Herod from his thoughts as a possible lover, and said to him as he resumed his seat, "Our encounter in person is most fortunate,

O valiant Herod. As the master now of Asia, I require men who can be of assistance to me. There is no doubt that you are the first soldier and civil administrator of Lower Asia. Between the Euphrates and the Delta of the Nile, and possibly beyond, you have no equal. You are cosmopolitan in your tastes and extremely witty, an amusing and stimulating companion. You are aware of the realities. To say all in a few words, we two can be of great service to each other—mutual assistance and all that it implies. You are of such reckless courage as to arouse my highest admiration, almost my envy. Then there is your unexcelled fidelity. Shall we consider from this night on, that we have a mutual assistance pact for our own advancement?"

Antony stood and extended his right hand, and Herod leaped to his feet and firmly grasped the hand of the Roman.

"Signed and sealed in our own blood, O Antony. Each to the death for the interest of the other."

Thus began a friendship which was to become famous over the world of that time, and was to have immense influence on the careers of both men.

CHAPTER NINE

THE ROAD TO ROME

Herod and Antony reclined informally in the headquarters of the Roman at Tarsus in Cilicia. The meal had been luxurious, and the two men were rather torpid from the numerous delicacies, but Antony was like that—sensuous and indulgent with himself no matter what the circumstances.

But Herod had taken almost no wine at all, and had eaten sparingly. He had something on his mind.

Antony belched lazily, reached for his wine cup, and spoke to his companion.

"It is good to see you, O beloved Herod, no matter what you have come to me to worry about. Never in my life have I had a better companion for whatever mood I might be in."

"I do have a matter which I wish to call to your attention. You are preparing to invade Parthia. In the case that you have not had a thorough report on climate, geography, and the internal state of affairs in both Parthia and Armenia, I beg you to allow me to get the information for you."

"Very thoughtful of you, you demon worker, but it seems unnecessary to my campaign. Romans are more skillful soldiers than those barbarian herdsmen. We are bound to win the campaign."

"But Crassus . . ."

"Was an utter fool, O Herod. The stinking herdsmen did not really beat him. His over-powering conceit blinded him, and he allowed himself to be tricked to his defeat and death. Orodes and his pup, Pacorus, will find no muddleheaded Crassus in me. And do not forget the crushing defeat that Caesar inflicted upon their Mithradates in Pontus . . ."

"*Vene, vidi, vici,*" Herod cried with admiration. "What military genius resided in that bald head of your kinsman! O to be Caius Julius Caesar for an hour!"

"I do not require his vast talents to beat the tricky, lying bandits, O Herod. Have no fear about that. Anyway, I have some information on the country and their methods of warfare. They are unexcelled bowmen and cavalrymen. But I have no intention of allowing their Surenas to maneuver me into a position where he can make use of these things. Why, their past wars indicated that they know nothing about the science of conducting a siege, nor defending themselves in such a situation. And that is where I shall crush them."

Herod sat silent for a time then said with slow urgency, "I wish that you would allow me to send three of my best spies into the country, nevertheless. Both Alexander the Great and your kinsman, the Great Caesar, held that you can never know too much about the enemy. As you probably know, they have been planning an invasion of Syria for six years now, and that Pacorus, crown prince, with their General Labienus, are eternally pestering King Orodes to allow them to proceed."

"What of it? We shall crush them with great slaughter. In any case, unless they strike immediately—before my plans for the invasion are completed—I shall pin them down within their own borders."

"And that is where they appear to be almost impossible to beat, O noble Antony. If my counsel is worth anything to such an experienced soldier and statesman as Marc Antony, I would ascertain everything about their internal affairs possible—their state of preparation, national spirit, geography, and winters. Your plan of campaign must rest upon these factors."

"Very well, O Alexander the Great, I shall allow you to attend to that later. But first, I have another matter which is annoying me and which I am resolved to settle before the invasion of Parthia. It concerns Cleopatra, queen of Egypt. As you may know, Caesar destroyed her brother and placed her upon the throne of Egypt. In spite of his infatuation with her, it was specified that she must bring her armed forces into any conflict, on the side of the Romans, and the party of Caesar. But what did she do while Octavius and I fought so desperately against his murderers? She kept very quiet in Egypt, not only avoiding the war in person, but failing to send a single legion nor even a ship to our aid! I am resolved that she shall be punished for this treasonable conduct. I care nothing at all about her great beauty. I have summoned her to me here in Cilicia and when she arrives, I shall treat her with the greatest severity. I shall deprive her of her throne, if indeed I do not punish her with death! If she does not appear soon, she shall not escape, for I shall march to Alexandria and seize her."

"I consider her failure to give assistance in the war as a criminal act, but then, she is a woman. It is probable that she does not understand such grave matters. I do not approve of women in public affairs, however beautiful."

"Nor I!" Antony blazed. "In fact, I hold that Caesar's infatuation with this woman cost him his life. Her insistence that he assume the crown and thereby make her queen of the Roman empire gave a handle to his enemies. I look upon her as a deadly serpent who should be exterminated. Do not be surprised if I behead her. And so incensed am I against her that I am determined to deal with her before Parthia. Then I can turn all my thoughts to the matter of the invasion."

"Good military strategy, O Antony," Herod murmured. "Leaving no enemy behind you. She might ally her country with the Parthians and afford you greater difficulties."

"Certainly! Consider how she slyly kept out of things while we fought for our very lives and the existence of Rome, when she had seduced my kinsman and persuaded him to restore her to the throne! Who knows what schemes she was devising? Possibly to join with Brutus or Cassius in case they won, or, as you suggest, the Parthians now? Remember they can all be reckoned as Asians."

"And with the ancient struggle which began with the siege of Troy and now revived with Parthia as the champion of Asia . . . a kind of Asia-for-the-Asiatics conflict . . ."

"Exactly! I have no intention of overlooking her default. My very blood boils at the thought of it."

"Understandable, O my excellent friend. But there is another matter. Will you consummate your marriage with Octavia, sister of Octavius Caesar, before the invasion?"

"Probably, but enthusiasm is lacking. You realize that the betrothal is a matter of state, not of the heart. That arrangement was thrust upon me in the forming of the new Triumvirate. I feel no urge to hurry it up, but perhaps it would be well if I had it over with also before going to Parthia. But do not deceive yourself—it will in no way interfere with any sexual pleasures I might come upon in the north. There will not only be a plenty of beautiful women who fall to a conqueror, but tender, youthful boys."

Antony looked slyly at Herod and laughed. "Though I know that you think little of such cosmopolitan pleasures."

"I can see no point nor pleasure to be had from such acts," Herod smiled. "Love to me means something between a male and a female, despite the discourses of Plato. Like yourself, at the moment I am not in love with anybody at all and, like you, I see no need for haste in consummating my marriage to the granddaughter of Hyrcanus. Not that she is not beautiful enough, but the betrothal, like yours, arose out of politics. Then again, I fear that she is stupid like her family, and in addition, she is fully two inches shorter than is necessary to make certain of tall, robust children."

From that point the conversation turned on trivial personal preferences in sex, horses, poetry, and the drama, provoking a great deal of laughter until they both began to yawn. As they rose to go to their beds, Antony stretched elaborately and said, "How would you like to sit with me on the tribunal tomorrow and listen to the cases which come before me?"

"Oh, nothing would please me more, O my firm friend! Human contention is ever the purest and the highest type of drama. And my curiosity about human behavior is insatiable."

Herod's inquiring mind was tremendously stimulated by the city of Tarsus, ancient in the fertile plain of Cilicia. It lay on both sides of the Cydnus, whose cold and swift waters were the pride of the city. This river bore traffic to the port city of Rhegma on the Great Sea. It was already considered a great town in the time of Xenophon, its civilization being mostly Semitic at that time. Its deities were Heracles, Perseus, Apollo, and Athena.

After Tarsus was Hellenized, the citizens then boasted that they were Argives sprung from the companions of Triptolemus, and Tarsus became the seat of a famous school of philosophy, and sent forth teachers as far as Rome itself, such as Athenodorus, the teacher of Augustus, and Nestor, the teacher of Marcellus. It became Roman in 66 BC and was a very rich city and province. It had received freedom lately from Antony, and later would receive the dignity of a metropolis from Augustus, and important immunities for its commerce. The inhabitants were vain and luxury-loving, and a statue bore the inscription, "Let us eat and drink, for tomorrow we die."

Antony had his tribune set up in the public square on the waterfront. This morning, as the chariot of Antony threaded its way slowly through the traffic of a great avenue along the river, the Roman satisfied the curiosity of his guest concerning Tarsus as they rode and observed. Boats of commerce and passengers moved briskly up and down, hailing and being hailed. Merchandise moved in from the sea through Rhegma, and outward from Cilicia. The traffic was very heavy.

Arrived at the park-like square, Herod took his seat beside his friend and the hearings began. The docket was crowded, for litigants had had a long wait for the arrival of Antony, and so the business had piled up heavily. Antony assumed a stern and judicial air as the litigants came before him. Roman justice was in operation. Antony, inwardly bored and callous, listened and dispensed justice. Herod was intensely interested. This went on for fully three hours, and yet there was a great number still to be heard, which might consume two or three days of hearing, waiting.

Then suddenly, a very curious thing occurred. Some commotion along the river, but the cause was out of the range of the vision of Herod and Antony. The waiting litigants turned, looked and listened, and ran away from the park, careless of their cause. Then even the men who were being heard followed the others, and Antony found his tribune deserted. Only he and Herod remained.

"What on earth is the matter?" Herod inquired.

Antony shook his head. "Never have I witnessed the like of it." A great, confused clamor arose on the river, but still invisible to the waiting and deserted officials. Yet, it was not the sound of strife. "It does not sound like a fight, but what can it be?"

"Let us run and see, O Antony."

The two men did just that. Pell-mell, they fled the tribune and ran towards the sound which grew greater by the moment.

Neither the two friends nor any of the spectators conceived of it at the time, but a great hour in the history of the Roman empire had arrived. And neither could Antony nor Herod imagine what changes were being brought into their lives.

Arrived at a place of vantage, they could hardly believe their eyes as they saw the reason for the clamor.

Moving slowly and, yes, majestically against the swift current of the Cydnus was a golden barge. The richness, the appointments, the beauty and dramatic arrangements of people and things—such as no man had ever seen before—evoked cries from the beholders. Applause, vocal and otherwise, mounted to the skies like the smoke of incense from a great altar.

"By Jupiter!" Antony swore and, forgetting rank and dignity, followed by Herod, elbowed his way rudely downstream as the gilded barge moved upward, so that in a few minutes, the vessel was very close.

"Diana of the Ephesians is come among men!" some voice in the packed mass shouted and it was taken up.

"It is Athena!"

Antony and Herod had their own eyes glued upon the surpassing spectacle, and Herod observed, "I see the *signia* of Egypt."

"It is Cleopatra of Egypt," Antony agreed. "What a great artist the queen is!"

"And the more you observe, the greater the wonder," Herod said in an awed voice.

For now with the gilded barge close at hand, Cleopatra, most gorgeously attired in silk almost as fragile as a spiderweb, and jeweled incredibly, glittered and shone from a raised dais forward on the vessel. The sort of reclining throne was draped in the most costly and eye-catching fabric, interwoven with gold thread. Six beautiful and richly dressed youths stood on either side of her, fanning her gently with fans made of the tail-feathers of male peacocks. To her rear posed a dozen beautiful maidens dressed as sea nymphs and Graces. The air was perfumed even beyond the packed masses ashore who craned their necks and fought for a chance to see, as the barge moved slowly towards the landing with its outspread sails of royal purple.

Without ceremony, Antony and Herod roughly forced their way to the pier to receive the Egyptian queen. Knowing Antony's sensual nature, Herod smiled secretly at the lack of rancor in the greeting of the Roman master of Asia. He heard Cleopatra's silken acceptance as she replied to Antony's invitation to a supper at his headquarters that evening.

Finally, they made their way again to the marketplace in the park-like square to resume the hearings. And just as slowly, the once-eager litigants drifted back to be heard.

"Well," Herod observed slowly, "the execution of Cleopatra will be the most gorgeous and sensational beheading in all history, my friend."

"I have not said that she will be beheaded," Antony snapped. "We shall hear what she has to say for herself. That is her right. That is Roman law. It is possible that she has a very good excuse for her failure to come to our support. At any rate, I shall not mention the matter this night. It will be a reception which is due her high rank. After that, the questioning can be arranged."

Antony sent servitors scurrying in every direction to find and buy the greatest delicacies that the province of Cilicia could afford. A most lengthy and sumptuous feast for Cleopatra was provided. Antony had been elaborately bathed and rubbed down, and appeared in his most gorgeous raiment and ornaments. Herod, though far from being charmed like Antony, dressed to do honor to the occasion. Antony sent an armed guard of 1,000 men to escort his guest to his headquarters. Cleopatra came surrounded by her beautiful boys and girls to add to the pleasures of the occasion.

A brief but curious incident occurred. All during the feast, Cleopatra had eyes for Antony only, scarcely noting that Herod was even present. This did not irk Herod, for while he regarded her as a marvelous spectacle, he did not think of her as a woman in connection with himself. Further, knowing the circumstance, it seemed wise and prudent on her part to play up to Antony, who was in reality her master and had the power of life and death over her. He neither expected nor yearned for her special attention. Yet, for a moment during the feast, he caught her eyes burningly upon him. It was a profound and yearning gaze. Almost immediately, she was turning on her charm again for Antony. When, at the end of the feast, she made Antony a present of the dozen beautiful boys who had furnished music and singing during the feast while the girls occasionally danced, a servitor, one of the boys, stealthily thrust a small, jeweled chest into his hands.

In the manner that it was handed to him, Herod recognized that the donor intended secrecy, and so he did not examine it until he was alone in his bedroom that night. The little casket was worth a great deal of money in itself. It was carved from ivory and inlaid with gold in the design of a rambling vine. The leaves were diamonds and the blossoms rubies. Inside was an ornament of magnificent design and great worth. Beneath it was a small strip of papyrus on which was written, "To the man with the most beautiful eyes and lips upon the earth. And to the arms most fitted for love."

So that was the translation of the look! But what was the real meaning of the whole matter? She was the queen of a country infinitely greater than his own; he was nothing beside her. When the infatuation of Antony was already plain, she had nothing to fear from that direction anymore. Why bother about a nobody like himself by comparison? She was indeed beautiful, witty, and charming, but for Herod, she held no allure. All her good female attributes were merely academic. She had been the mistress of the Great Caesar and had a son by him. He had seen her play for the favor of Antony. She was, therefore, tarnished goods. What was more, he had seen her effects upon Antony already. Antony was his friend. It meant to him that this seductive Egyptian was utterly forbidden to him. His woman must be one never touched by another man, nor ever to be afterwards. Possibly, that was nothing more than personal conceit and pride on his part, but that was the way it was. He concealed the costly trinket in his luggage and stretched out on his couch.

This night, Antony did not require his company. Without doubt, the sensual Antony was occupied with a careful examination of his gift of pretty boys. Herod had no wish to be present at such an orgy. His abhorrence of the practice all but choked him. Why, oh why was his friend Antony compelled by such practices?

Perhaps the answer lay in the dissolute youth of the man. His own father, a man never overburdened with moral concepts, had died while Marcus was a small boy, and his mother had married Lentellus, an abandoned wretch if ever one lived, and the young Marcus had been very fond of this dissolute scoundrel. Antony had been married to four wives now, and had been faithful to none. The muscles of Herod's limbs flexed as he stayed the impulse to protect the youth and rush in upon Antony with his naked sword.

In a moment Herod sank back upon his bed. What would become of his career, his soaring ambitions? Antony was the master of Asia, and consequently, the fountain from which flowed Herod's blessings. What madness! If he killed Antony, he could not even hope to escape with his own life. And what could he hope to accomplish by punishing Antony with death for a practice common over the known world. Nor was the act anything new. Socrates, Plato, and Pericles had engaged in it and endorsed it. The Greeks, the highest cultivated people of the earth for many centuries, practiced it; the Romans and all others now.

Who would praise him for his act of retribution? Nobody! For a few minutes, his protective instinct had gotten the better of him. All the world was not required to live by his father's abstemious and puritanical standards.

Now, Herod laughed cynically. He saw himself in a light he had never trained on himself before. He was no different from numerous men in public life before him. Antipater had been correct in his teachings to his sons. He was compromising his principles tonight for the sake of advancement through Antony. He knew now that he was not going to do anything to injure the friendship. He was going to seek every advancement possible. Having faced facts, he finally went off to sleep.

Herod, with his zeal for efficiency, was disappointed when he arose at his usual early hour just around dawn, to find Antony still abed. The Triumvir appeared at noon, went tired and irritable to the marketplace, but gave Herod no opportunity to mention the mission of Herod's spies to Parthia and Armenia. His talk was all of the beauty and charm of Cleopatra. Nor did Antony protest too vigorously when on the following day Herod announced that he must return to Judea.

Back at Jerusalem, on the surface, affairs appeared to be in excellent shape. The reports of his intelligence corps confirmed Herod's uneasiness. There was an unusual amount of correspondence between Ctesiphon and Dara in Parthia and Jerusalem. He worried about the firmness of fidelity of the legions at Apamia and Antioch. They had switched allegiance from the party of Caesar to that of Pompey once. Antony indeed had taken them over, but who could say whether they would faithfully adhere to Antony if actual warfare began with Parthia? Labienus, one of Pompey's most able commanders, was at Ctesiphon. He was there in 43 begging King Orodes to give greater help to Brutus and Cassius when the news arrived of the defeat of these two at Phillipi. Orodes had allowed him to remain ever since. With the Parthian Crown

Prince Pacorus, Herod knew that he had been pressing Orodes to allow him to invade Syria and wrest it from the Romans. The rumble from the north worried Herod, and particularly with Antony so wrapped up in his love affair, and his overconfident attitude concerning the invasion.

So he was overjoyed to learn that Cleopatra had at last returned to her kingdom, even if Antony was now her worshipful lover instead of her executioner. It was possible that the exactions of preparation for the invasion would cause the fickle Antony to put that woman out of his mind.

The year 40 BC strode across the world. Riders from the north arrived on spent steeds to report that the Parthians had themselves invaded, led by Labienus and Pacorus with a tremendous host of troops. Labienus drove into Asia Minor and took Lydia and Ionia. Pacorus in Syria soon had Antioch and Apamia. The Roman legions in Apamia had been followers of Brutus who had been taken over by Antony, and now these men fulfilled Herod's fears. They deserted to Labienus. Pacorus came down the great coastal road, gaining the submission of all the cities except Tyre, which was particularly attached to Herod. Simultaneously, Barzapharnes, a Parthian satrap, drove into Galilee. Decidius Saxa, Antony's legate, was defeated and fled the camp out of fear of treachery of his own men. He was pursued, captured, and put to death. Seven hundred and fifty Parthian horsemen appeared outside the walls of Jerusalem.

In such a gloomy atmosphere, Herod and Phasaelus conferred.

"What is to be done?" Phasaelus inquired of his brother with eyes bleary from worry and despair. "What *can* be done, O my beloved brother?"

"We must fight them, Phasaelus."

"Fight? Are you mad? Taking into account how the Roman generals have suffered at the hands of these Parthians, what can we do?"

"Fight. The welfare and protection of Palestine was placed in our

THE LIFE OF HEROD THE GREAT

hands by Antony. Not only have we been honored with citizenship by Rome, but we are the representatives of Rome in Lower Asia. We cannot evade our responsibilities. Nothing for us but to fight."

"And be destroyed," Phasaelus sneered. "With the sparse forces available, we shall suffer instant and total defeat."

Herod shrugged this off.

"Then if we *must* fall, Phasaelus, let us fall grandly. I shall fight."

"You must remember that numerous among us are partisans of the Parthians because of the historical ties with Old Persia. They will give all aid and comfort to the Parthians possible."

"That is to be expected, O beloved brother. In reality, this is a war between West and East for the mastery of Asia. Many honestly hold that we who have cast in our lot with Rome are traitors to the doctrine of 'Asia for the Asiatics.' This is merely a renewal of that ancient conflict. Personally, my face is towards the flexible West because there is progress and civilized advancement. I yearn for progress. Judea would be facing backward in time to fall under the influence of the barbarians—those culture-hating and seldom-bathed herdsmen of Parthia. That alone to me is worth fighting and dying for. I shall fight."

There was a long and troubled silence during which Phasaelus shook his head sadly.

"But it is useless, Herod. We shall be overwhelmed. The situation is such that we are no more than a point—with no dimension in space. We should pretend to submit, to join them, and wait to see if the Romans can come to our assistance later."

"Now I must inquire if *you* are not mad. It is too well known that we are Romans, and not only Romans, but of the party of Caesar. Too many of the old-time thinkers envy and resent us, and would lose no time in pointing out to the Parthians our affiliations. Have they not denounced us to Rome on every opportunity? Consider what they will pour into more receptive ears."

"But they have said to Hyrcanus that if we will but show friendliness and admit them to the city . . ."

"Bah! You must know that the word of a Parthian is worth far less than the excrement of a horse overnight. They delight in trickery. You know how Crassus was deceived to his destruction. You know that trickery and deception are their greatest arts up to the present. No, my beloved brother, our heads would roll before sunset of the day that we submitted ourselves to their mercy. No, I shall fight and, if I must die, all that I pray of my God is that I die with my face to the enemy."

The atmosphere was chilled between the two. Herod felt it with deep concern and sadness. After a while, he went to Phasaelus and placed his hand upon the shoulder of his older brother.

"Phasaelus, you must be aware that my love for you and for every member of my family is overwhelming. Let us prevent ill will and misunderstanding to injure such a profound affection. Let us . . ."

"Oh, of course, beloved brother," Phasaelus shrugged off the hand of Herod and sneered, "there can be no hurt to our affections for each other so long as the rest of the family submits to you and looks upon you as some kind of deity. I know that it will wound your gigantic self-conceit mortally when I tell you that in this grave instance, I am certain that the conclusions of Hyrcanus are more valid than yours. From now on, I am thinking for myself instead of being led around by you."

Herod, seated at his desk in the citadel, fiddled with his stylus for several seconds, then he looked up at the standing Phasaelus and smiled.

"I know, much beloved and admired brother of mine, that the times are full of peril for both our nation and ourselves. You labor under an unheard-of stress. But, troubled as we are, we must not forget that we are brothers, and seldom in history have two brothers been so close in heart and accomplishments. We cannot quarrel with each other. It could benefit none but our enemies. Rome has entrusted nothing to Hyrcanus. Except for the temple, he has nothing to do with public affairs. Ours is the responsibility. However, as co-governor of Judea, I ought to know these important conclusions which he has reached."

"Well, I suppose that the main thing he contends is that the Parthians are the defenders of Asia from European aggression, and that we too are Asians."

"Aha! Just as I thought. Exactly what a backward-looking priest would conclude. Throw down our defenses to Parthia. Desert to the enemy. Imagine such a saying, 'the sons of Antipater acting without honor or courage.' As to Hyrcanus . . ."

"Say no more, Herod. As always, you are right. I must go now and see if the watches we appointed are being strictly kept, lest the reactionaries steal a march upon us. What troubled times! The sons of Antipater whom everyone once thought the most fortunate of men are caught between the upper and lower millstones."

Phasaelus hastened from the room, and shortly Herod went out also. He walked slowly so as to observe the conditions in the city as he went. Eventually he climbed upon the massive wall of the city at a certain point and gazed down upon the camp of the Parthian horsemen outside. Their typical goat-skin tents spread out in a rude half-circle, their mounts grazed from short ropes. Six men were on sentry duty. Up and down they rode slowly, encased from head to foot in their scale armor which covered both man and horse completely except for the hands and feet of the rider. None were of exceptional height, but tough-looking men of wiry strength and endurance. Herod stood covered by his cloak to conceal his identity, and studied both camp and guards for a long time.

Deeply concerned about the attitude of Phasaelus, Herod decided to return to the citadel and leave word that he could be found during the evening at the home of his father. He would persuade Phasaelus to join him there for supper and, in the presence of his courageous mother, probe and purge the mind of his brother.

But as he returned to the citadel at a brisker pace than he had used to go to the walls, he noted an excitement in the population. Many strangers were in the streets. Something sudden was up. He all but ran the remaining few blocks to the fort.

His chief intelligence man was waiting for him.

"As you know, Antigonus has been in the north attempting to persuade some ruler to undertake to bring him back into Judea as king."

"That I know. Please go on without waste of words."

"It is said by some that he is now in the Parthian garrison near Drymi, that famous woodland not far from Ptolemais."

"I am familiar with it. Go on."

"Drymi was the gathering place of those favorable to Antigonus, son of Aristobulus. Not all of the people, but the Jews around Mount Carmel rallied to his cause there and are ready to march on Jerusalem. By their aid, he hopes to get some part at least of the country under his rule. Some of his party have already entered the city, and wait only for reinforcements to attack the palace. The hatred of Antigonus for Hyrcanus, his uncle, was all but feminine in its intensity. Therefore first of all, he hopes to eject Hyrcanus from the palace, seize upon him, and torture him horribly before he permits him to die. Next to Hyrcanus, he hates *you*, O noble Herod, because he fears you and sees in you a stumbling-stone to his ambitions. At this moment, he bears hard upon Pacorus to bring him back to Judea with power."

Herod nodded gravely, complimented his agent for his efficiency, and thrust towards him a generous sum of silver as a bonus. Then he sent immediately to the home of Phasaelus to hasten him to the citadel. They discussed the new emergency and began to make ready to defeat the attack. Under the pressure of duty, their brush of a few hours ago was forgotten.

Their combined forces were led out upon the parade ground of the fort, and possible maneuvers rehearsed hastily.

"Eight days of rain, O my commander?" Herod's captain of archery inquired.

"Yes, if the palace is attacked. Now you will dispose of your bowmen in this fashion, considering the structure and grounds of the palace. Leave no doubt as to who is concerned in each day of the rain."

The eight days of rain was a maneuver which the captain and Herod had worked out together years before, and they found it very effective in that there had not yet been found a defense against it. The bowmen—all extremely expert—released a discharge of arrows in eight relays. By the time that the eighth company had fired, the first had their arrows fitted to fire again so that the firing never ceased. It was literally a deluge and the carnage was tremendous among the enemy. Nor could the enemy concentrate on one quarter when they had gotten range, for the missiles confused by coming from too many directions.

Phasaelus was equally occupied with his foot soldiers for a time, then the brothers with their chief officers re-entered the citadel to plan, and the soldiers to rest.

This period of quiet lasted less than five hours. From the nearby temple of Zorobabel, Herod could hear the changing of the Levites at the end of the second watch. Herod and Phasaelus sat in the guardroom, each to his own silence, tense and watchful. Finally Phasaelus spoke.

"These years must be under a regency of Heaven. The original Creator is obviously dead and a regent governs until His son reaches manhood."

Herod nodded in confirmation. "I too have been trying to ambush a dream, but feel frustrated like you. Now I sit here waiting with the fatalism of a tree sensing the coming of a windstorm."

"O Herod! O Phasaelus! The palace is attacked!" came a desperate cry from the entrance of the massive building of the fort, and instantly the place came alive with the fury of a swarm of hornets whose nest has been disturbed.

The howling, hate-filled mob surrounded the palace of the Asamoneans. Arrows and stones pelted against windows and doors. Two thoughts came to Herod. The first was the inefficiency of any untrained group of fighters. The emotions ran too far ahead of effective effort. As if calling vile epithets won any victories. His second thought was for Mariamne. Where was the young princess hiding and how great was her fear?

The "eight days of rain" supported by the footmen of Phasaelus with blades quickly drove the mob from around the palace, running for their lives, but the leaders halted at the marketplace and firmed for a determined fight.

"Down with Roman oppression! Asia for the Asiatics! Drive the strangers back across the Great Sea!" were the battle cries of the attackers. "It is glorious to die for our Asia!" And glorious or not, they soon began to die in great numbers. The veteran troops of the brothers literally cut them to pieces.

Running in disorder, they took refuge in the temple, where Herod pursued them in great rage now. Then, finding it difficult to destroy them there or to drive them out without more troops, he sent armed men into the surrounding houses to prevent escape while he brought up additional forces.

But during the absence of Herod, the enemy stole forth and took revenge upon the men in the surrounding houses. The houses were set aflame and Herod's soldiers in them burned to death.

On finding this disaster to his men on his return with reinforcements, Herod became a demon. He shouted his doctrine with a loud voice.

"Every man who fights under me is a part of my own body. Who injures even one of my brothers in arms injures me. These men were murdered in the most brutal and inhuman manner by the enemy, and I shall avenge them in a like manner or die in the attempt. At them, my brothers!"

Nothing could have been more stimulating to his fighters than this declaration, which they had heard on several occasions, and the attack was utterly savage. And when the enemy was forced from the temple, the slaughter was terrible and thorough. The boast was that nobody inflicted injury upon the "body" of Herod without punishment condign. Herod had so bound his soldiers to him. And he ever was in the fore of the fighting, not somewhere safely in the background directing his men. Also he apportioned out the number of the enemy that each soldier was to destroy, and always selected more as his share.

"I only require each of you to account for five of the enemy. My quota is a minimum of ten."

And his reckless charge turned his men into demons, careless of death. This accounted for Herod's unfailing victories. The "body of Herod" could not conceive of failure.

With the great slaughter, the back of the enemy was broken, but hope still lived. There were daily skirmishes, with the Parthian party waiting for the influx of the nation at the approaching celebration of the fifty days after the Passover feast—the Pentecost.

But Herod and Phasaelus were alert. Herod placed a guard of sufficient men under a captain to keep eternal guard over the palace. Phasaelus guarded the city walls to repel attempts at breaching them. Herod then was free to go on the offensive. With his toughest men, he rushed outside the walls and attacked the enemy camped there and killed them or drove them fleeing in all directions, and, in general, kept them off-balance and from consolidating forces and building up confidence by any victories. On occasion, Herod and Phasaelus merged forces and erupted from the gates to inflict suffering upon the Parthian party.

Eternally defending the palace, Herod found himself more interested in Mariamne. Frequent conferences there to assure him that all was well brought the two into frequent contact—both Hyrcanus and Alexandra saying that since Mariamne was already betrothed to Herod, they were practically man and wife, and so there was no necessity to observe the customary separation until the final consummation. Besides, these were unusual times and circumstances. And Herod's excessive protective instinct betrayed him. The girl was so weak and helpless that her very weakness commanded his strength. And she was so small and soft. Like a baby chicken chirping. So he fought the enemy in a tigerish fashion for her sake. Only over his dead body should Antigonus seize and treat her with disrespect. Nor did he deceive himself that Antigonus would spare her because of her sex, youth, or beauty. He was judged to be effeminate generally, and no man can treat a truly feminine woman with greater cruelty than an effeminate man.

And Antigonus was becoming increasingly impatient to consummate the secret bargain which he had made with the Parthians. It was the strength and vigor of Herod which stood in his way. Through his supporters, he began to decry the disorders in Jerusalem—though it was his own party who brought them about—and to plead for the Parthian horsemen to be admitted to help quiet them. Antigonus realized that he could never climb the throne without the assistance of those Parthian horsemen inside the walls. But again, there was Herod obstructing his ambitions. So far, the promise of the Parthians to enthrone him was empty. Herod had stubbornly refused to open the gates to the horsemen, despite the blandishments of their leader, who was the butler to the prince, and called also Pacorus.

But now, Phasaelus and Herod again differed. Phasaelus favored admitting them. Seven hundred and fifty horsemen could not possibly overcome their forces, he argued. It would be interesting to meet and talk with them and, gaining their friendship, rid themselves of the necessity of all this endless fighting.

"No!" Herod bellowed. "You must be mad to consider stripping the city of its main defenses—those walls. You know that these herdsmen are excellent fighters in open country, but do not know how to conduct a siege. If they did, they would have been in Jerusalem already. It is not out of their goodwill that they are still outside, but our walls. And I pay no attention to their oaths of good intentions. They have not marched all the way down here for the pleasure of embracing the sons of Antipater. Our only safety lies in keeping those walls between us, and hoping that the Romans will arrive in time to assist us."

"Again you assume that your conclusions are the only ones thinkable . . ."

"They are, Phasaelus. Do not be taken in by their obvious deceit. Remember the fate of Crassus. This is the time for skepticism, not gullibility. We are allied to Rome. It is for Antony to say whether they shall be admitted or not. Until we receive such an order, our sole duty until that time is to oppose."

"And where is your noble Antony now? In Egypt, no doubt, indulging his lascivious pleasures with Cleopatra while we exist in deadly peril for his sake. All danger to us can be dispelled if we show ourselves friendly to these horsemen, and we can dwell in our own country in safety. What difference will it make? We dealt with the Great Caesar and prospered. We had to accommodate ourselves to the party of Brutus and Cassius and still prospered, then turned back to the party of Caesar under Antony and have been advanced under him also. It is too well known that we are the most capable men in Lower Asia, and if the Parthians gain permanent control, as it seems likely that they will, we will retain our present power if not advance.

What is so wrong about living under the rule of Asians? After all, we too are Asians, remember."

"I have no wish to quarrel with you, dear beloved brother. But I cannot, in honor, exhibit such a lack of fidelity. We are committed to Rome, whatever the circumstances, and I have given my right hand to Antony. He is my commander as well as my firm friend in spite of any social defects he might possess. It is not for me to judge. The decision to exclude or to admit these treacherous Parthians is his. I shall not admit them."

Seeing the stubborn expression on the face of Phasaelus, Herod rose and took his leave without another word. Something about the attitude of Phasaelus troubled him. It amounted to antagonism, a cold opposition utterly lacking in brotherly affection. Was his brother jealous of him? He decided to pay a visit to his mother and discuss the matter with her.

Over a cold joint of lamb and fresh figs, Herod told his mother all and waited for any comments that the shrewd Arabian woman might offer. She was a long time in speaking.

"It is my opinion that Phasaelus is envious of you, and has been so for a long time. Your successes have been almost miraculous, and he might feel that you have somehow deprived him of his birthright. Being the elder, it is natural for him to feel that the public distinctions should be his, and you the follower. However, it so happens that you were endowed with a greater intelligence and charm of manner. What has happened was inevitable and could not have been avoided by you at all. You are like Joseph among his brothers."

"Oh, I would not mind if he outstripped me, Mother, so long as I do not lose his love and companionship. I love him too fondly to care who is ahead in public affairs. I feel deeply injured because somehow I feel that he is not being open and frank with me any longer. Something is hidden. How foolish of him! If he has any hidden plan, I would be happy to do my utmost to gain him whatever it is that he desires."

"You were ever the most generous of my children, and the most affectionate. I am certain that you would assist him whatever may be his ambitions."

There was a long pause during which Cypros fixed her eyes upon the fountain in the side yard, the very one beside which the beautiful Egyptian midwife had all but seduced him years ago.

Cypros broke into his reveries now.

"Did it ever occur to you, generous Herod, that Phasaelus might be contemplating making himself as potent under the Parthians as you are under the Romans? The Romans have spoken of the possibility of making you a king more than once. Now, suppose that Phasaelus is tempted by the notion of being made king of Judea by these Parthians in the event that they prevail?"

"Oh, no! Not such barbarous herdsmen. Besides, they have brought Antigonus back with the promise to make him king. No move other than bringing him back has been made so far, however. The military to bring if off is not yet present. And the people have not risen in sufficient numbers to compel it. All but a certain priestly clique are still for me."

"That is true, beloved son." After another long wait, "However, that does not bar out the possibility of Phasaelus lying in wait to capture a dream."

"No, Mother, it does not."

Another prolonged silence. Each to a disparate silence, but it was a warm, mingling kind of silence.

"My weaving-women have all but finished a new robe for you, beloved son. It is the blue of the Great Sea, shot with threads of gold."

"How generous and thoughtful of you, Mother. You keep my maternal love aglow at your thoughtfulness. Allow me to embrace you before I return to that tiresome citadel."

Herod rose and gave his mother a warm, filial embrace. Then he must also kiss Salome, who was getting tall and showing signs of womanly development. At fourteen, she was thin and leggy like a colt. The girl clung to her brother and worshipped him with her eyes.

"Release him, Salome, beloved," Cypros scolded. "That is your brother by both mother and father, child, and not a deity as you make him out to be."

"Yes, I really must hurry back to the citadel. No telling what these Parthian partisans might do any minute."

Followed by his mother and sister, Herod started towards the door, when a house steward all but collided with him.

"O Herod, I have news for you! The Parthian horsemen have been admitted."

Herod reeled back upon his heels.

"What did you say? Parthian horsemen admitted into the city? By whom was this traitorous act committed?"

"They say . . . that is, I am not certain. But the leader, this freedman, Pacorus, is being received at the home of the nobly-born Phasaelus to sup this night."

When Herod had sufficiently regained his composure, he made his way back to the citadel in great haste and apprehension. And his discomfort was immediately increased as soon as he gained his quarters.

Phasaelus was there waiting for him. That alone did not upset Herod, it was the aura around Phasaelus, the smug satisfaction as of a great triumph. This was so intense that a kind of glow emanated from every pore.

"Ah, at last my resplendent brother! I was about to send an urgent message to you. Happily you have arrived."

"Some new emergency?"

"Yes and no. No more street fighting, thanks to my efforts."

"Such as?"

"Following the orders of the king, I have admitted the horsemen into the city."

"Which king, O Phasaelus? Has Jerusalem fallen to the unwashed Parni during the short time in which I visited our mother?"

Herod's voice had the coldness of a high mountain, and his reference to the enemy as the Parni dripped with scorn. It took the less agile-minded Phasaelus a full minute to get the impact of the insult, then his face flamed a deep red.

"That statement is very unfair, Herod. It is true that the original Arsaces, who began the revolt against the Greek Seleucids, was a leader of the robber Parni tribe, but that was all of two and a half centuries ago. All of what was once called the Persian empire are now called Parthians not from the Parni, but from the satrapy of Parthia."

"Yet strangely, the present-day Parthians have all the perfidious nature of the founders. Ancestry, my dear Phasaelus, is not only physical, but ideological, a kinship of soul and spirit. And it has been found that nothing so cements the mind of men together as the alliance of their manners. Hence we discover the backward in mind among the Jews sensing their kinship with the backward-looking Parthians, and indeed willing to slay the progressive minds among us so as to restore the government of their kind. They have great indignation that we are not willing to have our throats cut to bring this happy condition about."

Phasaelus flushed deeply.

"But you know that is not *my* intention, Herod. I wish to feint with them for time. No doubt the Romans will come to our rescue soon. I have calculated the risk."

The conciliating tone stirred Herod to hope. "A rank amateur should never risk a game with veterans, beloved brother. You, who have been trained to truth and honor, can never hope to match the wiles of those born and nurtured in deceit. I beseech you, beloved Phasaelus, to return at once to your ancestral virtues and luminance."

"In what way, dear Herod?"

"Join with me in fighting these horsemen whom you have admitted to the city. No, do not continue to deceive yourself that it is impossible. It will cost us something in lives, but as expert as they are said to be as bowmen, one hour of our eight days of rain will destroy the last one of them. They are too few. We command by four times 750 veteran bowmen. Shall we fight them?"

"Well, perhaps later, Herod. But tonight he is, that is, I . . ."

"You are honoring the captain of the horsemen with a feast."

"I was, but when I mentioned it to Hyrcanus, *the king* insisted that the feast be tendered him at the palace."

With bold eyes fixed on his brother's abashed face and his lips pursed, Herod continued. "It is possible, considering the fate of our noble father, that this captain will fall dead of poisoning before he leaves the table of Hyrcanus."

"Oh, no! *The king* has great admiration for this young man. Both he and I have hopes that you will attend yourself in order to meet him."

"I?" Herod's tone bristled with indignation. "First, I am a Roman officer charged with the welfare of this nation. Second, it is not my custom to dine with the servants. However, I will allow *my* butler to be present if he wishes to attend. That is, if Sabinus, my butler, is given an equal place of honor with Pacorus, former butler and freedman of Prince Pacorus."

Phasaelus did not press the invitation further, and Herod had the feeling that the whole matter was some scheme between Hyrcanus and Phasaelus, and he was wounded in his heart, and so said nothing more to his brother at that time concerning the Parthians. After the passage of five days, it was Phasaelus who broached the matter to him again.

"Beloved brother, will you come with me for a talk with Pacorus? He constantly pleads with both *the king* and myself for the honor of meeting you."

"Not at my home, nor the home of our murdered father, since the servitor who gave him the poisoned wine found a ready refuge in Parthia. Nor shall he enter the citadel. At an inn perhaps, and very briefly."

The encounter was indeed brief and frustrating to Phasaelus, Hyrcanus, and Pacorus, for Herod was positively rude to Pacorus. He met the flood of flattery from the Parthian with silence. Total silence that was insulting, and intended to be so. Likewise, he refused to partake of the lavish meal before him, letting it be noted that he did not eat with the enemy. He did speak, and that crushingly, when the captain urged upon Herod that they confer about the welfare of the city.

"The responsibility for the public affairs of Judea were conferred upon myself and my brother Phasaelus alone. Neither your name nor that of Hyrcanus was mentioned. Only an order from Rome will make it possible for me to discuss the affairs of Jerusalem with you. Have treaty-making powers been conferred upon you by King Orodes, or by Prince Pacorus?"

"Not in exact terms," the abashed captain murmured.

"Then we waste time here. My position does not permit me to confer with anyone of your nation below the head of government. And now I must excuse myself and attend to the safety of the city."

"But wait, Herod," Phasaelus pled as Herod rose to his feet. "The generous captain has a proposition which seems worth consideration to both myself and Hyrcanus . . ."

"Oh, yes, yes, yes," Hyrcanus got out despite a mouth full of food. "Pacorus is much loved and has great influence with Prince Pacorus, after whom he is called. He can gain us the goodwill of the prince. Yes, yes, yes, we must listen."

Herod still made as if to depart, but again Phasaelus halted him.

"Look, Herod, beloved brother, Pacorus admits that he has not the power to negotiate, but he says that if we will go with him to Galilee where Barzapharnes has his headquarters, he can persuade him to withdraw his troops from Judea, abandon the cause of Antigonus, and the two countries live in peace with each other." Herod's stony gaze halted Phasaelus momentarily, then he braced himself and went on. "I consider that I would have done my country a tremendous service if I can turn away the threat and the horrors of war from it. Hyrcanus and I have pledged ourselves to accompany Captain Pacorus to near Mount Carmel in Galilee. As co-tetrarch of Judea, it would be more effective if you went with us to Barzapharnes on this embassage. I plead with you to accompany us."

"No! And do not insult me by repeating such a proposition. By the powers vested in me as tetrarch, I am in the position of a father to my countrymen. I was not made tetrarch to betray my country into the hands of perfidious barbarians."

Herod's hand fell instinctively to the hilt of his sword; he turned sharply on his heels and strode from the inn.

So now, with a defiant manner towards Herod, Phasaelus prepared to go with Hyrcanus and Pacorus to the camp of Barzapharnes in Galilee. There was a poorly suppressed air of triumph about him as he prepared a guard of 500 horsemen to go with him. Hyrcanus had an equal number. Both behaved towards Herod as if he were of no importance in government, and so Herod was confirmed in his suspicions that they expected to return with one or the other supreme in public affairs under the Parthians. He was not surprised at the eternally scheming cretin, Hyrcanus, but his heart contracted painfully at the wounds of Phasaclus. He was amazed, from their past experiences with Hyrcanus, that Phasaelus did not even suspect that if there occurred any shift in power, that Hyrcanus intended that it would be to himself, and not the credulous Phasaelus. That meant that Phasaelus had been flattered into believing that he himself was going to be elevated. Poor fool!

So Herod, enslaved by love and fidelity to Phasaelus, swallowed his pride, sought out Phasaelus, and pled with him earnestly not to leave Judea. In the face of Herod's show of affection, Phasaelus was pleasant enough, but stubbornly held to his plans.

In the dawny morning when the cavalcade set out, Herod insisted on riding as far as the Gate of Damascus with and beside Phasaelus. Pacorus interrupted when they arrived at the gate to inform Herod, with deceitful smiles, that he was taking only 450 of his horsemen with him, leaving 300 of his "freedmen" to assist Herod in maintaining order in Jerusalem. Herod did not even make a reply, but expended these last moments in taking a most affectionate farewell of his brother.

Herod then returned to his cares and immediately increased the guard of his body to 3,000 men, those men of the greatest skill as soldiers and who he knew were eternally faithful to him. The majority of whom were Galileans.

WHAT HEROD HAD predicted but could not know about for many weeks later, Phasaelus began to have suspicions of as soon as the cavalcade entered Galilee. The governors of cities and towns met them in arms and with a hostile, sullen air. He wondered that Hyrcanus made so light of these manifestations. When he called the attention of the high priest to it, he hurriedly answered that it was not really directed at them. The times were troubled, and they must expect things like that. Nothing to worry about at all.

At Carmel, Barzapharnes received them warmly and made them expensive gifts, and Phasaelus was calmed. What Phasaelus did not know was that the satrap was keeping him free of suspicion until Herod could be taken. In spite of this, Phasaelus felt disappointment that Prince Pacorus was not there to clasp them to his bosom as the captain had said he would. Something seemed wrong and inimical. And now, he wished that he had listened to Herod.

He could not know that back at Jerusalem every effort was being made to lure his brother outside the protecting walls of the city. The Parthians outside the walls sent messages that letters had arrived from his brother in Galilee, telling of the success of his mission, and waited for Herod to come out and receive them. This Herod sensibly refused to do, but rather countered with the accusation that Barzapharnes had imprisoned his brother and Hyrcanus, and that he would believe nothing they said until he saw his brother safely returned.

Herod's spies in Galilee had already sent word that the lives of Phasaelus and possibly Hyrcanus also were in peril. Their execution waited only upon the capture of Herod, lest Herod, learning of the fate of Phasaelus, should flee beyond the reach of the Parthians in Judea. When Prince Pacorus arrived at Carmel, it was with the intention of turning the two prisoners—and Herod also if possible—over to Antigonus to deal with them as he pleased, providing he had paid the price promised to Prince Pacorus and Barzapharnes. The exact terms had not been learned, but they were understood to be enormous. So Herod was extra wary, and would not listen to the flattering Parthian messengers further.

Two days after this report, Alexandra sent an urgent note for Herod to come to the palace. She had most important and urgent information for him. In a matter of minutes, Herod was on the way.

Alexandra, clothed in black and without a single ornament, ran to meet Herod in the wide reception hall and tearfully flung herself upon his bosom.

"O my strong and protective son! O you who loves and takes care of his people! Know with what depth of villainy and uncleanness Judea is now threatened."

"Please lose no time nor waste words, Alexandra."

"The case is this: That vile creature, spawned in Hades, I speak of Antigonus, no less, promised the Parthians 1,000 talents *and* 500 virgins selected from the first families of Judea to bring him back and make him king."

"What? Did I hear you correctly—500 virgin daughters of Judea's principal families?"

"That is exactly what I said to you, O Herod. This soulless monster, even though born of the priestly line, offered this to the Parthians, and they accepted the offer of this enormous sum of money, naturally, as not caring a fig for what becomes of the nation, but more readily did they accept the offer of our virgins of high birth."

"How horrible!" Herod gasped. "It is infinitely better to slay them all than to allow them to fall into the hands of these barbarians. Infinitely better, unless this vile bargain can be prevented from going through."

Herod thought and spoke from his experience as a soldier. Too often he had witnessed the unspeakable fate of female captives of war. Women tossed to the soldiers to do with as they pleased. A woman would be taken by a higher officer and treated well until he tired of her, then she was either tossed to the common soldiers, or sold into slavery, never, never again to see her native land, nor associate with the class of people to which she was born. Nor would she be received by them should she find the opportunity to return. She would be looked upon as if she were a leper. Yes, those who died immediately were the more fortunate of female captives. And this horrid fate to come upon 500 of the best families of this country?

"No, I will prevent this Antigonus from carrying out his vile trade. Never will I suffer such a thing to happen to us. How, I do not know at this moment, but rest assured I shall save you. I shall let you know what is the plan before sunset tomorrow." He was on the point of leaving the room, then whirled. "Aha! So that explains why the Parthians have made no move to place Antigonus on the throne, eh? They held back until the price is paid, and so far as the girls are concerned, never will it be paid."

The short distance to the citadel was rapidly covered as Herod burned with revulsion, horror, and indignation. His own pure, beautiful, and talented sister being touched by such beasts, possibly his mother, the young wives of his brothers, and even Mariamne. No! The time and the cause had come when he must risk his very life, and he was fully resolved to do so.

The rumor had reached the citadel by the time that he returned from the palace. A half dozen men of the principal families were there, Sameas among them.

"But Antigonus could not possibly have descended to such moral depths," was the general conclusion. "He is of the royal line, and therefore could not be so cold and cruel even to reach the throne. Besides, he must know that when the people discovered his infamy, he would be slaughtered like the monster that he would be. No, the thing is too foul for even Antigonus."

"Yet, I believe that the rumor is founded on truth," Sameas said emphatically. "The history of the Asamoneans since John Hyrcanus has been full of the shedding of blood unjustly, and every kind of vile crime. Recall the crimes of the grandfather of this Antigonus, Alexander Jannaeus. His crucifixion, in one night, of 800 innocent patriots who differed with him, indulging his bestiality with his numerous concubines in tents set up at the spot where these noble men were being murdered. Full of wine, Alexander Jannaeus swaggered from tent to tent while his victims agonized on the stakes. Then, thinking that they were not suffering sufficiently, he had the wives and children of the patriots dragged to the feet of the stakes so that the dying men must witness their throats being cut. No, O Herod, do not discount the rumor too hastily. Somehow, knowing your protective attitude, I believe that you will find some means of frustrating the vile deed, this unbelievable and soulless crime against our nation."

"You are the victim of clever slanderers," one bearded Gour asai snarled. "You who favor strangers from across the Great Sea to us of Asia. It is time that we governed ourselves. Have we not been robbed and oppressed sufficiently by these foreign, soulless tyrants to which our customs are not only strange, but abhorrent? Not one word of this vile rumor is true. Neither the Parthians nor Antigonus would commit such a deed. I contend that we of Asia should be allowed to enjoy our freedom from the monsters from across the sea."

Sameas smiled triumphantly. "If it is a wanton lie, then it emanates from Antigonus himself," he said. "He boasts that Hyrcanus and Phasaelus are already the prisoners of the Parthians in Galilee and he will himself slay them as soon as Herod is taken, which is expected within the next three days. Then he will journey to Galilee, where he will hand over the 1,000 talents in gold to Prince Pacorus and Barzapharnes, and return to Jerusalem to ascend the throne with the support of Parthian soldiers, and deliver the 500 aristocratic young women immediately to the Parthians. The Thracida!"

The outraged Herod had said nothing so far. Now, he sent Sameas a quick, conspiratorial glance, then dissembled, "I hear so many contradictory rumors that I do not know what to believe. So I shall take no steps until I am assured of some facts. Please excuse me, you potent men of Jerusalem, so that I may sleep and restore my nerves."

But Herod did not sleep. Far from it. As the men talked, he had already formed a plan, a desperate plan, which appeared his only means of survival, and the rescue of the flower of Jewish womanhood. So in less than an hour after the departure of the men, a score of his agents were speeding through the streets of Jerusalem to the homes of upper-class citizens with a certain message. By now, the fearful rumor had reached every home of the prominent in the city, and there was terrible fear and the feeling of helplessness behind every door. The confidence of Antigonus that he could afford to be reckless was behind it all. His most hated adversary would soon join Phasaelus and

Hyrcanus in prison. He meant to slay each one with his own hand, and to torture each before granting him the blessing of death. The 1,000 talents and the girls were well spent.

And while the triumphant Antigonus dreamed, the messengers of Herod were busy. His agents softly knocked upon specified doors and delivered the message. Purpose: To save by flight the proscribed young women. Place: The empty square hard by the Gate of the Essenes. Time: The following night at first dark. Requirements: Secrecy except to other families who might be threatened. Bring along enough provisions for a day's march.

Herod's first move was to send Joseph with 2,500 fighting men south to Idumea. Joseph, with the help of Pheroras, was to move the money, coined and uncoined, in the houses of Herod, Joseph, and their late father, Antipater, along with the most valuable ornaments and the like and take them with them hidden under farm produce. Joseph was to meet Herod at Tressa, the first town over the border in Idumea. The distance was not much in actual miles, but the difficulties could be insurmountable. However with the men all mounted and heavily armed, and more important, unsuspected by the enemy, he saw no reason why Joseph should not make it in two or three hours at the most. Before noon, the men in small groups had reached the meeting place outside the city gate and were galloping towards the land of Edom, homeland of the family.

Early in the day, Herod prepared four mule-drawn wagons. One for his mother, sister, the wives of Phasaelus and Joseph. Phasaelus had a son of six years who rode in this conveyance. The second wagon was for Mariamne and Alexandra and one female servant for each. The third wagon bore a female servitor for each of the women of the family and eatables for the household and clothing. Also a supply of lightwood for torches. The fourth wagon carried additional arms and lightwood. The two last wagons, loaded to appear as the conveyances of tradesmen, went outside of the gate in advance, since they would hardly be interfered with.

The plan Herod had formed was desperate to the extreme, but he was sustained by four things: his exaggerated protective instinct, his pride of country, the faith of the people that he would save them in this extremity, and the prayers and praise whispered in his ears by those in the plot. Yes, under such stimuli, he happily risked his life.

And things certainly began well. By the second hour of darkness of this moonless night, Herod saw that many times the 500 virgins were milling about the square hard by the Gate of the Essenes. The darkness prevented any count, but it was easily discerned that his dangerous adventure was over-subscribed. For a while, he was dismayed to find mothers with small children clinging to their robes; aged men, heads of families whose young women were in danger, and who knew that they would be killed without conscience when it was found that they had moved their daughters or wives of their sons out of the reach of Antigonus, making it impossible to hand them over to the Parthians. Herod was dismayed because he knew that these small children and aged people would slow his march, and the essence of his plan was speed. Two of his officers ran to Herod tearing at their hair.

"Naturally you will send them home, O leader. They cannot stand the pace; they will collapse after a few furlongs and bring us all to a cruel death. Shall we send them away?"

"We cannot, O Captain. Their presence attests to the faith of Judea in the love and faith of Herod. No, we must take them with us to safety, or die with them on the road. I see just what you see from a military point of view. We are burdened with this unwieldy mass of slow-moving non-combatants, but it cannot be avoided. All that is left to us is to pray to our God and fight like fiends from Hell. Great danger goes before great glory. Remember that hour on the narrow, rocky beach of the Sea of Galilee when we faced Hezekiah?"

"Will I ever forget it, O my leader. I had given up hope of life when that huge brute of a bandit sprung suddenly from behind a boulder with his javelin poised and I was off-balance to defend myself. Luckily one of our men ran the brute through from behind. That is the benefit of an army. Never are you fighting alone."

"The real secret of military victory lies in hard fighting," Herod reminded the officer. "When you make a hole in the body, the blood, which is the life, runs out and flows down and dies. All of his power to injure you passes with his blood. In your mighty right hand and arm lies your safety. Battle is no place for delicacy and indecision. Hard! Waste no motions. Try to make every stroke account for a man. Preach that again to your men. When too many of the enemy begin to fall quickly, the others lose heart and flee away. I know you remember our past victories. A body thrust is always good, but one in the head and neck is better."

"I am encouraged already. And I recall that the rabble who might pursue us will not be led by Herod. Not a man of the 3,000 who follow you can conceive of your being beaten. Lead on!"

"Aha! Now you speak like a man again, and a part of Herod's body. Can Herod's body forsake these helpless people who look to us as their only salvation? In what other body in the whole nation would they repose such trust? Even in such a desperate and hopeless situation, they evidently believe that we can save them. Does that not elevate your soul and make you the equivalent of twenty men?"

"No, a hundred, O Herod. We shall win their safety."

"Excellently spoken, O captain. Now, I shall give you the honor and privilege of taking 1,000 men and leading forth. With the other 2,000 I shall protect the rear where the real danger will lie."

Out through the thick walls of the city, the procession marched. Westward for nearly two miles they moved to connect with the ancient highway running north and south from far up into Asia Minor and south to the Sanai Peninsula and on to Egypt. There they turned south and had proceeded eight furlongs before the first band of pursuers overtook them. It was a small band of hate-yelling fanatics who attacked recklessly.

"Keep the procession moving and permit no panic nor even cries. That can only serve to slow us and invite the wolves."

Herod then wheeled, contained the reckless attackers, and wiped them out to a man. Leaving no bodies upon the highroad nor close enough to be seen, he again whirled and caught up with the hurrying crowd. His heart bled to see these women who had never been forced to even care for their own bodies fleeing afoot, many of them dragging their small children along this dark rocky road and weeping. His rage and sense of injury rose as he thought. He trotted his stallion up the line until he rode beside the wagon bearing his mother and sister.

"It is very hard to conceive of; these ravening beasts, every one of them reared to uphold the sanctity of virginity in Jewish women, now rushing forth with the intention of slaying their protectors in order to lay in a stock of merit with the Parthians. They do not even have the honor nor the compassion of stray dogs. And I shall ruthlessly kill everyone that I can catch. If any escape and can be identified when I return from Rome, I shall put them to death without exception."

"O my beloved and courageous son," Cypros murmured. "Then you intend to take refuge in Rome until times are better. I am very glad to hear you say that."

"But I did not say that, Mother, I said that I was going to Rome. I shall return as king of Judea and kill without compassion the men who have made the horrible ordeal of this night necessary. Rome must and will make me king, not for my own greater glory, but for the benefit of Rome itself in Lower Asia."

"Oh!" Salome shouted and stretched out her arms to embrace her brother. "Allow me to embrace you, beloved brother. I always knew that you would wear the diadem someday."

"That is, if I survive the terrible ordeal of this night, my beautiful and beloved Salome. This mission, this road to Rome, began really on the day that the Parthians erupted into Syria; as you know, we have had to surmount numerous dangers, but what lies between us now and the Idumean borders is the greatest of all. It is possible that I shall never arrive there alive."

"As I told you, over-bold son," Cypros said determinedly, "you need not have so burdened yourself and endangered your life. You might have accepted only the women of your immediate family—all of whom ride well—and dashed into the safety of Idumea promptly."

"But the return from Rome, Mother. Even *you* have not considered that? How could I, in conscience, return to pose as the governor of a nation whose finest women I had abandoned to the horrors of rape by foreign soldiers? In the high esteem in which the purity of its women is held by us, what excuse could I offer and still expect to be regarded as a protector—for that is what a king is supposed to be to his people? I would be no better than this Antigonus, who is content to buy his seat upon the throne by an enormous sum of money, which must be paid out of the taxes of the people in time—forcing the nation to buy its own chains of slavery—and worst of all, by the most brutal sacrifice of the reason for existence of the nation. What a king! No, I must protect them or die in the attempt. Those barbarians shall never know the feel of a single Jewish woman's body while I am alive."

"And your position is just and honorable, my son. Gladly will I die with you if that is to be."

"And I also, beloved and noble brother. You are already a king at heart, and always were."

Herod leaned from his saddle and was embraced by mother and sister, and had reined his stallion into a turn to go back to his place in the rear when it happened. A front wheel came off the wagon, and Cypros was catapulted over the rail of the wagon to the ground, her left shoulder bearing the weight of the fall. She cried out in pain and lay there helpless for a minute while the other occupants of the wagon scrambled to right themselves, and wept.

Herod dismounted and bent over his mother, calling her name frantically and weeping.

"Halt! Halt! Where do we go when my mother is in danger of death? This delay is enough to allow the enemy to overtake and destroy us. Time is our only friend, and this happening has caused time to desert us. It is a signal that this is the hour of my death, for I will not live to see those whom I have taken under my protection captured."

Herod drew his dagger, but was instantly overpowered by a dozen of his guard, who disarmed him. The host set up a great outcry of alarm for Herod, but more for themselves. Who would lead them and take care of them if he destroyed his life? What was to become of them? They pled pitifully with him to spare himself.

It was a very moving episode while it lasted, but it was brief. Three of Herod's Galileans put the wheel back on the axle and secured it with a hastily whittled pin. Cypros, moaning with pain, begging Herod to abandon her and go on with his mission, was laid out in the bed of the wagon and made as comfortable as possible, and the procession, quieting down, took up its motion. A little faster now in terror of being overtaken.

An attack came, but it was a smaller body than the first, and easily disposed of. Herod did not allow the procession to halt as his men wiped out the attackers, collected the weapons of the enemy and went on. A third attack was absorbed in the same manner. Herod was obviously in good heart again and showed relish in doing away with his attackers.

Herod now set a lookout relay of three men, each four furlongs apart to his rear, to pass a signal along until it reached him of the approach of the enemy from Jerusalem.

"The repeated attacks prove that the news of our escape is spreading wider over the city. Larger attacks will build up to catch us before we cross into Idumea, which is friendly to us and very hostile to them. I can make no more speed with the type of non-combatants that I have, but all that we can. If God is merciful, we may not be assaulted by a strong Jewish-Parthian military aggregation. If they attack . . ."

A full hour passed without the pre-arranged call of a night-bird from the rear. Knowing this road as well as the palm of his hand, Herod was uplifted to note that they were more than half the way to the border and safety. Ahead of him loomed a hill, rising gently and symmetrically like the rounded breast of a virgin from its surroundings. He took it to be a good omen.

But as his advance guard reached it and began to follow the road around half of its base, came the call. It was repeated three times, which meant that they were pursued by a considerable military force.

Herod had a choice. Idumea was not too far off now, and he could make a run for it. With only his fighting men, he might have tried it, but with all the women and flagging old people and children, he ran the risk of being attacked while in great disorder. Herod chose to fight. The dangers he had suffered during this night, no, all that he had suffered since the invasion of Pacorus, his worry and uncertainty concerning the fate of Phasaelus, the injury to his mother, and the horrible threat to his young and beautiful sister and to Mariamne—everything—had charged his tissues highly with adrenalin. He yearned now to fight, whatever the outcome.

Turning his stallion across the road, he summoned his officers about him.

"I am going to fight here. Get all the non-fighters to the crest of the hill. All the baggage and vehicles below them on the hillsides as far from the road as possible. Tell the six elders who have been caring for the fire-pots to call all the men too old to fight to bring all the bundles of twigs and have them ready for torches at a call. We fighters will ring the base of the hill ready to defend it with our lives. Not one sound must be heard from *anybody*. Warn the women that all our lives depend upon silence. Look to their children in this respect. See that these things are done then return to me here."

The officers to the last corporal hastened to duty. Motionless in alertness, Herod sat Nicator like a Centaur. This veteran of many battles swung his head to the north, pointed his ears forward, and breathed more rapidly, informing Herod that he heard something which Herod himself could not catch as yet. What was a loud clamor nearly two miles to the north was as yet the slightest whisper to the sensitive horse.

The three sentinels rode up, saluted, and reported.

"In excess of 2,000, but scarcely 3,000 men all fully armed. Many torches being carried. No Parthians among them. In poor order and discipline. So certain of easy victory that no effort at concealment is made. Their gloating shouts can be heard at a long distance . . .

"'The Parthians have drawn the claws of the lion of Idumea. His fangs have been broken off against the iron of the sword of Pacorus.'

"'Let us hasten to where he lies hidden in the woods and give him the justice of death. Death by a thousand thrusts.'

"'Orodes will roll the head of Herod across the floor of his palace as they sing a song of triumph as they did with the hated Crassus. And also his right hand which has killed so many of the righteous.'

"'Down with the hated foreigners from across the Great Sea.'

"'Asia for the Asians! We have the same customs.'

"'Down with Herod, servant of Rome!'

"'Let us make haste to where he hides. To me the first stab into his pretty body.'"

The darkness prevented the sentinels from seeing the savage glow in the eyes of Herod. His body stretched, and his nerves tingled. Like the warhorse in the Valley of Jehoshaphat, he yearned for the conflict. But all he said at that moment was, "Well, I shall give them the meeting."

The officers returned. Herod did not need to be told that they had done their duty expertly, for with the mass of humanity upon that rounded hill, not a whisper of a sound could be heard. From the road, not a man nor a horse could be seen.

"Well done, my limbs," Herod spoke to his officers. "Do not attack until half of the enemy has passed the center of our line at the foot of the hill where it turns. Do I need to tell you that we may all die to a man? With that in mind, conscious that you are defending the most righteous of causes, you are this night angels of God, but fight like the utmost demons from Hell. Under the circumstances we take no prisoners. Leave no wounded if possible. Let us be spoken of in history as the greatest warriors of the known world. In this our probable last battle. As you know, I ask none of you to do more than I do myself. Great will be your reward—both in glory and wealth—if we are victors this night over those who run after us to murder us for our virtuous deeds. Avenge yourselves against such vile intentions. Remember we are charged with the crime of preserving our virgins from the rape of the Parthian soldiers."

As the Trojans must have watched the landing of the Greeks on their shores during the night, Herod and his party, still as death in the darkness, watched the enemy army come pouring up to the point where the road touched the hill and wound gently along it for perhaps a fourth of its circumference. They were entirely afoot, and as had been reported, in poor discipline. The lines were very ragged, some eating, drinking from up-tilted wine-skins, boasting, laughing, and generally celebrating their victory in advance. No doubt most of them were already spending the money they expected from both Parthians and Antigonus. Herod knew that Antigonus had offered a fabulous reward for his head.

"THE LION OF JUDAH!" Herod shouted suddenly and charged down the incline into the ranks of his pursuers and began to hack and slash down the surprised footmen. Instant disorder among them. Those who had already passed lost valuable minutes in trying to form into an orderly body and turn back to the support of those under immediate and savage attack. But Herod's right wing charged down and began its enveloping movement, while the left was closing in on the enemy's rear. A figure eight was the aim with Herod's center forming the junction of the two circles. The plan was to contain and swallow the enemy like a python. Allow no chance for escape, or die to the last man in the attempt. When this terrible struggle was well underway, Herod shouted as loudly as he could to be heard over the tumult of clashing arms and cursing and yelling men, "THE HOSTS OF GIDEON!"

It was answered after a small delay by the voice of a priest on the hilltop—an eminent man of Jerusalem and very high in the priesthood: "AND THE HOSTS OF GOD!"

Hundreds of torches flared so that Herod's fighters would not attack each other in the struggles of the desperate battle.

This little-known conflict around the breast-shaped hill was probably the most savagely fought battle in the history of the world. The enemy, sensing the plan, fought furiously to prevent being enclosed in those circles of death. When that failed, they fought even more desperately to break out. Herod himself was fighting for everything—for everything he loved on that hill, for injuries he suffered, for the past, for the future, for the justice of his cause, and lastly for his very life. Not even against Hezekiah had he fought so desperately.

However, there was no conscious fear. This night beside the rounded hill, he was no longer the elegant, sophisticated Herod that the world knew. Here was a primitive, atavistic animal clubbing the saber-toothed tiger who had thrust his terrible head into the mouth of his cave. He exposed himself recklessly and shouted like a demon as he cut down the enemy.

Finally, it was over. Two or three score had escaped and fled back towards Jerusalem as fast as they were able. One fleeing man Herod recognized as one of the Sanhedrin who had sought to sentence him to death six years before. He put Nicator into a fast gallop, overtook the man, and hacked off his head as he ran. He had been the general of the army pursuing Herod. Then he rode back to the foot of the hill laughing. He waved his bloody sword above his head in a rhythm.

"Plunder the bodies of the scoundrels, my men!" Herod shouted and sang. "Now, we are free. We have won the gift of our own lives. Hooray!"

Torches ran everywhere over the bloody field as the soldiers plundered, and as they did, gave the *coup de grâce* to those found still alive.

Those upon the hill cried, sang, chanted, and wept their gratitude at still being alive and able to continue their escape.

With her mother calling after her to restrain her, Mariamne, all disheveled, flew down the hill with her unbound hair streaming out behind her and threw herself upon Herod's bosom. Her slim arms encircled his waist, and she pressed kisses upon his armor, his arms, and finally and feverishly upon his mouth.

"Ah, my beloved, my dearest, my husband, my lord, you are the greatest man of all the earth, and God has been good enough to give you to me as my very own, to love and to possess, to live with in joy and affection, and never will I wish to live a moment after you are dead. I love you, I love you, and take all my happiness from you. Life would be a curse to me if you should die before I do."

At the first touch of her warm, tremulous body, Herod, anew, was shot through with a bolt of lightning. It was a thunderous, miraculous revelation. This was the something he had sought all the adult years of his life in vain. This was femaleness at last. Involuntarily, his strong arms went about the slight, but soft form and pressed Mariamne tightly to him, forgetting the thousands of eyes upon them by the flickering flames of the torches. He stood there holding her like that as the revived multitudes moved on down the hillsides to the road again.

"Mariamne! My daughter! You stupid thing!" Alexandra screamed. "To shame me and yourself before the public in such a manner," her mother jerked at her.

Herod did not release the girl.

"Shame, Alexandra?" Herod snapped. "Who is it in the inhabitable world that does not know that Mariamne, your daughter, is betrothed to me? I now love her for her warmth of heart and her sincerity. With my own hands I will cut out the tongue that speaks unflatteringly of her. She is the betrothed of Herod." He embraced her again warmly and kissed Mariamne on her lips.

"Betrothed, yes," Alexandra said with an acid tongue, "but you neglect to marry her."

Cypros and Salome, making their way towards Herod down the uneven surface of the hill, and in semi-darkness, now arrived at where he stood. They had overheard the exchange, and Cypros looked hard at Alexandra and, being a woman, and a very intelligent woman, saw something that escaped the notice of her son, and it made her very uneasy.

"From this night on, we are married," Herod said as if issuing a decree from his office. "As Mariamne, my profoundly beloved said, we shall live happily together as no other man and woman ever lived, nor will we allow ourselves to be separated even by death itself. If one or the other of us dies, the other will also seek death within the hour of learning it."

"Ah, yes!" Mariamne almost sang. "That is the way I wish it to be. Ah, my beloved."

Cypros held her gaze upon Alexandra. The woman visibly shrank and dwindled and her face was bleak. *Medea*, Cypros thought instantly. *This is how Medea looked when she learned of the unfaithfulness of Jason. This woman is in love with my son. This woman is in love with my son and jealous of her own daughter, and her heart is as ruthless and as cruel and vengeful as Medea. God have mercy upon them all. God have tender mercy upon us all.*

And as Cypros looked, Alexandra awoke from her crushing defeat. Her eyes shone with an almost demoniac light. Her body grew rigid and taut, and she took a step forward towards the couple.

"Ah, put an end to this shameful, disgraceful spectacle, Mariamne. The daughter of royalty allowing herself to be treated like a *pornai*! The troubles of the times have driven you mad. No, you were born stupid. Haven't I always said so? Come away!"

But Herod did not release the girl, nor did she make any effort to break away from his arms. But this did not foil the fury of her mother. Alexandra, her face contorted with rage, seized her by an arm and jerked her free. Mariamne, harshly dominated from her birth, tucked her head and went meekly.

Cypros, watching her son closely, saw him tense and his eyes blaze momentarily, then he relaxed, and turned abruptly about the business of getting his charges on the road again. Cypros was to remember this scene all the days of her life and to continue to draw meaning from it.

As a matter of sentiment, Herod made it his business to be the last of the contingent to cross the border. As he did so, he looked to the east, across the wastes of Moab and the Dead Sea, and saw the red sun leap up and begin its tour of inspection of the firmament. Herod took it as a good omen. *The Lord of Light salutes me on my way to Rome. I am*

congratulated on my work of the past night. May never such a night befall
me again before my dying day.

Joseph, with his armed men, met Herod at Tressa, a small town just
over the border, and they embraced each other almost hysterically.

"O beloved Herod, you have arrived! I have been so worried, for the
odds were so heavy against your making it. What with Phasaelus . . ."

"What have you heard about him, Joseph?"

"Nothing definite, Herod. There is a rumor that both he and
Hyrcanus are imprisoned, but there is no definite proof. I believe it,
however, because I have had no letter from him. Have you?"

"No and, like you, I fear the worst." Tears escaped from Herod's
eyes. "You know how hard, how persistently I sought to prevent him,
do you not, O Joseph." A tremor came into the voice of Herod. "Why
he allowed himself to be persuaded by that degenerate Hyrcanus instead of his own brother, I cannot understand."

A significant silence fell between Herod and Joseph. Neither
wanted to examine the motives of Phasaelus too closely.

"No matter the cause of his strange behavior, he is my beloved
brother, and if he is still alive and held by those barbarous herdsmen
for ransom, I will pay as much as 300 talents gold to ransom him. If he
has been murdered, I will avenge him. A hundred lives for his own. I
make a vow of it."

Herod's eyes emitted a sulfurous blaze and his fists clenched into
hard balls.

"Of course, I must continue my journey to Rome. Everything
hinges on that. But my plan is to ransom Phasaelus first of all. To this
end, I will halt at Petra in Arabia long enough to collect the large sums
that Father left with Aretas Malchus, king of Arabia, and to several
other chiefs there. I will also ask for a loan from him to make certain
that I have sufficient moneys to pay whatever ransom is demanded

for Phasaelus's life. I shall take with me the seven-year-old son of my unfortunate brother to leave as a hostage with Malchus until the loan is repaid. With the 300 talents secured and sent on to Pacorus for the release of our brother, I shall then continue on to Rome with all haste so as not to be prevented from crossing the Great Sea by winter storms."

"Excellent, O Herod. The plan is certain of success for the reason that in addition to the loans made to Malchus by our father, you yourself have done him numerous favors. He is bound to do all that you ask of him. Do you wish me to be your emissary in dealing with the Parthians?"

"Ah, no, beloved Joseph. The matter shall be conducted through that close and eminent friend of Father's, Saramalla of Syria. Your task is to hold Masada against the forces of Antigonus and to prevent the capture of the refugees there. Not one woman must fall into those brutal hands. Antigonus must not be allowed to fulfill his bargain to the Parthians, which he must be extremely anxious to do to secure the government from them. Defend this fort, Joseph. It must not be taken. You understand that, do you not?"

"I get all the implications, Herod. This fort shall not be taken with a woman alive in it."

"And kill Mariamne, Salome, and our mother first of all in the case that you are overwhelmed. A love superior to any felt by any man since the beginning of the world now possesses me for Mariamne, Joseph. It is a mingled thing, hard to explain. It is not only her beauty, but a female softness, warmth, her helplessness and dependence upon my strength and . . . well, it cannot be described, but no man must even touch her hand before me, nor after me, even if I am dead. That will give you some idea of my emotions."

"Even though she is of the perfidious Asamoneans?"

"Even so. This is something between Mariamne and me. Nothing else matters, nor ever can." Herod's facial expression broke like day. "With Mariamne sharing my bed, I shall conquer the world for her sake. She will be more than a mere wife to me. She is my woman."

AS JOSEPH HAD observed, Herod's plans were both meritorious and logical, but the sections concerning the release of Phasaelus were to fail for two reasons.

The first was that Phasaelus, seeing the hopelessness of his situation, was already resolved upon taking his own life while Herod and Joseph conferred.

The situation was this. Prince Pacorus and Barzapharnes had received Phasaelus and Hyrcanus with a great show of admiration and respect on their arrival at the camp. They made them impressive gifts, but strung out negotiations while they waited for the word from Jerusalem that Herod—the man they wanted most—had been captured. The two Parthians exclaimed over the excellent plans for peace that Phasaelus and Hyrcanus presented and pretended to agree with every point. What they did not tell Phasaelus was that information from Jerusalem indicated that they would never get their hands upon Herod. He scorned their stories and traps and, recognizing his tremendous prestige with the Jewish population, the two Parthians realized that it would be the height of folly to attempt to seize upon his person by force.

So there was no longer any point in dragging out the pretense. It was resolved to place them under arrest and turn them over to Antigonus, who was impatient of the delay. So Pacorus excused himself by telling Phasaelus that he must absent himself from Galilee for a few days, but that, on his return, he would sign a treaty of alliance on the terms suggested by "this most intelligent and charming son of the noble Antipater." He took an affectionate farewell of Phasaelus and Hyrcanus, and rode away.

The first discord which Phasaelus noted was that his camp on the beach was secretly but securely guarded. It was surrounded by horsemen who kept their distance in the woods, but except for that side which fronted on the sea, the camp was surrounded. He became uneasy.

Then a hurried but secret message arrived from Saramalla, the longtime intimate of his father, to prepare to flee without delay, as he had learned that Phasaelus and Hyrcanus were to be arrested and turned over as prisoners to Antigonus by the Parthians. Antigonus was already on his way to receive the prisoners. Therefore, in a matter of minutes, the trusting Phasaelus was tumbled from the apex of exultation and triumph to the depths of despair. But, putting aside his emotions, he prepared to embark upon the ships which Saramalla had provided, for all means of escape by land were cut off.

But the bird of ill omen of the family, Hyrcanus, again stood in the way. He was still in the headquarters of Barzapharnes, rolling in false glory and gabbling away, and would not hasten to join Phasaelus on the beach as he was urged. Saramalla, aboard a ship, sent word that Phasaelus, the beloved son of his beloved friend, was to come aboard immediately, abandon the foolish and possibly treacherous Hyrcanus, and save himself. Phasaelus, true son of his father, could not bring himself to abandon Hyrcanus, and was still trying to induce him to come to the beach when he was arrested.

It served Phasaelus nothing to reproach the Parthians for the perfidy, for they only laughed at him. What if they had lied? It had served their purpose, had it not? The end justified the means. Why such indignation at a few lies?

And now Phasaelus discovered the profound depths of Hell. The attitude of his captors was inconceivable to him. How could they regard the decencies so lightly? And what of Hyrcanus? He could not avoid the suspicion that the high priest had played the Judas goat, leading him into the trap, and also depending upon the fidelity of

Phasaelus to prevent his escape. What to do? There was certainly no escape from the massive and closely guarded prison. The windows were too far from the cobblestone floor for him to reach and attempt his escape that way, even if he had not been chained to the immensely thick wall. There was but one way out of his hopeless situation—the ever open door of death. Never could he expect an iota of mercy from the hate-filled, effeminate Antigonus.

A meagre slit of light of the setting sun lay on the floor of his cell when a woman selling eatables through the prison—or so she was disguised—halted before the bars of his cell door and solicited trade. She managed to convey the news that she had come to bring: of Herod's dramatic escape from Judea. Further, that the Parthians had been so enraged at both his escape and the loss of the 500 virgins that they had plundered Jerusalem and, that not sufficing, they had gone out into the country and destroyed Marissa and another smaller city. The results were that many who had favored the Parthians because of Asiatic ties were now enraged at them, and looked upon Herod as a glorious hero and savior of the people.

Phasaelus had laughed bitterly and whispered to the woman, "I shall not submit myself to the fate the Parthians and Antigonus anticipate. I die gladly knowing that Herod can and will avenge me."

He dashed his head against the rough stone wall of his cell and died. Later, some said that he died from his self-inflicted wound, but others said that he wounded himself severely indeed, but would have lived if the physician, sent by Barzapharnes and Prince Pacorus to attend him, had not been bribed by Antigonus to rub poison into the wound. The courage and fortitude of Phasaelus had so impressed the Parthians that Antigonus feared that they might discard him and turn to the able sons of Antipater. No one has been able to establish the entire truth of what happened behind the cold walls of the prison.

The second obstruction to Herod's plan was that when he arrived at Petra with the son of Phasaelus perched before him on the saddle, Malchus, in a huddle with the Arab chiefs—all of whom owed Herod money—would not allow his party to reach the palace. As Herod approached the rose-red city—called that because of the profuse growths of red and pink oleanders through the narrow, rocky defile that suddenly burst upon sight of the city from the tunnel-like way— sentinels had been posted to prevent him. To Herod's astonishment, he found them sullen and threatening. He and his men noted that the inevitable symbols of friendship were withheld from him. Nobody offered them fire nor water.

"Begone, you Herod," the surly captain of the armed band snarled. "King Malchus sends word that the Parthians have laid a charge upon him not to receive you. Begone!"

Herod's astonishment was complete, for he knew that the Parthians could not have done any such thing. And such behavior from a relative, for Cypros, his mother, was a niece of Malchus. Both his father and himself had done this man numerous kindnesses both as a relative and as a friend. Herod's quick intelligence told him all. Now that he was persuaded that Herod was in no position to do him any more favors, nor punish him for his insolence, he had taken such a step to avoid paying his just debts. Herod was learning at thirty-five what he might have learned many years before had he not been born to wealth and power. That the world fawns upon success one day and kicks failure in the same individual the next.

Herod pressed his lips together and said almost lightly to the captain, who had considered himself honored to perform the slightest service for Herod on numerous occasions, "Say to King Malchus that I had no wish to burden him in any way. I merely wanted to discuss a matter that is of some importance to myself."

With that, he turned his horse and rode away over the heated protest of his own bodyguards, who were enraged to the extent of begging to be allowed to slay the insolent captain and his whole company and then attack the palace itself.

"The nature of man is displayed, that is all. Do not be disturbed by it. Besides, we are in a vast hurry at this moment. We can instruct the improperly-born scoundrels later on."

When the party had emerged from the rocky defile again, Herod called a halt. He sent an escort of ten men with his small nephew to return him to the fort of Masada, while with the others he went on southward. Having spent so many summers of his youth in this vicinity, he knew it like the back of his hand. He led his men down a sharp declivity along a little-known path and halted at a bright spring that bubbled up from the rocks. It was surrounded by a pleasant grove of ancient trees. There they rested for an hour and Herod headed for the temple of Jupiter-Ammon, that same temple which Alexander the Great had honored with his presence nearly three centuries before and identified himself with the Egyptian deity.

Herod had no such exaltation. For the first time in his life he was profoundly depressed, and for sound reasons. Too many tragic occurrences had befallen him recently—things he would have held to be not only improbable, but impossible. The beloved of God indeed! These were Herod's morbid thoughts as he came in sight of the age-stained stone walls which enclosed the ancient temple.

The massive, creaking gates swung open as he approached them with his cavalcade. Unsmilingly, he leaned from his saddle and handed the old gate-keeper a drachma and walked his horse slowly into the roomy enclosure. Suddenly a great flock of doves came whirring in close circles around him. Round and round they flew, coming closer to him all the time until he halted his mount in confusion, when the doors of the temple itself were hardly fifty feet away. Finally, several of the birds settled without seeming fright upon rider and horse.

The double doors of the lotus-columned ancient sanctuary swung open and an old man in the robes of the chief of the priests emerged and, standing on the raised platform before the door, stood staring. He was immediately joined by two others of lesser dignity, and they all stood staring and beaming. Seeing this, Herod put Nicator to a very slow walk and arrived at the portal.

"A very good omen," the abbot said, and his assistants nodded and beamed. "You have already been welcomed by the gods. Dismount, and favor this place by entering and accepting our hospitality."

Perceptibly lifted in spirit now, Herod got down, mounted the steps, and bowed respectfully.

"A rare thing has occurred," the chief of the priests repeated. "The doves of the temple have shown the approval of the gods. You are destined for rare good fortune. You bring also good fortune to the temple. Enter and sup with us. We pray that you will spend the night under this roof."

"I came for that purpose," Herod spoke very humbly. "God has not shown himself so favorably to me for many months. I know that many men troubled of spirit, or possessed of a demon, come here to pass a night to find peace. That is why I have come. Is, is it indeed rare for your doves to so greet a man entering these sacred gates?"

"Extremely rare. Not for thirty years have they done so, my lord. You can understand the tremendous excitement among us here. Enter, enter, and do us the honor of sharing our diet and root-trees. Come into this reception chamber and be seated."

Herod sank wearily upon a reclining couch, and servitors, all dressed in the habits of religious recluses, began to minister to his physical comfort. The shoes were gently removed from his tired feet and a bowl of water placed on the floor and his feet were washed, dried, and anointed. A cup of wine was offered him, then a bowl of fresh fruit placed at his side.

Not until these comforts had been furnished was Herod asked his name, his country, and his troubles.

Herod told the Prior these things, and would have talked more, so broken was he in spirit, but it was not permitted. Not until his sleeping-cell was prepared for him, and his body-servants had assisted him to a full bath and change of linen, and he had been directed to the spacious, scantily adorned dining room. There was the long wooden table with the patina of great age upon it. Along each side were back-less benches highly polished by generations of use. Many sconces were fastened to the walls, the flames supported by olive oil. Nor did any Roman feast cause the board to groan, but there was a bounty of wholesome, well-prepared, plain food. Pitchers of rich fresh milk from the temple cows, mounds of warm little loaves of bread, deep-brown roasted flesh-meat, and an abundance of fresh fruits. As Herod sur-prised himself by eating heartily, he could hear the murmur of his 100 guardsmen bivouacked on the grounds of the temple. He was grateful that they could at last gain a night of peaceful sleep.

As soon as the meal was over, Herod left the dining room where each of the guests had eaten in silence. Each was like himself, a trou-bled man, and each kept his own secrets to himself. No doubt each man had been so counseled as he had been.

"When you have retired for the night, I will visit you in your cell and hear your story," the chief of the priests had told him.

And Herod had hardly been stretched on his narrow couch for half an hour when the priest entered and sat on the stool beside the head of the bed and signaled Herod to begin. Herod told all. He thoroughly emptied himself to this keen-eyed old man with the shaven skull. And he found peace flowing in as the telling of his story went on.

"Peace be with you, my son," the old man said at last. "The resolu-tion to all of your distress is within this cell with you. In addition, the doves have spoken. Your road to Rome holds further difficulties, but *you* will surmount them all. Sleep, sleep, sleep deeply now, my son," chanted the man of religion as he passed his long, thin hands back and forth slowly before Herod's face, "and arise with the morrow and proceed on your way."

Herod found himself sinking quickly into a deep, dreamless slumber. Well rested on awakening around sun-up, he was on his way and arrived at the small city of Rhinocolura, very near the Egyptian border, and in mid-afternoon pulled up for refreshments for himself and his men at a prosperous wayside inn.

As he entered the large public room, a man rose from a far, dim corner and approached him respectfully.

"You are Herod, second son of the lamented and noble Antipater of Idumea and Judea, are you not?"

"I am Herod. What do you want of me?"

"To deliver a message which I have waited here two days to give you."

"Well, speak briefly."

"It is this: King Malchus of Petra Arabia, your kinsman and friend, repented within the hour of his treatment of you, and sent me on a swift horse to overtake you and beg you to return so that he could restore to you what is yours. He begs your forgiveness most humbly, and offers to you every assistance possible. But I could not overtake you on the road, nor did any man see you pass along the road so could not direct me to where you could be found."

Herod laughed for the first time in many days. "I am overjoyed to receive such a message from my kinsman, because there has ever been warm love between him and my family. My heart was indeed paining me because of what appeared to be his defection in my hour of distress. Your message from him restores my soul. But I am too far on my road to Rome to turn back. I must contrive to sail before the winter storms prevent me. Go back and tell him that his very words have helped me, and embrace him warmly for me. Tell him that my younger brother Joseph is in the fort of Masada, perhaps soon to be besieged by Antigonus, and to give Joseph what help he can if necessary."

"King Malchus will be happy to do so. I have another piece of information for you that is not so happy, O Herod."

"It concerns my brother, Phasaelus, does it not?"

"Yes. He is dead."

Then he told Herod all that he had heard concerning the tragedy, and added, "Hyrcanus, whom many suspect of acting the traitor to your family for the Parthians, did not escape punishment as he had believed that he would. He has been carried a prisoner to Parthia."

"No doubt his being carried away was looked upon by neither himself nor Pacorus as a punishment, but as a rescue. He knows that Antigonus hates him to the extent that he would kill him quickly, and by as prolonged and painful a means possible. And if Antigonus did not, that I would myself if life remained in my body."

"But it is rumored that neither Pacorus nor Barzapharnes any longer desired the death of either Phasaelus or Hyrcanus, seeing the weakness of Antigonus and his unpopularity with the people. But Antigonus was determined that Hyrcanus should never contend for the high priesthood again with himself. When Hyrcanus was turned over to Antigonus by Barzapharnes, he made it impossible for him to do so, though he was not permitted to destroy Hyrcanus as he intended."

Then this courier of Malchus told Herod in great detail the account of what happened at the prison in Galilee that was in circulation all over Lower Asia.

While the handsome young Phasaelus lay in his cell, in a coma from a terrible concussion of the brain, Antigonus arrived from Jerusalem to receive the prisoners. On hearing that the 500 virgins had escaped from under the hand of Antigonus, the Parthians were wavering in their firmness to Antigonus and, in fact, considered transferring their allegiance to the sons of Antipater if they could be persuaded. Hyrcanus, whom they considered too foolish for any practical use, they would remove to the safety of Parthia as a reward for bringing Phasaelus into their hands.

But when Hyrcanus was brought into the presence of Antigonus, the Asamonean leaped to his feet, denounced Hyrcanus in the vilest terms for several minutes, then advanced upon him.

"O you sly old hyena, you who are responsible for the deaths of my beloved father and my brother Alexander, you who, under a pose of modesty and caring nothing for public life, have committed vile crimes too numerous to mention to obtain it and remain in it. You have betrayed not only us, who justly despise and hate you for your lies, but lured to his death your supposed friend who had done so much to gain the diadem for you. You lured him to his death at your table, as you have betrayed Phasaelus, and attempted to lure Herod also. But you shall not profit any longer from your crimes. I shall render you such that never again can you be a high priest, since our laws demand that a man holding that dignity must be perfect in body and lack no part."

And though Hyrcanus screamed in abysmal terror, prayed, and pled, falling upon his knees, the younger man, son of his brother, seized and attacked Hyrcanus in a most savage manner. He tried to drag Hyrcanus back to his feet, but failing in that, wrestled and struggled with him on the stone floor, the two rolling over and over, Hyrcanus trying to protect himself, but unable to do so. Sometimes, Antigonus, with his strong teeth bared in utter hatred, had Hyrcanus by his beard, sometimes by one ear, sometimes by the other, until finally, Antigonus succeeded in grasping the old man by both. Then with an inhuman snarling he bared his strong white teeth to the limit, and fastened them at the root of the left ear of Hyrcanus and tore it from his screaming head.

This one mutilation was sufficient to disqualify Hyrcanus for the priesthood, but the atavistic hatred of Antigonus for his uncle was still not satisfied. His mouth, chin, and the front of his rich apparel were streaming with the blood of Hyrcanus, and he too snarled and screamed insults as he contrived to pin Hyrcanus in a position to tear off the right ear with his teeth. Triumphant and sated at last, he had risen to his all-fours when a detachment of the guard of Barzapharnes broke into the room. The great thickness of the walls of the prison had smothered the shrieks of Hyrcanus to a great extent but, finally, they had penetrated to where Pacorus and Barzapharnes conferred. The detachment was sent on the run, but arrived to find the Asamonean prince slowly rising from his act of vengeance, his inhuman hatred of his uncle.

"But . . . but this you . . . tell me, is . . . ," and Herod began to retch. When the spasm had been overcome with the help of a servitor, Herod reflected. "Antigonus is truly a monster. Nothing but a beast could bring himself to such an act. I thought that the selling of the virgins could not be outdone for debasement of soul, but he has added to it this latest enormity. It indicates the extent of his hatred for any and all who stand in the way of his ambitions, whether justified or not, for certainly neither his father, his brother, nor himself have any legitimate claim to the throne. I will state that ambition without ability is the greatest evil in the world. It ever fathers monstrous crimes against mankind. As to the sorrowful end of my brother, my poor deluded brother, it shall be paid for in blood."

Herod and his men ate heartily but hurriedly and, early the next morning, arrived at Pelusium in the Delta. Several ships were tied up in this busy port and, after some dickering, Herod was able to charter three to transport himself, his men, and horses to Alexandria.

"What a man was Alexander the Great!" Herod mused as he came
in sight of the towering lighthouse which guarded the harbor of the
city named after the great Macedonian. "What a mark he has left upon
Lower Asia! During his short lifetime, he governed the men of the
earth by the glory of his sword, and now nearly three centuries after,
by the splendor of his mind. Like the Great Caesar, I envy him, and
feel humble before his mighty achievements. Oh, to accomplish even
a tenth part of what he did."

He stood on the forward part of the deck of his ship and watched
the approach to the magnificent city. First he was impressed, as always, by the expert engineering feat which had made this great port
possible. There was the long, long mole extending far out into the
Great Sea to receive the ships. The Pharaohs pointing up to the sky to
light and warn the ships, then the abundant wharfage and warehouse.
Then up rose the magnificent buildings of the royal palace libraries,
museums, universities, and other public buildings flanked by the rich
and well landscaped gardens. Palms, palms, wide spreading trees, and
flowering shrubs everywhere. His beauty-loving soul was nourished.

On receiving Herod's message that he had arrived, Cleopatra hurriedly sent word begging him not to disembark until she was ready to
receive him fittingly. In haste to continue on his way to Rome, Herod
fretted aboard ship for three hours. Yet, being the type of individual
that he was, Herod used part of those hours in bathing and adorning
his person. He gave orders to his men to make a fitting appearance.

Herod glittered like a heathen deity in white and gold as he descended the gangplank. His guard glittered; the horses glittered, and
delighted the eyes of the many thousands who had gathered at the
waterfront to be entertained by the sight.

Need it be said that the beautiful queen of Egypt shone like a sunset as she and Herod took their places to review her troops? A great
roar tore the throats of the populace at their joint appearance. They

THE LIFE OF HEROD THE GREAT

had seen Caesar with this beautiful woman, they had seen Antony likewise displaying his armed might with her, but these two as man and woman together seemed more fitting. The people shouted their approval.

Herod was a lover of beauty and splendor, but the palace of Cleopatra, enriched with the spoils of Europe and Asia by both Caesar and Antony, was far and away beyond his most extravagant dreams. Images in pure gold and richly jeweled from the temples of far places had prominent places in her hall of reception, in her dining hall, and everywhere that the eye could find. The richest rugs, hangings, carvings, objects of art, and everything filled the place.

But Herod was repelled by it all. He sought to be just, but to him, the unbelievable display meant that love to this beautiful and cultivated Greek meant gifts, not warmth and fidelity. Those qualities intrigued him most. If she had really loved Caesar, as she had pretended that she did during his lifetime, how could she now be what she was to the earthy Antony? Then there were other indications of her greed for both power and material wealth. She had brought about the death of both her brother-husbands and apparently thought nothing about it. Then there was the pathetic case of her younger sister, Arsinoe.

That no member of her immediate family should be left in position to challenge her sole claim to the throne of Egypt, she had tried to persuade Julius Caesar to put her to death after her two brothers had been disposed of. Infatuated as Caesar was by Cleopatra, he agreed to use the gentle, inoffensive girl in his triumph at Rome, but could not be brought to kill the girl. He arranged to have a sum of money settled upon her, and forbade her to ever live again in Egypt. A modest household was set up for her in distant Cilicia.

After Cleopatra had encountered Antony at Tarsus and enslaved him, Cleopatra then decided that she should take advantage of the nearness of Ephesus, where Arsinoe lived, to put the girl out of her way forever. It was well known that the unhappy girl, deprived of everything due her by her birth, and barely escaping with her life, went daily to the famous temple of Diana at Ephesus to pray. When Cleopatra had gained this information, she persuaded Antony to send a group of his armed men to the temple to slay her. Arsinoe was kneeling in fervent prayer when Antony's soldiers arrived. Arsinoe was seized upon, dragged from the temple, and a few feet from the doors, hacked to bits.

Therefore, when the lengthy and sumptuous state dinner had ended, and he and Cleopatra were alone in a luxury-loaded alcove of her reception hall, and Cleopatra began to pay him too-intimate attention, he was repelled. As if he had been kissed by a python. He was polite, but evaded her skillfully. To ward her off, he repeatedly spoke of his utmost fidelity to Antony.

However, Cleopatra knew more ways to kill a cat besides choking it to death on butter.

"Perhaps it is fortunate for you that affairs have turned out as they are in your small country, O Herod. Your abilities are far too great for such a tiny country. It so happens that there is no Egyptian capable of being the general of all my armies. Now, in your unhappy situation, I will place you in command. Not only will you be in full authority over all military affairs, but advise me also on all matters of government. I am aware of your luxurious tastes, and will build you a palace to suit your love of elegance."

"You are too generous, O beautiful and competent queen of a great and ancient nation, for I do not think myself worthy of the great advancement you offer me. Then you forget that I am not free to act on my own inclinations, but have a master, Antony. As you know, he made me and my lamented brother tetrarchs of Judea and responsible for the public affairs of that nation. I must run further risks of my life to hasten to Rome and report to him the state of affairs there at this moment."

How naive and faithful is this magnificently-made man! Cleopatra thought. *Yet those very qualities heighten his charm and worth to me. Almost a virgin among men, and yet such extraordinary abilities. At the head of my armies, and with his tremendous influence in Celesyria, my rule can be extended at least as far as the Euphrates. I need no longer fawn upon that dissolute Antony. I can wrest Lower Asia as well as Egypt from the rule of Rome. And, ah, such nights of love! It will be my privilege to train him in the arts of love.*

Aloud the queen said casually, "You take these matters too seriously, my Herod. You are too intense as a man of affairs, and take yourself too lightly as a man. Never do you take time for rest nor pleasures. That is necessary also. Leave Antony to me. I will make him understand my need of you as a general. Egypt is of importance to Rome also, but you would never realize it by listening to that priggish Octavius Caesar. No more human emotions or juices than a pebble. His father must have begotten him with a finger."

Herod chuckled. "Yet, it is rumored that he is madly in love with Julia, the wife of another man, and considers a discreet purchase of her from her husband."

"And the rumor is true, and that is why I am enraged at his criticism of my affair with Antony. Let Octavius take the beam out of his own eye before he trips over the mote in mine. So far as he is concerned, I am no better than a dancing girl in an inn."

Herod ostentatiously swept his eyes around the great room with its enormous treasures obtained through love and commented dryly, "But what a dancing girl!"

Cleopatra broke into a delighted laugh. "But you are really the witty, delightful companion that Antony insists you are. I *must* keep you here with me to assist me. You are indeed a jewel without price."

Impulsively, Cleopatra rose from her long chair, rushed to where Herod lounged in another, and knelt beside him. As she walked,

Herod could not avoid seeing that her gossamer-thin robe of fine silk clung to her legs like the drapery of the *Winged Victory*. Her perfume made a night-blooming flower of her. Her touch was soft and alluring.

"Do not leave me, Herod. It might be difficult for you to believe, but I am perhaps the most lonesome woman upon the earth. I feel that you, and you alone understand me. I cannot allow you to depart from my life. Stay, Herod."

"Your words all but persuade me, O wondrous Cleopatra. If only I could spend the rest of my life here under the spell of your great beauty, charm, and tact. But then, considering the perilous state of affairs in Asia, I would be the utmost traitor to Antony to do so. Do not tempt me further. I must hasten on to Antony at Rome. Those beastly Parthians must not gain further at his expense. I must go as quickly as possible."

Cleopatra rested her perfumed head on Herod's chest and sighed.

"But beautiful and bewitching queen, you honor me too much by your touch. You must not profane your body by resting your head upon me. Such a glory is reserved for Antony alone. I would be insanely jealous if I were in his place."

By these words, Herod dissembled. Had Cleopatra known his real thoughts, she would have contrived to put him to death the next morning. What Herod really felt was that her touch was common to at least two other men, and that was far too promiscuous for him. Further, in spite of her exalted position and wealth, his betrothed was infinitely her superior. Mariamne's little finger was worth ten Cleopatras. Instead of the physical touch being alluring, it was indeed in the same class as the endearments of a dancing girl so far as he was concerned. Love for sale.

"But, you foolish warrior," Cleopatra cooed, "do you not realize that you cannot sail to Rome until the winter passes? You will be destroyed by the storms."

"But I might not encounter a storm at all. It is a little early for them, and if I hurry . . ."

"And the news has just arrived of the terrible riots in Rome. Civil war, in fact. You would be drawn into the conflict by your close association with Antony, and perish. Consider yourself to be very, very fortunate to be here and out of it."

"Then there is a greater demand upon my fidelity to Antony. If he is under such peril, then I must do all that is within my power to fight by his side. He is not only my benefactor, but my friend. I have given him my right hand."

There was a silence. It continued long enough for Cleopatra to think of a way to extricate herself from a trap which she now saw.

"Your noble sentiments do you credit, O faithful Herod. Since I feel exactly as you do, I make your difficulties my very own. After the terrible experiences you have had to reach this far, your splendid body requires rest . . ."

"But I cannot so indulge myself at such a time. The winter . . ."

"I understand and plan against the storms. I will send the steward of the palace to men of influence who, if there are worthy vessels to be found, will know where to find them, and arrange everything for you. Rest yourself here with me for tomorrow, and on the morning of the following day, you can sail for Rome."

Herod's impatience showed in his face, so Cleopatra went on to convince him.

"I share your concern, O worthy Herod. You and I, of all the people of the earth, are closest to beloved Antony. Only we two really love him. Naturally, we wish to do all for his sake. However, we must get our hands upon the means to reach him. You cannot sail for Rome until you have a vessel."

"That is true," Herod conceded grudgingly. He somehow did not believe Cleopatra. He was convinced that he could obtain the ship he required with more speed than her steward, and inactivity was driving him crazy with the strain he was under. But what could he do? He could not call the queen of Egypt, whose hands he was in, and who was the fanatically beloved of Antony, a liar and stride from her sumptuous palace as he so yearned to do. Silently he cursed her devious cleverness, and pretended to be convinced. But he had existed too long in public life to be without resources. When his valet dressed him for supper, Herod sent word to his man of business to exert himself to find for him at any cost the type of vessel he required as quickly as possible.

Outside of his urgency to report to Antony at Rome, Herod considered himself in even greater danger than on the night of his hazardous flight from Jerusalem. Was this woman actually in love with him, or seeking to use him as a tool? If a tool, to what end? To turn against Antony and make Egypt independent of Rome by seizing, through him, all Lower Asia? But the idea in her head could be even more sinister. Recognizing the attachment of Antony to him, Cleopatra might well resent his strong influence as a stumbling block to her avarice and ambitions. She might well be setting a snare for him so that Antony would destroy him. He must guard every moment and be utterly circumspect.

His anxiety was increased when the next darkness arrived and Cleopatra prettily bemoaned their lack of good fortune in even hearing of a suitable ship. This in the face of a secret report from his personal steward that the report had gone along the waterfront that the queen did not wish for any shipowner to charter or sell a vessel to Herod. This was unwelcome news, because the rumor was that Herod was extremely wealthy, and it being late in the season business was dull; thus shipowners were, in spite of the secret warning, hungry to deal with Herod.

When on the third night Cleopatra, weeping in pretended frustration, summoned her palace steward to report to Herod himself of his lack of success, it was all that Herod could do to keep a straight face,

for his man had a vessel under charter. It was being outfitted and provisioned at this very moment under an assumed name. Captain and
pilot had been hired, and he was assured that he could sail on the tide
around dawn of the morrow. The road to Rome was indeed difficult
in this instance, but he had high hopes that he would make his goal.

With the last course of the lavish meal, Herod sprang his surprise.

"A ship belonging to a man from Tyre, an old friend of my family,
had unexpectedly come into port here, O faithful friend. You need not
worry yourself any longer. I have been far too heavy a burden upon
you. He has some urgent business at Rome, and sends me word that
he will take me there also. But everything has a price. To obtain this
boon, I must be on board before midnight, since he plans to depart
before the morning, and therefore, cannot enjoy the wealth of your
company as I wish."

Cleopatra played her game well. She pretended the greatest happiness at Herod's good luck, but could find no way to detain him even
for an hour, for Herod's valet had already moved his wearing apparel to
the ship while Herod rode with the queen that afternoon to view some
ancient monuments along the river. Nor was there opportunity for the
queen to concoct any scheme to meet the surprise move, for Herod
had departed the palace in ten minutes after his announcement.

Having successfully fled his Circe, Herod's voyage to Rome was as
full of adventures almost as that of Ulysses on that same sea. A violent
storm and shipwreck drove him onto the island of Rhodes. While there,
Herod, seeing the destruction which Cassius had made at Rhodes,
made the city a gift of a large sum of money to restore it. Further, he had
built a large three-decked ship in which he and his company continued
on to Italy. He landed at the port city of Brundusium.

When he disembarked, he gave a shout of joy and, going to a temple, poured a libation to Apollo. Then by swift chariots, they set out
for Rome.

Herod's arrival at the gates of Rome was far different from what
he had dreamed of since early childhood. There was neither time nor
mood to stand in awe of the ancient structures on the Seven Hills. Day
was breaking, and he merely noted the fog hanging over the Tiber as
the red rays of the rising sun attacked it. The driver went as swiftly as
possible to the entrance of the palatial home of Marcus Antonius, the
Triumvir, and master of Asia.

In spite of the early hour, Antony leaped from his bed to receive
him as soon as his doorman announced Herod. They flung themselves upon each other with rude affection and welcome.

"But I am happy to see you, old friend!" Antony slapped Herod on
the shoulder after embracing him many times. "You must tell me everything. But I am most unreasonable, O my friend. You wish to bathe and
refresh yourself, I know."

Herod did desire a good bath and a change of clothes, but these
activities did not hold up the report, because Antony came on into
the sunken bath with him. They both took a bath and were rubbed
down by the attendants. Herod made a detailed report on everything
that had happened from the invasion on to his arrival at Rome. Every
phase of the struggle in Asia was followed by a penetrating though
succinct analysis. Both men were lying prone on the rubbing tables
when Herod ended. The rubbers were kneading their backs.

After a silence of several minutes, Herod glanced across at Antony,
and slowly the Roman spoke.

"You are magnificent, Herod. You have performed a superhuman
task in your fidelity to Rome and to me. Rome is at fault in not having
made you a king when you were made a tetrarch, and given you greater
military forces. But how could I know that those treacherous officers
at Apamia would defect to that Pompeian traitor, Sabienus? In any
case, that round-headed, thin-lipped, small-mouthed Caius Octavius
who now goes under the name of Caesar is going to place the blame

at my door. That young serpent is just as poisonous as an ancient one. Every bit of our disaster in Asia is going to be whispered around by his minions as due to my attachment to Cleopatra. To hear him talk, the queen of Egypt is no more than an avaricious whore."

"Oh, but I was under the impression that all was very goodwill between you. You are married to his sister."

"Another aggravation, Herod. Octavia beside Cleopatra is like a drink of watered wine. Stiff as a stone in the bed. I curse this winter season that forces me to send my men into winter camp and return to Rome. But it is absolutely necessary now for me to be here. Those Parthians are much better organized than I had thought. Privately, I wish now that I had permitted you to scout both Parthia and Armenia. But I trust you to never allow Octavius to know that it was suggested to me. My difficulties with him are too formidable already. Ah, how he hates Cleopatra!"

"Then for the sake of peace between you, and your security at Rome, why not abandon her?"

"Abandon my love? No, by Jupiter! Cleopatra is my very life. She is my soul. She alone understands me and is faithful to me. She merely gave herself to Caesar to promote her own interests, and I believe her and do not blame her for doing so. But now, we have discovered each other, thanks to the Gods, and she would not even look at another man."

Feeling deep pity for his friend, Herod urged Antony as he slipped into a short robe, "I understand, but for the sake of your great career, could you pretend to have abandoned Cleopatra while this war with Parthia continues so as not to give Caesar a chance to undermine you in Rome while you must be absent in Asia?"

Herod suggested this, hoping that Antony would come to himself during the time and forget the Egyptian queen.

"No, my faithful friend. If circumstances ever came to that point, I would forsake Rome and spend the rest of my days with her. I am conscious that you seek only my good in making such a suggestion, but I am too possessed by love for her to even consider it. You see, O beloved Herod, my early youth was not so fortunate as your own, though I was born a patrician. I remember well the luxury of your father's estate and the sheltering influence when I came to Jerusalem with Gabinius in the war against Aristobulus. You were a small boy then. Such a home and such a father as you had never were mine. Rather, I was reared as a wolf on the hunt for prey. Cleopatra is the first softening influence in my life. She provides me everything which I have lacked. I have reached middle-life now, and before I found her—. No, I cannot bear the thought of turning away from her for even a moment.

"Octavius accuses me to members of the Roman senate of bestowing the spoils of war upon her, which rightfully should be brought to Rome, but what are the little baubles she craves? A handful or two of jewels; an image or so from some heathen temple, some gold and silver for coining. She is like a little girl crying for glittering toys. It is charming. I love to give them to her and watch her gladness. Besides, Rome is stuffed already with the treasures of the inhabitable earth. Besides, I confide to you, my closest friend, that if worse comes to the worst, I am putting aside in Egypt a little something to retire upon. It pays to be prudent."

Hearing these things and remembering his own encounter with Cleopatra, Herod was infinitely sad. But perhaps it would cost him his career, and probably his life, to press the matter further. Besides, his body now cried for sleep. To change the subject, he yawned elaborately.

"How thoughtless I am to forget that you have been riding all night long while I slept!" Antony said contritely. "You must go to sleep in my very bed. Will you break your fast before sleep or after?"

"Before. Then I shall sleep an hour or so, and be ready to continue our conversation."

Antony followed Herod foot to foot. As he ate the warm meal, Antony talked.

"You must be made king immediately, Herod, not only for your elevation, which is long overdue, but for the benefit of Rome itself. You are the most able soldier and administrator in Lower Asia, and your fidelity to Rome is unequalled. Even that purse-mouthed Octavius will agree with me on that. He and the senate will be as outraged as I at the insolence of that Antigonus accepting the government of an ally of Rome from our enemies."

"Oh, I can beat him with little trouble, as you are aware that I have done before. He's no soldier. The Parthians had to bring him in and heave him up by main force upon the throne. You drive the Parthians back to above the Euphrates, and I will deal with the spiteful and womanish Antigonus."

"That is well underway. Since you left Judea, we have shown those barbarians who is the greatest military power of the world."

"Joyful tidings! Tell me, what is the posture of affairs at present?"

"On the table beside the bed is the report from my best general, Ventidius Bassus. He has had two decisive victories over those perfidious herdsmen. Briefly, he drove Labienus and his provincial levies as far as the Taurus without their even giving him battle. There, joined by the main army of the Parthians, they gave Ventidius the meeting, and suffered a crushing defeat. Labienus fled to Cilicia, but was captured and beheaded."

"Ave, Antony, and Ventidius and the Roman eagle!"

"The Parthians reformed and attacked Ventidius in the passes of the Amanus, but he made a stand at Trapezon and overwhelmed the herdsmen. Pacorus himself was slain. It was a rout. Phranipates, the ablest general of Parthia, also fell there north of the Orontes Valley. The Parthians began a hasty withdrawal from Syria. The head of Pacorus was cut off and sent about to the cities of Syria to prove to them that he was indeed slain so that those who had hopes of a Parthian victory might be depressed, and those faithful to Rome might be in good heart and stiffen their resistance."

"But, excellent! Most excellent!"

"But when Ventidius had scattered his men into winter quarters, the treacherous Parthians massed 20,000 troops and attacked him with a great number of free cavaliers in their full armor. The Parthians had great hopes of victory, because the battle was fought on the anniversary of the defeat of Crassus. The forces faced each other at Gindarus in Cyrrhestica and the enemy were utterly routed. There is no further resistance except from Aradus and Jerusalem."

"Which I will put down with an iron hand."

"I am confident of that, O daring Herod. Rome must quickly put the diadem upon your head and arm you properly."

"But I must deliver the charge that my future mother-in-law laid upon me. My betrothed has a brother of thirteen years. She asks that you make him king, since he is of the royal line."

"Are you mad, O Herod? I understand, I suppose. Being an honest man, you but delivered the message handed to you."

"That is the case, O Antony."

"Good, for you would get nothing but a most decisive denial of such a foolish request. Rome has no need, nor interest in a youthful priest. Why, the very name of the Asamoneans is utterly hateful to the Romans. Not one of which but has not been troublesome to Rome. Under the present circumstance, Rome requires an experienced and skillful military leader. I am highly incensed at the insolence of this woman to try to send a man of your eminence on an errand. Or to attempt to tell *me* what to do. I have the impulse to slay her immediately because her spirit too much resembles that of another, a sly, deceitful, greedy person who delights to reap where others sow."

"And who is this detestable person, O Antony? Remember I am your utterly faithful friend."

"Of that I am utterly convinced by your actions. It is none other than Caius Octavius. Who was beside Caesar as he strove to rise to power, even when in Gaul?"

"Marc Antony," Herod answered.

"Who was wielding a slashing sword beside him at Pharsalus?"

"History says Marc Antony."

"And who sailed to Egypt and risked death in the difficult fighting there?"

"History and my beloved father say, 'Marc Antony.'"

"Who stood faithful in the civil strife that followed and until he was made dictator for life in Rome?"

"Again, Marc Antony."

"Who therefore aided Caesar to bring to Rome the booty so great that the world has never seen such an accumulation, and which caused the people of Rome to worship Caesar as a god?"

"Marc Antony."

"And when the abhorrent deed was done—when noble Caesar had been murdered in the senate house, and his murderers had all but persuaded the people of Rome that they had done a noble deed in destroying the greatest man of all the world, who was it saw what was needful if liberty were to continue in the world, and did it?"

"Marc Antony. The moment and place of history was when the body of Caesar arrived in the marketplace. It arrived at that place of the gathering of the people of Rome merely the body of a dead man, an evil and oppressive man, scarcely more than the body of an ox, but, by the intervention of one Marc Antony, left that spot the remains of a god."

"Well said, O noble and discerning Herod. And now for the point: Had I not turned the tide at that moment, the party of Caesar would have been exterminated by the party of the dead Pompey. Cassius and Brutus would have hunted us down like wild beasts of the forest and hacked us down like brutes. And Caius Octavius, Caesar's adopted son, first of all. But what happens? When he learns in Illyria that Caesar has been murdered and that I have gained safety and control of Rome for the party of Caesar, who comes galloping to Rome to claim 'the estate left him by the dead Caesar'? The still milky stripling, Caius Octavius! He does not appear in gratitude and goodwill, mind you, but full of glitter-eyed suspicion that the man who hand labored to create the estate had perhaps spent a sesterce of what he had helped to accumulate. The stripling did not once say that he was grateful, nor offer to reward me by a sesterce for what I had done, but, 'Give me both the power and wealth that my grand-uncle, my adopted father, has bequeathed to me, you scoundrel.'"

"I had not thought of the matter too much, but you really have a case. You did preserve the estate, and with it, his very life. Yes, you deserved something."

"And so do you, O my faithful friend. You have served both Rome and Judea well. You have saved the very life of the woman who now hastily seeks to displace you with her useless son, and the useless life of the son of a now degenerate line. So far as Rome is concerned, no royal family exists at this time in Judea. The mentally enfeebled Hyrcanus was only allowed to continue his pose as a favor to your noble and beloved father. Remember what happened to him?"

"With fire in my blood, O Antony."

"And your brother Phasaelus, lured into the trap of the Parthians?"

"I am beside myself with rage until he is avenged."

"So this woman sends a charge to have you set aside and her and her son given the reward for your fidelity to both your own nation and to Rome and then will have you disposed of next. For do not be deceived. Human beings detest feeling gratitude. You would shortly be done away with as soon as they felt that your services were no longer necessary to prop them up in power."

"Oh, I can see the possibilities. As you suggested, I made no request of you, I merely delivered a message. If you had thought that desirable . . ."

"By Jupiter, no! I repeat, Rome needs a capable man more than ever in Lower Asia. To be specific, Rome needs Herod in Lower Asia. The numerous reports concerning the acts of Herod, his brother, and their father before them are here for all to read. Never, never mention that criminally foolish message again. The senate must be called into a special session to deal with the matter of making you a king. If then, I placed such a mad proposal before them when they all—as well as the people of Rome—are so concerned about the threat of Parthia, they would behead me."

"You have no worry on that score, my friend."

Antony arose from the side of the bed and reached the room door, where he turned.

"I go now to confer with Caius Octavius and certain other influential Romans. A swift message will be sent to Ventidius to proceed to Masada to aid Joseph. I realize how worried you are lest Antigonus overpower the fort and seize the women to bribe the Parthians to return to help him. That is against the interest of Rome. I need not tell you that my home is your own. I commit you to the care and protection of my Lares and Penates until I return. Sleep long and well."

But sleep was long in coming. Herod worried about those in the fort at Masada. His terrible night of flight and struggle would count for nothing if Antigonus took the place. Herod refused to think of the horrible fate of those inside. Then his thoughts turned to the love affair of his friend and protector, Antony. His sympathy was profound. Antony's love for the perfidious Cleopatra was so all-consuming, and his faith so perfect. Herod shuddered to think where it might lead him.

If only Antony could be persuaded to turn from her! Yet, he knew that he dare not suggest such a thing to his friend again. Every man must go his road alone. How fortunate he was in Mariamne! Simple, sweet, and lacking in ambition. Just a dear, soft, sweet, beautiful thing for him to love and cherish. Her need of his strength made her all the easier to love. And being as she was, he could pour out all the abundant love that he had held in check all his adult life. He was putting all of the happiness of his life in her beloved little hands. It was safely deposited. God was indeed good. Then he drifted off to sleep.

It was mid-afternoon before Herod awoke and dressed. He was brought food by Antony's servitors, and ate it before the wide hearth in the reception hall. It was his first time to observe the interior of a Roman house, and he made a careful comparison with the Asian homes. He realized as he did so that the house of Antony was not typical. First, Antony was a man of extreme wealth. Then, like Alexander the Great, Antony was enamored of eastern luxury. It was elaborately adorned with couches, rich drapery, and cushions. The trophies of his conquests outside of Italy were everywhere. Rich and voluptuous, it still fell far short of what he had seen in the palace of Cleopatra.

Finally, he sat before the fireplace, and noted the small clay figures— the Lares and Penates which guarded the home. They stood, one on each side of the hearth. Then he unrolled the report of Ventidius and read it carefully in detail. He indulged in a broad grin when he came to the details of the last battle at Girdna, near the temple of Hercules. Ventidius Bassus had out-deceived even the Parthians until he could bring up troops from Cappadocia to beat them. *Wonderful!* How Herod wished that he could have been in that battle. How he wished that he might have looked on the dead head of Pacorus and spat in the deceitful and cruel face. *Ah, poor beloved Phasaelus!*

"If this is the end of my long journey to Rome—that is, I am made king, beloved brother, I shall avenge you. The disaster lies at my own door, brother. I recognized years ago that I was the stronger, and should have protected you by preventing you from leaving Jerusalem, even if I had to have you put in chains." Tears began to seep from his eyes.

"And what of Joseph? Has he been overpowered and slain? If I am to become a king, may it come swiftly so that I can return and rescue all of those whom I love from even a worse fate than that of Phasaelus."

As he sat dejected, staring into the flames on the hearth, Antony entered with several men, whom Herod could see were of some consequence by their apparel and bearing. Their egos were well nourished, from the looks on their faces.

Antony greeted him with a great show of affection, and made the introductions. But as he lifted his hand in a kind of salute to begin, two young men ran forward and flung themselves upon Herod.

"Messala!" Herod cried in delight. "How pleasant to see you again! And Atratinus! This is a surprise. What excellent company you were when I saw you last in Syria with Antony!"

"And what excellent company you were, O handsome Herod!" Messala spoke first. "And what a magnificent host. Remember that I was the advocate of you and your lamented brother Phasaelus when Antony made you tetrarchs."

"And now we are to introduce you tomorrow when Antony, Octavius, and the Roman senate will elevate you to a king."

"King?" Herod answered in mock surprise. "You think me worthy of such a dignity?"

"Oh, cast aside the mock modesty, O Herod," Messala laughed. "You are one of those men who carry around a throne in the seat of your pants. All that is required is a diadem."

There was a burst of good-natured laughter in which Herod joined. Antony took advantage of this to make the introductions. And naturally the first presentation was made to one Caius Octavius Caesar, who would be known to the world and to history as Augustus Caesar. Only

Antony would not be alive to hear this title. The man whom he despised as a fool would see to that.

Herod was aware of the searching eyes of the young man, and scarcely that, as Caesar was eleven years younger than himself at thirty-two. Octavius Caesar was large-boned and husky with a thick neck, round head, with short hair combed down from the crown of his head all around. Tall, blonde, and well set. Keen, penetrating eyes in an otherwise placid face. Herod, a better judge of men than his friend, Antony, did not make the mistake of despising this youth as Antony did. He saluted respectfully and allowed Caesar to speak first.

"By an unfortunate late birth, I did not have the pleasure of being a guest at your magnificent home as did my father—adopted—but never did he cease to sing the praises of the noble Antipater," Caesar said slowly and deliberately, but with a gleam of sincerity in his eyes. "As you know, your father fought beside Caesar in Egypt, and rescued him when he was plunged into the sea at Alexandria. Caesar could swim well of course, but the missiles that rained around him, while he struggled in the water, to prevent his escape nearly took his life. Antipater, a magnificent swimmer, and reckless of the darts of the enemy, plunged in to his rescue."

"My father never spoke of that," Herod replied modestly. "But that he worshipped the Great Caesar as the greatest mind as well as soldier of the inhabitable earth was no secret."

"He was a man of virtue, bravery, and generosity, in the opinion of my father. Due to his rescue of my father at the risk of his own life, I owe to him and his family my own life and good fortune, for at that time, he had not officially adopted me. So I and Rome owe everything to Antipater. My obligation extends to his son."

"Perhaps I do not deserve such sentiments in you, O Caesar, the Younger."

"But you do, and more. We have been on Capitoline Hill this day reading the decrees and records laid up there. Your own acts in fidelity to Rome occupy a great deal of space. They show you to be a man of genius in military matters and also as an administrator. And your reckless daring is hard to equal anywhere. As Messala says, you are one of those rare men who were born to rule. We are shamefully late in elevating you to the royal dignity."

"Ah, yes!" Antony said forcefully. "And I need a man of his qualifications very badly now. Why, according to Sextus Caesar, this handsome young Herod has all of Celesyria under his influence, with the exception of the few Parthian partisans around Jerusalem. He wrote a very lengthy and detailed account of the occasion when they tried to sentence you to death for doing your duty."

The room burst into raucous laughter. It appeared that they had all read the account. Herod's eyes went quickly to the face of young Caesar. His eyes swam with laughter, but it was quiet laughter. The youth had restraint.

"I was very amused. I would have loved to have been present at that trial," Caesar said in his slow, quiet way. "Even then you were serving Rome creditably. As I look at you, listen to you, with the accounts of your exploits in mind, I cannot conceive of you being an Asian. You seem to be one of us."

"Did I not say that earlier as we conversed at the temple of Jupiter?" Messala demanded. "I remember how much Herod and his brother impressed me when I met them in Syria."

"And so my father said of Antipater and his sons," Caesar nodded, "that they might have been born of the patricians in Rome. When you are king in Judea, you must invite us all to be your guests and feast us as Antipater did my father and Antony years ago."

"Ah, yes, Herod," Antony smacked his lips. "That lavish amount of broiled quail, oysters from Britian, tender roast lamb, wines from Gaul, well iced in snow from the mountains, but do not take the advantage of the rest of us because of your vast wealth and handsome looks, and make off with all the young and beautiful women as you served the Parthians."

More loud laughter, and Antony went on.

"Why, this Herod brought off the rape of the Sabine women all by himself. Most men consider themselves lucky to make off with one beautiful woman, but Herod runs off with more than a thousand and still has them all waiting for his return. What a man!"

"Oh!" exclaimed Atratinus, "even he needs assistance on that task. We must hasten to his assistance."

"I have not overlooked that possibility. Having driven the barbarous Parthians out of Syria, I have sent word to Ventidius Bassus this very day to hasten down into Idumea and to surround the fort of Masada, where they are to insure a more equitable division of the spoils."

"Yes, Herod," Caesar added in his dry tones as the laughter died down, "we do not make you king to be the *father* of your country, only the *king*."

"Have a care, O Herod," Messala issued a mock warning. "It is myself and Atratinus who will introduce you into the senate tomorrow and speak of your loyalty and services to Rome, as well as that of your noble family. Then we will lay before the senate the character and evil acts of Antigonus. But unless you promise here and now to allow us to share your raptures, we might confuse matters. Have a care! We are desperate men. You might be pictured as using virgins for coins and biting off the ears of your uncle."

Herod was fanatically patriotic and did not relish these jokes about his countrywomen, but his position did not permit him to show resentment. He made out to laugh with the rest, knowing that few of the dozen men here would ever cross the Great Sea. But he found a way to turn the trend of jests.

"Oh, if I were only the stallion that you flatter me to be! You make me out to be the Camel Driver of song."

He told them about the lengthy ballad, and allowed himself to be persuaded to sing a few verses, which instantly found great favor. Then the supper was announced, and the men surrounding the table went into detail about the matter of elevating Herod to the kingship of Judea. They discussed how the senate would be convoked and how everything would be carried off. When that was over, back to the Camel Driver, and the type of humor that men, and particularly young men, were apt to indulge in. This went on far into the night.

As Herod returned to bed that night, he asked himself if he really had ended the long journey. Had he really reached Rome? In reality, it had been a journey of three generations in distance. His grandfather had seen the vision and thrown up the roadbed through forest and sea-lane. His father had set forth on the journey, but fell by the way-side because, to be honest, Antipater lacked the toughness for such travel. He had refused to face the realities. The same thing hindered his older brother Phasaelus. But here he was, almost at the end of the long journey, delayed by merely a group of hours measured by the sun. He thought he would go to the temple of a deity who ruled over destinies, and would chant words pronounced by the Pythoness. Tomorrow.

The day arrived dressed in red and purple raiment which trailed the skirts of its robes along the Tiber, which parted Rome into halves. In mid-morning, a group of Herod's new-made friends called for him in five chariots. Antony had departed two hours before to see that everything, every detail, went as he had planned it. Even before he left Judea, Herod was aware of the great ability of Antony as an orator and a soldier, but now, he realized his genius as a politician.

Herod was brought into the senate chamber by two of his associates of the night before and was seated between them in an inconspicuous place in the rear. The dignified senators, all dressed in their white togas, pretended not to notice his entry. His companions did not need to point out the two consuls, Caius Domitius Calvinus and Caius Asinius Pollio. He could tell from their seats and their dress the difference. All faces were stern and alert.

When the dark-haired, supple-bodied Messala mounted the speaker's rostrum, Herod noted that the gay blade of the night before was regarded with deep respect. From the time he lifted his right arm in a gesture of oratory, men leaned forward to listen. In a sentence, he stated why the senate had been convoked. Then he launched his effort. While he told in moving language of the great help which Antipater had given the Romans from the provisioning of the expedition of Mithradates on his way to join Caesar in Egypt to his raising of 3,000 troops of his own and smoothing the way for the general, Octavius, from his place as president of the senate, leaned forward, nodding his head in agreement, and wiping away a tear as he contemplated the services which Antipater had rendered to Caesar later.

"With these eyes I beheld the wounds upon the body of this noble man, received in his courage and fidelity to Rome and to Caesar! Antipater was in no way compelled to be at the scene of conflict in Egypt at all. But admiration for the great principles emanating from Rome placed him there. The first man to scale the walls in the great battle of the Jews Camp, the first to make it possible for the Roman forces to enter the city, and when he had beaten the enemy which faced his wing, and seeing the men under Mithradates in full retreat, Antipater ran along the beach and attacked the enemy so violently and successfully that Mithradates was able to turn back and inflict terrible defeat upon the enemy. This account was later written by Mithradates to Caesar, and indeed he stated that Antipater had been his savior, both as to the victory and his life. But that is not all; we cite the tremendous services which he rendered to Rome and Caesar in Judea, as the champion of Rome and its noble principles of government in

Asia. And this noble and faithful friend of Rome died for his devotion
to Rome. He was treacherously slain by partisans of Parthians to open
the road for their invasion of Syria."

The senate was visibly moved.

Then Messala turned his oratory upon Herod himself—citing his
record, and printing up his virtues. Herod smiled inwardly at the tremendous histrionic powers of the speaker. He played on his vocal cords
like a ten-stringed lyre. His gestures were dynamic. When he came to
the night of the flight of Herod with the virgins, his voice dropped to a
husky whisper as he described the passage from the Gate of the Essenes
to the Idumean border. He was interrupted many times by cries of applause or indignation at what Herod had suffered. The senate was in a
loud buzz for minutes after Messala spoke. The Consul Pollio was so
excited to admiration of the deeds of Herod, as Messala recited them,
that he threw aside dignity and bowed to Herod in salutation.

Atratinus was equally effective when he rose to lay before the senate
the crimes of Antigonus. In mid-speech, as Atratinus told of the use of
the virgins of the first families as coin with which to pay the Parthians
for the throne, many leaped to their feet in indignation. The trouble
that the family of Antigonus had caused Rome, the hatred that the
Asamoneans bore Rome, the insulting behavior of his seeking the kingdom from the Parthians, and his injuries to the Roman party in Palestine roused the senate to great fury. Shouts of anger broke in upon the
speaker.

Then Antony, whom Herod now saw for the first time in the room,
spoke of the grave threat to Roman power from the barbarous Parthians,
and the need of a rashly-courageous man like Herod, who had shown
himself so faithful to Rome as attested by his fabulous record of achievements, who should be elevated to a dignity which was comparable to his
services...

Octavius rose and added to the urgency of what Antony had said.

The young man was no orator, but conveyed great sincerity. Because Herod, son of the noble Antipater, had demonstrated his abilities and his fidelity, his unshakable fidelity to Rome at the repeated risk of his fortune and life, with the Parthian ambitions in Celesyria, Rome should at last do what was honorable and right to do—elevate Herod to a royal status.

The vote was quick and unanimous. Herod was king of Judea from this hour on. The decrees were made and read aloud in the senate house. The special session of the senate was then dissolved.

Pollio, consul for the second time, ran to Herod, where he bowed and stated that it was Rome who should be congratulating itself for the king they had just made.

"Never in my life had I been so fascinated by a personality. I offer you my right hand in eternal friendship. Every time that you have the opportunity, come to Rome and make my house your own."

Thus began a very firm and faithful friendship. It was to have effect upon Herod's later life.

Both Octavius and Antony realized that they had done a very popular thing, and the personality of their candidate was capturing everybody present. Indeed, he was about to be snatched from them. They nodded to each other, and fell in on either side of him, excluding others.

"We now march to the capitol to offer sacrifices and to lay up the decrees."

Thus everybody marched out of the senate house, Herod between Antony and Caesar. The consuls, followed by the magistrates, led the procession; Caesar and Antony, with Herod between them, came next; and then the senate.

"And remember," Antony said to Herod as soon as they were outside, "that it is I who will feast you on your first day as king. I have to say it now because numerous others will make the offer as soon as we leave the capitol, especially the Consul Pollio. Never have I seen him so charmed by anyone."

"And of course, I will be present at the feast," Caesar said quickly. "Antony shall not have you all to himself."

This boyish spontaneity pleased Herod very much, yet surprised him too. Octavius had impressed him as rather grave for his age. Now he realized that this adopted son of the Great Caesar could not be taken for granted. He was much more complicated than he seemed. Octavius reasoned. Allowing for bias in Antony, the young man had a strong feeling for justice. Certainly he was also gracious.

"How can I show my deep gratitude, O Caesar, for your generosity in thus honoring me before all Rome by attending the feast in my honor?"

Octavius made no attempt at flowery words, but he flashed Herod a very warm and brilliant smile.

Then the whispering ceased and the procession, with solemn faces and mien, moved sedately into the great temple of Jupiter Capitoline.

The solemn hour was present, then it passed, and the eminent men emerged into the sunlight. Without exception, they said a word or two of congratulation to Herod and began to disperse. But the tight little band who had carried off the elevation of Herod remained about him and Antony, and proceeded towards their conveyances at the senate house. For the first time, Herod had a chance to look at part of the city well.

He noted with disappointment that most of the streets were crooked and narrow, as if they had been laid out by the cows. The majority of the homes were made of wood. Rome, at the time, was far from the magnificent city of marble that Augustus Caesar was to boast of, that he had found it of wood and left it of stone. However, emotionally, it gleamed and glittered from the splendor that was in the heart of Herod. Though Herod said little in the midst of the witty band, his feeling of exaltation was sensed, and Messala prodded Herod.

"How does our new-made king feel at this moment?"

To hide his deep emotions, Herod brought a smile by striking a mock pose of Antony, and declaimed: "Triumvirs, consuls, magistrates, senators, tribunes. Lend me your ears. I am in Rome, the capital city of the inhabitable world. Rome, the home of my soul. All of my conscious years I have yearned to reach my spiritual home. Rome, the center of the world, and will remain so for at least a thousand years, sending out her light of peace, progress, and justice over all mankind. As a private man, I would love to linger here in contemplation of her spiritual and material marvels forever, but gracious Rome, through the ingenuity of my assembled friends and supporters, has made me a king. As a king, I must hasten back to Asia to fight with the valor of a Roman for my country and the glory of Rome."

Pollio was the first to embrace Herod, but they all did.

"This is no outsider," Pollio said, as if ready to defend his statement to the last ditch, but there was no contest. "King Herod was born a Roman. He is one of us. His words show his spirit, and his spirit is reflected from the shield of Apollo."

CHAPTER TEN

HOME AGAIN

On the seventh day after Herod arrived at the door of Antony's house, he sailed for home. A large cluster of eminent Romans saw him embark, and in a very warm atmosphere of departure, Herod said: "I confess to be overwhelmed by the personality of the Romans. The first striking characteristic is the adaptability of the Romans. They take and use everything that is good from everywhere. In that respect, they surpass the Greeks. Second, they amuse themselves in a great way, but play never interferes with work, and work does not prevent play, so necessary to humanity. I was feasted by my friend and benefactor, Marc Antony, in a lavish fashion where the wit and the wine both flowed freely, yet no detail of the necessary preparation for my campaign in Asia was overlooked. Here, on the seventh day since my arrival at Rome, I sail, having been made a king, and furnished with everything necessary to fight. The Roman is a practical man, but O, so delightful as a companion. How I love and respect you all."

"But do not forget one thing, beloved Herod," Antony cautioned.

"We have one prevailing fault. Roman officials, especially in the provinces, look at the *hand* of the petitioner first. They never even see the *face* of the petitioner if the hand is empty."

There was a loud burst of laughter at this.

"Bribery," Antony continued. "Eternal hunger for bribes. Because you have an enormous task before you, and I know your capabilities, I shall appoint no Roman pro-consul or any other official to trouble you in that respect. We will deal with each other directly. And if any of my commanders attempt anything of the kind, all you need do is report it to me."

"That is a healthy saying, O Antony," Herod agreed, "and the provinces of Asia have been ravaged sufficiently by the Parthian barbarians to be unable to bear more at this time." Herod nodded emphatically. "Your compassion is commendable. And the people will make a comparison that will be to the utter disfavor of those herdsmen, and make the reputation of Rome ring like silver and shine like gold."

"Exactly." Antony snapped. "Give no bribes and permit no extortions from the people. See to it that the rule of Rome is not detested in Lower Asia."

PROVIDED WITH MONEY and arms by Rome, Herod landed at the port of Ptolemais, and immediately began to gather himself an army. From Asia Minor, he secured two legions of mercenaries, and would have hired more, but there was no necessity. Galilee ran to Herod's standards almost to a man. Herod's former followers being in the lead, he was greeted with wild cries of joy.

Nor did the appearance of the king do him any injury with the people. From his diadem to his high-laced sandals, he shone and glittered. His horse gleamed in his rich furnishings. The whole was a composition in white and gold.

"King Herod! Hail to our own Herod, protector of the people, who has returned to defend us! Herod, of the sun-like splendor."

Yet, Herod was deeply concerned. He had had no communication with his family shut up in Masada since the morning that he parted from them on his way to Rome. And his fears for them were justified, for Antigonus had sent an army to besiege Masada three weeks after the departure of Herod, to seize the women and present them to his benefactor, the Parthians.

But the walls of the fort were thick and strong, and Joseph had plenty of armed and experienced fighting men around the place. He had plenty of provisions and water as well, so merely scorned his besiegers outside. However, on the day that Herod was made king at Rome, Joseph saw himself in grave danger. His water supply was all but gone. Every soul in the fort realized the danger of their situation, and there were frightened faces, dejected looks, and quiet tears.

Joseph now considered a desperate expedient. He would take 200 persons, the family and those closest to them, and attempt to flee to his kinsman, Malchus, in Petra Arabia. Before the siege had begun, a man had come to the fort to sell oil, and had told Joseph of the repentance of Malchus. So now, he considered slipping from the fort under cover of darkness and attempting to duplicate in a small way the exploit of his brother. He found some of the 200 willing to follow, but others preferring to die of thirst rather than be seized by Antigonus.

In this desperate situation, relief came in the form of a tremendous downpour of rain. The cisterns were filled to overflowing.

"It is a sign from Heaven!" Joseph shouted. "God approves of our behavior. Herod will return and rescue us all."

Joseph now went on the offensive. He took a group of his fighting men and went outside in repeated frays and drove the enemy back to a distance, but dared not attempt to lead the whole party of his charges from the fort. He had no way of knowing that the Parthians had withdrawn from Celesyria, nor of the victories of Ventidius. All he could do was maintain a desperate hope that Herod would return and raise the siege.

This was the posture of affairs while Herod now marched through Galilee. The emissary Delius had received the urgent message directing Ventidius Bassus to Masada to aid Joseph, but upon hearing that Herod had been made king and would soon return to Celesyria, the Roman general realized that his time of opportunity was growing short. With the Parthians driven out of Syria, he knew the weak position of Antigonus at Jerusalem. Antigonus would be an easy mark for a considerable bribe. So Ventidius pretended to march south in pursuit of the Parthians who were no longer there, and instead of going on to Idumea to raise the siege, he camped on the outskirts of Jerusalem and there extorted a huge bribe from the quaking Antigonus. But that was not all. Silo, next in command of the Roman forces to Ventidius, complained that that was very well for him, but he had gotten nothing. Now, in case Ventidius cared to share with him what he had frightened out of Antigonus . . .

"No. An officer expects to gain *something* to take back to Rome to provide for the future. As you know, I gained very little in the north. Never will I part with this sum which I have gained, and Herod, the intimate friend of Antony, will certainly not part with a drachma. He has no reason to fear anything from us. Antony has made him king. This is my last opportunity to get money. And a Roman is due to get more than his pay for being exiled among the heathens."

"But I too am a Roman exiled among the heathens and have gained practically nothing. What about me?"

"I have a plan. I will take with me the main body of my men, but leave you behind with enough to make a show of assisting King

Herod. Then, under the pretense of sympathizing with his case, you wring what you can from Antigonus."

This was done, and Ventidius had time to withdraw with his booty into Syria before Herod landed at Ptolemais. Silo was lingering about Jerusalem when Herod landed, and hearing news of Herod's landing and successful gathering of military force was most unwelcome to the Roman commander—what profit was Herod's presence to him?

Herod, full of anxiety for all those whom he loved, burned to march straight for Idumea to their relief, but the seaside city of Joppa alone offered him resistance. He was too experienced a military commander to leave an enemy in his rear. Annoyed at the delay, Herod planned to attack Joppa with fury, but he was delayed in that.

Silo, afraid of being caught red-handed at his game, who thought he saw an opportunity to place himself in a good light before Herod—and through him, with Antony—now broke camp and planned to join Herod in the siege of Joppa. But Jews of the Parthian party fell upon him, and would have defeated him, had not Herod hurried to his support. The Jews were beaten off, and the two now turned to punish Joppa. The port city was quickly reduced to submission, and Herod then joyfully and hastily marched to Masada.

All along the route, Herod's ranks were swelled by volunteers.

"We have received nothing but benefits from you and your family in the past. You alone preserved the national honor by saving our women from the barbarians. Accept us in your army that we may have the honor and pleasure of avenging the injuries done us by Antigonus and his Parthians."

With such a formidable and willing legion of fighters, Herod marched to the fort of Masada without any real fighting. The enemy fled at his approach.

For obvious reasons, few reunions in the history of the world have been so poignant. The great doors swung open and Herod rode through to tumble from his mount into the arms of the tearful Joseph. They hugged fiercely in the intensity of their affectionate and tearful embrace. The inmates, weeping, laughing, a little gaunt from doled-out food, less elegant than formerly, poured down the narrow stone stairs and fell upon the brothers in a flood.

"Herod! Herod! The king! He has returned a king! Our preserver! Our noble and valiant king! But let me touch him. Touch his garments. Herod! He has no equal upon the earth."

They poured through the grim portals and out into the sunlight leaping, crying, and some moving slowly and quietly weeping.

And Mariamne, disdaining all decorum, did not wait for him in the guardroom above. She was in the struggling mob fighting for her chance to reach him. Herod heard her voice, and fought to get to her as she fought to touch him.

"Beloved of my soul," Herod flamed at this proof of her love for him, "why did you not wait above for me?"

"Because I could not, my love. I have waited so long. Often my soul fainted as I waited, longed, and feared. O my love! O my love, my blessing, my gift from God!"

And seemingly blind to the multitude about them, Mariamne flung herself upon Herod's bosom, clung to him, and kissed him repeatedly upon his lips.

Shamelessly, Herod returned her kisses. His arms wrapped about her and lifted her from her feet so that her face was opposite his own.

"My queen, my beautiful and beloved queen. For the joy you have given my soul this moment, I shall employ all I have in repaying you. You have made me your humble slave. From this moment my mind, my body, my sword shall exist only to serve you well, beloved."

"My poor daughter who is without shame," came a muted voice from the stairs, and Herod looked up to find Alexandra standing on the landing of the stone stairway. She drooped on the stone railing, and looked down with displeasure. "Like a female camp-follower. But then I always knew that she was stupid."

However, Mariamne did not skulk away now. Holding her still tightly against him, Herod allowed her slim body to slide slowly and gently to the stone pavement. With his eyes still lifted to where Alexandra stood, Herod let one arm drop protectively about the slender waist of Mariamne, and thus they began to mount the stairs. When they came to the landing, Herod spoke lightly but firmly.

"Perhaps you do not know yet that I was made king of Judea while in Rome, dear Alexandra."

"Yes, I heard the shouts here below," Alexandra replied in a tight voice. "Naturally, I was surprised, because . . ."

"Since I am now king, and Mariamne being not only betrothed to me, but beloved as no woman on earth has ever been, nor shall ever be again, she is the future queen of Judea. I cannot permit her to be spoken to nor of as likened to a camp-follower, nor yet as a stupid fool, not even by her own mother."

"So there!" Mariamne said triumphantly like a small child. "Nor can Aristobulus treat me spitefully anymore, or I shall tell Herod about it."

Mariamne could be seen sticking out her tongue at her mother.

Alexandra longed to slap Mariamne's face but realized that it was no longer possible. She simply made an adjustment and smiled.

"My daughter knows that I mean no harm. Merely am I very happy over the turn of affairs, and stand ready to serve you, my son."

Herod was steadily climbing with his arm still about Mariamne. Now he had passed Alexandra. He looked back and asked off-hand, "In what capacity, O Alexandra?"

"Being of royal birth, I can instruct you in the ways of royalty, my dear. I can . . ."

"But first I am my mother's son, Alexandra. I must see and embrace her and my extravagantly beloved sister."

Herod removed his arm from about the waist of Mariamne, and ran two steps at a time up the stairs.

Here in the inelegant but spacious guardroom occurred another tender and touching scene. Herod was extremely devoted to his family. When the tension lessened, he told Cypros of his proposed plan—to transfer them all to Samaria where they could live more comfortably, and be more accessible. There was a house of forty rooms in which he would establish his mother and sister and Alexandra and Mariamne, and the wives of Phasaelus and Joseph. Naturally, his mother would govern the domicile until the war was over. Their old house servants would be sent. Also, his agents had found housing for the others who had been shut up with them in Masada. All would be pleasantly situated now.

"And today, since I have seen Mariamne again, and find myself as deeply in love with her as I felt on that night of my victory at the hill, I will build a city on the site as a memorial. And why not? At that hill I preserved the life of my beloved mother, my sister, and my betrothed among many others. I removed the obstacle on my road to Rome on that night, Mother, I found love—the purest and most enduring love that the world has ever known."

After a long, subduing silence, Cypros spoke in a whisper. "I understand. I beg God that you never find disillusionment, my son. You are so intense, you are a perfectionist and seek perfection in others. Fidelity in love and friendship is a religion with you, but you must not expect to find other worshippers on every hand. You must *not*."

"Why such an unhappy face, beloved Mother? You know me to be the least credulous of men." Herod stooped and embraced the shoulders of Cypros. "All will be well."

"And I do not like Alexandra either," Salome pouted. "She says that we are only half-Jews." The budding girl fiddled with a slender circle of gold about her wrist. "And that awful Aristobulus! He has received no proper training at all. Full of conceit and boasting. Says that he will cure me of my insolence when he is king. Ha, ha! Now *you*, my beloved brother, *are* king. Serves him right."

Herod's face clouded momentarily, then cleared.

"So you see you do not have to pay any attention to the bad-mannered puppy. But Mariamne herself said none of those things. She is completely different from the rest of her family. She has been imposed upon also by her mother. My pity for her was the beginning of my love. She will rejoice in being freed from the domination of her mother, and be bound closer to me out of gratitude."

Cypros shook her head silently.

"Once an Asamonean, forever an Asamonean. No matter what they experience, they feel no gratitude to anyone. Keep in mind the terrible fate of your father and beware."

Silence fell automatically as the sound of voices echoed from the bare corridor.

"Alexandra and that spoiled son of hers," Salome murmured.

Almost immediately, the two erupted into the guardroom.

"Herod! Herod! I hurried to tell you that while you loiter in here, the people are all outside of the fort, wandering about as they please."

"And why not, O Alexandra?"

"You ask such a thing? Suppose that Antigonus attacks?"

"Nothing would please me more, Alexandra. It would bring the war to an abrupt end. In fact, I would give him fifty talents in gold out of my own pocket if he will only attack me. But that cruel beast knows who his master is. Nothing could persuade him to come out from the security of the walls of Jerusalem." The face of the king was hard and grim. "However, he and his supporters deceive themselves if they fancy that this protection is anything more than temporary, for I shall dig him out shortly and destroy him."

"Very well," Alexandra said approvingly, but at the same time in a patronizing manner. "I am certain of your ability to defend and re-store order to the kingdom." She patted Aristobulus's head reassur-ingly. "And I am here to advise you and assist you in the conduct of the government, you know. Being royal by birth, I can be of continual service to you in the ways of royalty."

"Thank you, for your offer, Alexandra, and if I ever require such service, I shall call upon your talents."

Alexandra and her son swept from the room.

Cypros and Salome, at the point of exasperation, spoke out.

"Be quiet, Salome!" Cypros snapped. "I'll address your brother, if you please. Now, Herod, why did you allow her to offer you such insolence?"

"Mother, can't you see that I am laughing at her? What can she do against me? I humor her out of the consciousness of my strength. I indulge her stupidity because I love her daughter so profoundly, and do not wish to give pain."

"How foolish! Your beloved father said the same to me of Hyrcanus many times. And his indulgence cost him his life. Make this insolent woman know her place immediately and hold her to it. That is the voice of wisdom. Already, she is trying to usurp your power."

"And how can you endure a woman who sticks her head and neck forward like a parrot when she speaks, then snatches it backward when she finishes?" Salome asked. "It makes her detestable."

Herod laughed freely, and touched his sister's cheek with his fingers.

"You will see that I will be able to defend myself against anything that she can conceive of in her childish brain, Mother, and keep laugh-ing at her all the time. Salome, you had better be a very good girl, or I shall give you to Aristobulus as his wife."

Still laughing, he threw up his hands to defend himself against Salome's mock blows, laughingly demanding to know, "What! You will threaten the life of the king? Have you no reverence?"

Joseph, tall and athletic, entered the room, and again Herod embraced him and praised him.

"O Mother, Joseph caused me to be exceedingly proud. Because of his defense against that monster, I shall make him second in command, though he is inclined to be a bit rash in his bravery."

"Your praise, O beloved brother, is meat and I intend to earn it. I now submit to you my plans for moving the people to Samaria. We move tomorrow at dawn."

Herod quickly scanned the tablet and nodded approval. Then he lifted his head and spoke.

"I could not have planned better, O beloved and faithful Joseph, but I must make an important change. I cannot spare you to remain with our refugees. You must lead a legion under me in the fighting."

"Oh, how I hoped that you would say that, adored King-Brother. Give me action. Now, if only Pheroras . . ."

"No!" Cypros all but shouted. "I am happy to have him with us so that I can keep an eye on him, but give him no responsibilities, O Herod. I regret to say that my youngest son is interested only in amusing himself. With girls."

WITH HIS BELOVED charges safe in Samaria, Herod's soft mood vanished and he marched to Jerusalem—his own army joined with that of Silo. The winter of 39 was approaching, and it was Herod's hope to make a quick conquest and restore order to the province of Judea and begin his reign. He was highly encouraged when a steady stream of the citizenry ran to join him. As many as were fit for soldiers, there were many who were not, but all hailing him as the preserver of the nation, their protector, and the like terms of praise and approval. Herod was moved.

"These are all my people," Herod said in consultation with his chief officers. "I have no wish to fight and destroy them any further."

Herod sent a large number of the Roman soldiers into quarter for the winter so as to be available to Antony if he had need of them. The remainder were distributed over Galilee, Samaria, and Joppa. Herod and his soldiers were aligned before the walls of Jerusalem.

So far as Antigonus was concerned, he felt like he had fallen off a cliff into nothingness. Not one Roman, least of all Silo, spoke a word. Total silence. While Herod, so splendidly attired, walked up and down, showing himself to the people on the wall. He was not only restraining the attack of his men, but commanding them to do no more than defend themselves when attacked by the men of Antigonus. It was making a very favorable impression upon the spectators. Dismayed at the silence of Silo, and the fears boiling up from his belly, Antigonus ordered his men to attack and drive Herod's men back. And to the surprise of the multitudes, and to their pleasure, Herod's men fell back to safety without firing a single arrow nor dart. Herod's act was convincing. The people believed that he wanted to spare them, and he gained in stature.

But a frenzied undercover drama was being enacted. Antigonus hurriedly returned to the palace and got off a secret message to Silo. He reminded the Roman of the favors he had received from him.

Herod could catch no glimpse of Antigonus. That young man was only too aware of his peril. Seeing Herod's huge army, the Romans under Silo, and the citizenry running to join Herod, he secluded himself in the palace of the Asamoneans, looking to the north in desperate hope of seeing the Parthians returning to defend him, and alternately cursing Herod and weeping. Nor were his comments on Alexandra, her daughter and son in any way complimentary. His only hope rested in Silo, to whom Antigonus had handed over a substantial amount of money to hinder Herod in every way possible, and to persuade Rome to change its decrees and declare him king instead of Herod. So he issued orders to his men to attack Herod's army, and to kill and injure as many as possible while he waited upon the results of Silo's efforts in his behalf.

It is hardly necessary to say that his hopes were vain there. Silo knew only too well that it would have cost him his life had he dared to broach such a suggestion to Antony. He knew that it was only a matter of time before Jerusalem must fall to Herod.

*   *   *

So those contingents guarding the west wall of the palace immediately fired darts at Herod's front ranks, and sallied forth to fight hand to hand with them.

But now Herod played his high card. Three heralds from his camp paraded up and down barely out of the range of injury, and chanted in loud, very clear voices, Herod's proclamation.

"I am here to neither kill nor in any way injure a single person of my countrymen, my beloved fellow countrymen. I have come for the *good* of my fellow citizens, and for the preservation of our ancient and holy city. I am not here to take spite nor revenge against even my most bitter adversaries. I bear no grudge against even my most open enemies. Let us forget old grudges and unite as brother-Judeans for peace and progress. I am your king, and it is therefore my duty to preserve each of you, and care for you like a father over his children. Meet me in a like spirit and allow Judea to return to its old eminence, prosperity, and glory."

Seeing the hopeful, uplifting effect that this proclamation had upon the citizens and soldiery upon the wall, and the enervating effect upon the fighting men, three of the most eminent men among the party of Antigonus hurried to the palace.

"The men are now murmuring that Herod is most magnanimous of soul and are ready to submit to him," they informed Antigonus. "Never should you have included the virgins of our first families in your price to the Parthians."

"But, but it was necessary to fight against those from across the Great Sea. We are Asians, and any means are justified in defeating them."

"But not our women, especially our virgins, Antigonus. Few of us had ever really approved of that, if you must know. Now, you must get up and do something, or Herod will win everything without even having to strike a blow. Many of your soldiers are now fraternizing with Herod's. Everybody is hungry for peace. Some complain that our taxes are backbreaking, and all to furnish bribes to first the Parthians and then Ventidius Bassus to prevent Herod, and here he is before the city with a vast army in spite of the huge bribes to Ventidius. We are all in terrible danger from Herod. You must become a man of action. You must match Herod in energy."

"I laugh at your fears. I have given Silo half a talent to exercise his great influence with Rome to set aside Herod and make me king instead, now that the Parthians are gone. I have promised him five talents when he has succeeded. Herod is due for a terrible shock. When I receive him as my prisoner from Silo, I shall torture him unmercifully."

"You must do something now. Issue a proclamation to counter Herod's, or we are all dead men."

Instead of being alarmed, Antigonus was sullen.

"I will compose a proclamation, but you will see that it is useless, for in a few days, Rome will turn its favor to me and might even denounce Herod this day. I will appear on the wall in no more than an hour."

The magnificent appearance of Herod in his diadem and royal apparel, and the assurance that they would not be the targets of his soldiers' arrows and darts, had attracted thousands to the west walls to see and to satisfy their curiosity. Trust Herod to furnish excitement. It was something of a spectacle for Herod to even ride through the streets of the city. Everybody wanted to see and to hear the hero who had preserved the virgins. Would they hear any account of that romantic and historic night? The man who had fled the city in dire peril had returned a king! Judea—the people and his wife!—were upon that west wall, which they remembered that Phasaelus, as governor of Jerusalem, had restored. It had been thrown down by Pompey, and rebuilt by the handsome, ill-fated son of Antipater. The poor young man! They waited impatiently for the proclamation of Antigonus. "I address myself to the Romans. They will do unjustly if they persist in bestowing the kingdom upon Herod, son of Antipater. This Herod is first only a private citizen with no connection with royalty. In addition, he is not of Judea at all, but an Idumean."

* * *

CHAPTER ELEVEN

HEROD AT JERUSALEM

I t was little more than rutting like a senseless bull in the spring. Mariamne did not deserve Herod and so her downfall would be just, righteous. And now as the wife of Herod, she was queen of Judea—which rightfully belonged to Alexandra as the daughter and heir of Hyrcanus, which she should be allowed to exercise through her son—but Herod had gone to Rome and bewitched them and returned with her rightful crown upon his own head and making this stupid daughter of hers his queen instead of herself. Well, all was fair in love and war and this was both. Let Herod and Mariamne look to themselves. The die was cast.

The sounds of Herod's deep groans and grunts in the torture of procreation and the inciting squeals of her daughter, confirmed Alexandra in her resolution to oppose, to throw down and to destroy. Complete innocence could not produce that effect upon Herod nor any man.

* * *

A very sumptuous meal had followed the presentation of gifts by all the wedding guests. Both Herod and Mariamne had been in very high spirits, in the course of which something had occurred which elevated the bride considerably and depressed Alexandra to the same extent. As the food was being served, the spoiled young Aristobulus, seeing the under-butler attending upon Herod first, who indicated that he was to serve Mariamne always before himself, screamed: "Are you crazy? You are neglecting to serve me first. I will have you whipped!"

"Quiet," Herod ordered. "The butler will not be punished at all, for he is correct in his procedure. Your sister is now the queen of Judea, and I, the king, order that she must be served even before myself. You must get accustomed to seeing her preferred before everybody, for that is the honor due her and which I will insist upon at all times and upon all occasions."

"But my sister is only a woman, while I am a prince and Mother says—"

"But I am the *king* and your sister is now my wife and queen, and it is my wish and will that she be honored beyond all others, even myself, and I will visit punishment most severe upon any who do not so honor her. I am the power in this kingdom and my wishes must prevail."

"So now I am no longer compelled to submit to your insolent impertinences," Mariamne gloated while she shook her finger at the raging Aristobulus. "I am the queen, do you hear? Thank God, your tyranny is at an end at last." Mariamne flung triumphant eyes in the direction of her mother. "And I shall be the first one to remind you of your place if you dare to insult me, you undisciplined whelp!"

Alexandra's hand ached to slap the face of her daughter, but she could see the infatuated Herod would not bear it, so she sat in red-acid rage while Mariamne preened herself and eyed Herod with love and worship.

You stupid lump of flesh! Alexandra raged inwardly. *The day will not be long in coming when I shall tumble you off your throne and put my son in your place. That I know! Your Herod is no match for my cunning.*

Herod, utterly unaware—and if he had been, untroubled by the enmity of his mother-in-law—spent ten passionate days in Samaria with his bride before the news came to him that the foot soldiers of Sosius were approaching through the midland road while Sosius with 6,000 horses came by the coastal highway. So Herod betook himself immediately to Jerusalem to meet Sosius and to press the siege of the city in earnest.

He took a most affectionate farewell of his bride and promised to write her every day, which he did, no matter how pressed he was for time.

Nevertheless, at Jerusalem he was the dedicated soldier and commander. He set up his plan of attack against the outside wall of the temple as Pompey had done, and began to direct his war machines, his catapults and machines for scaling the walls.

With 80,000 experienced fighting men at his disposal, he felt confident of success. His adversary had only the stout walls which Phasaelus had erected to protect them.

Antigonus first relied on the scorched earth strategy to drive off his formidable foe, but Herod countered this by sending to Arabia, Syria, and even Egypt for foodstuffs and soon had the armies bountifully provisioned and sat down the siege. As usual when the city was attacked, the nation was inside the walls to celebrate Passover and Herod saw this to his advantage, for the food supplies inside would be soon exhausted. With this in mind, he set ambush to prevent anyone from running away from the city for food or trying to bring in any food.

But before he began the actual assault upon the walls, he tried psychological warfare. Again, he had it proclaimed that he was not there as the enemy of the people, but as their friend and protector. It was not his wish that a single individual of the nation should perish through this civil strife, and if those inside would but accept the decree of Caesar and the Roman senate and open the gates to him, no one would be injured, but if they refused and chose to fight him, why their blood would be upon their own hands.

To this, Antigonus made his same answer—a plea to the Romans for the preservation of himself and the priestly line since it was the tradition of old.

The eminent Pharisees Pollio and his distinguished pupil Sameas were upon the wall at the time and heard both proclamations and said, "The gates should be opened to Herod. We must be for him, for he has spoken for the people, while Antigonus, as usual, has been concerned only for himself. The gates should be opened to Herod and needless slaughter avoided."

However the followers of Antigonus had great indignation at Pollio and Sameas and had promised to have them strangled in the event that Antigonus defeated Herod and drove him away. So bitter had the partisan fighting become that neither side considered anything less than the extermination of the other. This mutual hatred was strengthened each day that the siege was prolonged.

The siege kept Herod away from the enjoyment of his bride because of the useless stubbornness of Antigonus, and the soldiers, both Roman and Jewish, became more hardened in their hatred of the foe, and one incident brought it to the boiling point.

The priests in the temple complained to Herod that they had no more victims for the daily sacrifice and begged Herod to allow them to receive some. Herod agreed readily, for he thought that this act of generosity on his part would induce them to open the gates to him, but to the contrary, they taunted him on the following day for his credulity. Five months passed before the city fell.

Herod selected forty of his dare-devil Galileans to attempt to climb the walls and open the gates. These were followed by a dozen of the Roman centurions. This group fought their way upon the walls, descended, and opened a gate. The huge army poured into Jerusalem, and first seized the temple and that part of the city nearest to it, and then spread outward over entire Jerusalem. But in his hour of triumph ... was tragedy.

Many of the Judeans or Galileans, who had retreated to join him— some out of hatred and contempt for Antigonus and some out of admiration and worship of Herod for his glorious deeds of the past— but all partisans who fell upon the partisans of Antigonus with the utmost in fury, refused to spare them even when Herod ordered them to shed no more blood. They ran into houses and slew, sparing none, they pursued them in the streets and chopped them down without mercy. They dragged priests from the temple and beheaded them and cut out their throats.

And the Romans. Herod was forced to stand with drawn sword to prevent their entering into the forbidden parts of the temple to see what they could see.

"I would consider victory worse than defeat if the temple is violated and defiled," Herod explained to Sosius. And so the Roman soldiers were driven out of the temple and as Herod and Sosius stood side by side in the Common Court, down came Antigonus from the citadel at the top and was face to face at last with his conqueror and hated successor. The eyes of the two locked in the extremes of hatred. Antigonus was beaten and he knew it. There was nothing more material that he could do against the victorious Idumean, but he could and did refuse him the honor due him. Though he realized only too well that the last word would have to come from Herod, he refused to acknowledge that he had been beaten by Herod but chose to pretend that his defeat was due to the Romans, so he went and prostrated himself before Sosius.

In a moment he realized that he had made a poor choice, for when he sought to propitiate the Roman by embracing his feet, Sosius drew them out of his reach, spat down into his face, stood upon his outstretched hands, and cried so that all could hear him, "Get to your feet, Antigonus, your charms might have had some effect upon Pacorus and Barzapharnes, they being Asiatic barbarians, but neither Roman law nor Roman custom provides for the keeping of harems. We do not maintain households of women. Unless Herod sees room for you in his household, I regard you as a prisoner of war who has shown himself the enemy of Rome and as such, subject to Roman justice and punishment."

"Though I am an Asian, Sosius, Antigonus knows only too well that it is a tradition of my family to indulge in no concubines and dancing women. I have only recently married his cousin Mariamne and therefore have no need of any other woman. Bind him and let him be sent to Antony to dispose of as he pleases." Herod then turned to the soldiers and ordered Antigonus to be put in bonds and in close custody until he could be taken to Antony.

But now another difficulty presented itself, for Sosius, being a Roman, thought that his men should be allowed to plunder Jerusalem. The siege had been long and trying and it was customary to permit the men to repay their privations by plundering a place when it was taken.

"No!" Herod shouted and bared his sword. "Do you Romans have a mind to leave me the king of an empty desert by emptying my capital of men and money? No, I tell you! If one house in Jerusalem is entered by your men or one woman violated, I will fight you!"

"My men will be terribly disappointed at receiving nothing after the long siege."

"Oh, I know the hunger of you Romans when you plunder in the provinces, Sosius, and I will not allow you to go away empty-handed. Out of my own pocket I will reward you. The people have suffered enough through Antigonus and the Parthians. It is my purpose to make their burdens lighter rather than add to them."

So Herod not only gave Sosius a gift of a generous sum of money, but to each of his soldiers as well, and sent them away happily. Hereupon Sosius dedicated a crown of gold to God and marched away, leading Antigonus in bonds to Antony, who beheaded him promptly.

Herod now suspended all official activities for three days while he rode to Samaria to move his household to the royal palace in Jerusalem, which he prudently placed under the administration of his mother.

This was done because complaints had reached his ears from the serving men and women. Their former servants were all free men and women because Antipater would have no slaves on his premises, and now there was unrest among the servants of the Asamoneans who naturally wanted the same status as their new associates, and in addition they craved to escape the domination of the Ethiopian Eunuch who had managed the Asamonean palace for many years and resorted to the lash for the slightest matter. The lash was unthinkable in the Cypros ménage. And they were treated like intelligent, reasoning beings. Cypros had the custom of calling a conference in her apartment of every servitor of her household each morning immediately after breakfast, where each submitted the requirements for his or her tasks, voiced their complaints, or expressed any other matter which moved them.

Now in the months in Samaria, all of the servants of both families had been accustomed to this system and the Asamoneans were determined not to submit to the old way, and so Herod knew it would be easier to make the change of systems with his mother in control rather than under Alexandra, who was fond of the methods of the Eunuch and would not gainsay him. This merciful change was to stand Herod in very good stead later on.

CHAPTER TWELVE

KING OF JUDEA

For the first month of his actual reign, Herod was very busy with settling government affairs by dividing tasks and making appointments and, as natural, all was done on the assumption that to the victor belonged the spoils.

Herod's well-known generosity showed itself plainly. He richly rewarded Pollio, Sameas, and numerous others of his loyal supporters with both honors and wealth as he ruthlessly stripped the adherents of Antigonus, some of whom he put to death and seized upon their wealth to bestow upon his friends. And since this category ranged from the highest Sacerdotal Pharisee to the Sadducee, Scribe, and working man, there was not a clear-cut line upon which his opponents could make a stand and rally others to them, so Herod and his party swept all before them.

His coronation was a gorgeous scene indeed. Everything was done on a magnificent scale. The rich dress of Herod and his queen evoked involuntary expressions of admiration. Both were in white and gold, and Herod's tender and fond presentation of Mariamne to the nation was unforgettable. It satisfied the dreamiest romantic, so beautiful they both appeared. Sameas said after that it was worth the war to present so beautiful a vision to the nation.

However, Herod could not exempt himself from the mutations of fate that overtake all mortals. Antony was leading his armies northward to reopen his campaign against the Parthians, and Cleopatra insisted on accompanying him as far as the Euphrates. The infatuated Roman was persuaded that the queen of Egypt did this out of fondness for his company. In reality it was to take advantage and partially satisfy her greed. She looked and estimated what was to be gained—Arabia, Palestine, and Syria—and came with the modest demand that he put to death the kings of these countries and turn the territories over to her. Having murdered all the members of her immediate family, she was now setting out to extend her activities to strangers.

Antony was deeply in love, but still he had not the urge to slay these men in such a ruthless and causeless manner, though he did bestow upon her some parts of each of the three countries. Perhaps he saw the folly of extending Egypt up to the Euphrates, which was her dream. Cleopatra then accompanied her lover as far as the ancient river, then turned back for a visit with Herod.

To his dying day, Herod could never be certain of Cleopatra's motives in this visit. Seeing Herod's tremendous hold upon Antony, since Antony had rejected both the idea of slaying Herod and of depriving him of his kingdom for her satisfaction, the Egyptian might have considered Herod a dangerous rival for the influence of her lover and resolved to turn Antony against him in another way, by making him betray himself into a dangerous position by succumbing to her overtures. Or was she really attracted to him as she had professed?

At any rate, on her return to Jerusalem she made open show of her admiration for Herod and offered him every chance to possess her. Boldly she went into his private apartment in the palace as if neither his wife nor mother or mother-in-law existed and flung herself upon him. He was offered every provocation, but Herod prudently refrained from responding. His virility revolted against his will on occasion when she flung herself down upon a couch and called to him to come to her so that she could kiss him and, clasping her arms about his neck, drew his face down and pressed her inciting kisses upon his lips.

What supported Herod most was his philosophy of friendship, handed down by his father. Rather death before the betrayal of a friend. Antony was his sworn friend, therefore romantic exercises with Antony's beloved were out of the question—not even possible. In fact her attempts to seduce him filled Herod with loathing. She had shown herself unworthy of his friend's love and devotion.

So Herod, out of his deep devotion to his friend, considered a very drastic step. This he discussed with King Malchus of Arabia, his cousin. Herod would kill Cleopatra, this unfaithful woman, while he had her in his power.

"Oh no, Cousin Herod!" Malchus admonished. "You see how insane Antony is over this woman, vile as she is. You could never bring him to see your killing her as an act of friendship. He will look upon your depriving him of her company as the worst crime of the universe and utterly inimical to himself. No, do not injure a single hair of her head, dear Cousin, if you wish to survive, for Antony instead of being grateful would surely kill you."

"It is hard to believe that a man of Antony's force and intelligence could fall so deeply under the spell of a woman. His passion passes all understanding. I do not believe that sexual intercourse, however adept she might be in pleasing him, could do all of that. What do you suppose it is?"

"I wish I knew, but do her no injury if you wish to live. In fact, do nothing that she can represent or construe as an injury when she converses with Antony. Failing in inducing you to try to seduce her so that she can accuse you of it before Antony, an insult or injury, would serve her equally well."

"That I can see now."

So Herod, while resisting Cleopatra's seductions, did her favors; he bought up the taxes of the provinces which Antony had so recently bestowed upon her to the injury of himself, of Malchus and the king of Syria to the amount of 200 talents, and accompanied her as far as Pelusium on her way back to Alexandria. Then he sighed with relief, but much too soon, for though Cleopatra was gone, she had left a manifestation behind. At first to his amusement and then to his dismay, his wife and mother-in-law were imitating every gesture and mannerism of Cleopatra as closely as possible. It was as ridiculous as it was distressing, for they seemed to reason that her moral approach to life must be estimable seeing how far it had carried her. And Herod was utterly outdone when he perceived the artificial airs that Mariamne was assuming.

"Am I not more beautiful than Cleopatra, beloved? And more seductive?"

"Why do you ask me such a silly question, Mariamne?" Herod cried as he released himself from what had been a most satisfactory embrace until she spoke. "You are nothing alike, thank God."

"But I must be more alluring, my husband, since you preferred my embraces to hers."

"No, your purity of soul and body makes you preferable to her. Do not look upon Cleopatra as a pattern neither of beauty nor of behavior. I prefer you innocent as I found you."

"My mother says that since you prefer me to Cleopatra, who is almost old enough to be my mother, probably Antony would also prefer me."

"What nonsense you have gotten into your pretty head, my treasure. Forget it all and just remain sweet and pure in body and soul as you have always been. Give me another kiss, now."

To his astonished displeasure, his wife now assumed that she was in a position to bargain with him and demanded a ring of great value that his mother owned and which had been in the family for three generations, and it was with difficulty that he made Mariamne see that it was not his to give, it being the property of his mother. He was so disturbed that on the morrow he took counsel of his mother.

"I am glad that you have come to me, beloved son, for you appear to have every kind of knowledge except the nature of women. I want you to realize that you have two implacable enemies, both women, and for the same reason. Did it never occur to you that up until the very hour of your marriage to Mariamne, her mother had the hope of becoming your wife?"

"No, because the idea is too ridiculous, not only because of her age, but she is too interfering and would try to assist me in affairs of government. Few women of the earth have the ability to offer advice as you did for my noble father, and never did you thrust it upon him, but gave it only when he asked it of you, but this pushing woman would drive me mad in a few days with her importunities. I have had to tell her on three different occasions that I do not require her assistance in government."

"No woman likes to have her affections scorned and rejected and that is what you have done, and she will never forgive you because of it. The same with the queen of Egypt."

"That cunning, conniving creature. Why, I am not certain that she loved me at all, but set a snare to destroy me with Antony."

"That could be true, Herod, but still she had been told repeatedly that she is a beautiful and irresistible woman who has brought down such game as the Great Caesar and Antony. Her self-love could not fail to be cruelly injured by being scorned by the king of a small nation. She will never forgive your indifference to her charms."

"But I cannot go about making love to every woman who is attracted to me for one reason or another, Mother. They are legion. Like my esteemed father, I require the attentions of but one woman at a time and that of my own choosing."

"Correct and honorable, but now without your willing it, you have these two implacable women as your enemies. At one time, I thought to advise you to separate Alexandra from her daughter to prevent her corrupting Mariamne, seeing that she has been so thoroughly dominated by her mother all of her life and that her mother can make disturbances between you, but now I think differently. If you sent her away from the palace it would merely free her to plot and conspire against your reign with your enemies. You must keep her under your eye. Being an Asamonean, she is fond of intrigue and never will accept the facts and will continue to conspire to get the throne for her son."

"You are very observant, mother, and I agree with all you say. I just hope that she cannot corrupt the mind of Mariamne."

*　*　*

"I have told Alexandra, this poor, grief-stricken mother, that I would make her case my own, beloved. When I think of that poor innocent youth done out of his life like that, I cannot bear it! The case cries out that justice be done, and this time Herod should be brought to justice and executed for his numerous crimes of barbarity," Cleopatra prevailed upon Antony.

It would be excellent drama if it could be set down that Antony had asked Cleopatra, *Was this Aristobulus younger and more deserving of life than your brothers—neither of whom were allowed to attain the years of twenty—or than your younger sister Arsinoe, who was very young and innocent and had no ambitions for government when you had me drag her*

from her prayers in the temple of Diana at Ephesus and hack her to death?
Why is it that the death of this young Jew whom you have never seen affects
you and stirs your sense of justice so deeply, beloved? Why are you so eager
for the death of my friend, Herod?

Antony might indeed have made such queries, but if he did, it has
not been set down by any of his numerous biographers. What he actually did was to promise to send for Herod to stand his trial on the
accusation, which he did.

Overjoyed, Cleopatra sent off a letter to Jerusalem immediately to
Alexandra advising her to send along every scrap of evidence against
Herod that she could find. She was disappointed when Alexandra's answer came, for even Cleopatra could see that it was very weak: 1. Herod
was not at the scene—near the fishpond when and where Aristobulus
was drowned. Many witnesses could and would testify that Herod was
inside the house in plain view of several house guests. 2. The drowning occurred after dark, when many young men were swimming in the
pond because the night was very hot, yet not one could testify when
and how the young high priest had drowned. They were all splashing
around in the water and, after a time, it was discovered that Aristobulus
had drowned. That was all. Had he merely lost his footing in the melee
and drowned by accident? Or had some hand held his head under until he suffocated? Nobody could be found to testify to either theory.
Aristobulus was merely found to be dead when the majority decided
to leave the pond because of darkness. In the seventeenth year of his life
the youthful high priest was dead by drowning. That was all.

So Antony came to Laodicea in company with Cleopatra and commanded Herod to come and defend himself against the charges which
Alexandra and Cleopatra brought against him.

In preparation for his journey into Asia Minor, Herod appointed his
uncle Joseph, brother of his mother, as procurator during his absence.

"I know that I am innocent of the charge, Uncle Joseph, but I am

THE LIFE OF HEROD THE GREAT

uneasy because I am aware of Cleopatra's ill will. She may over-sway Antony against all Roman law and he behead me.

"I have a private charge to give you. You know my vast affections for my wife. So great is my love that even in death, I cannot bear to think of any other man possessing her. In the case that Antony be-heads me, I command you to kill Mariamne so that she remains mine alone, even in death. In addition, often in our amours we have sworn to each other that neither of us wished to survive the other. Promise to do this for me, Joseph, or I will not rest in my grave."

"Your love for Mariamne is truly a marvelous thing, Herod. It is like a poem by a great Greek artist like Homer. It is for the ages. I pray of course that you will escape blame for the death of Aristobulus before Antony, for the accusation is unjust. But in the event that Cleopatra prevails over reason and justice, I will immediately slay Mariamne. But if I were you, and you win your case before Antony, I would slay Alexandra immediately upon my return to Judea. That vile maker of trouble and spreader of scandal. She is the one who should have been drowned."

"True, Joseph, and someday if she keeps to her present course I shall have her strangled, but the time is not right as yet. I will allow her to contrive her own execution. Being an Asamonean, her unbalanced love of power will bring her to her end as it has the other members of that miserable family. My beloved wife is all that is good of that tribe. It is a mystery how anything so beautiful and good as she could have come from that house."

So assured by his uncle Joseph, Herod set off for Laodicea, a city in Phrygia founded by Artiochous Theos and named for his wife.

Herod found Cleopatra there with Antony and very zealous in her accusations, but finally Antony interrupted to insist that, by Roman law, a defendant must be allowed to state his side of a case. He pointed out before Herod spoke that no evidence had been presented that

Herod was at the scene of the drowning, and his only connection with the murder, if it was a murder, which had not been established, could easily have been an accidental drowning there in the darkness, and if it was a murder, Herod could not be connected with it for under the political situation, there must have been many men who desired the death of the youth. It was impossible to condemn a man under such slender evidence. It would be the rankest injustice to do so. Herod could only be connected by the suspicions in the mind of Alexandra, who stood to gain—in her hopes at least—by the death of Herod.

In dismissing the charge against his friend, Antony told Cleopatra that she was, in the future, to refrain from meddling in affairs of Herod's government. She was to keep in mind that Herod was a king, not a subordinate officer in Antony's army, and kings should not be required to give an account of every move they made or they would not be kings indeed. Then he instructed Herod on his return to Jerusalem to command his mother-in-law to keep her mouth out of affairs of government under pain of severe punishment. There could be no peace and order with women meddling in affairs.

Then, seeing the unhappy face of Cleopatra, the fond Antony explained himself to her.

"Well, beloved, leave Herod's kingdom and revenues alone. He is much too valued a friend and assistant for me to injure. Remember his valuable assistance to me at Samosata only recently. I will bestow upon you certain provinces in Syria with their revenues in place of Judea, which you want."

Cleopatra leaped to her feet and ran to where Antony reclined on a long chair and, wrapping her arms about his neck, kissed him repeatedly on his mouth, his forehead, his cheeks.

"Under such circumstances, I am persuaded of the complete innocence of Herod as you are and from this very hour on, I abandon the cause of Alexandra and her offspring. When do I take possession of my new provinces in Syria and begin to collect my revenues?"

Antony looked up at the woman who cold-bloodedly displayed her greed and smiled fondly.

"How covetous you are for things, but as long as you are as greedy for my company as you appear to be, I don't object to your insatiable craving for little things like jewels and ornaments—female playthings."

ALL THIS OCCURRED on the first day of Herod's arrival at Laodicea, but Antony, ever fond of his company, detained him for a week more, insisted on Herod taking every meal with him, sitting with him on the tribune, the constant companionship of former times. And as usual, they made each other presents.

Overjoyed at the outcome of his trial, Herod sent off letters to his wife, to Joseph, to Pollio, and to his mother relating what had happened.

It was on his fifth day with Antony that Herod wrote these epistles, and his disposition was that the time he was away, even including the five days it required to journey to Phrygia, that he had been away from Jerusalem no time at all. But everything is by comparison or relative.

On this tenth day of Herod's absence from Jerusalem, Alexandra ran to Joseph with great alarm, or simulated alarm, on her face and demanded that he arrange a heavy military escort to conduct her and Mariamne to a Roman camp just outside of Jerusalem for their protection.

"Protection? Where is the danger?"

"Have you not heard the rumor that is all over Jerusalem to the effect that Antony has tortured and killed Herod?"

"Not a word of it. From what source did you hear it?"

"Oh, it's just all around. No particular source. And I think it prudent for us to seek safety in the Roman camp in case disturbances arise in the city on hearing of Herod's death and we can be with the Romans and friends of their commanders and dispose them to restore the government to my family."

"But I have heard no such report, Alexandra, and even if I did, I could make no move until I was assured that report was true."

However, Alexandra was hard at him to get her and Mariamne to the Roman camp anyway, just in case. For once in the Roman camp, she could induce them to conduct her and Mariamne to Antony, wherever he might be, and when Antony was confronted with the beauty of Mariamne, he would bestow the government of Judea upon her as the Great Caesar had done for Cleopatra in Egypt. Alexandra was eager and anxious to depart at once for the Roman camp in any case.

* * *

CHAPTER THIRTEEN

MARIAMNE ACCUSED

H erod had his right hand upon the rod of authority, and that was the way they operated. It proved so satisfactory to both Caesar and the Roman senate as well as to the people in the provinces that the moment that any Roman governor in Asia complained of any difficulties, Caesar sent him word: "O, turn that province over to Herod and come on home."

It was particularly satisfying to Herod and the Jewish nation that there was not a single Roman official in Palestine. There was of course a Roman president of Syria, but his power was emasculated by Caesar for whoever he was, he was instructed to take no action until he had consulted Herod and had his proposed step approved by him.

With his new honors and added promises, Herod returned to Jerusalem in a softened mood. Again he was conscious of the pulse of night and day and Mariamne was a heart-remembered name. Travel weary and finding several documents on government affairs awaiting his perusal, he gathered them and stretched out on his bed to read them and called Mariamne to come and lie beside him as he read.

Mariamne came into the room, but refused to lie down beside him, telling Herod in a most insolent manner that she detested him and could no longer bear the thought of living with him.

"Have I not always been kind, generous, and indulgent with you, Mariamne?"

"If you call murdering my brother and my grandfather kind and generous, yes!"

Now Herod flung the scrolls aside and leaped to his feet.

"I will not tolerate those slanders concocted by your lying, covetous mother anymore, Mariamne. Lies made to cover up the gross crimes and numerous murders of your own family. My noble father was poisoned at the table of your grandfather who pretended to be his bosom friend, my beloved brother Phasaelus was lured to his death by that same feeble-minded monster, Hyrcanus. Your vile slut of a mother has urged and prodded her own son, her father, and possibly her daughter to their death to satisfy her own unholy greed for power. If you utter that atrocious lie again that I killed your criminal grandfather and stupid brother, I will strangle you here and now with my own hands. Get out of my presence at once. I no longer wish to lie down with you again. Your evil spell over me is broken at last, get out!"

Herod's rage was so great that he might indeed have slain Mariamne if his valet had not heard his loud and angry voice and run into the room and restrained him. Mariamne, at last awakened to the perils of her insolence, fled away in fright. She told her mother of Herod's threatening behavior, but Alexandra was in no way disturbed.

"What can come of it, my beautiful baby, but further submission on your husband's part? You know how insanely he loves you. Out of his enslavement to your beauty and your royal birth, Herod will merely look upon it as another instance of your fits of ill-humor, and seek to dispel it by petting you and buying you off with presents of new ornaments. Do not let his show of temper depress you. Return to him now and smile affectionately and his anger at you will be instantly dissipated."

From past experience, this view of affairs seemed reasonable to Mariamne and she acted upon her mother's advice.

But she did not find the Herod that her mother had predicted, nor that she expected. As she entered the room, Herod's cup-bearer was taking his leave, and for a second, new fear attacked Mariamne, for she remembered the little matter of the love potion she had given the man to mix into the wine which he served to the king. Then she grew firmer. This servant would not dare to accuse her to Herod. The loyalty of the king to her would never hear it.

*   *   *

"I am aware of your cold-blooded villainy, Mariamne. You and Alexandra are less intelligent and therefore less sensitive than swine who at least have some consciousness of family relations; and Time, that sun-made treasure, brings you nothing.

"You have taken pains to have me understand that you do not love me. Very well, I accept your conclusion and match it with equal indifference to you in the future, for I realize that I have brought it upon myself by my excessive love and worship of you and to my own injury, for a man in love cannot be true to his own interests. It is impossible to love and be wise, for no man ever thinks as much of himself as he does of the one he loves; his weakness is not only plain to others but also to the one he loves. And it has been proven repeatedly everywhere that if the love he offers is not felt to an equal degree by the object of his love, he is rewarded by a secret contempt. In every love affair there is either reciprocation or contempt and my love for you has been rewarded by contempt. And out of your own mouth I learn that my love is rewarded by your hatred."

"Oh, I was mad. I do not hate you."

"Your actions prove that you do, Mariamne. Deianira, the wife of Hercules, caused his death by presenting him with a poisoned cloak. You have tried to bring about my destruction through a potion in my wine cup, which you tried to persuade my cup-bearer was nothing more than a love potion to increase my love for you. He was too loyal to give it to me without advising me about it first."

"The man lies. You will not allow him to calumniate me so, I am certain."

"Why should I doubt him? I have been shown the container, which originated in Egypt. He could not have obtained it himself, Mariamne. And further I have the memory of other attempts of you and your mother upon my life. Such as the lying accusation to Antony through Cleopatra in the death of your brother. You sought to have my friend Antony take me out of your path to power for you. With your own mouth you accused me of the murder of your grandfather because I defended myself against the snare that he and your mother laid for me. These slanders you and Alexandra caused to be spread all over Jerusalem in the hope that the nation would rise and kill me.

"With all these instances of your hatred in mind, why should I refuse to believe that you would draw back from taking me off by stealth as your grandfather did to my esteemed father at your grandfather's own table? And all of these attempts you have made upon my life not because I have failed to treat you with love and indulgence such as few women of the earth have ever enjoyed, but at the urging of your mother who is mad to rule. To the extent that you have rejected the fact that I picked you up from nothing and made you a queen, but you must be persuaded by Alexandra to wrest the throne from me and rule through a line that has been rejected by both the people of Judea and Rome, which alone has the power to choose and name the ruler of Palestine.

"And now, no longer blinded by love, I am resolved to give you the opportunity you have so long sought. I will allow you to stand your trial for your crimes against me and the peace and stability of the nation. So long has your insane mother deluded you that the nation craves to restore your family to power, that I shall allow your pretensions to meet the realities. Turnabout is fair play. For at least six of the eight years since our marriage, you have been accusing me, but without success. Now I shall accuse you this day and let the 100 judges decide your guilt or innocence."

"You would not do such a thing, my Herod."

"Oh, but I shall, and I am no longer your Herod. It is you who said that you could no longer bear to live with me. I now free you to exert the tremendous power over the nation of your dreams. Now I realize how strongly you depend upon Sohemus to assist you in government once you are rid of me, and that your asking a position for him in government the day I left for Egypt was so that he could gain experience. I know how he has been conspiring with you and Alexandra for the entire year since I went to Rhodes to stand my trial before Caesar and your disappointment and rage when I returned not only safely, but with added trust and responsibilities under Caesar and the Roman senate. You could not bear my touch for you had dedicated yourself to Sohemus."

Mariamne sat with bowed head and in silence now.

"Sohemus I shall order to be slain immediately, but I shall allow you to stand your trial on the morrow, so that it cannot be charged that I have acted without justice towards you. If the judges free you of the charges, then you are free. Now go seek the counsel of your brilliant mother and otherwise prepare yourself to stand your trial tomorrow."

Mariamne went precipitously to the apartment of Alexandra and told her of the alarming development and was comforted.

"I always told you that Herod was a fool and not the ingenious man that the nation is deceived that he is. You have two weapons that he cannot combat successfully: your eminent beauty and your noble birth. The judges will never condemn you, and the city will rise to your defense. Fear nothing, beloved. Tomorrow is our day of triumph, Mariamne. Show no fear but contempt of your husband before the judges and walk out in triumph."

"You do not think then that I should turn aside his anger, prostrating myself before him and begging his forgiveness for my past arrogance and promising to submit myself to him in the future as a wife is supposed to do?"

"By heavens, no, Mariamne. When we have this opportunity at last to defy him and accuse him of his cruelties before such eminent men of the city? No, let us bring about the destruction of this half-Jew and restore the power of the Asamoneans."

"Do you think Herod's Idumean birth matters to many, Mother? It has not appeared so in the past. He has brought security and peace and such wealth as the nation has never seen before in all its history and so the Soffereim even praise him."

"You are deceived for many who praise him with their lips hate this outsider in their hearts and pray for the restoration of the line of Aaron. They will support our cause, have no doubts."

"Herod wields a tremendous influence everywhere in the nation, Mother. He is fortified on all sides and hard to defeat."

"But I shall defeat him, beloved. I shall send around word to all members of my party this day to make your trial a show of our strength and a public defiance of Herod by acquitting with a censure of Herod."

"Well, all right, Mother, I trust my fate to your hands and rest on it."

"You do well, my child."

CHAPTER FOURTEEN

TRIAL OF MARIAMNE

The hour of trial in the hall of justice was set for the hour after noon so that all could be completed by sundown according to Jewish law.

Herod did not enter the court in triumph, as might have been expected by the unthinking. He all but crept in and took his seat without any response to public salutation. The worshipping multitudes outside in the streets could not see what Herod saw. The woman who had spent the night in bonds and close custody was the tender, sweet bride of less than ten years before, the soft-eyed mother of his five children, with Herod seeing the pictures as she presented each infant for his inspection and approval. Five infants as fruit of their passion—three boys and two girls. Hours of consummation, confirmation, and reconfirmation. Love pure, love unabashed, with the illusion of bliss eternal hanging over them.

So how had they reached this present dismal point? As an individual, no doubt his sins and deficiencies were many, but his conscience was clear in the matter of kindness and appreciation and protection of his wife. But had he failed in the matter of protection? Long before his marriage he had been aware of the ambitious domineering nature of Alexandra and her ruthless methods, also of the weak will of Mariamne. Why had he allowed Alexandra to remain in his household and thus expose Mariamne to her ruthless tactics? To prevent Alexandra from fomenting trouble for his government. Why had he not expelled her from his household and when she made trouble, executed her like any other seditious malefactor? Because Alexandra was the mother of Mariamne, and love had made a coward of him.

Well, here he was facing cold facts at last. On at least two occasions, Mariamne had conspired for his death and showed sharp disappointment at his survival. His was no longer a marriage, they were just meeting and rutting like a pair of animals in the darkness and parting just as coldly at dawn. The fact that she was willing to accuse him so readily where there was no valid evidence told him all, and he should have taken this attitude on her part more seriously long before. The only generous thing to do was to allow her choice, and if it led her into water above her head, that was her own concern, no longer his.

God knew that he had defended and protected her in the past, not only against his mother and sister, but her own folly. Well, she wanted to be rid of his presence, and now she would get her wish, whatever the judges found. They had shared the same bed and roof for the last time.

The judges, the learned men in their official robes, entered almost in a body and took their seats. The seats of the spectators quickly filled, the people as always licking their lips for the sight of cruelty and suffering, and especially of those in high places. The story of his extravagant love and indulgence of Mariamne was well known all over the nation and indeed over Asia. To see this pampered and indulged one on trial for her life drew spectators like flies to honey. The accommodations were overrun in a matter of minutes and the aisles filled with standees.

Into this packed and highly charged room Mariamne was led, closely followed by Alexandra. In spite of everything it tore at his heart to behold his wife in the unbecoming black of a defendant and with her wrists bound with heavy cords. But an inner voice bade him to control his emotions for these two had tried very hard to bring him to the same place, impatient to hear that his head had rolled. He at least refrained from exhibiting morbid pleasure in any unhappy termination. Their eyes did not meet, but Alexandra took pains to stare him down in a very defiant manner, indicating that she expected to vanquish him in this room this day.

Mariamne's slow mind had not yet calculated the possibilities of the situation and she appeared unconcerned. Her face did not even change color as her husband was called upon to state his accusations. Not until Herod's recital (which covered the time from his journey to Laodicea to stand his trial before Antony to the revelation of his cupbearer of the potion and compositions Mariamne had counseled him to put in Herod's cup) touched upon the name of Sohemus, was there the slightest reaction on the part of Mariamne. Then the upper part of her body shook slightly as if she shivered from cold, and blood stained her otherwise pale cheeks a deep pink.

One Amos, who was a ramrod of tradition and naturally contemptuous of women, noted this and nudged Pollio, who sat next him. "But observe her now, Pollio. The scarlet of her cheeks and the shiver no doubt from the memory of pleasant embraces with this Sohemus. I always contended that Herod violated our traditions by allowing his wife and that contentious lover of strife, Alexandra, too much liberty of action, setting a bad example for the women of the nation. And when it comes to the place where a wife feels secure in plotting to replace her husband in government and boldly telling him that she hates him and refuses to lie down by him, you can be assured that the other man has already taken the place of her husband in her affections. It is not to be borne or Jerusalem will become a very nest of female infidelity."

"Perhaps it is only her stupidity instead of actual infidelity. It is my opinion of Mariamne that she is no better endowed mentally than her grandfather Hyrcanus was. And bear in mind that she was exposed to the influence of that bold ambitious and trouble-making Alexandra, who will not abandon the impossible dream of becoming governor of our nation."

"Which our nation would never bear." Amos threw a look of utmost distaste in Alexandra's direction. "This tendency must be put down with the utmost in punishment to teach all of the women of our country to know their place. This is not Greece, this is Jerusalem, nor are we a race of degenerate Greeks. I am now fully persuaded that what she represented as a love potion was in reality a powerful poison, for, disappointed that her husband escaped the ax of Caesar, disrupting her plans to rule with the assistance of Sohemus, who had become her lover in Herod's absence, she then resolves to remove Herod from their path by poison."

"If your conclusions are correct, and it is indeed possible," Pollio ruminated slowly, "this Mariamne is certainly a dangerous woman. And what need had she for a love potion, for it is universally understood that Herod loved her to an extravagant degree and indulged her slightest whim. No request that she made was too hard for him to grant her. Therefore her insolence and hatred of him are hard to understand."

"Not for me," Amos snapped. "When a woman has transferred her affections, she can be the utmost in contention and cruelty. She yearned for the company of Sohemus and, being barred from it by the presence of Herod, she hated Herod to the last extremity. When a woman does not gain the man she wants, God help the one she does get. In the past I have not approved of Herod because I was persuaded that he tended to ignore and violate our traditions, but in this matter he is correct, and who could fail to pity his case today? So successful and fortunate in all else, yet the humblest laborer in the fields has been more fortunate than he at home."

"And being often with him and at the palace as you know, he deserves better than he got from these women. And all the fault lies at the door of Alexandra. Indeed, it is she who ought to be tried instead of her stupid daughter whom she has so corrupted. Nowhere on earth could you have found a more affectionate and devoted wife than Mariamne in the early years of her marriage. But it did not satisfy Alexandra that her daughter had been made queen by Herod, for no opportunity for her to seize power came of it. Hence the creation of disturbances to do away with Herod so that she could gain the government herself."

Alexandra was not blind. As the testimony of Herod and other witnesses—most of them of his household—went on, showing the hard nature and insolent behavior of Mariamne and her bold and open statements of her hatred of her husband, and regrets that he had not been slain by Caesar, more judicial brows lifted in astonishment at her boldness and hardness under overwhelming kindness and indulgence of her fits of temper, even to the slapping of his face on occasion; their faces hardened as they glared at Alexandra. And her cock-sure attitude collapsed after the judges had conferred briefly after hearing from Mariamne that she did indeed hate her husband because she believed him responsible for the deaths of her brother and her grandfather.

"And what proof did you have of your husband's guilt in these deaths?" Eleazer, the president of the court, asked her. "Did you not know that Hyrcanus was brought before this same court and condemned on abundant evidence of his guilt? Only a mind poisoned against your husband could have produced the suspicions which you say made you hate Herod. As to the end of your brother, there is not one of us here who is not familiar with all that has been learned about that situation."

*   *   *

The wife of Caesar wielded much less power in Rome than Mariamne did in Judea. And now the bailiff, a very common, rude man, was pulling and shoving her around without peril. She was still the daughter of the Asamoneans, still as beautiful as she was yesterday, but different from what her mother had assured her, it availed her nothing. The only change in her situation was that she was no longer regarded as the wife of Herod. She stole a glance at his unhappy face. A smile and a nod from that handsome head and all this nightmare of horrors would vanish. But how could she seek it now, when she had scorned it in the palace?

Mariamne had not been led away to her execution immediately because of Sameas. He was extremely fond of Herod and, seeing the misery in his face, Sameas leaned forward and suggested to the president that Mariamne not be put to death but confined in one of the strong fortresses for the rest of her life.

"The love affair between Herod and Mariamne has been a thing of such beauty as to shed a rosy light over all the world. Indeed it has equaled or surpassed those romances famous in history like Hero and Leander and not even inferior to Astarte and Adonis. It is my belief that if Mariamne is preserved alive that she and Herod will be reunited to each other."

"The suggestion is worthy of consideration, Sameas. After all, she is the mother of five children by Herod, and perhaps she is the victim of false testimony by her former servants."

It was at this moment that Alexandra, terrified that she herself might not escape the same sentence as her daughter, leaped from her seat and put on a show of ignorance of her daughter's behavior towards Herod. She ran to where Mariamne sat and began to denounce her so that all could hear her. She cried that her daughter was an evil woman and most ungrateful to her generous and indulgent husband, and therefore her punishment was just for her arrogant and insolent behavior in not making proper returns to Herod, who had been a benefactor to both of them. To give verisimilitude to her hypocrisy, Alexandra now began to tear her hair and disarray her clothes.

However, she convinced nobody, and there arose sounds of disgust and disapproval from among the spectators.

As for Mariamne, she sat in silence for some minutes as Alexandra went on in this distasteful and deceitful manner, but finally she said, "Please, Mother, have some regard for decency and personal dignity and do not expose yourself in a manner so unbecoming. You have proved a bad advisor as well as prophet. Now hear the consequences of your activities with whatever composure you can muster."

Sameas threw up his hands in despair for, without being told by the president, he knew that any chance of commuting the sentence of Mariamne had now been destroyed by her mother, especially in view of the fact that Cypros and Salome were present and a handle had now been furnished for objections by them to preserving the life of Mariamne. The testimony of Mariamne's own mother had done her more damage than anything Herod or his witnesses had uttered. The president gestured for the queen to be taken on to her execution.

Mariamne went to her death without casting one glance at Herod or even her mother, in a manner so stolid that some wondered if she really comprehended what was happening. But Herod wept without control as she went by.

Mariamne did not lose her composure until she saw her executioner approach her with the cord in that desolate spot outside the city walls. Involuntarily then, she covered her throat with her hands and cried out to Herod. This was too awful. Twenty-four hours before, had she but cried out in fear, Herod would have summoned every man in his armies to defend her but now that loneliness that surrounds every human at the point of death was upon her. The hour when none can reach nor help. Even though in bed and surrounded by a host of relatives, friends, physicians, and spiritual advisors, one walks those final steps alone. Mariamne felt it and rebelled against departing the warmth of life for the cold loneliness of death.

"Keep your hands off me. I am the queen of Herod."

"You were the queen, Mariamne, but you hated the man who made you queen and lavished his love, power, and wealth upon you. All of you accursed Asamoneans suffer from the same disease—the will to rule where you are not wanted—and one by one you all pay with your lives for your unholy ambitions. Will none of you never learn to be content with your good fortune?"

"I will if you will spare me long enough to make an appeal to my husband for forgiveness for my crimes against his love. He will make you rich if you will spare me and hide me somewhere until he can talk with me and compose our differences. For now, I see that my enemy was not my husband but my vile mother. Spare me for but one night and notify my husband."

"The court did not order me to compose your quarrels but to strangle you. I am not so foolish as to risk my own execution to spare you. As always, Asamoneans are happy to sacrifice the lives of others to spare their own. Joseph, a good man, gave you his sympathy and you betrayed him to his death. I am glad to destroy the last of you who have shed rivers of Jewish blood and have been such a burden and trouble to our nation. My hope is that I will be ordered soon to perform the same task upon your hateful mother. Down with your hands, woman!"

With composed dignity, Mariamne lowered her hands, felt the harsh cord touch and tighten, then a loud ringing in her ears and her eyes straining from their sockets, then blessed nothingness. And just as Sameas had feared, Mariamne was punished for her sins, by death, but Herod was punished more drastically by life.

As in those final minutes of Mariamne in the boulder-strewn desolation of the Hill of Skulls outside the city walls, Herod, too, awakened to the fact that he had reached the point of no return. Now there could be no reconciliation and beginning all over again to recapture his lost love. Mariamne was dead. Dead. Never to burn away annoyances with her hot, soft body. It was too late to do what he should have done years ago and rid his house of Alexandra, if even by death. Now he blamed himself bitterly for not having protected his wife from her bold and conscience-less mother. He was therefore more responsible for Mariamne's death than she was herself.

Herod fell into a melancholy mood of self-accusations and memory of lost love, and as days and weeks passed, sank so low that his physicians despaired of his life. He could find comfort nowhere and in nothing. He came to the point where he forgot that she was dead and went about calling her name and conversing with her as if she were present.

He was persuaded at last by his mother to leave the place where he had lived so intimately with his wife, in the hope of lessening his grief and self-blame, and at last he consented to go to the estate of a friend in Samaria.

Now Alexandra remained at Jerusalem, though not at the palace, for neither Herod nor his relations would have tolerated that. On hearing of Herod's serious illness and of his absence, because of his illness, from the city, her old ardor for power came down upon her. She made a serious attempt to get the two fortresses which commanded Jerusalem into her hands by a stratagem.

Alexandra went to the commanders of these strongholds and said that they should deliver them into her hands to hold for the sons of Herod so that in the event that Herod died of his present malady these indispensable strong places would be in the hands of one who would defend the rights of Herod's sons, and prevent anybody else from seizing upon the government. And in case of his recovery, nobody would be more zealous in preserving them for him as one of his own family as she was.

However, these arguments did not make a favorable impression upon the commanders. Both were old and firm friends of Herod's and were familiar with what he had suffered at the hands of Alexandra. One of the commanders, Achiabus, was his cousin, German and extremely attached to Herod. Now both of these men, after a conference, sent messengers to Samaria to let Herod know of Alexandra's scheme.

Herod lost no time over his decision in reply to his faithful officers.

"Slay that evil woman at once and purge the nation of infamy."

This was done at once and with alacrity. Alexandra was loved by few and her death was welcomed by the multitudes.

It is possible that his order to destroy Alexandra freed Herod from his sense of guilt in the death of Mariamne, for he began to recover almost immediately. It was at this time that Herod met with one Judas, a very old man who was eminent not only among the sect of the Essenes, but honored all over Jerusalem for his virtues and his ability to foretell the future. He was at the head of a school of the Essenes and numerous young men gathered there to be taught by him. Judas journeyed to Samaria to where Herod lodged and revealed to the king that he had long been the intimate friend of his father, Antipater; therefore Herod's distress concerned him greatly. He now proposed to heal Herod of his despondency of soul.

"But peace is not in Samaria, nor yet in Judea, my son. Arise this very hour and be off to the community of the Essenes, which is situated in the Desert of Quietude east of the Jordan, and submit yourself to the ministrations of the brethren there. I have sent word that you are coming to them."

And to the surprise of his host, Herod made no objections, but gathered his clothing and departed immediately for the place which was very near the east bank of the Jordan as it approached the Dead Sea.

The head of the monastery received him very kindly and assigned him to the same cell which Antipater, even unknown to his family, had once occupied for a week.

"Cease to torture your soul over the death of a woman who had a great capacity for pride and ambition, but little for love, son," the director told him. "Never did Mariamne really love you, but at first she was content with the extreme pleasure which she obtained from your magnificent body, for she was, by nature, addicted to the lusts of the body. You have lost nothing but an evil obstruction to your abilities. Your finest hour is yet to come."

To aid in his recovery, Herod was assigned work like the other brethren and began to learn to cut stone. Hence forever after, his sympathy and affiliation with the guild of the stone-cutters and masons. He even provided himself with a suit of their working clothes and went from his palace on occasion to be present at the meetings of the guild, which was a great source of Herod's power with the multitudes, for these men would circulate among other workers speaking in support of the policies of the king and opposing those among the wealthy who opposed Herod.

After a month at the monastery, Herod was dismissed as cured and returned to Jerusalem. It was from this experience that the influence of the Essenes was to cling to Herod until the end of his life, and to be so obvious that it was complained of by the Pharisees and others, but without effect upon the king. But Herod was not the only instance among the wealthy and powerful who had Essene sympathies. Numerous men among the principal families of Jerusalem were secret friends of the brethren, and held them in esteem for their virtuous way of life, and it was commonly said that the simple word of an Essene was worth more than the oath of the high priest.

On his return to the capital, Herod astonished the city by taking up the administration of government in a vigorous manner as if nothing had occurred. His younger brother Pheroras had a new pair of hunting dogs sent to him from Armenia, and he and Herod spent a happy day hunting to try out the dogs.

Herod further demonstrated his return to himself by sending to Cos, a small island off the coast of Egypt where the finest silk was to be obtained, for lengths of white silk, for a new tunic and outer robe. The sewing women of the palace were set to work embroidering the scenes of Herod's military victories on the tunic so that they marched round his body like the frieze on the Parthenon.

Now Herod had brought expert gold- and silversmiths from Damascus and established them in a house in the Valley of the Cheesemongers so that the young men of Judea who had the inclination might become proficient in this art. He now commissioned them to create for him costly and unique ornaments for himself and his family. He was very zealous about it because Caesar was about to finish with the settlement of affairs in Egypt and had notified Herod that he would return to Rome through Asia in order to pay him a visit and would spend two days in Jerusalem.

In addition to his own personal appearance, Herod set thousands of men to work to have Jerusalem and the roads leading to it in every direction in splendid appearance.

When Caesar arrived at Jerusalem, Herod entertained him in a very splendid manner, and on the second night gave him a feast to which he invited the principal men of the city, who enjoyed both the rich foods and wines and the company of Caesar immensely and had nothing but praise for Herod because he made it possible. This universal approval of Herod indicated the subtle change which had come over Judea in regard to Herod. With his victory over Antigonus, many were reconciled to his rule, then became proud of him as he defeated the Parthians, and now had become fond of him. Now their attitude was, "Just leave it to our invincible Herod, he will come out best with everybody and every thing and occasion—even to Caesar."

For Caesar had expressed open admiration of Herod's tunic and the odd design of his ornaments and announced that he intended to copy them on his return to Rome.

"Herod, you have the most exceptional and agreeable taste in dress of any man in the inhabitable world!" Caesar had exclaimed before all of the assembled company. "Caesar can only follow your splendid example."

Jerusalem was delighted to hear their ruler so spoken of by Caesar as taking part of the glory to themselves for having such a king. So numerous of them followed Herod to Ptolemais, where Herod put on a magnificent military parade and review before Caesar, causing the men of Judea to be very proud of their army and also the man who had created it. Gerovsai, Soferin, and Dibre Soferin all joined in approval of their king now.

The nation was at peace and prosperity was increasing daily. They were utterly satisfied with the reign of Herod now.

But all was not well with Herod. There was more family trouble, for at this time, his sister Salome asked his permission to divorce Costobarus, her husband.

"But by the law of our nation, a man can divorce his wife, but a woman has no hopes of dissolving a marriage unless her husband puts her away, Salome," Herod objected.

"Do you think that is just and fair to women, Herod? That we must suffer every injury and indignity without hope of relief, while men can thrust us out at will."

"Has Costobarus been treating you ill?" Herod demanded, his temper rising. "I gave you to him because he was an old and trusted friend of mine, he was also very rich and of high birth in Idumea. If he has dared to behave towards you in an unjust and unpleasant manner, I shall deal with him as he deserves."

"No, beloved brother, my husband has not beaten me nor treated me with a lack of courtesy, but he has again been unfaithful and treacherous towards you. And loving you as I do and have done always, I want no husband who conspires against you."

Herod lounged in the hall of reception where sat his mother and Pheroras. His mother put down the scroll of poetry she had been reading and asked, "He cannot be beseeching Cleopatra again to induce Antony to tear Idumea away from you and bestow it upon him, thus affording him a handle to overthrow you, for now both Cleopatra and Antony are dead. What is it this time?"

"It only proves I should not have overlooked his former crimes," Herod said in a very harsh and determined tone. "It was solely that Antony refused to agree to the importunities of Cleopatra that I was not removed as king in favor of the man I had advanced so far. But you two women cried out for me to forgive him his sins against me and decency."

"And that is exactly why I do not feel that this second offense should be overlooked," Salome said with firmness, "this flagrant betrayal of a solemn trust. To me it indicates that he still intends an attempt against you as he would not have concealed and protected your enemies for all these years to be of assistance to him when he makes the attempt."

"What enemies? All of the Asamoneans and their close friends are dead."

"The sons of Baha are certainly blood kin to the Asamoneans and most assuredly your enemies and they are certainly alive."

*   *   *

And not only were the two sons of Baha flushed out, but also the others accused by Salome. So Herod concluded that his men had suppressed a political mutiny of importance. All of them, including Costobarus, were beheaded. Now indeed and finally, the last of the Asamoneans were dead.

*   *   *

CHAPTER FIFTEEN

GAMES, GOLD, GENEROSITY

J udeans expressed their surprise at the magnificence of everything provided. They were very proud to point out that Augustus Caesar and his wife Julia had sent to their king furniture and rare and costly objects to the games. Oh, yes, their king was the intimate friend of the Caesars.

In such an atmosphere the pious objectors were regarded as fanatical nuisances and in general disfavor, so when ten of them planned to assassinate Herod in the theater, he was immediately informed of the plot and the ten were captured, all armed with their daggers, and executed. This happened because their understanding of how the games developed was faulty. Herod was not leading but following the people. He had merely and satisfactorily bodied forth the Jewish dream. Who but a fanatic was going to object to the Jewish people being mentioned among the great of the earth in display and performance? Leave it to their Herod to bring this off in a fitting manner.

There was something about the games to interest everybody. There were the sideshow booths of the magicians, fortunetellers, merchants of things like rare birds, dolls, candies, and dried fruits and small novelties crying out their wares to attract coins, but there were also concessions dealing horses, statuary, camels.

Famous orators always followed the games and spoke from movable pedestals, attracting crowds who tossed them coins; famous actors delivered recitations.

* * *

Families of Samaria were settled in the homes which fringed the city proper, for Herod argued that it was of no profit to the family to have a home but no way of providing its own food and possibly a little something to take to the market.

For the protection of the city in case of invasion, Herod enclosed Samaria with a very strong wall which surrounded an area considerably larger than the old city had been, it being now twenty furlongs in circumference.

In the center of this circuit Herod created a masterpiece that was to bring him fame in every part of the known world. On a space a furlong and a half in circumference, Herod erected a temple which became famous both for its size and its perfect beauty, and with other objects of beauty and decorations of the city, it became a monument to future generations of his fine taste and beneficence.

Herod changed the name of Samaria to Sebaste as a compliment to Caesar, and as the fame of the temple there spread, people came from everywhere to see it as they did the Parthenon.

* * *

The prosperity and splendor enjoyed by the people was gradually displaced by misery. Fortune gave way to the misfortune of several continuous years of drought. Barren land yielded nothing, and the shortages of food ushered in a famine. Herod would alleviate circumstances in time to save them. The solution was made more difficult because Syria had neither any food supplies to give nor even to sell to Judea.

The solution came to Herod quite simply one day when a crowd of hungry people gathered before the palace to protest their condition and to denounce the king for it.

Herod would not drive them away by force as his servants urged.

"No, invite them into the kitchen and allow them to share what we have," Herod said calmly.

The people came in a belligerent mood, but when they had been fed exactly as the king, their attitude softened, because the Jewish people, being unalterably democratic, when they saw that their king did not exalt himself above them, they were more patient. Then they got another shock. The king did not hustle them from the palace, but to the contrary invited them all to make themselves at ease in the hall of reception and help him to figure out a way to feed the nation in this extremity.

* * *

. . . ahead of which was to report to the king what they had found.

* * *

The servants of one man had assisted the king in assembling all of the treasures and ornaments of gold and silver in the palace, when the man arrived to report the gold decorations of the beams of the palace were being chopped down to take to Egypt to exchange for corn.

The man rushed away to report to his assistants of Herod's sacrificing of all of the saleable things in the palace. The account spread quickly over Jerusalem among the poor, and enthusiasm ran high. There was a surplus of wagons, beasts, and drivers ready to make the journey into Egypt.

Petronius, who had been of the number at the feast given to Herod by Antony on the occasion when Herod was made king, had been a longtime friend of the king since then and was now governor of Egypt. When he received the letter from Herod telling of the desolate conditions in his kingdom, he readily consented to export corn and oil to relieve the kingdom of his friend. So when the wagons arrived he exchanged the gold.

* * *

CHAPTER SIXTEEN

LOVE AGAIN FOR HEROD MAGNUS

With the nation at peace and in a prosperous condition, Herod was at peace with himself. When not occupied with administrative duties, he amused himself bringing his concept of a beautiful garden into reality. With his grove of trees, shrubs, and flowering plants strikingly arranged, his fountains and his flocks of doves, he succeeded in creating a garden that was a showplace of Asia, until Titus sacked Jerusalem in 70 AD. In his frenzy of creation and with the unhappiness of the past, remarriage had no place in his heart.

Herod had been a widower for five years now and had told his family and friends repeatedly that he would never remarry. The River brethren were correct in their estimate of women. None or very few were ever really true to a man and were best avoided unless one yearned to become a father, and he was already the father of six children. One son by Doris, his first wife, and five children by Mariamne. He saw no need to entangle himself with another woman.

Then his friends began to tell him of an extremely beautiful girl also named Mariamne, the daughter of Simon, a high priest at Alexandria. Simon had recently moved to Jerusalem with his beautiful daughter who, being Alexandrian, was also an accomplished young lady in her knowledge of music and poetry.

These reports kept up until Herod's interest was aroused in the girl, and he induced Sameas to give a feast to which Simon and his daughter were guests so that Herod could see her.

Herod was more vulnerable than he realized; he found himself instantly carried away by the beauty and cultivated manner of this Alexandrian Mariamne, and allowed his impression to be known to his friends.

Not expecting the king to ever consider marriage, it was taken for granted that Herod would take her as his concubine, and even her father hoped for nothing better. Who was he to expect a king to marry his daughter? She would be highly honored as a concubine.

When a group of Herod's intimates brought the matter up to Herod, he amazed them by his attitude.

"But that is unthinkable. No nation on earth so values the purity of its women as the Jews, as you well know. Therefore it would ill-become the king of the Jews to set the example of violating virgins."

"But you have abundant precedent in our kings, ancient and recent. Alexander Jannaeus had a score at least of concubines."

"It does not matter. I am not an Asamonean. And my father's admonitions and example oppose any such destructive actions. An honorable man occupies a bed only with a wife, he taught."

"But you cannot marry this girl. Her family is not sufficiently exalted to mate with the king. The people would never bear it."

"We shall see!"

What Herod did was to deprive Jesus, son of Phebet, of the high priesthood and confer it upon Simon, thus augmenting the family dignity so that the king could ally himself with the family by marrying the daughter of Simon.

Perhaps his wedding reminded him strongly of his night of flight to save the virgins long ago, for now he went about performing his vow to memorialize his victory over the pursuing Jews at the rounded hill. He encircled it with round towers with a flight of steps of polished stone to the crest of the hill. Inside the enclosure of towers were exceedingly rich apartments of extraordinary beauty of material and concept. In midst of these structures, Herod constructed his place of burial and named the whole after himself—Herodium, The City of Herod.

His old vow performed, Herod now turned to body forth another old dream: a city of polished white marble climbing the long gentle incline from the jewel blue of the Mediterranean.

The site was marked by a morbid enclosure known as Strato's Tower. Years before, when he was governor of Galilee, Herod had passed there and his beauty-worshipping soul had revolted at the spectacle of the ugly tumbledown structure on so beautiful a site, and over the years he had dreamed what could be done there. It was in Pheonicia between Dora and Jappa, both port cities but neither really satisfactory as a haven for ships, for the north wind drove such waves against the rocky shore that ships were forced to ride at anchor offshore while being loaded or unloaded.

Strato's Tower was even less favorably endowed by nature as a haven for there was not even the slightest indentation of the shore there.

* * *

Herod sent his older sons Alexander and Aristobulus to Rome for education and mentoring. Caesar received the sons of Herod as princes of the first order and invited them to make his palace their residence, but this was overborne by Pollio, the Roman magistrate who had been one of the guests at the feast which Antony had given Herod on the occasion of Herod being made a king and who had formed a tremendous attachment to Herod and had insisted on taking Herod's sons into his own home, and Caesar gave way to the magistrate.

Herod had sent his boys off to Rome with such an abundance of fine wearing apparel, ornaments, and spending money that they attracted favorable notice at once among the Roman patricians. The youths soon discovered that it was a tremendous advantage in Rome to be the son of King Herod. It was to be sought after by the sons of the patrician houses, and petted and pampered as a possible future son-in-law, and to be deferred to everywhere. So they were very proud of this birth and to announce that they were the sons of Herod, king of Judea, and intimate friend of Caesar and other powerful Romans. Herod was accumulating some weight due to middle-age, and with a brush of gray at his temples felt that he was introducing his sons to practical politics and politicians and thus giving them a leg-up in what was necessary when they succeeded him. Each month he sent off a long, affection-filled epistle to his sons and Pollio urging energy and application to their studies, and instructions in human relations.

* * *

Meanwhile, Trachonitis, in the province of Trachon, was full of robbers who were given to pillaging the Damascenes for a living and so addicted to the practice that when there were no others to prey on they would plunder and slay each other. Then Zenodorus, instead of restraining these lawless characters, joined with them for a percentage of the plunder and thus greatly augmented his income.

Now as the Damascenes, the people of Bätanea and Auranitis, suffered greatly from the Trachonites, they finally complained to Varro, the president of Syria, and entreated him to write to Caesar about the corrupt Zenodorus. Varro did so and Caesar immediately replied for

Varro to give the land to Herod that by the care of Herod the neigh-
boring provinces might be no longer troubled by these crimes of the
Trachonites.

Caesar recognized that it was no easy task to break up these
mobs, since this wicked life was all that these men had ever known
and they knew no other way of earning a living. There were no cities in Trachon nor did these outlaws own any land. They lived in
dens and caves in the earth, which their domestic animals shared
with them. However, they had contrived two basins inside which
they conducted water and, although the openings of these caves
were so narrow that only one person could enter or leave at a time,
they were very spacious inside and there was room to store corn and
other edibles. But the ground over these dens was not very high,
the area being a boulder-strewn plain. Travel was very troublesome
therefore, unless one went by the narrow winding trails, and this was
impossible to know unless led by a trained guide.

But the difficulties did not appear insurmountable to Herod. Since
these robbers were addicted to preying on each other as well as out-
siders, presents of money judiciously bestowed soon procured him
six guides from among the robbers themselves. His blows were so
crushing that the robbers were stamped out; the robberies came to
an abrupt end; peace and quietude came to the people of the neigh-
boring provinces. Caesar now bestowed these three provinces upon
Herod—Trachonitis, Bätanea, and Auranitis. Suce had been king of
Arabia for ten years now, his rule extended from the Delta of the Nile
to the Euphrates on the north and east.

Caesar now designated Herod as Herod Magnus, Herod the Great,
and it was understood all over the empire that Caesar had no friend
closer to him than Herod except Agrippa, and Agrippa loved and respected no man more than Herod except Caesar. These three men
governed the empire. Herod ruled western Asia, Agrippa Asia Minor,

and Caesar Europe. Thus far Herod had come from the governorship of Galilee.

Zenodorus was deeply hurt on seeing his income cut off by Herod's extermination of the robbers and, in addition, the principality of Trachonitis had been snatched from Zenodorus and transferred to Herod. Consumed by envy of Herod, Zenodorus sailed for Rome to denounce Herod, but when there, discovered that he could not even get a hearing. Neither Caesar nor the senate would receive him.

About this time Agrippa went to Asia Minor to take over the government of that area. Agrippa decided to winter at Milylene, and there he was joined by his warm friend, Herod. Herod passed a pleasant week with Agrippa then returned to his duties at Jerusalem.

Now Zenodorus thought he saw his chance to dispose of the hated Herod, who had ruined him. He stirred up a group of men from Gadara to go to Agrippa and accuse Herod of malfeasance in office. Instead of listening to the charges, Agrippa arrested the delegation and sent them hand-cuffed to Herod to dispose of them as he pleased.

And now the eternal envy of the Arabians of Judea broke out. They joined Zenodorus and the Gadarenes in trying to raise a sedition against the government of Herod, but had no success.

Shortly after Caesar came to Syria on a tour of inspection of all parts of the empire, and the never-say-die Zenodorus stirred up another group of Gadarenes to run to Caesar and complain of the harshness of Herod and to beg that Gadara be cut off from Herod's rule and be put directly under the Romans. The disturbance got Zenodorus nowhere, for Caesar would not allow Herod to speak in his own defense. Caesar gave Herod his right hand and the Gadarenes, perceiving the indignation of Caesar, fled away in all directions, some in such dread of what might be done to them that they killed themselves. Zenodorus probably suffered from appendicitis or ulcers, for he died

suddenly of a ruptured abdomen, thus relieving Herod of his malig-
nant intentions towards him.

And as an enemy of Herod's in Jerusalem had complained earlier,
Herod drew splendor from his very dangers. The destructive and evil
activities of Zenodorus from which, in the end, he gained nothing,
but rather lost his principality to Herod and served as a ladder to make
King Herod, Herod the Great, and with both Caesar and Agrippa still
insisting that Herod's abilities were too great for the territories he
governed.

CHAPTER SEVENTEEN

HEROD BUILDS

I n the eighteenth year of his reign and with so many other successes to his credit and the great extension of his kingdom, Herod now undertook the major work of his entire reign, that is the replacing of the temple of Zorobabel with a structure of his own concept of what was fitting.

First he called the principal men of the nation together with the multitude and spoke to them thus: "I think I need not mention to you, my countrymen, about such other works as I have done since I came to the kingdom, although I hope I may be pardoned that they have been performed in such a manner to bring more security to you than glory to myself; for I have neither been negligent in the most difficult times about what tended to ease your necessities, nor have the buildings I have made been so proper to preserve me as yourselves from injuries. And I imagine that with God's assistance, I have advanced the nation of the Jews to a degree of happiness which they never before had; and for the particular edifices belonging to your own country and to your own cities as also to those cities that were lately acquired, which we have erected and greatly adorned and thereby augmented the dignity of your nation, it seems to me a needless task to enumerate them to you since you well know them already.

"But now as to that undertaking which I have in mind to set about at present, and which will be a work of the greatest piety and excellence that can possibly be undertaken by us, I will now declare to you that our fathers, indeed, when they had returned from Babylon, built this temple to God almighty yet does it want sixty cubits of its largeness in altitude of that first temple which Solomon built that exceeded this temple. Nor let anyone condemn our fathers for their negligence nor want of piety herein for it was not their fault that the temple was no higher, for they were Cyrus and Darius, the son of Hystaspes, who determined the measures of its rebuilding and also the subjection of those fathers of ours to the Macedonians that they had not the opportunity to follow the original model of this sacred edifice, but since I am now doing God's will, your governor and I have had peace for a long time and have gained great riches and large revenues, and what is the principal thing of all, I am at amity with and well regarded by the Romans, who are the rulers of the whole world. I will do my endeavors to correct the imperfection of our temple, and to make a most thankful return to God for what blessings I have received from Him by giving me this kingdom and that by rendering His temple as complete as I am able."

This speech to prepare the mind of the nation for the mighty task was received with a thunderous roar by the men of the guilds of builders, but with incredulity by some others and still others—mostly of the priesthood—who feared that the existing temple would be torn down, and the king then find that he could not replace it. The undertaking appeared too vast to their minds, and impossible of accomplishment.

Herod became aware of this and reassured them and announced

he would not pull down the temple till everything—materials and skilled workers—was on hand to build it up again.

So Herod got ready 1,000 wagons that were to haul the stones for the new building. He chose out 10,000 of the most skilled workers and bought 1,000 sacerdotal robes for as many of the priests and then taught the arts of the stone-cutters and carpenters and then began to build, by taking away the old foundations and replacing them immediately with the new. The new structure was 100 cubits in height and built of stones white and strong and each of them was 25 cubits by eight in height.

In this manner was built the fabulous temple, the third temple at Jerusalem, the temple of Herod that, when completed, for perfection of architectural lines and rich adornment, became one of the show-places of the world of the time until it was destroyed by Titus when he sacked Jerusalem in 70 AD. This temple was built in a year and six months, "upon which all the people were full of joy and when all was ready the nation returned thanks in the first place to God" and in the next to the king for his alacrity. They feasted and celebrated this rebuilding of the temple.

Herod was his open-handed self on the occasion, for he sacrificed 300 oxen to God, for it so happened that the dedication of the new temple fell on the day of his inauguration, which he celebrated annually as a festival. Because of the coincidence of the two, Herod made the dedication most illustrious.

CHAPTER EIGHTEEN

RETURN OF THE TWO PRINCES

Herod combined business with pleasure. Being notified that his sons Alexander and Aristobulus had satisfactorily completed their studies in science at Rome and feeling the necessity for a conference with Caesar, Herod decided to go for his sons instead of sending to them to come home.

Herod was an extremely proud father when he was greeted by his tall handsome boys, who had the finish of long residence in a great city, a flavor of scholarship, and the patina of association with sophisticated people whose egos were well nourished. Caesar spoke very kindly of the boys and made them presents to take with them as keepsakes. As a parting admonition, he expressed the hope that the young princes appreciated this rare good fortune in being the sons of so able, eminent, and amiable a man as Herod.

Both of the young men hastened to assure Caesar that they did, and at the time, they seemed utterly sincere, and Herod blazed with pride and paternal love. He suggested to Caesar that he immediately turn the government over to his sons and retire as a sort of advisor to them, and Caesar, a very disappointed father in his daughter Julia, promptly refused to allow it.

"At your death will be time enough." Caesar added, "Or perhaps too soon."

On their arrival in Judea, the proud Herod lost no time in presenting his sons to the nation, and let it be understood that they were his successors in the government. He had enough territory to divide between them, Herod observed.

The boys were admired and flattered because of their eminent position as the sons and heirs of Herod and their good looks and extreme wealth, all of which pleased Herod mightily.

However, three months had not passed before the disillusionment set in. Herod's old-time opponents went to work to use these shallow youths as tools against Herod. Instead of continuing to be proud of and affectionate to their father, they were persuaded that Herod was a usurper, and that they were indebted to him for nothing. The government really resided in the family line of their executed mother; that she had been murdered by Herod without cause and that they should be ashamed to associate with such a criminal as the king. Further, it was their bounden duty to overthrow Herod and take the government through their descent from the Asamoneans.

Forthwith these stupid youths, who were persuaded that they were greater and more deserving than their father, began to make such observations in Jerusalem, and there was no lack of individuals to bring the report of their gross indiscretions to the king. His worshipping sister, Salome, and his brother, Pheroras, were among scores of others who reported to Herod of the disloyalty of his two sons.

But Herod's paternal love and pride were not easily destroyed. Even when he was forced to believe that Alexander had said these disloyal things, he thought that it was his duty to recall his son to a proper attitude by pointing out to him first the error of the accusations and then his own profound love for them, which his sons should return instead of allowing themselves to be lured into such an ugly and unprofitable posture by those who were no more their friends than his.

While Alexander denied the allegations to Herod's face, he went right on behind his father's back in the same strain, and further inside the palace he took up the custom of his late grandmother and mother of boasting of his royal blood and speaking of Herod and his family as being of mean birth, and also of Herod's wives and their children in the same fashion, so that a great tumult was stirred up in the palace because of this.

On one occasion Herod entered as Alexander was thus holding forth and snapped with heavy sarcasm, "Oh, nobody is royal around here except Alexander." As for Aristobulus, he was not aggressive, but concurred in everything that his older brother did or said. Herod decided that Aristobulus was like his mother—with little initiative nor intelligence of his own, thus easily persuaded to his own hurt. He too lamented publicly the mean birth of his father, who was usurping the government left to them by their mother, and said he spurned the company of the murderer of his mother.

Now, Herod bore with this slander of himself by his sons very patiently for a long time.

Sameas, about Herod's own age and full of admiration for the king, without being told by Herod, decided to see if he could not bring the young men to their senses. He therefore invited them to a private supper at his home and during the meal spoke to them quite boldly.

"What madness has come upon you young men since your return from Rome that you go about the city uttering slanderous remarks about your father to anyone who will listen to you to the effect you scorn his company because he murdered your mother, which he did not. And that he is wrongfully usurping the throne of your mother."

The face of Alexander flushed red with anger and he said shortly,

"It is well known that you are a worshipper of King Herod so we should not be surprised that you exert yourself to protect him."

"Protect Herod? You are indeed mad, Alexander. Your father, like the lion, has no other weapon besides himself, and requires none. Protect him against whom?"

"The people of Judea who will rise to restore the government to its rightful owners—the royal line."

"The government is already in the hands of the royal line. It is possible that you do not yet know that the Asamoneans are no longer royal, and that the power now resides in Rome, and that whom Caesar and the Roman senate name as king is king in Judea. As to the rising of the people against Herod on your behalf—that is in no way a possibility. Your father has conferred too many benefits upon the nation for them to change from his care and protection. You were in Rome for a number of years and while there, frequently in the company of Caesar, did you ever gain the impression that Caesar did not know that your father was in possession of the government here?"

"Certainly not."

"Or that if he were, that he was not approved by Rome?"

"To the contrary. Caesar is ever full of praise of our father, but that is because Caesar is ignorant of Herod's evil deeds."

"Such as—"

"His murder of my mother and grandmother and Hyrcanus, my great-grandfather, in order to obtain the government."

"Lies, all lies, for in the first place, he was made king by Rome while all of them were alive, and it was known in Rome that they were alive, as the Asamoneans had been rejected by Rome, as of no use to the empire and as enemies of Rome.

"The making of Herod as king was a very deliberate act on the part of Rome, and the proof that Caesar has not regretted the act is the enormous increase of the territories under Herod's administration. As you know, he is esteemed the third man in power in the empire, and how he is honored and esteemed by Caesar and Agrippa, so the delusion that you can overthrow him is madness. Caesar knows you only as the sons of his friend, Herod. As a descendant of the former royal line of the Asamoneans, of which you appear so mistakenly proud, you would be nothing more than outcasts and perhaps even hunted down as criminals and enemies of Rome."

"So you readily excuse the murder of my mother, her mother, and her grandfather, Sameas?" Alexander asked with hatred in his tones.

"They were not murdered by Herod. They were not murdered at all. They were tried and condemned by the Sanhedrin, each for treasonable acts against the king and government of Judea. If they were murdered, then they brought their deaths upon themselves. Would you like to examine the transcripts in each case? I think when you have read the evidence you will alter your opinions."

"Not one bit. For the Sanhedrin merely followed the dictates of Herod!"

"That is a convenient and comforting lie but a lie nevertheless," Sameas said. "It is an insult upon the honor of the members of our judicial body. Therefore, seeing your state of mind, I will not attempt to persuade you to a more just and sensible frame of mind, and that for your own security; for those who encourage you to make treasonable statements about the king are not your friends, but hasten to repeat to the king or members of his family your every word. Nor will the time ever come when they will raise a sedition against Herod, as you are led to believe. Not a soul raised a voice of protest when your mother, her mother, and Hyrcanus were led to their execution. Bear that in mind. And none will start a revolt from Herod's government if the same fate comes to you. Keep that in mind and conduct yourselves accordingly."

"When I am king, I shall remember your enmity to my mother's family and act accordingly, Sameas. You remember that and conduct yourself accordingly."

"Thanks for the warning, Alexander. What you have said goes to convince me that many thoughtful people of the nation are correct in their conclusion that all that was worthwhile in the Asamoneans died with the noble John Hyrcanus. I remember that it was his bloodthirsty son Aristobulus who first set himself up to be a king by murdering his own mother and brothers, then follows the terrible Alexander Jannaeus with his wholesale butcheries of the people, who was the father of the degenerate and tricky Hyrcanus who was rejected by the nation, and only restored to power by the influence, wealth, and energy of Antipater the father of Herod, who exerted his influence with the Great Caesar to allow Hyrcanus to be high priest again. This madness for power at any cost which began with Aristobulus seems to repeat itself in every generation since, and you being sons of the able Herod disappoint me in appearing not to have escaped it."

"So we are now madmen because we resent the murder of our mother, and scorn accepting the government from her murderer?"

"Perhaps you assume too much by being so positive that your father will bestow the government upon you. He has many other sons, and as you know, Caesar has given him permission to transfer it to any one of them that he wishes. He even has a son older than you."

The flag of alarm flew in the face of Alexander first and then that of Aristobulus. Such a possibility had never occurred to them.

"But our mother was of royal birth," Alexander said weakly after a pause.

"There is no royal descent in Jerusalem except from Herod," Sameas said coldly. "Thus any son of his is as royal as you are. Do not continue to deceive yourself that the nation holds your Asamonean blood in any high esteem. That is the delusion which brought your mother, her mother, and Hyrcanus to their end. Be wise and hasten to effect a reconciliation with your father before it is too late."

But in spite of this sincere and timely admonition, the sons of Herod did not cease their folly, in spite of the fact that Herod treated them with continued forbearance and indulgence. He turned aside those who ran to him to report the indiscretions of his sons, reiterating his love of them and his pride in them. Now that they both were of legal age, he got them suitable wives. To Alexander, his oldest son by Mariamne, he married Glaphyia, the beautiful daughter of the king of Cappadocia, and to Aristobulus, Bernice, the daughter of Herod's sister Salome.

CHAPTER NINETEEN

REUNION IN IONIA

erod received a letter from his friend Marcus Agrippa advising him that he was sailing for Pontus to prosecute a military campaign there. Herod replied immediately saying that since his friend was coming into Asia, he must come into Judea and allow Herod to be his host, as Agrippa had been to him, and thus repay some of the kindnesses received.

Agrippa agreed and Herod spared neither pains nor expenses in the entertainment of his friend. First Herod took Agrippa and his party on a tour of inspection of the places he had built, for example Caesarea, Sebaste, and the fortresses of Alexandrium, Hyrcania, and Herodium, then he brought the party into Jerusalem.

The inhabitants turned out in festival mood and garments and gave Agrippa a great reception, and Agrippa met the people more than halfway. He offered a hecatomb of sacrifices to God and feasted the entire population without stint, providing the greatest dainties that could be had, and altogether he and the people of Jerusalem enjoyed each other so much that Agrippa had a mind to prolong his stay, but winter was approaching.

*   *   *

Herod later joined Agrippa on his tour of various cities in Asia Minor, often functioning as an intercessor for supplicants. In Ionia, Herod was of some help to his own people, for some Jews heard that he was there with their governor. They ran to Herod and begged his intercession with Agrippa, because they were not allowed to live by their own laws and were otherwise treated unjustly.

Agrippa agreeably summoned the principal Romans of the area as jurors to hear the case and Herod appointed Nicolaus of Damascus to appear for the Jews. The Greeks, who were the majority population of the area, offered no defense to the argument put forth by Nicolaus and so Agrippa ruled that on account of Herod's goodwill and friendship, he was ready to grant the Jews whatever they should ask him provided the requests were in no way to the detriment of the Roman government.

At Samos, Herod decided it was time that he returned to his own kingdom, and landed at Caesarea and, on reaching Jerusalem, called the people together and gave them an account of his travels and a report on the condition of all of the Jews of Asia. Then, being in a very happy mood, he remitted a fourth part of the collected taxes for that year, which caused the people to be so pleased with him that they wished their king all manner of happiness.

BACK UPON THE GRILLE
Excerpts from Hurston's Letters

A s to Herod's reputed harshness, [Josephus] says, "Herod was the first man of the world in excusing offenses against himself. When seditious men were brought before him, he gave them a talk and dismissed them. Yet he was the first man in the world to punish unfaithfulness in his own family."

That is not hard for me to understand for I think that all of us expect greater fidelity out of our own than others. . . . Herod's two sons by the Jewish princess[,] and naturally [the] daughter of the high priest who repeatedly plotted against him, he had strangled, a very hard thing for a father to do, but as the Encyclopedia [Britannica] observes, "Herod but outdid those who sought to do the same thing to him." Josephus, traditionalist and bent on the restoration of absolute power to the priesthood, seem[ed] to take it very hard that Herod did not allow the family of his wife to put him to death.

AS TO THE philosophical side, Herod lent his aid to the movement out of which Christianity evolved. Thus it is ironical that he should be [. . .] the *boogerman of our religion. When you review the tenets of the Essenes, the third philosophical sect in Palestine, you will find that everything Christ did or said according to the Four Gospels was straight from it. Other things tend to confirm that both Jesus Christ and John the Baptist were Essenes. Of Herod's attitude towards the Essenes, Josephus complains, "Herod paid the Essenes a reverence greater than their mortal nature required." They were scattered all over Palestine, but their stronghold was Galilee, and that was Herod's favorite province, though as you know, both Essenes and Galileans were held in low esteem by the powers in Jerusalem. "The Fringes" (Pharisees), Scribes, and priests in general could not lay a finger on Herod's pets while he was alive. So the doctrine of brotherly love, God the father of all mankind equally, and not just the Jews, gained ground in his reign. Not only would Christ never have been put to death under Herod, but the [S]anhedrin would not have dared to even start the commotion. As we Negroes say, Herod would have been all over them just like gravy over rice. It is possible that our American leftists borrowed that habit of getting up a rabble and "demonstrating" from the Jewish priesthood, for it was a favorite maneuver of theirs[.] Only one occurred during Herod's reign, and that was when he was on his deathbed, and they therefore thought it was safe. But the old boy (68) sprung out of bed, polished them off, and went on back to bed with his ulcers.*[1]

AFTER THIRTY-SEVEN YEARS *on the throne, and with enemies within his own kingdom (the Pharisees and the Sanhedrin)[, Herod] died peacefully in his bed and was borne to his tomb in splendor.*[2]

1 Zora Neale Hurston, letter to Mary Holland, June 13, 1955, in *Zora Neale Hurston, A Life in Letters*, ed. Carla Kaplan (New York: Doubleday, 2002), 731, 732–33.
2 Hurston, letter to Mary Holland, June 13, 1935, in *Zora Neale Hurston, A Life in Letters*, 731; Zora Neale Hurston, letter to Burroughs Mitchell, October 2, 1953, in *Zora Neale Hurston, A Life in Letters*, 703.

A STORY FINALLY TOLD

I n her autobiography, *Dust Tracks on a Road*, Dr. Zora Neale Hurston testifies that she was—as the saying goes among many of us in the South—born and raised in the church. And many of us in the South, like a great number of Protestant Christians and Catholics the world over, have been taught to accept the Bible—Old and New Testaments—as the infallible "Word of God," or, at the very least, the word of men inspired by God, and therefore as "the gospel truth." And as a stratagem to ensure we did so, we were warned to never question God about any of it. "But as early as I can remember," Hurston writes, "I was questing and seeking. It was not that I did not hear. I tumbled right into the Missionary Baptist Church when I was born. I saw the preachers and the pulpits, the people and the pews. Both at home and from the pulpit, I heard my father . . . explain all about God's habits, His heaven, His ways and means. Everything was known and settled."[1]

---

1   Zora Neale Hurston, *Dust Tracks on a Road*, in *Zora Neale Hurston: Folklore, Memoirs, and Other Writings*, ed. Cheryl Wall (New York: Library of America, 1995), 754.

So though she was practically "born with God in the house," Hurston still had many questions on the subject.[2] Her mind was never "settled." Her curiosity about the personality of God and her interests in biblical figures and events inspired an ongoing desire to poke and pry, to search out the inside meaning of things and to know and understand the cosmic world. Rather than settle her mind, the sermons of her father, the Reverend John Hurston, and the Sunday school lessons of her mother, Lucy Ann Hurston, inspired a lifelong inquiry into spiritual traditions, biblical events, and religious doctrine and teachings. Among the many questions that unsettled her mind were those pertaining to Herod the Great (Gaius Julius Herodes), which led Hurston, as a veteran cultural anthropologist and ethnographer and a seasoned cultural critic, into more than fourteen years of research on the life and times of Herod the Great. In a letter to the editor Burroughs Mitchell of the publisher Scribner's, Hurston described with delight her intense and absorbing investigation into the contours of Herod's life. "Under the spell of a great obsession," she wrote. "The life story of HEROD THE GREAT. You have no idea the great amount of research that I have done on this man. No matter who talks about him, friend or foe, Herod is a magnificent character."[3] But it was the voice of his foes that history sanctioned.

Hurston had found the legendary and historical accounts of Herod to be perplexing. On the one hand, within Christian traditions—based on New Testament accounts—Herod was the Antichrist, "the monster of the first Christmas."[4] On the other hand, in Jewish traditions—in which the historian Flavius Josephus's *Antiquities of the Jews* and *Jewish War* figure prominently—Herod was the iconoclastic and wicked

---

2   Hurston, *Dust Tracks*, 754.

3   Zora Neale Hurston, letter to Burroughs Mitchell, October 2, 1953, in *Zora Neale Hurston, A Life in Letters*, ed. Carla Kaplan (New York: Doubleday, 2002), 702.

4   Paul Meir, "Commentaries," in Flavius Josephus, *The New Complete Works of Josephus*, revised and expanded ed. (Grand Rapids, MI: Kregel Academic, 1999), 567.

usurper of the Jewish throne. But her own research contradicted both accounts and would challenge the long-accepted, one-dimensional depiction of Herod as (1) the evil tyrant who ordered "the slaughter of the innocents"; (2) a repugnant and illegitimate king; (3) a Romanized Jew whose Hellenic tendencies undermined Jewish tradition and culture; and (4) an impious and sinful reprobate whose awful illness and death were punishments from God.

Hurston contended that not only did Herod not order a massacre of baby boys "in the hope of catching the infant Jesus in the dragnet," but moreover, that such an event never happened. According to her research, Herod lived "72–4 BC while no one can say when Christ was born, since he had no biographer, and there was no interest in the matter until generations later when Christianity was an established religion. The synoptic Gospels, Matthew, Mark, and Luke, were all written so long after His death that legend crept in, so that even they differ on events of the life of Christ. Nobody can be sure even of their authorship."[5] And even if Jesus were born during Herod's reign, from 37 BCE until his death in 4 BCE, Hurston argues that an attempt on Jesus's life would have been improbable, given that Herod was sympathetic to and supportive of the teachings and mission of the Essenes, the mystical Jewish sect with which the Christ is believed to have been associated. Even though the dates of Herod's reign and his death are still debated, contemporary historians nevertheless retain the traditional chronology.[6]

A story of the slaughter of the innocents is not recorded in Josephus's histories. Given his anti-Herodian bent, it is doubtful that Josephus would have overlooked an opportunity to add to the compilation of malicious deeds in his vilification of Herod. Hurston's work acknowledges Herod's evidenced acts of violence, but rather

5   Hurston, letter to Mary Holland, in *Zora Neale Hurston, A Life in Letters*, 729–30.
6   Kimberley Czajkowski and Benedikt Eckhardt, *Herod in History: Nicolaus of Damascus and the Augustan Age* (Oxford: Oxford University Press, 2021), 1n1.

than condemn and dismiss Herod, her work seeks to understand his inclinations, actions, and motivations. As Hurston pointed out in her introduction, Herod was "a part of his time and of the customs of those times," and the kind of brutal violence that characterized Herod's time figured into his career. Political executions were political expediencies, and close ties of blood did not stand in the way.[7]

And yet, like the Marc Antonys, Augustus Caesars, and Cleopatras of his time, there was more to Herod than episodes of violence and tragedy. Hurston's contextualization of Herod within the customs of his times does not constitute an excuse or justification for the cruelties of Herod's reign. What Hurston was working to avoid in her approach was what contemporary scholars call presentism, that is, the tendency to interpret the past in terms of present-day sensibilities, moralities, and ethics, which "usually leads us to find ourselves morally superior." Assuming a morally superior stance invariably leads us to obscure, obstruct, or forget aspects of our historical experience.[8]

In *The Many Faces of Herod the Great*, the historian of ancient history Adam Marshak cautions against taking moralistic and judgmental positions in our approach to history, in general, and in our inquiry into the life of Herod the Great, in particular. "By consciously avoiding value judgments about his moral worth as a king and person," Marshak writes, "we will avoid the two major mistakes of past studies of Herod and his reign: (1) an unrealistic emphasis on his wickedness that does not take into account either the complexity of the Roman world, especially Judea, and the reality that his behavior was not particularly unique, and (2) an overemphasis on force and repression as the sole factor in his success."[9]

---

7   Zora Neale Hurston, introduction to *The Life of Herod the Great* (Amistad: New York, 2025), xxiii.

8   Lynn Hunt, "Against Presentism," American Historical Association, published May 1, 2002, https://www.historians.org/perspectives-article/against-presentism-may-2002/.

9   Adam Marshak, *The Many Faces of Herod the Great* (Grand Rapids, MI: William B. Eerdmans Publishing Company, 2015), xxviii.

Hurston realized from her research that brute force alone did not explain Herod's successful thirty-seven-year reign. Herod, contrary to popular opinion, *was* a popular king. He provided economic and political stability and promoted education, the arts, and the Olympic games. "And the nation took to these things like ducks to water," Hurston writes. "They loved Herod, threw garlands at him when he appeared in the streets. . . . He was beloved by the nation. Even many Pharisees and priests went over to him."[10]

Adam Marshak's observations support Hurston's findings:

Oppression and repression certainly had their role and function within the Herodian regime. However, they alone cannot account for his ability to minimize or quash dissent, nor can they explain why he was so popular with his Roman patrons, his royal neighbors, and the myriad of cities dotting the eastern Mediterranean, with whom he had rather friendly relationships. Some other factor besides oppression had to exist, and I believe that this factor was his ability to tap into the cultural mindset of his audiences and fulfill their expectations of him and his position.[11]

Through an analysis that focuses on the politics of self-representation, Marshak concluded that fundamental to Herod's success was his genius capacity for self-representation and his uncanny skill at negotiating the Roman, Hellenistic eastern, and Judean cultural realms. He became the trusted Roman ally, the ideal Hellenistic monarch, and to present himself as the legitimate successor to the Hasmonean dynasty, "a glorious Jewish king in the vein of David

10 Hurston, letter to Mary Holland, June 13, 1955, in *Zora Neale Hurston, A Life in Letters*, 730–31.

11 Marshak, *Many Faces of Herod the Great*, xxiv.

and Solomon."[12] During his reign, Judea experienced unprecedented prosperity and extended periods of peace. And he was called great, "Magnus," not only because Caesar Augustus bestowed the title upon him for his many services but also "because his reign in Jerusalem was the most splendid since the legendary days of Solomon."[13]

According to Marshak's criteria—a long, relatively peaceful, and stable reign culminating in a natural death and the ability to pass on one's realm to one's heirs—Herod was a successful king. Minor revolts and riots notwithstanding, Herod maintained his rule. His protection and support of Jews living in the Diaspora spoke to Herod's strength and authority beyond Judea. In chapter 19 of this book, "Reunion in Ionia," for instance, Hurston depicts Herod's efforts to secure the civil rights and liberties of the Jews of Ionia. And as Herod's building programs made Judea a place of pride and transformed Jerusalem into a pilgrimage destination for Diaspora Jews, so their patronage reflected a recognition of Herod's legitimacy and contributed to his prestige as "not only king of Judea, but also king of the Jews," making Herod "arguably the most powerful king in the history of Judea."[14]

Herod was the astute politician and statesman who was able to parlay his relations with Rome into benefits for both Judean and Diaspora Jews as well as for other ethnic populaces in the vicinity of his kingdom. But even as Herod's reign was accepted and respected by Rome and a majority of the Jewish people, there were yet those who perceived his reign as a disruption of the Hasmonean royal line, and it was "the traditionalist minority," Hurston points out, "who happened, however, to be setting down records."[15] Flavius Josephus was among the traditionalists.

---

12 Marshak, *Many Faces of Herod the Great*, xxiv.

13 John J. Collins, foreword to *Many Faces of Herod the Great*, by Marshak, xiii.

14 Marshak, *Many Faces of Herod the Great*, 301, 302, xxiv.

15 Hurston, letter to Mary Holland, June 13, 1955, in *Zora Neale Hurston, A Life in Letters*, 731.

In any case, as the chief source of information regarding the life and times of Herod, Josephus drew heavily from *The Commentaries of Herod the Great*. This authorized account of Herod's life, written by Nicolaus of Damascus, Herod's friend, advisor, and diplomat, has been lost. Josephus, however, followed closely Nicolaus's narrative in terms of the chronology of events, "except for his added opinions." His re-interpretation of events and Herod's motivations in relation to those events registered Josephus's personal biases and resentment of Herod and his reign. The priestly scribes, bound by tradition, Hurston writes, "detested" Herod.[16]

In *Antiquities of the Jews*, Flavius Josephus outlined his own personal genealogy. He writes that he is not only sprung from a priestly line, "but from the first of the twenty-four courses" and "the chief family of that first course also." He speaks of his Hasmonean "royal blood" and his forebears who "had both the office of the high priesthood, and the dignity of a king, for a long time together."[17] For Josephus, Herod was anathema; he "regarded [Herod] as a sort of sacrilege."[18]

Hurston assessed Josephus's writings on Herod as "a poisoned source."[19] She took umbrage with his disparagement of Nicolaus, as a propagandist court historian, while relying heavily on Nicolaus's work. Ironically, as Josephus relied heavily on Nicolaus, Hurston relied heavily on Josephus, including passages and language from Josephus's work in her manuscript drafts. Though many of the details of Hurston's *The Life of Herod the Great* are derived from the works of Josephus, Hurston argued that the historian's portrayal of Herod was

---

16 Hurston, letter to Mary Holland, June 13, 1955, in *Zora Neale Hurston, A Life in Letters*, 730.

17 Josephus, *New Complete Works of Josephus*, 17.

18 Hurston, letter to Mary Holland, June 13, 1955, in *Zora Neale Hurston, A Life in Letters*, 731.

19 Hurston, "Introduction," *The Life of Herod the Great*, xxv.

not to be trusted. She noted that Josephus embellished or traduced actual events narrated in Nicolaus's account and introduced legends, fables, and other fictions into his portrayal of Herod. The works of contemporary scholars substantiate Hurston's assessments and provide insights into Josephus's practices as a historian of classical antiquity. For example, in *Herod in History*, Kimberley Czajkowski and Benedikt Eckhardt, historians of antiquity and classical Europe, write that Josephus criticized Nicolaus "in the extreme" and was "determined to undermine the credentials of Nicolaus." They caution that "Josephus's more general criticisms of Nicolaus's writing should be taken with a rather large pinch of salt."[20]

As to Josephus's embellishments and inventions, modern historians explain that ancient historiography made use of highly stylized rhetorical devices for dramatic effect. The practice allowed historians and biographers to draw from a stock of earlier models and prototypes of events, situations, and human behavior to enhance the narrative plot of their writings. Such is the case, for example, with Josephus's description of Herod's death. Because Josephus's account of Herod, overall, cast him as an evil, impious, and maniacal tyrant, the demands of the script were that Herod die a tyrant's death.

Presumably detailed in Nicolaus's lost biography, Herod's last days and death were briefly alluded to in Nicolaus's biography of Caesar Augustus. Thus, drawing on other, anti-Herodian sources and previous models of a tyrant's death, Josephus fashioned a horrible end for Herod. According to Josephus's account, Herod's last days, around the age of seventy, were filled with family turmoil, revolts, a suicide attempt, and an agonizing death from symptoms associated with a disease termed phthiriasis, an infection caused by mites: "But now, Herod's sickness greatly increased upon him after

20 Czajkowski and Eckhardt, *Herod in History*, 9, 124, 96.

a severe manner, and this by God's judgment upon him for his sins," writes Josephus.

Accordingly, Herod suffered from an appetite that could not be satisfied, ulcers, swollen feet and belly, rotting genitals that produced worms, difficulty breathing, and a case of bad breath, and he was taken with convulsions "in all parts of his body." Diviners and prophets declared "that God inflicted this punishment on the king on account of his great impiety." Said suffering drove Herod insane and inspired insane decrees; five days later, he died.[21]

According to Hurston's research, "Herod died peacefully in his bed and was borne to his tomb in splendor."[22] In "Worms and the Death of Kings: A Cautionary Note on Disease and History," the historian Thomas Africa observes that phthiriasis was diagnosed for the likes of Roman emperor Galerius, Roman general Sulla, and Philip II of Spain. Though the disease is real, Africa suggests that historical reports, absent a physician's confirmation, are suspect. Further, he writes:

> Most accounts of the ailments of prominent persons in antiquity are found not in medical works but in the writings of historians, who at best are imprecise when describing illness. . . . While Heaven bestows this affliction on the just and unjust alike, the disease is an appropriate punishment for cruel tyrants and enemies of God. The temptation for moralistic historians to inflict phthiriasis on hated rulers is obvious, and each episode must be judged on its own merits.[23]

---

21 Josephus, *New Complete Works of Josephus*, 565.

22 Zora Neale Hurston, letter to Burroughs Mitchell, October 2, 1953, in *Zora Neale Hurston, A Life in Letters*, 703.

23 Thomas Africa, "Worms and the Death of Kings: A Cautionary Note on Disease and History," *Classical Antiquity* 1, no. 1 (April 1982): 1–2, https://www.jstor.org/stable/25010757.

The Herod of Fact Rather than the Herod of Folklore

In *The True Herod*, Geza Vermes, a historian of Jewish studies, writes that Herod's "persistent ill repute is founded on the massacre of the innocents, a crime which he never committed." He describes the birth stories of Jesus in Matthew and Luke as "fictional or twisted," legends patterned on Pharaoh's decree against Jewish baby boys in the age of Moses at the time of the Exodus from Egypt. The legend of the massacre decreed by Pharaoh, which was "taken literally for more than 1,700 years," states Vermes, became "the protype of Herod's massacre of the innocents whose source is more likely to be Jewish folklore than genuine history."[24]

Hurston dramatized this probability in her novel *Moses, Man of the Mountain* (1939). When the infant Moses was born to Jochebed and Amram, they placed him in a woven basket and set it afloat upon the Nile, in hopes of preserving his life. They left his sister Miriam to stand watch. But Miriam fell asleep and so lost sight of the basket and the fate of Moses. Too afraid to repeat the truth of what happened, Miriam lied that Pharaoh's daughter had retrieved the basket from the river and took the infant Moses with her into the palace.

In this parallel story, Herod assumes the role of the wicked tyrant Pharaoh and the Christ child that of Moses. As Hurston interrogated the myths and legends surrounding Moses and questions his identity in *Moses, Man of the Mountain*, she works to debunk the folklore surrounding Herod in *The Life of Herod the Great*. In the canon of Hurston's writings, then, we can conceive of *The Life of Herod the Great* as a sequel to *Moses, Man of the Mountain*, Hurston's third novel, and a continuation of the saga of the Jewish people.

Hurston's efforts to have us see the Herod of fact versus the Herod

---

24 Geza Vermes, *The True Herod* (London: Bloomsbury, 2014), 106, 42,113, 119.

of folklore were intended to bring us not only to a better understanding of the real Herod and his reign but also to a better appreciation of the evolution of the history and culture of the Jewish people, from their crossing the River Jordan into Canaan, to the birth of Jesus the Christ. Hurston wrote in her introduction to the Herod manuscript that "the evolution of Jewish culture and thought from the time of Moses to the fall of Jerusalem to Titus in 70 AD" had been neglected. "Therefore, it appears that the Jews had and have no life except in the Bible. Like a pressed flower between the leaves of a book."[25]

If culture is human personality writ large, as the anthropologist Ruth Benedict theorized, then the extent to which Herod has been reduced to a stock, villainous character of history is the extent to which the personality and genius of the people he led and represented, during his thirty-seven-year reign, are also stereotyped and their humanity diminished. Through the prism of Herod's life, Hurston captures the complexities and textures of the history of the Jewish people, their triumphs and setbacks, their internecine conflicts and their struggles in a world dominated by Roman imperialist rule. And through tracing their resilience through hardships and political strife and their capacity to endure and continue, she reveals a particular expression of the human condition and the capacity of the transcendent human spirit.

Let There Be Light

"Like the dead-seeming rocks, I have memories within that came out of the material that went to make me. Time and place have had their say. So you will have to know something about the time and place where I came from, in order that you may interpret the incidents and directions of

---

25 Hurston, introduction to *The Life of Herod the Great*, xxii.

my life."[26] These are the opening lines of Hurston's autobiography, *Dust Tracks on a Road* (1942). And it is this cosmic approach that she takes in writing her revisionist novel of the life and times of Herod the Great. It was impossible to know him, Hurston reasoned, without knowing something of the time and place that birthed him—that first century BCE, the century of decision.

Compelled by the captivating story of Herod the Great, Hurston was equally compelled by the era that gave rise to Herod's reign. *The Life of Herod the Great* is something of an abbreviated universal history. In her preface to it, Hurston discussed this tumultuous and momentous time in human history. She saw spinning within it the ancient struggle between the East and the West and the concomitant struggle for the minds of the peoples of the world. She saw that the pattern of the struggles has repeated through time and across geographies. And in tracing these patterns and their reproductions from antiquity to her own time, Hurston saw that in two thousand years, the wheel of history had come full circle. "What *was* in Herod's day *is* again"; history was repeating itself. And Hurston advises that "the First Century BC has important implications for present-day western civilization." And what was so in Hurston's day is so in this twenty-first century.

I Corinthians 3:13–15

"The role of Herod in History is not just an antique preoccupation," write Czajkowski and Eckhardt, "but a topic beloved of modern scholars."[27] Indeed, Marshak writes that, until recently, Herod has been seen "as one of history's *untouchables*, that group of individuals whose behavior and regimes defy objective analysis." In order to become knowl-

---

26 Hurston, *Dust Tracks*, 561.
27 Czajkowski and Eckhardt, *Herod in History*, 173.

edgeable about the real Herod of history, Marshak urges us to "shed our preconception of the Herod of the New Testament."[28] Twenty-first-century scholars have evolved the courage to break taboo and to touch the untouchable. They have developed methodologies and approaches designed to "uncover the 'real' Herod."[29] But before these and other scholars made available the works that would help us to grow and develop our knowledge of the real Herod and his times, before Ehud Netzer excavated Herodium in 1972 and before Netzer's publication of *The Architecture of Herod, the Great Builder* in 2006, Zora Neale Hurston had already begun her archeological dig into the life of Herod and the first century BCE. She had already conducted the years of research that allowed her to pull back the veil that has kept Herod a man half in shadow. She had initiated that work, but it was not to see the light of day.

At the outset, Hurston was "burning to write" the story "of the 3,000 years struggle of the Jewish people for democracy and the rights of man." She conveyed her interests in a 1945 letter to her friend Carl Van Vechten.[30] The tentative title was "Under Fire and Cloud." Over time, Herod moved from the margins of her manuscript to center stage, and the biographical approach to the life of Herod shifted to a novelistic approach. Researching, writing, revising, editing, researching, Hurston was "passing through the most formative period of [her] whole life." She wrote passionately about the life and times of Herod, her "great obsession."[31] Even after her editor Burroughs Mitchell rejected the manuscript, she "took it easily," she told Mitchell. And she continued to revise her work. "Perhaps it is because I have such faith

28 Marshak, *Many Faces of Herod the Great*, 301, 302, xxii.
29 Czajkowski and Eckhardt, *Herod in History*, 173.
30 Zora Neale Hurston, letter to Carl Van Vechten, September 12, 1945, in *Zora Neale Hurston, A Life in Letters*, 529.
31 Hurston, letter to Burroughs Mitchell, October 2, 1953, in *Zora Neale Hurston, A Life in Letters*, 702.

in the material."[32] In 1958, David McKay Publications declined to publish her manuscript, and on January 16, 1959, a letter to Harper Brothers would be Hurston's last query on behalf of the manuscript of "The Life of Herod the Great."

In 1960, the "Herod the Great" manuscript was nearly lost to us and to history. A few days after Hurston's funeral, a crew was hired to clear out the little green cinder block house at 1734 School Court, in Fort Pierce, Florida, where she had lived. They were in the process of burning the contents of an old trunk in which Hurston stored her papers, letters, and manuscripts. Deputy Patrick Duval, of the St. Lucie County Sheriff's Department, happened to be driving by and saw the smoke. Deputy Duval was a friend of Hurston, knew she was a writer, and presumed that the contents of the trunk might be important. With a nearby garden hose, he extinguished the fire, saving many of Hurston's papers. Among the papers rescued, many with charred and burnt edges, was the manuscript of Hurston's novel "The Life of Herod the Great." Details of Hurston's last days, days she spent passionately enthralled with her great obsession, are recounted in Valerie Boyd's *Wrapped in Rainbows* and Lynn Moylan's *Zora Neale Hurston's Final Decade.*

After hundreds of years, King Herod the Great is coming out of the shadows. After decades, Dr. Zora Neale Hurston can finally tell her untold story. Both Herod and Hurston have "come out more than conquer."

---

32 Zora Neale Hurston, letter to Burroughs Mitchell, August 12, 1955, in *Zora Neale Hurston, A Life in Letters*, 742.

ABOUT THE AUTHOR

Zora Neale Hurston wrote four novels (*Jonah's Gourd Vine; Their Eyes Were Watching God; Moses, Man of the Mountain;* and *Seraph on the Suwanee*) and was still working on her fifth novel, *The Life of Herod the Great,* when she died; three books of folklore (*Mules and Men* and the posthumously published *Go Gator and Muddy the Water* and *Every Tongue Got to Confess*); a work of anthropological research (*Tell My Horse*); an autobiography (*Dust Tracks on a Road*); an international bestselling ethnographic work (*Barracoon*); and over fifty short stories, essays, and plays. She was born in Notasulga, Alabama; grew up in Eatonville, Florida; and lived her last years in Fort Pierce, Florida.

ABOUT THE EDITOR

Deborah G. Plant is an African American and Africana Studies independent scholar, author of *Of Greed and Glory: In Pursuit of Freedom for All,* and literary critic specializing in the life and works of Zora Neale Hurston. She is the editor of the *New York Times* bestseller *Barracoon: The Story of the Last "Black Cargo"* by Zora Neale Hurston and the author of *Alice Walker: A Woman for Our Times,* a philosophical biography. She is also the editor of *The Inside Light: New Critical Essays on Zora Neale Hurston* and the author of *Zora Neale Hurston: A Biography of the Spirit* and *Every Tub Must Sit on Its Own Bottom: The Philosophy and Politics of Zora Neale Hurston.* She holds MA and PhD degrees in English from the University of Nebraska–Lincoln. Plant played an instrumental role in founding the University of South Florida's Department of Africana Studies, where she chaired the department for five years. She presently resides in Florida.

A NOTE FROM THE COVER ARTIST

What an immense honor it is to have my work be forever paired with Zora Neale Hurston—the Queen of the Harlem Renaissance—whose work transcends time and space! My heart is glad to reveal the pictorial of *The Life of Herod the Great*. King Herod was not a disastrous king as depicted in the Bible, but a religious and philosophical man who lived a life of adventure. I chose a white dove to deliver a purified message from the divine as it relates to King Herod's persona. His eyes are closed in a type of meditation that is looking inward to an innate part of the psyche. The yellow halo surrounding his head depicts the glory of the sun that shines on his royal majesty. From the seed of an idea, to a sketch, to reality, King Herod is here to grace us with his presence!

—Akindele John